RYAN BAKER

Ugley and the Silver Scales

Kay Sung Park

authorHOUSE®

AuthorHouse™
1663 Liberty Drive
Bloomington, IN 47403
www.authorhouse.com
Phone: 1-800-839-8640

First published by AuthorHouse 5/25/2010

ISBN: 978-1-4490-8368-7 (e)
ISBN: 978-1-4490-8367-0 (sc)

Library of Congress Control Number: 2010906307

Printed in the United States of America
Bloomington, Indiana

This book is printed on acid-free paper.

Hannah who is like Ella except she never goes out in pajamas; Daniel who is like Ryan except he never forgets; Ha-rhim who is like Laxan except he never likes swim

Contents

PART 1 LEINAD

PART 2 UGLEY

PART 1 LEINAD

Long, long time ago far away in the ocean down came a Goddess called Neptess. She was so happy to see beautiful sea creatures in the ocean. However, soon she saw the darkness in the deep ocean floor. This made her feel so sad that she could not enjoy the journey anymore.

Far underneath the ocean floor, there were compact layers of various pressurized unusual minerals. It was the mineral layers that kept substances with remarkable potentials to generate essential gases for living organisms. However, they were hidden and had never been useful.

Finally, the power of the Goddess triggered them out, and a vast number of gaseous substances in huge bubble balls were released from the minerals underneath the ocean floor. As bubble balls were constantly produced for so long, the mineral layers of the ocean floor were pushed up at once in one piece. Accordingly, a whole new land appeared beneath the hemisphere mineral layers. The layers of crystal-clear mineral films were well supported by countless bubble balls. Then, the sky was filled with groups and layers of gleaming bubble balls in a spiral.

From the world above the ocean, invisible rays out of the sun light passed through the surface of the ocean and traveled all the way down to the millions of bubble balls beneath the hemisphere mineral layers. As soon as the rays touched the bubble balls, they become brighter like recharged light bulbs. The light was amassed during days, and nights fell under dim light. Thus, the bubble balls in groups and layers glittered all year long.

After many years the land became beautiful and rich for living. Then, Neptess invited many humans and animals from other worlds to live on this remarkable new land with peace and joys. She built a magnificent castle made up of pure silver that could last forever...

Chapter 1
TURNING TWELVE

"Leinad!" A spirited voice echoed in the morning sky.

"Coming, grandpa," replied Leinad lively, jumping out of the porch.

"My apology, Master Rupidd," said Leinad regretfully.

"All right, provided you slept well."

"I did, master," declared Leinad, beaming.

"Well, that's what you need today," said Rupidd merrily. "OK, we'd better hurry up now unless you want to drop the opportunity."

"Nice try, master. After waiting for twelve years for this moment, yes, master, I can easily do that," said Leinad sourly.

"I'm telling you now, master, all this is…for you."

He was going to say 'for my father,' but changed his mind. His father was the most important reason, but he had decided not to tell about his father.

"Generous, Leinad, but I will save my thanks until the end of the day."

"Fair enough, master."

"Then, shall we?" asked Rupidd, his hands smoothing the manes of two horses gently. "Cobah and Rhodin are doing pretty good this morning," exclaimed Rupidd, smiling at the horses.

"That's great, master!" cried Leinad brightly.

"Cobah," called Rupidd pleasantly, drawing the rein of the white horse for Leinad, "if Leinad gives you a hard time by any means, let me know, OK?" He tapped Cobah's back gently as Leinad handed over the rein.

"Exactly. Cobah, you heard him," said Leinad radiantly.

"So, if my apprentice is performing well today," said Rupidd, surveying Leinad's expression briefly, "tomorrow, I would like to take him to the forest."

"Blue Forest, master," said Leinad, taking the saddle on Cobah.

"Correct." Rupidd said, getting into the saddle on Rhodin.

"Why, Leinad!" exclaimed Rupidd, narrowing his eyes. "Are you all right? You look nervous." He said with a look of anxiety, his face forming a bitter smile. "No worries, Leinad. Soon or later, you will be enjoying it."

"I am OK, master, seriously," said Leinad, trying to cloak his nervousness with a grin, but his master only chuckled lightly.

The truth was Leinad could never conceal his thoughts and feelings from his master ever since he had become an apprentice of Rupidd; his father had dropped him off at Rupidd's house and disappeared five years ago. Leinad remembered that his father had said, "Son, someone must do this before too late." But Leinad had never understood why and where his father had to leave in that instant. When Leinad had once argued for that, his father had only said, "Son, when you turn twelve, I will tell you everything." Now it has been over a month since Leinad had turned twelve, but his father would never explain a thing because he had never come back home. If it was ever possible, Leinad would have gone to find his father long ago. Whenever he had tried, his master was always there for a critical lesson, shaking his head. And only recently, he had decided to wait patiently for any words from his master.

"Want a race, Leinad? That's the best way of washing off a complex mind," said Rupidd, his voice was highly spirited like it was intended to wake Leinad from the daydream.

Leinad looked around the scenery briefly and realized that he dreamed for more than a while. Smiling awkwardly, he yelled, "Race!"

Then, his attention moved to his horse. "We would love to, right, Cobah?"

Cobah responded quite promptly. She ran off without delay even before her opponent was ready for it.

"Wait! Apprentice! Fair play is the first and everything you need to learn, you know that?" yelled Rupidd, running after him.

"Sorry, not this time! I am only your grandson, you know that?" Leinad shouted back to the chaser, cackling ever merrily.

"Very well, then. Regret no fun! Rhodin, please!" Rupidd called out, zipping up fiercely. "Here I come, my evil foe!"

For sure the master was skillful and fast, but it was not an easy task for him at all. During the five years of training, if there was anything that Leinad could not pick up from his master, it might be only the age.

"Wow! Master, are you sure they only select twenty-eight people?" cried Leinad anxiously as they entered the city gate of Iridion. Obviously streets were unusually populated with a large number of people.

"My! You worry about it, Leinad, don't you?" said Rupidd teasingly. "Well, it's not too late to withdraw your pride for winning the race."

"Master, it's not that. Please, stop it. I'm just amazed by the number of people here," cried Leinad naturally, but he could not hide the emerging nervousness by the sight of the hurly-burly of the people of his age.

"Oh, is that right? That certainly makes me feel better," said his master lightly, examining Leinad's expression.

"Confidence is everything you taught me, master."

"Aha! Yes, yes, confidence! That's all you need now, definitely," exclaimed Rupidd cheerfully, giving him a smack on the shoulder. "Come on, Leinad, people are waiting to see your performance," said Rupidd brightly, directing them toward the busy throng.

The street was well paved with coral clay and pearl white pebble stones. Along sides were lined up tall trees with large leaves which looked a lot like maple trees except for the color of the leaves; one side was ivory white. A few storey houses, which were made up of ashen stones and cardinal woods, were visible on both sides. The street ran straight down and intersected with the main road of the market place which lay along the shoreline. On one end of the road was a large pier, and on the other end an open arena called GIA. It was Great Iridion Arena for sports activities, games, seasonal events and qualification tests. And it was these tests that have been scheduled for today. It was an exciting event for those who turning twelve by August 28 every year. They were officially independent and qualified to participate in the tests. Any individual who passed the tests would obtain an honorable invitation card from the king for the events and the activities at the castle.

Leinad quietly followed his master, but his mind was soon stolen by the sight of the young people moving to the arena.

"Seriously, it wasn't this crowded last year," muttered Leinad. "Something must be going on, master, otherwise –."

"Otherwise, you are too nervous, Leinad. I see nothing but the same thing," said Rupidd plainly, gazing straight at the entrance to the arena right ahead.

"OK, this is it," cried Rupidd, jumping off the horse. His expression turned serious. "Listen, Leinad," said Rupidd, looking Leinad straight in the eyes. "I congratulate you for turning twelve. There is no doubt that you are a big lad. And now, how many people are competing is not an issue for you. I am sure you know that."

"I will do my best, master," said Leinad optimistically.

"That's my apprentice. And don't forget your motivation," advised Rupidd.

Yes, I have an important motivation.

Leinad has waited for this moment for five years, and now he would challenge the opportunity to go and find his father. Without such a reason Rupidd would have been only a grandpa.

Chapter 2
QUALIFICATION

It was a big oval-shaped arena which was filled with water up to near the spectator seats. The water was so clean that anything could be seen from above. It was like a huge aquarium with various living creatures. For the actual tests there were two transparent reservoirs underwater on both ends of the arena. One of the reservoirs was occupied by some numbers of large grey fish resembling dolphins, except that they had a stripe of navy blue scales which ran down on their back. The other reservoir was empty. These two reservoirs were connected through a huge transparent wave-shaped tube oriented vertically. There were small air gaps with emergency egresses on the peaks of the waves. Outside, above the daises were two platforms on both sides of the oval stand.

In the preparation hall the organizer explained the rules and regulations to the participants. It would be the last part of the tests for the qualification. Leinad's eyes were at the wall impassively while his mind was floating on an empty sea. Sailing on an empty sea... But, Leinad had an aim. He saw an image of the castle beyond the ocean of the confidence. *I must go to the castle.*

Leinad looked at the platform before him, getting ready for the race. His main duty was to take one of the fish from one reservoir to the other in a fast manner. But first, he would have to ride a maddening bird successfully without falling. The bird would try hard to shake him off from its back while carrying him over to the other platform. If he could remain on its back long enough, definitely he would have a better chance to dive right onto the reservoir. Then, he would catch one of the fish in there, racing over to the other reservoir to finish the performance.

Leinad heard the spectators yelling from every seat of the arena. He would only end up making more fun for them if he ever fell into the water effortlessly.

Vigilant, Leinad! Confidence!

After breathing in deeply once more, he stepped up on the platform where a big grey bird was waiting for him.

As his name was called out loud in the air, he waved his hand toward the audience, smiling awkwardly. Then, he turned, stepping back to the bird which glared at him mercilessly as if to say, 'Don't even think about it, you sucker!' Leinad smiled with intent at the bird, but it was only a silly attempt before the fight.

The bird looked at Leinad with loathing. Its featherless small head and its long neck, which was heavily wrinkled and crooked with two irregular humps, were constantly moving back and forth while its two big bulging never-blinking yellow eyes were fixed on Leinad. Relatively small dark grey feathered wings were half opened down, partially covering its two brown short bare legs which were ruffled like wrecked wood. It looked now very much ready to perform the show for the audience who were craving for mishaps and collapses.

"Ready!" The organizer shouted.

Leinad wished he could see his master one more time, but his master seemed miles away. He closed his eyes quietly and inhaled fresh air as much as he could, and discharged it very slowly along with the image of the monster bird and the cravings of the audience. Then, he saw his master yelling at him cheerfully.

Leinad, you can do it! Go and knock them down! Go, Leinad, go!

Leinad approached to the bird cautiously. He stretched his arm and soothed its neck gently first while forcing a smile at the yellow eyes which were now staring shrilly as if to measure the nerves of the rider. Then, he placed one hand on its rock-hard hump and climbed on its back very carefully. It was barely half a second after his feet left the ground when the bird kicked the platform and soared up into the sky, rattling radically. Shortly, the view of the crystal clear water came to his senses along with a big laughter from the stand down below.

"Whoa!" shouted Leinad as the bird jerked without warning.

The bird started to shake its body hysterically. It moved unpredictably to any possible direction to shake off the daring rider and earn the cheers from the spectators, yet advancing to the platform on the other side of the arena. Leinad's head and arms danced up in the air vigorously. He endeavored to balance on the crazy vehicle for what seemed like hours, yet the target was far away. But, by some means, it was not too bad at all now. Has this bird been milder? Or it was because he had well managed to ride frenziedly behaving Cobah in the past? He was not sure.

Now, as the platform was nearing, the bird became even gentler for Leinad. After stroking its neck softly (to thank for the wonderful ride), he let his weight off the back of the bird. With a cheerful splash he landed safely in the center of the reservoir in one piece. And there, he saw a charming fish approaching him. After swallowing a good portion of fresh air, he dived into the tube promptly and headed toward the destination along with the fish.

Leinad managed to pass ten waves to begin with, then, he had to stop at the next peak to breathe. When he got there, however, he realized that there was not much air isolated in the peak. He advanced hurriedly to the peak of the next wave. And there, he found a fair amount of air reserved for him. After breathing briefly, he resumed the race to the destination with his companion.

It was not so long before he needed air again. Unfortunately though, there was not much air left in the next few peaks. The water would march in to his lung any second. There was a very little hope for him now. An emergency egress came into view irresistibly, but he shook his head at once. In desperate he clutched the tip of the fish's tail tight in his hand and pointed to the wave ahead. The fish seemed aware of the situation. It jerked back abruptly once and dragged him forward. Shortly, it dashed toward the destination at full speed. Eighteenth, nineteenth …twenty-fifth, and at long last, the fish entered the reservoir, pulling Leinad into it. But, the fish did not stop there. It raced all the way up and tore out of the water along with Leinad.

Cool air rushed in and delivered to his lung at once, but Leinad did not feel anything for real until the big cheers and applauses broke into his eardrums, followed by a huge smash of his own body on the water. He indeed made it one way or another. Thankfully, not only did the fish help him, but also saved his life!

Chapter 3
SORA

"At long last!" exclaimed Leinad, approaching to his master.

He hoisted a thin silvery card ineptly.

"Indeed!" cried Rupidd happily.

"Thanks, master," said Leinad, smiling bitterly.

"Thanks for what? You are my apprentice if you ever forget," declared Rupidd, chuckling softly. "And my apprentice just made one step forward. Now I owe HIM a thank-you," said Rupidd encouragingly.

"OK, Leinad, we have a little time to look around before we go."

"Where are we going, master?" asked Leinad, brushing Cobah's forehead with a thank-you smile.

"To the market place," said Rupidd, carrying his smile over to the busy road.

"What about Rhodin and Cobah?"

"Don't worry. We are not going far," said Rupidd.

The market place was very crowded with many spectators, shoppers, and merchants. There were stores along the street, attracting customers with various items from mountains and oceans, including minerals, gems, coral as well as food products such as grains, nuts, groceries and preserved or dried vegetables. Certainly, it was not the first visit for Leinad, but there was something weird. The shops, the goods, the events, and even the people were different in some way. *Am I haunted by something?* He wondered.

"Everything looks different, ah?" asked Rupidd lightly.

"That's what I meant, master. Is this for real?"

"I already said, Leinad, for sure everything is the same. If there is any difference, it's YOU, Leinad," said Rupidd wittily. "See, you are big enough now to have the responsibility of yourself," he said, sounding optimistic. "Anyhow, it is a good sign if you see things different," he added, nodding with a pensive expression which then brightened by the sight of a shop before him.

"Ah, here, Leinad, I wanted to show you some drawings in this shop."

Right above the entrance door, there were four capital letters in a strange format, and each letter was held by a certain animal. Leinad was not sure their identities, because they were all in silver, appearing very aggressive.

"SORA?" Leinad read it out faintly, his expression perplexed.

"Singular Odd Rare Atypical," said Rupidd in a peculiar voice. "You will see what I mean shortly."

And the moment he opened the door, he saw what his master meant. The floor was occupied by grey white shelves which were fully loaded with various immobilized living creatures including stuffed animals, pinned creatures, fossilized fish, and calcified birds, none of which were familiar to Leinad. Even the pinned creatures, which resembled certain insects, were much bigger and creepier with their firm razor sharp pincers and obtruded pitch black eyes.

Along the wall were drawings and paintings of buildings, trees, rocks, fish, birds and inland animals. But they were all uncharacteristic, irregular, or abnormal, giving an impression that they were only imaginary. At the end of the wall, there were fine drawings and paintings of a silver castle.

"Is this the castle, master?" asked Leinad unsurely.

"Well, technically speaking, yes," replied Rupidd, sounding incorrect.

"No, not that I know, sir, if you meant the castle where they go for the competition and stuff," intercepted a voice from their back.

Leinad did not notice that there was a boy behind him.

"Oh, sorry to bother you. I just overheard you," said the boy regretfully.

"Not at all, my lad. You seem to know about the castle," said Rupidd curiously.

"Not much, sir, but I am still trying. I have discovered only a little bit of the story, I should say, the history of the castle, sir," said the boy.

"Is that right?" asked Rupidd with interest.

The boy took it as a question, and he began.

"Long, long ago an ocean Goddess built a silver castle which was this one here," said the boy brightly, pointing to a small drawing framed on the wall, "but then, in recent year for some reason it changed into the one like this over here." With this, the boy screwed his face as if to show how awful it meant.

Leinad surveyed the drawing intently for a few seconds, and then his eyes moved to his master's with a daunted look.

"That's a sand castle," cried Leinad.

"Inspiring," said Rupidd cheerfully, nodding. "So," he said, looking at Leinad briefly, "you also came for the tests, my lad?"

"No, no, sir. I am, well, my sister and I will just turn nine in two days," cried the boy defensively at once. While his eyes were wandering around the back side of the shop, he mumbled, "Oh, where did she go?"

Then, his eyes stopped at the stairs located far at the back. "Excuse me, please, both of you, I must go find my sister now." With a gauche smile the boy darted away. "Ellaxia! Sister!" He shouted anxiously, running up the stairs.

Meanwhile, Leinad was quite moved by the attitude of the boy.

"You don't have to feel ashamed, Leinad," said Rupidd willingly. "You grew up with your own pride and strength to become independent. And you are one of twenty-nine selected people, if you have forgotten. See, you will be on your own journey in two days."

Just then, the boy reappeared with a thud, jumping down the stairs.

"Sorry for my rudeness, sir," cried the boy with a sour smile, panting. He carried the smile over to Leinad. "Hang on!" he divulged, his eyes grew bigger. Then he suddenly threw his hand into his pocket and pulled out a notepad. After inspecting the notepad briefly with a clumsy expression, he cried out, "There! R11G17P38, yes, I knew it!" His face returned to Leinad with a hazy look. "Mr. R11G17P38…"

"Excuse me?" demanded Leinad with a grimace, turning his eyes to his master who shrugged vacantly.

"Oh, sorry, my bad. No offense. It's only for my convenience, i.e., rider number 11 in group 17, and 38 points," cried the boy, throwing the notepad back into his pocket. "I am so pleased to meet you, rider 11. That was awesome! Wow, 38 points! That's my dream number, you know." The boy exclaimed.

"Thank you," said Leinad with embarrassment, his eyes turning to his master.

Rupidd only shrugged with a broad smile as if to say, 'See, I told you.'

"Anyway, I was going to tell you about my sister. She was upstairs, being captivated by the drawings of hemabies. Sorry, but, I had to watch her, always. She is only a little child," said the boy like a grown-up. With an emphasis on 'always' his words sounded repentant, yet his expression happy.

"Aha! Hemabies," cried Rupidd. His eyes filled with visible joy.

"Drawings of hemabies!" exclaimed Rupidd, smiling happily at Leinad like he was only talking to Leinad.

"Yes, but just a baby hemaby, sir," uttered the boy, sounding dejected. "I am not sure for real, though, because never seen one before," he added unsurely.

"Leinad, you might want to see them," suggested Rupidd brightly, and turning to the boy, he asked politely, "My lad, could you lead us to the location, please?"

"Love to, sir," said the boy gaily. "Then, this way, please."

The boy directed them to the upper floor.

Leinad had half a mind to ask his master about hemabies, but he decided to wait and see the drawings of the creature, first.

"Hey, sis! I have people like you. They wanted to see your hemabies," said the boy as they approached to a girl facing large framed drawings and paintings.

"Hi, there," greeted the girl pleasantly. The next second, she rolled her eyes at her brother, "Brother! They are NOT mine," hissed the girl. "Just checking how cute they are...," she added exuberantly. Half of her words seemed melted in her throat.

"See this," said the girl, stepping aside for Rupidd and Leinad. "Don't you just think so?" She asked, nodding vigorously, as though egging them to agree.

Leinad examined the drawing and then the painting with great interest for her, but he was not sure if it was cute at all. It was only one of those peculiar animals displayed on the shelves. It seemed that even Rupidd did not accept her egging.

"Yes, it is quite a creature, young lady." He said politely, nodding gently.

"Wait!" blurted the girl, gazing at Leinad. "I have seen you before...," said the girl faintly, endeavoring to remember.

Her brother whispered something to her brightly.

And of course, Leinad knew what was going on, and he said with the same clumsy smile, "Probably, yes."

"Yes, I was sure," cried the girl keenly, "you were the –."

"Best participant, rider 11 in group 17, 38 points!" finished the boy on behalf of her animatedly. Then he amused with his own way of cherishing.

"Double Ps – Prompt and Precise! The most thrilling rider ever!"

Leinad now began to feel embarrassed again by the boy's exaggerated sense of humor. He knew that his pride and strength brought him there. But, under the given circumstances he would happily give the credits to Cobah and the fish for the triumph in the final tests.

Thanks to the boy who now seemed to move on.

"Mohzake," began the boy with a look of disappointment.

"That's our cousin," intercepted the girl, beaming innocently.

The boy grimaced at the girl briefly and continued, "ended the tests with 29 points. Poor Mr. R7G21P29."

"Actually, brother, it wasn't so bad, though, considering his situation," said the girl with a satisfied look. "He has been in a bad shape for long, right, brother?" asked the girl.

The boy nodded for her instead of saying yes, but rather ineptly.

In Leinad's mind there was a sudden thirst to know about their cousin, but he quenched down as they already moved on the conversation.

"We came here for the events many times," said the girl casually.

"Four times," corrected the boy for her.

"But, never seen such a remarkable performance." She finished her sentence.

"To me you both are equally remarkable," said Rupidd, chuckling mildly. "O.K. – Organized and Knowledgeable! The most brilliant adventurers!" He exclaimed spiritedly, imitating the boy's way of cherishing.

"So, tell us now, what do you know about hemabies?" asked Rupidd.

"If you asked my opinion, double Cs double Fs – Cute Charming Fabulous Friend," said the girl bashfully.

"Nice try, sis. But, it's more likely Cleverly Cooperative Flying Fish, if you insist double Cs double Fs," said the boy arrogantly. "And I can add two more Fs – Fast Faithful, if you like. Of course, all this is only based on my studies."

"Your studies... Inspiring!" cried Rupidd. "How did you carry on your studies?" he asked with interest.

"Well, I discovered it from people around, sir. Once I also looked into a history book, but could not completely understand what was described in there. The only thing I understood was the legendary tale," said the boy.

"And what was that about?" asked Rupidd with great attraction in his expression.

"Allow me, brother!" interrupted the girl breathlessly. "Let me!"

And she did not wait for her brother to say a word.

"Long ago," she began, looking at her brother briefly and then at the old man who was gazing at her with bated breath, "according to the tale, somewhere in the ocean lived unique fish called hemabies. They were said to be smart, energetic and cheerful creatures, but never appeared in the human world. For many years these hemabies had a wish and a belief; if they would endeavor to jump high out of the water persistently and merrily, one day they would be invisible like thin air, and fly like clouds. So, every night herds of hemabies swam, jumping out of the water in groups, and sang happy songs for many hours. However, the songs, which meant to be joyous, sounded very sad to all other creatures. In the end, their work brought sympathy to the heart of the ocean Goddess. And she was touched by their endless efforts toward the wish. Thus, she offered an opportunity to them; those who served the kingdom of Bubble Land for a hundred years would turn invisible and fly to the world beyond Bubble Land. It was the land in the sky which was only visible and accessible to those who came from there."

The girl paused there with a sigh, looking at her brother, and she uttered words that sounded like a disappointment.

"I guess hemabies are certainly some kind of fish, but they are only available at the castle because of this reason... Of course, it is only a legendary story; they will eventually fly to an invisible world. They call it Sky Land or something like that, right, brother?"

"Silane Land, sis. Yeah, you got it right. And hemaby means a flying sea horse, if I remember correctly," cried the boy egotistically.

At a loss, Leinad turned his attention to his master who seemed very impressed.

"Remarkable," said Rupidd, nodding. "Tell us more about the history book you mentioned. You actually have that book?"

"Well. No, sir. It belonged to our uncle," said the boy.

"Samahan, that's his name, if you want to know," added the girl, sounding proudly honored.

"Kangryn?" asked Rupidd curiously. "Interesting. Surely, you both are kin of Kangryn?"

"Yes, we are," said the girl, her eyes brightened. "You know him, don't you, sir?"

"Well, of course. Archeologist Samahan Kangryn. The name is well known. In fact, he is more than just an archeologist, I can guarantee that," said Rupidd, sounding very certain. Then, turning his eyes to the boy once more, he asked inquisitively, "Anyway, is he around?"

"Actually, no, sir. Only visited us in Humington a few weeks ago," said the girl in aid of her brother.

"Two weeks and, and two days ago, precisely, sir," said the boy.

"And he spent three days there before he left for the forest, right brother?"

"Yes, after three days he left for Blue Forest. He had only said that he would need to go check something there," uttered the boy.

"Blue Forest?" asked Rupidd with a look of concern.

"He always brings something unique or at least interesting stories whenever he comes to visit us... I wonder what he would bring this time," said the girl, her eyes blankly looking at her brother.

"Arch Cliff, precisely, sir." The boy corrected.

"Arch Cliff? Hmmm," mumbled Rupidd, looking at Leinad worriedly. Then, turning back to the boy again, he guessed, "He's gone alone, I suppose."

"I think so. He only looked very excited…," said the girl on behalf of her brother. She looked at her brother for a moment.

"Actually," began the boy, sounding remorseful to his sister, "he went with our cousin…"

"What? You didn't tell me that!" barked the girl at once, sounding badly hurt.

"Sorry, sis. Didn't get a chance to tell you yet… Cousin Zake told me only this morning, though," said the boy apologetically.

"OK, but, what about uncle Kan?" asked the girl.

"Don't know, sis. He only said he had to come back alone," said the boy. Then, returning his interest to Rupidd, he asked apprehensively, "Is there something wrong, sir?"

"Oh, no, not at all. There is nothing really to worry for both of you. Yes, I am sure he will be back with exciting news shortly. You just wait and see," said Rupidd encouragingly.

But the two innocent faces turned even darker with Rupidd's words.

"Well," said Rupidd brightly. "It was very, very nice to hear the story of hemabies. Very interesting. And good luck to both of you. Now, we must be aware of time, Leinad."

"Very nice talking to you, both," said Leinad with a mild smile, walking toward the stairs. He had to hurry as he noticed that his master was already out of sight.

"All the best at the castle!" shouted the boy and the girl almost at the same time. Leinad waved his hands toward the two in reply.

Chapter 4
SECRET OF RUPIDD

"How had my father been doing, master Rupidd?" asked Leinad.

"Oh, Hasyn…," said Rupidd indecisively, drawing in the reins a bit.

His voice was soft, but Leinad felt a hint of darkness in his expression. He must have been quite surprised by the unexpected question, Leinad thought. For long Leinad had endured well without a word about his father, yet he had no complete control of his mind; questions had often slipped from his troubled mind.

"You should feel proud of your father, Leinad," said Rupidd gallantly.

He quietly turned his head to a distant view without any further explanation. Leinad's eyes followed his master's, and stopped at the view where his master was mesmerized. Far away in the distance was visible a peaceful green field which was expanded endlessly toward where the sky fell. And there, among the flickering lights, Leinad saw his father smiling mildly at him. Leinad knew that his father concealed his own troubles with the smile, but Leinad only smiled back.

Father, where are you now? Can I assure myself you are OK?

"We will shortly get to the edge of a large field; a richly green meadow along the river that runs down from the mountains. And we will follow the meadow path today. Now, afar the field, you can see a seemingly never-ending forest," said Rupidd, narrowing his eyes at the distant view.

"Well, my thanks to Cobah and Rhodin," exclaimed Rupidd brightly, patting Rhodin on the neck gently, "We will have enough time for our exploration there, provided everything goes well."

"So, that's Blue Forest, master?" asked Leinad.

Leinad did not ask further about his father, but now he could not help pondering why his master told him to be proud of his father. Of course, he knew that his father had been one of the most devoted persons in the country, and he was always proud of it. Leinad wondered why his master said 'feel proud of your father' when he asked how his father did as a trainee. He worried. He hoped that his master did not mean something really bad had happened to his father.

"Yes, Leinad, that's the forest," said Rupidd thoughtfully. "Now, tell me, Leinad, what you know about the forest."

"Father said a bit…," divulged Leinad, but his voice disappeared in his throat as he realized that he was talking about his father again. "But, it was more than five years ago, master." He tried to fix it.

"Then, you can tell me the stories you heard from others," demanded Rupidd wittily.

Leinad knew that whatever he might say, it would be nothing new to his master, but then, there was a chance to hear something more from his master; maybe something about his father. So, he explained briefly.

"Blue Forest was once the home of all animals. But one day, a horrifying monster showed up, threatened and killed humans and animals regardless of their reasons.

Then, the forest dreadfully became the home of the monster."

Rupidd approved with nodding, but his face hardened.

"What is that 'a bit' you heard from your father?"

"It's..." Leinad replied at once. For half a second he was delighted because his master at last brought out the matter of his father to discuss. But the next words were stuck in his mouth as there was nothing much for him to say about. In fact, what his father had said was even less than 'a bit.' Equally, Leinad considered that his master asked it because he wanted to say something about his father.

"Actually, he only said about something bad happening in Blue Forest, and he'd tried to stop it. But until now I have had no idea what was going on," said Leinad, sounding suddenly very down.

"I see." Rupidd said caringly. "Your father might have thought that it was too much for you at your age."

"I was already seven at that time, master, old enough to understand the situation," argued Leinad with a broad grin, letting his master chuckle for a moment.

"I had objected, but he only ignored me by saying that he would tell everything when I turned twelve."

"He promised that?" asked Rupidd, sounding surprised.

"I see now what he meant," said Rupidd tentatively. "Five years, Leinad! Notice the remarkable changes in you. Only your father had guessed that such a stubborn little dumb child could grow up to a fast and intelligent lad."

"Master Rupidd!" yelled Leinad as if being insulted badly, but his expression was contented.

An impulse to tease his master seized upon Leinad, but he had to surrender as his master's expression suddenly turned serious.

"Rhodin!" Rupidd called out calmly, reining up Rhodin.

"Easy, Rhodin, easy," cried Rupidd, jumping off the horse.

The horse moved restlessly against the rein, neighing.

"What's the matter, master?" asked Leinad worriedly, coming down from his horse. "Is he in depression again?"

"I can't tell…," said Rupidd, inspecting the surrounding briefly.

"No, it's not that. There is something nettling him this time."

While his hand soothing the horse on the neck, his eyes stopped at a spot which was crammed with pale green reeds. Virtually it was invisible through the tall wall of overpopulated reeds.

"Leinad, watch Cobah. Easy her, if you can," suggested Rupidd with composure.

"Yes, something must be…" His voice dissolved in his mouth while he was assessing the reed forest.

"Well, not anymore, I think," said Rupidd, softening his voice.

Releasing a negligible sigh, Leinad complained, "This place… I can't see a thing, master," uttered Leinad, his eyes moved ahead to the trail which was curved into the forest of weeds.

"That's right, Leinad. Although it is a shortcut, this trail has never been useful because of this creepy silence and invisibility along the way," said Rupidd sourly. "Well, despite of that, I personally think it is a safer route." He added affirmatively, examining the expression in Rhodin's eyes.

"So, what's the matter, Rhodin? It's not him, is he?" asked Rupidd tenderly, scratching Rhodin's forehead. "Well, always good to let us know any danger you feel, though."

Rupidd mounted on his horse, now turning his attention to Leinad who was yet marked with a visible concern on his face.

"If you two are all right?" asked Rupidd caringly.

"I think so, master," replied Leinad with assent, his eyes on Cobah's like he was talking to her.

"Rhodin, you heard him now?"

With that, Rupidd patted Rhodin's neck gently twice, and Rhodin in reply to his master's request strode forward submissively, and Cobah shadowed behind him. Meanwhile, Rupidd's eyes advanced toward the path ahead of them and examined the reed walls for any sign of an unpleasant surprise.

"Rhodin, if you feel comfortable, would you speed up a bit?" asked Rupidd brightly, withdrawing his awareness back to Rhodin.

The horse reacted quite promptly. He expedited his paces bravely to a sprint. And shortly they resumed their usual momentum, racing toward the green forest over the waving sea of rustling reeds.

Chapter 5
HIDDEN PASSAGE

"Rhodin!" called Rupidd brightly when they were nearing the forest.

Rhodin slowed his paces without delay. Peeking at his master briefly he neighed lively as though to request anything better than just 'Rhodin' from his master.

"Well done, Rhodin. Excellent, Cobah!" exclaimed Rupidd joyfully.

Then, both horses thanked him with cheerful neighs almost in one voice.

"OK, we stop here for a second, Rhodin, Cobah, please."

As they brought to a halt side by side, Rupidd released a faint exclamation with the view before him. The ground was gradually ascending now, turning into a broad hill in the distance. Near at hand were yellowish green reeds which without much leaves stood like bamboos. As going further up, the population of reeds decreased significantly, blending with slim plants possessing healthy green leaves. Then, at some point the reeds were completely replaced by green plants, stretching all the way toward the visible end of the green forest.

"See that?" exclaimed Rupidd attentively.

Leinad at first thought that his master meant the trail ahead because it narrowed significantly with heavily crowded reeds. But his master made it clear with another question.

"So peaceful, isn't it? It always has been…" cried Rupidd, sounding captivated. "I can hardly believe it all happened there…," he added quietly. His regretful words disappeared in his throat and barely reached to Leinad's ears.

So peaceful it is… Leinad thought over his master's words, and he considered a link between two words; blue and peaceful.

Maybe the forest was once so peaceful like a blue ocean.

"Why they call it Blue Forest, master?"

"Because it appears blue, Leinad," replied Rupidd bluntly.

"But, it's just natural green, master."

"Close. But precisely speaking, it only appears green, Leinad."

Rupidd fixed his eyes on the forest as if to make sure everything turned green.

"Blue Forest may be very little to do with its appearance," said Rupidd composedly.

"I don't get it, master," cried Leinad, his expression bemused.

"Leinad, have you ever contemplated a world beyond Bubble Land?" asked Rupidd appealingly, ignoring Leinad's confusion.

"No, but, is it something to do with Blue Forest?" asked Leinad.

Rupidd paid no heed to his apprentice again. He said quietly what seemed like an answer to his own question, his eyes appearing blank yet remained in the distant forest.

"It is near, but it could be a long way, Leinad, a very long way...," said Rupidd calmly, his faint voice for the last few words died in his mouth.

He turned his head to Leinad with an encouraging expression.

"I hope one day you will be able to explore it, Leinad. I very much hope so."

Rupidd's eyes grew brighter. "Yes, Blue Forest is very much to do with all that, Leinad. It is the key to the good and the hope of Bubble Land. And at the same time, it is the key to the world and beyond," exclaimed Rupidd.

"I am afraid I can only assure you of it this much, but when the time comes, you will understand what I mean accordingly," added Rupidd.

His master's voice was encouraging, but Leinad did not miss to spy a barely discernable woe on his master's face. Then Leinad decided to wait for the time to come.

"Well," began Rupidd, amending his interest to the surrounding, "hopefully we have enough time to visit Arch Cliff as well."

"That's the –," uttered Leinad, remembering the story of the boy at the shop, but his last words were collided with his master's.

"Yes, that's where your father was."

Rupidd said lightly, but Leinad was sort of surprised that his master mentioned his father first. He would not miss the opportunity to talk about his father.

"My father was there, master? I thought Arch Cliff is a dangerous place in the forest," said Leinad attentively.

"Right." Rupidd said, his eyes turning toward the forest again. "Yes, it used to be..."

"I don't understand why my father was there, though," cried Leinad impatiently, wanting seriously to hear more.

"Don't worry too much about it now, Leinad, you'll figure it out soon," said Rupidd decisively at once.

Leinad did not bother him further.

"Meanwhile, Rhodin will lead us to the hidden passage," he said, gently tapping his horse to draw his mind.

"Rhodin," called Rupidd softly.

Rupidd's eyes were fixed on the trail, on both sides of which were populated with tick reeds. As his eyes followed his master's, Leinad just spotted that right next to the trail there was another trail which was well hidden; the view was practically obscured with reeds like no one had set foot on it for years. Rhodin forwarded his steps to the hidden trail and Cobah followed silently.

Rhodin trotted through with difficulty until it curved to a small clearing which was surrounded by walls of tall slim plants. There appeared at least five visible trails now, mostly rough with the plants all around. Rhodin stepped back a few feet, hissing to the air lively once, then, dashed straight to one of the trails ahead. Leinad was troubled with a sudden jolt, but he got over it the next seconds. To his surprise the horses passed though without touching the plants on both sides.

As they progressed, at some point the plants in the surrounding were dramatically replaced by tall tree; nearly over ten straight feet. They were very slim, possessing almost no branches except for the tree tops. There were large numbers of healthy leaves on the tree tops, covering up the entire sky on their way. The first thing Leinad noticed was that it was so bright like a lighted tunnel. And the brightness was from the silver white color of the leaves as visible from below. Apparently the other side of leaves was green as judged by the leaves on the ground. The weird mechanism of the passage was another thing he noted. Unmistakably the passageway disappeared instantly after they passed, and virtually there was no trace of their way. As the horses advanced fast, in effect the trees on their way ambiguously opened up room briefly for the runners to pass through.

Feeling half confused and half amazed, Leinad looked at his master who was ahead of him. Even from behind Leinad could almost see his master's neutralized face. His master sat quietly on his horse who seemed to know the way so well to the destination. Leinad decided to reserve all the burning questions that arose ever since they had left home.

The horses ran through the emerging passageway for what felt like hours. When they finally slowed down, there was a visible decrease in the density of the tall slim trees, and the trail widened significantly. Shortly, there appeared trees with ivory flowers which were blended with green leaves under bright open sky. The aroma of the flowers and the shape of leaves told Leinad that they were acacia trees. Leinad inhaled deeply over until he had no sense of the smell.

Soon the passageway was homogeneously enveloped with tall acacia trees, leading to a forest of thick aroma of acacia. As they passed through, there appeared a huge oval-shaped clearing right before them. It was a wide green field filled with velvety grass, surrounded by seemingly invulnerable layers of walls of acacia trees.

"This is the hidden passage, Leinad!" cried Rupidd lively while his horse was marching leisurely along the perimeter of the clearing.

Leinad was a bit surprised to hear his master's voice. It seemed like years since he had heard his master's voice last. The sparkling voice of his master stirred Leinad's mind to realize that he bore hundreds of pressing questions.

"Do you want to know why they call it Hidden Passage?" asked Rupidd joyously, but he did not wait for Leinad's reply.

"Well, what is it that hits your mind first when you see this beautiful setting, Leinad?" asked Rupidd cheerfully.

Leinad knew what his master meant by that, but he was still unsure about Hidden Passage. Rhodin, who seemed to think faster than Leinad, already started to gear up. And surely, Cobah did not wait for Leinad's request, zooming to join their joys.

"Why not!" Leinad yelled eagerly. *On such a beautiful field!*

One exciting call seemed enough for Leinad to bury all the imperative questions inside. His mind raced with eagerness as Cobah carried him fast, following Rhodin. Now his intent was set at winning the race, requesting Cobah to run to her best. Cobah worked hard and caught up Rhodin progressively, yet remained behind Rhodin. Rupidd peeked back at Leinad with a teasing gesture.

"Hah! What's the matter, Leinad? You are so slow today! Why, is that it? Why don't you cheat me again now?" yelled Rupidd playfully.

"Cobah!" demanded Leinad, but sincerely, "Please!"

Cobah was fast, yet behind Rhodin. Until they almost completed one full lap, Leinad besought relentlessly, but his efforts were only vain. Then, he witnessed something very unusual.

"What the…!" shouted Leinad in disbelief. "Ma, master, Rhodin's…flying!"

"I know that! Does that bother you?" Rupidd's voice tore off the air.

"Er, no. But…, whoa!!" Leinad screamed as his horse also swiftly kicked the ground, following the imaginary trail of Rhodin in the air.

Leinad's heart almost stopped for the next few minutes as they soared up the treetops, and bravely dashed into the sky.

"Master! You didn't tell me about this!" yelled Leinad, sounding upset, but that was only a fake.

"Wow!! Master, it's great!"

It was simply breathtaking with the scene of the acacia forest and beyond. Leinad had never been this high. Besides, he was on a flying horse! While bearing down the feeling of thrill mingled with decreasing fear, Leinad surveyed the forest amusingly. Cobah, following Rhodin, was gyrating in mid-air above the clearing. The forest now appeared deep blue as if it was transformed into a peaceful blue ocean spanned to every direction from the clearing. For a split second he expected to see the castle and the real ocean beyond the forest. What he saw was, however, nothing but a blue forest as far as his eyes could reach. To the nearest, villages, fields, mountains, and even meadows with endless width of reeds, were all invisible from there.

Leinad attempted to spare his thought with a phenomenon beyond the reality. *Is it the limit of this world?*

He turned his head to his master who was still ahead of him. *Only master Rupidd can explain this.* He decided.

At that point Rupidd looked back at Leinad as if he was called.

"Are you all right, Leinad?" shouted Rupidd, sounding worried.

"I think so…" Leinad managed to reply unsurely, now turning his head to the sky. Then, he just noticed that the sky was totally different. Blue… It was a bright blue sky which he had never seen before.

"Master, the sky…is blue!" Leinad shouted in amazement, his eyes still remaining on the sky.

"Leinad!" called out the master decisively. "Rhodin, we are going back!" shouted Rupidd, disregarding Leinad's claim.

As Rhodin glided down, Rupidd made sure with a yell at the followers, "Come along, Cobah!"

Both horses swooped down toward the clearing peacefully. Leinad glanced back at the sky once more, but his mind was preoccupied by the thoughts of the unfamiliar events and phenomena he just experienced. He wondered why his master had never told him anything about it. And he considered that he was the only person on Bubble Land who actually was unaware of all that.

Leinad came back to reality by the thick aroma of acacia flower bathed the clearing. He just noted that they were already on the ground, and Cobah neighed cheerfully once as if to wake Leinad. Urgent questions streamed in his mind. He tapped Cobah's neck gently to advance.

"Explain it to me, please, master," demanded Leinad as Cobah kept her paces beside Rhodin.

"Explain," copied Rupidd wittily, "That is the first word my apprentice said. Well, what you have seen just now explained everything, Leinad," said Rupidd, looking at the sky over the acacia walls. "Yes, we might be able to have some time at Arch Cliff if we head off now."

"Master, please!" insisted Leinad. "You never said about flying."

Rupidd reined up Rhodin, quietly looking up the sparkling sky. Leinad's eyes traced his master's, then, voluntarily traveled around the sky, attempting to locate any trace of the cheerful blue sky which had vanished long ago.

"If you run through the hidden passage toward northeast, you will get to the border of Laneless Shrub, and from there to Arch Cliff it will take Cobah an hour…," said Rupidd, his eyes turning to the heavily jammed acacia forest. "And from Arch Cliff, if you race toward southeast, you will be out of the forest in two hours. There, you will see the mountains over the field. Then, you must be out of Blue Forest, and you are safe."

Feeling confused, Leinad looked at his master awkwardly. Above all that his master explained, Leinad revived an urge to remind him of the question, but he decided to wait. He knew his master never said anything directly.

"I am sure my apprentice can do it alone," said Rupidd affirmatively, "in any case, if you must."

Now Rupidd turned his head to Leinad, smiling.

"Yes, the hidden passage," said Rupidd, directing his interest to the empty grass field. "This clearing, Leinad, is hidden. No trails. The sky, Leinad, blue sky you referred."

"Yes, master. I was amazed, actually," said Leinad brightly.

"That's the hidden passage. What I mean by this, it is hidden, and only visible…," said Rupidd, looking Leinad straight in the eyes, "to anyone who came through the passage."

"I don't understand it, master, I –," said Leinad.

"Yes, you could see it because you were with Cobah. Or maybe, because they accepted you," explained Rupidd, breaking off Leinad's bewilderment.

"You mean it is something to do with Cobah?" asked Leinad, casting a quick slant at Cobah's eyes.

Rupidd nodded. "Earlier, we talked about Blue Forest, Leinad."

"Yes, master. Actually, it was really blue from up there. It seems that the white acacia flower blends with the green leaves to show something like blue color from the distance. But then, I cannot explain the blue sky…"

"Seeing the sky blue means a lot, Leinad, indeed," said Rupidd thoughtfully. "It's about the privilege one can have. Yes, it is very exciting, but at the same time, it's very fearful," added Rupidd, his face darkening with anxiety. "It can cause a lot of things – mostly unexpected and bad – sometimes, even horrible," said Rupidd remorsefully.

"You see now what I meant, Leinad?"

"I think so…," replied Leinad, sounding unsure. "Wait! Master, what about Rhodin and Cobah?" asked Leinad, his eyes shifting to Rhodin's.

For a moment Rupidd quietly watched the distant view as like he was not told anything.

"Yes," replied Rupidd thoughtfully, "they are from another world."

"That's why they have been distressed, master." Leinad uttered quite promptly.

"Yes, mental struggling with a different environment could be a reason, but there is a foremost reason, Leinad," said Rupidd painfully, "which, I am afraid, I cannot put into words."

Leinad nodded pensively. He was happy with that. His master had at least unbolted the answering chest for him. Then, there came another question he wanted to ask.

Is master Rupidd also from another world?

But in the last seconds he changed his mind.

"Master Rupidd, who brought them here, anyway, I mean, how did they end up here in the first place?"

"Now that's another question hard to answer," said Rupidd apologetically. "I am sorry, but I am not qualified to verbalize for that," declared Rupidd decisively. "Leinad, how they did end up here is not important to you. The fact is that they are here with you. And someday, you will stamp out the pains from their hearts and fill them with happiness. I believe that's what they wish," said Rupidd caringly, his eyes on Cobah's with a soothing smile.

More than half of his mind forced him to ask why his master was now exposing things which were unseen and untold for over five years of training. Then, he decided to surrender with a simple reasoning; his master waited until he turned twelve. *Now I am independent and I can make my own judgment. With my own decision I can go to a faraway world out of the blue sky as long as Cobah takes me there.*

Leinad gazed at Rhodin's eyes which appeared so attentive to their conversation. Certainly, Rhodin understood what they were talking, he thought. Rhodin's eyes suddenly looked so sorrowful to tell that they were badly long for homecoming.

Yes, someday I will take you home, my friend.

Leinad himself would happily see to it.

While Cobah was stalking Rhodin through Laneless Shrub, Leinad's mind drifted onto the unseen world:

Bright blue sky sparkles over the castle
A land as wide as the blue ocean floats on cotton-white clouds
Astonishing creatures play peacefully on the land
Dazzling flowers cheerfully dance with streams of cool misty gust
Gorgeous birds or wondrous winged animals sing enchanting songs in the air.

Out of the blue Leinad recalled the story of hemabies he heard. And he began to believe it for real. *Hemabies must also have known the world beyond the blue sky. Was it called Silane Land?*

Chapter 6
ARCH CLIFF

From the scenery of the surrounding Leinad could guess that Arch Cliff was nearing. There were various ashen rocks scattered along the crooked trail through the valley. Rhodin and Cobah slowed their paces notably now.

"Get your spear handy, Leinad," suggested Rupidd tranquilly, looking back at Leinad with an encouraging smile, "and be aware of your bearings."

Shortly over a rocky grove was visible a gigantic figure which stood on top of a broad hill in the distance. Its contour was like an odd-shaped rock half buried or an aged tree decayed badly, but the color of the figure was nearly black.

"Rhodin," called Rupidd gently, reining up. "What do you think?"

Taking notice to Cobah who just came along side, Rupidd said, "This is the reality, Leinad, not the story you were told. If you can find any hint of peace here, I daresay we still have a hope," said Rupidd bitterly.

"That black figure...," began Rupidd, pointing at it, "looks odd, but it is actually a giant cliff, Leinad."

"Arch Cliff, master," corrected Leinad.

"Right."

Rupidd narrowed his eyes at the figure for a few seconds quietly.

"Hard to tell at this point, but its shape is like a small letter h that people took it as happy home, holy heaven…," cried Rupidd, sounding very painful. "It is only hopeless hell now…," added Rupidd, his expression full of distress.

"Is there any reason why it's black, though, master?" asked Leinad uncertainly.

"That could be a premonition of it, Leinad. You see, the holy symbol is tilted quite a bit, and now completely covered by vicious black creatures called Dark Choppers, or DCs, if you like," said Rupidd solemnly.

"I doubt they are nocturnal, but mostly they are there, resting on the cliff just like that. Rumor has it that they are rarely out for preys, but once they are, and set on a target, they work as one until they finish the last scrap of bone," explained Rupidd, shooting another glance at the giant cliff.

"People ask where they came from, but my questions are when and what happened to those inhabitants of the forest," said Rupidd, gesturing with his head to advance toward the hill.

"Forward, Leinad. We will need to go over the hill. Now, Rhodin and Cobah! Both of you, take it easy, OK?" Rupidd said openly, patting Rhodin's neck. "We should be all right as long as we breathe very slowly," he added.

Leinad was not sure if he understood his master's 'when and what' questions.

"You mean, they used to be normal birds in here until –."

"Shhh!" cried Rupidd abruptly, interrupting Leinad's inquiry.

He lifted up his right hand cautiously, turning to Leinad slowly. His eyes looked very stiff, focusing on scattered rocks on his left. Rhodin, with troubled eyes, seemed struggling to keep himself under control. Leinad soothed Cobah's uptight neck while his eyes searching for anything suspicious around the rocks nearby, his hand holding his spear tight.

Rupidd gave an eye signal to Leinad to go to the front. Cobah silently stepped over.

"Watch out!"

Rupidd called out at once, throwing a dart in that instant.

Leinad turned his head hurriedly to his master, but he only saw a dark grey animal falling down behind him. Rhodin and Cobah neighed vigorously, their forelegs kicking the air.

Now around seven wild animals came out of the hideouts very quietly at the same time. They were wild dogs or wolves for sure, but now licking gross saliva constantly from their fangs and half opened mouths, they were only hungry beasts.

"Leinad, keep on forwarding," suggested Rupidd calmly.

Rupidd's eyes were fixed on the beasts, his left arm up in mid-air with a pack of blue metal pieces in his hand. The next seconds, two more beasts jumped toward Leinad, but in a flash they fell down, howling sharply. Now even before the two touched the ground, the remaining beasts leaped toward Rupidd all at the same time, snarling revoltingly. This time Rupidd was even faster, his darts did not let them roar twice. In half a millisecond the rage of the hunger turned into tormenting yowls, and the wild hunters tumbled onto the ground helplessly.

Leinad released a sigh of relief, his eyes moved to the dark cliff again. He did not use his weapon, but he felt a pain in his grip. Rupidd briefly studied the motionless animals on the ground and moved his interest to the hill over the trail as though they were nothing but warped woods.

"Keep on going, Leinad," cried Rupidd brightly, patting Rhodin's neck.

As they advanced, the actual profile of the black figure became apparent. It certainly was a huge rock, except for the surface which was entirely covered up with enormous numbers of black birds. At first Leinad thought they were crows, but that was not right because some of them actually dangled underneath like bats. They kept their spots awfully silent and absolute unmoved. Half a second Leinad considered they were all dead, or fakes glued on the rock permanently. But Rhodin and Cobah seemed to believe what Rupidd had said. Their steps kept advancing, their eyes firm on the cliff. Rupidd gently soothed Rhodin's neck, his eyes surveying the surrounding carefully. Leinad replicated his master exactly the same.

The area was filled with large rocks, shaped like sea shells. The tips of them were well buried in the ground, standing upright as though they had life. Leinad thought that they were perfect shelters for animals. But it was so quiet that nothing seemingly existing, making them even creepier.

Leinad once speculated what his father was doing in this horrible place at that dreadful time. Anything could have happened, but his father came back home without a bit of injury. Leinad's eyes moved around as if to find anything that could have been his father's ally.

"I was told there was a human shelter over the hill, but I am not sure how we will hit upon it," said Rupidd anxiously, his eyes looking up the hill. "I believe that's what he's been after. But I doubt he made it safely," muttered Rupidd composedly.

For a brief second Leinad thought that his master was talking about his father, then, he remembered another person.

"The archeologist you meant, master?"

"Yes, Kangryn. A brilliant man, but his enthusiasm always goes too fast, way before the safety issue. Well, he managed well to find the way out so far, but I wonder how his life has been going on over the life-risking bridges," uttered Rupidd, freezing his stare briefly at every suspicious spot as if to demonstrate he was different from the archeologist.

"Nevertheless," Rupidd added, but Leinad could not listen anymore. His mind and eyes were stolen by the black creatures which were now so close while they were passing the cliff. He genuinely wanted to beg his master to stop talking, but the words could not leave his mouth.

"He is such a gift, I should point that out," said Rupidd approvingly, his eyes studying the cliff briefly.

As their steps slowly moved on toward the other side of the cliff, there appeared a huge field full of sanctuary rocks in various sizes and shapes widely spread to the distant surroundings which ended by densely populated green trees stood like a grove fence. Nature had reserved remarkable features for animals to live with peace and joys, but there was no hint of any small activities whatsoever under that concept. Leinad for a moment made an unsuccessful attempt to locate the natural shelter which his master referred.

"I have a very bad feeling about this place, master," whispered Leinad, his eyes back wandering around the giant cliff agitatedly.

"Well," chuckling softly once, Rupidd said, "that's for sure, Leinad. No one would ever have a good feeling up here."

"Master, I can't spot the human shelter you mentioned," said Leinad dejectedly. "See, they just –."

"Naturally," said Rupidd spontaneously. "It is not that easy for sure."

Rupidd's attention moved over to the giant cliff again. Narrowing his eyes at the cliff he mused silently for a few seconds.

"Leinad, if you ever able to go up there...," said Rupidd, sounding rapt.

"Hmmm, why I didn't ever question about it until now...?" muttered Rupidd, drawing his awareness to Leinad now, looking quiet serious.

Sharp chill came across Leinad's spine. His eyes nervously moved to the giant cliff which now looked very much like an enormous beast crouching before attack. Words jumbled inside and he could not make a humble sentence.

"Are, are you serious...?" He managed to make one out.

"That's right. But how...," said Rupidd, releasing a faint regretful sigh, "is the question."

"But, it's out of the question s. It's obvious, master," protested Leinad as if being hurt.

"Listen, Leinad," began Rupidd, looking at Leinad's eyes thoughtfully, "first, I am not going to throw you anywhere without knowing your safety. And second, it's you, Leinad, who have to find the shelter."

"I don't understand, master Rupidd. Why is that?" asked Leinad at a loss.

"Because…your father had asked you to," said Rupidd resolutely now. "Yes, he had taken care of animals in this forest, and came back home in one piece… Is it convincing?"

Leinad's heart turned still, his mouth half opened as though Rupidd's words just charmed him to a statue.

Rupidd examined Leinad's face and formed a trifling smile.

"When your father in the end came back home he had only said that things were turning positive." Rupidd's eyes moved over to the field down the hill, and he said decisively, "Yes, I was optimistic. I had believed that he wouldn't end up here hopelessly."

"What about the monster? It should have killed him anytime," said Leinad with difficulty.

"That's right, Leinad. The monster must have been here, threatening animals and, of course, your father," said Rupidd, sounding unrealistic. "But, see, your father came back just like that."

"Just like that with a smile…," recited Leinad with a glum look.

Rupidd nodded approvingly once, hardening his face.

"After all that, you father never came back from the castle," said Rupidd regretfully.

"But, master, why did he go to the – ?"

Leinad stopped as he was nearly startled by a sudden loud shriek echoed in the quiet area. It came from the complex of stone shelters down the hill. Rupidd's head sharply responded to the direction while his hand patting Rhodin's neck softly. Leinad eased Cobah's neck at once, but his eyes promptly directed to the cliff. The Dark Choppers were yet intact.

"Come with me now, Leinad. We will have to figure out this one first," said Rupidd briskly.

Rhodin set off at once and Cobah followed accordingly. Leinad mind ached with his previous feeling that he had expressed to his master; *I really have a bad feeling with this place.* While his eyes were engaged in scrutinizing the area attentively, he spared his mind to spot the human shelter; or at least some kind of hint which could change his master's mind. Now all the rocks which once he had considered as shelters were like countless sinister hidey-holes from which any unseen nasty creatures could pop out and gnaw his back any time. From the distance they were only small identical pieces of odd-looking rocks or sea shells, but now they were all different in some ways and much bigger. In dismay Leinad considered them all as human shelters.

"Master," called Leinad cautiously. He wanted to ask his master about the contour of the real human shelter.

Rupidd hoisted his hand, reining up Rhodin, his eyes fixed on shelters dotted ambiguously on the left side of the trail. Leinad, who held his weapon tight in his hand, kept silent right behind his master, his eyes nervously tracing his master's. Then he heard growling sounds; very faint, but a lot from shelters here and there. Now, they were snarling at one another like quarreling about their shares. It was not a good sign at all. Rupidd took it very seriously.

"Listen, Leinad," he began, turning to Leinad with a solemn expression. "You've seen enough of Arch Cliff already. And so, we'll change our plan here. You are going home now, Leinad. Run fast over and down the hill, and through the forest straight toward southeast, and you will get home in no time. Don't look back or stop no matter what happens. And tomorrow, you must get going to the castle. You heard me?" said Rupidd determinedly. "Now, Cobah, it's your duty. I leave him to you."

At that juncture, with thundering roars a huge rock fell right before them with a loud thud. Rhodin and Cobah jerked with sudden fear, hissing recklessly at once.

"Samahan Kan!" shouted Rupidd in dread.

Leinad was not sure if it was a rock at the present, but then he saw someone being fossilized inside, visible through the semi-transparent surface of the object. In the next seconds a deafening voice whacked his hairs erect.

"WHAT DO YOU THINK YOU ARE?"

Roars came with echoes, but the figure was yet out of sight.

"Sneaking in my territory, indeed!"

"Leinad, NOW! Cobah, run as fast as you can!" hissed Rupidd, ignoring the furious roars.

"Run, Cobah!" he cried again.

Leinad did not have any choice because Cobah was already on her way as she was ordered. *Grandpa!* He shouted only soundlessly to curb the fear. And he had to work very hard to press down an excruciating impulse to look back.

Cobah ran fast out of the hill of Arch Cliff along the trail then dashed into the forest. Leinad was unable to think anything properly until Cobah abruptly stopped with a loud neigh, almost throwing him into the air. For a moment he believed to face another group of wild beasts. But it was only a small figure up in the air right before him. Surely it was not like a bird. Then he considered it to be a nasty creature, Dark Chopper, but it was rather endearing for that; despite having no feathers, with a sparkling skin it was quite an appealing animal. And one way or another it was very familiar to Leinad. Cobah seemed to have a similar impression. In fact she even looked happy to see the creature. Not only that, as this little creature set off toward the hill, Cobah turned around and followed it.

"Cobah, what are you doing? We have to get out of here now!" cried Leinad in panic.

But Cobah seemed to have decided to follow the little animal for any reason. Ignoring Leinad's panicked cry, she simply kept trailing it. Maybe she just wanted to go back and make sure that her friend Rhodin (with master Rupidd) was all right, Leinad considered. Then he did not ask Cobah twice.

Shortly, they were back on the hill which was very quiet now. In the absence of his master, Leinad felt that the hill and the cliff were awfully chilling. There was no hint of the winner of the battle between a master and a monster. Leinad had a very strong itch to go check the site, but he was too afraid to know what might have happened.

Moments later, Cobah stopped as the flying animal perched atop a shelter. The trail ended there in front of the shelter. Leinad then figured out that it was not actually the front of the shelter where the trail ended, but at the back of it. There was no particular difference in the appearance of the shelter. The front was left widely open and a roomy stony shelter was revealed as he entered. Nothing particular to notice. Then again, why the trail ended there? His mind came back to the question. He returned to the rear and examined the surface of the stone wall with his hands. Some parts of the surface were slightly protruded with a certain angles in a broad line, but virtually indistinguishable. He followed the obtruded line carefully and confirmed that the line ended in a shape of an octagon which was taller than his height. And there were a pair of small lumps in the center.

He absentmindedly held his hands on the lumps and pushed to his left and then to his right. Nothing happened. This time, with intent he placed his hands on the lumps and pushed outward both ways (left and right) at the same time. When he was almost in need of oxygen, it cracked to life, appearing a visible vertical line in the center. Now, with a feeling of winning he pushed even harder to both ways, and ultimately, the entire wall separated into two pieces, giving a large gap that looked like the main entrance to the shelter.

Feeling eager to see what's inside Leinad gestured to Cobah with a nervous smile, and he carried the smile to the top of the shelter, but the flying creature was not there anymore. It was gone. He stepped in without delay. And as they entered, the door slid close.

It was not the shelter which he had entered before. Surprisingly, it was now a neat space lit mildly with the light coming from the flat ceiling. There were four stone walls that stood smoothly, making a robust square room. Except for the floor which was tidy and elegant with one piece of granite, the room was like one piece of an empty rock. Leinad wondered if it was really made up with a single rock. Its shape and structure with a thin ceiling were too elaborate to be natural. However, without any articles within the room, and with the light coming from the ceiling, it was almost like a large empty diamond box. Nevertheless, there was nothing particular to reason the hidden entrance.

Now Leinad turned his interest to the wall that hid the exit. He walked to the wall and tried to feel the cracks with his hands while looking vaguely at Cobah. No, there was no crack as far as his sensor told. Cobah was staring at the floor with a reason, and his eyes followed. Then, he spotted something from his location. They were thin lines of cracks, which were shaped like a diamond, visible right in the center of the granite floor. He threw himself there straight away, but then, he found nothing on the spot.

He wiped out the surface willingly several times with his sleeves and hands. Interestingly, some words gradually appeared in emerald and a horizontal line in red below the words. Leinad read it out cheerfully for Cobah and the imaginary master to hear.

If you inscribe animals
You are twelve and
Go fit to love
Challenge to free nature

It was a riddle.

"If you inscribe animals, you are twelve and go fit to love challenge to free nature." Leinad repeated it several times without getting any better ideas or a foreseeable clue to inscribe.

The whole sentence only gave an impression to call attention to animals and nature. But it would not be that simple, he thought. He then studied the riddle with each word separately, striving to make any possible sentences by taking out words systematically. He took the first words of each row and read down the lines.

"If you go challenge…."

It also made sense. Then, he worked for the second, third, and fourth words in the same way. The result was not disappointing. It read, "you are fit to," "inscribe twelve to free," and "animals and love nature."

Now he linked all together and read it aloud.

"If you go challenge you are fit to inscribe twelve to free animals and love nature."

It made some sense. In fact, it sounded perfect because the riddle unearthed the right person. He was now cherishing twelve.

Leinad wrote 'twelve' right above the specified line with his finger. Shortly, there was a cheerful crack sound from the floor, and then, another crack from the wall. In a moment the stone wall in front of him slid open smoothly.

"What?" cried Leinad, making a face.

"The riddle was only to open a hidden exit, Cobah?"

Flummoxed, Leinad walked to the exit which was now left widely open. And there, what he saw was a straight trail to the giant cliff which looked so close now. And at once he realized that something was missing on the cliff.

"Look, Cobah! Dark Choppers are gone!" cried Leinad in surprise.

Now the cliff was much like a tilted alphabet – small letter h. Otherwise, it was like number 6 with the bottom half earthed. Whichever it resembled, the figure formed a remarkable arch underneath the figure.

Leinad stepped out of the room, his eyes surveying the trail and the sky. Yet, all clear and quiet. Courage grew inside without knowing it.

This is it. This is the moment. Leinad believed that his master should be somewhere down the hill, wanting to see him up on the cliff in this very moment. *I can find the location of the human shelter now, master!*

Cobah came beside like she knew what Leinad would do next.

"I will go climb up the cliff now, Cobah. You just stay here, wait for my signal, OK?" he said, making an effort to cover his feeling.

With the spear in his hand, Leinad sprinted toward the cliff without delay. When he was a little more than half way, some of his senses told him that he was not alone. He turned his head to conform. Sure enough, a wild animal with two frenzied eyes was after him fast. In the next few seconds, however, many more jumped out of shelters and joined the hunt. No choice now. He ran toward the cliff as fast as he could. At this moment there was a loud screech from the sky, but he had to keep on running fast. Another screech fiercely hit his eardrums. Now the surrounding darkened, and the air turned chilly. He looked up the sky, and the instant he did, he was frozen on the spot. A flight of Dark Choppers! They were swooping down toward him very aggressively. And they were very close already. Down on the ground the wild animals were even closer. They would not give up their portions of the prey. They opened their mouths wide, their greasy fangs aimed at Leinad. Then, they jumped toward Leinad all at once. Leinad shrunk his body, his arms wrapping around his head, screaming.

Leinad was not sure what was going on. It was only so dark and very noisy for the time being, yet he was breathing. Knowing he was still alive, he did not want to find out what was going on beyond his eyelids for now. *Pretty soon, they will finish me without leaving a tidbit of bones, anyway.* He bolted his eyes tight and started to count the seconds he could breathe. When he counted around twenty, he sensed brightness, and it was awfully quiet again. He unzipped his eyes. The sky and the ground were all clear like what had happened was not for real. The truth was that he was still in one piece, breathing.

His immediate thought was running back to Cobah, but somehow he found more courage inside now. Whatever the reason, Dark Choppers did not even touch him at all. Besides, the empty cliff was right before him. Then, without second thought he ran toward the cliff again.

"At last!" Leinad cried nervously, climbing up the naked giant cliff.

As his breath gradually grew faster so as strength in him. Until he reached the very top edge, he thought only about the whereabouts of his father and master. Moments later, Leinad stood on the zenith of the cliff, and he saw the world down below. He felt it was so high that he was in Saline Land; maybe heaven. Then there was no room for fear whatever may bring.

Master, you were wrong. It can't be a hopeless hell. Or can there be heaven right atop hell? Heaven and hell... Are they that close?

It was wide, spanning over an ocean of green tree tops swaying toward the distance with wind. Down below were small ashen solid rocks scattered over the field. Leinad studied the shelter rocks thoroughly from one side. By doing so, he discovered that they were in fact in certain forms of clusters. And there were tapered trails between every group of rocks, narrowing to the center. It was like a huge spiral spider web network. It was a labyrinth.

While he was tracing the trail to the shelter where Cobah was, his eyes stopped at the shelter rock right in the center of the network. It was very identical to all others except for the fact that it was the only one with a straight trail to Arch Cliff, and that was where Cobah was. *That is the human shelter!*

Now Leinad's interest moved to the cliff where he stood. He could not believe he was right at the home of the creepy birds; the pinnacle of the cliff. There was no sign of Dark Choppers appearing from anywhere in the sky. But he spotted a creature flapping gently in mid-air behind him. He at once knew that it was the same peculiar flying animal. He was pleased to see it again.

"Hello, there, my friend." Leinad greeted cheerfully. "My thanks for helping me find the human shelter."

The creature made a faint sound, wagging its tail. Then it landed gently on the cliff. Leinad now noticed that there was a thin circled line of crack on the surface where the animal perched. He stepped toward it, and the creature flew up again. He sat down beside the circle, his eyes moving to the companion in the air.

"You came to help me again, my friend?" asked Leinad, beaming.

He brushed, tapped, and smacked the area. Nothing happened. Now he just caught a glimpse of a pair of very faint hand prints in the center of the circle. It was nearly obscured.

Leinad hesitantly placed his hands and pondered what his master would suggest for him, his eyes looking at the creature as though it was his master who came to deliver any useful advice.

"Well, you wouldn't find any answer on my face, would you? I would close my eyes, instead, and try to think something that might help," said the imaginary master.

Leinad closed his eyes and opened his mind wide to let any helpful words arise and float in the sky.

Blue Forest, Arch Cliff, Dark Choppers, monster, flying creature, human shelter, master Rupidd..., and Father? Motivation...

Yes, it was the word that he would never forget. It has been the origin and the reason of his courage and strength. Now, Leinad attempted to draw a world where his father could have been. Then, suddenly he heard someone calling him in the dark. Startled, he opened his eyes. The voice died away with the brightness. The next moment, he felt the stone under his hands crackle. He withdrew them swiftly as the stone slid open. *It worked!* In delight his eyes searched for his cheerful companion in the air, but it was gone again.

Chapter 7
LAND OF FINIXIES

The first thing Leinad saw was darkness, and then, the steps of a spiral staircase became gradually visible. While he was hesitating, he saw an image of his master nodding with an encouraging smile. He reluctantly moved his feet down the steps. His hesitation step by step diminished with increasing interest in an unseen picture down the well. It was a dreadful long way down. When his feet after some time touched the ground, unexpectedly the whole area turned bright. And this instant, his mouth fell open by the sight that came with the sudden brightness.

It was a miniature of Arch Cliff, but now Leinad was not sure if he called it Horrible Hell or Heavenly Home. The letter h of Arch Cliff stood straight on the hill, and down below was a broad field filled with a large number of silver stones resembling tombstones, whose sizes decreased as they were close to the center. To his amazement there were some kinds of animal figures engraved on every stone. Leinad stared at the stones for a while as if to mesmerize whatever the animals to pop out at once. Around the stone there were very narrow circuit-like trails just like the real ones outside. And lastly, in the center was a diamond-shaped silver statue that stood like a memorial tower. The whole structure must have meant to be a charming miniature world, but Leinad could not smile. It only made him think of a graveyard for the animals killed by the horrendous monster. With all the tombstones it only suited Horrible Hell to memorize.

Leinad's stare stopped at the silvery statue in the center. There were some letters carved on the surface, but they were nearly hidden under the brightness. With the help of his finger tips, he figured out the article written on the silver statue. It was a story about the cliff of h. His mind hovered hopelessly after reading it.

> h cliff
>
> heart of animals of all kinds once made for
>
> happiness they share in
>
> harmony they live with
>
> hope they wanted it to be
>
> holy place
>
> hence
>
> he who reads this
>
> help the land he must
>
> holler two words

"Here comes another riddle," cried Leinad, feeling irritated. "And now TWO words this time."

But, after reading several times, he realized that he already knew the answer. And he called it out almost by a sudden instinct.

"Heavenly home!"

And the response came right away. Now the diamond statue started to illuminate, and at some point the surrounding suddenly filled with piercing light which was so strong that Leinad jerked by surprise, covering up his face with hands. His eyes bolted tight, but he sensed the light scattering brilliantly. He had a strong intuition that there were some figures actually moving in the air, but he was not brave enough to swear it. When the diamond statue was settled with a peaceful silence, Leinad undid his eyes cautiously. Now the surrounding was vague, and virtually nothing was visible except two objects.

Behind him was the silver statue, yet stood like a memorial tower. And in front was a huge figure, shaped like a fork. In fact, the outline of it was much like two of alphabet letter h; one of them was backward, close enough to make a shape like a colossal fork. Leinad decided it was an entrance of a peaceful land because 'Heavenly Home' was written on the top of the structure. There was no actual gate in there, but he could not see a thing behind the structure from there. He forced himself to step forward cautiously. As he passed through the arch, a peaceful motion picture with cheerful sounds gradually appeared before him.

Remarkably, it was indeed a heavenly home. There were animals playing leisurely on a green meadow, birds somersaulting gaily up in the air. Along with tall healthy green trees there were animal shelters arrayed in groups endlessly toward the distance. And cheerful chirps in various colors came from the rich leaves of a forest. The animals on the land, the birds in the sky, even the trees on the ground looked so blissful. And no one seemed bothered by a strange visitor.

"Hello, there!"

Leinad was momentarily frightened by an audible voice from behind. When he looked back, there was a girl with a pleasing smile. She was slim and small.

"Welcome to Heavenly Home, the second visitor," said the girl happily.

Feeling stunned, Leinad gawked at the girl for a moment.

"This is Vixie, and she is a caretaker here," said the girl spiritedly.

"Nice, that's nice name," said Leinad awkwardly still in disbelief.

"But, is this for real?" asked Leinad, forgetting to introduce himself.

"For real?" recited the girl with a grin.

"I mean, it's not a…." he began, but he could not complete the sentence because her eyes were so real and vivacious.

It is real. He decided.

"I mean, I am not sure where I landed unless you tell me a bit…"

"This place is concealed as you may have noticed. See those animals? They are never bothered by a human like you because they have never met any human. Well, technically, humans are forbidden here by the nature. Sorry, but they only tend to kill animals," said the girl disappointedly.

"Aren't you a human?" asked Leinad, sounding obvious.

"Vixie is only a Finixie."

"Finixie?" asked Leinad in bewilderment.

"We Finixies have an ability to communicate with all animals on this land. Of course, we Finixies can do with humans just like you, although we Finixies have never gone to their world before," said the girl proudly.

"I don't understand, Vixie. You are like us, but not a human?"

"First of all, we Finixie were not born, but made by the nature. We Finixies never eat; never die, if you ask me. And of course, we Finixie can talk just like you."

That was a big difference. But yet, Leinad could not convince himself completely. Her eyes innocently sparkled as if there was pure light behind.

"OK, that's fine. Although there is no reason, but I still think it is only a dream," cried Leinad. "So, please, if it is not, tell me how I can get back."

"Not so fast, Leinad, you came here not by an accident," exclaimed Vixie.

"What do you mean not by an accident?" asked Leinad, his face befuddled.

"Well, it went all as expected," said Vixie.

"What?" Leinad cried in disbelief of what he heard.

"Hold on, how do you know my name?" asked Leinad defensively.

Then, he remembered what she said in the very beginning.

"Did you say that I was the second human to visit here?"

Leinad's eyes fixed on hers with a feeling of growing contentment.

"You know my father, aren't you?" asked Leinad decisively. "And he was the first one who visited here. That's what it is!" exclaimed Leinad confirmatively.

He began to understand his master's intension now. It was all convincing.

"Can you please tell me about my father?" asked Leinad sincerely.

There was no doubt that the Finixie knew something about his father. Without any objection she kept silent for a while as if assessing the first visitor.

"Hasyn was a remarkable human. He really was," said the girl thoughtfully. "He helped Vixie with a lot of things for animals, to tell the truth."

Leinad was now more than thrilled to hear his father's name and his father's deed for the good. Whether it was a dream or for real, it was still exhilarating to learn about his father.

"On the land where he lived, Hasyn had said, there was an atrocious killer monster. He'd worked hard to settle with peace, but he could not succeed it because the monster's power grew incredibly. So, he'd decided to go to the king to appeal. You see, he wanted to build a heavenly home for animals like here, but obviously it was impossible," explained Vixie regretfully.

"In the presence of such a monster...," muttered Leinad remorsefully.

"Do you know..., did he say anything about how he managed his life in the presence of the monster? He could have been killed any time."

"Well, not precisely. Vixie remembers she'd asked once," said the Finixie.

"And?" demanded Leinad mildly.

"Yes, he had only said there was a friend helping him," said Vixie with an effort to recall something.

Leinad thought of his master or the archeologist.

"Harf... Harfhas. Yes, that was his name," said the girl after a while.

"Harfhas?" repeated Leinad blankly.

"Look, Leinad," began Vixie, her voice sounded suddenly serious. "Vixie senses that you must go now. Vixie will tell you briefly at this point. Your father knew that you would go all through on your own and make it to this point on this day. And that's why Vixie waited for you."

"What do you mean you waited for me? You mean he already knew that he would not return?"

"Vixie thinks so," replied Vixie, her expression was murky. "Sorry, Leinad, Vixie had no idea what was with him. He'd never said anything bad, and that was him. Vixie really doesn't… you know all these years Vixie really wanted to know what had happened to him," said Vixie desolately.

"Vixie is sure he is OK, Leinad, but… Vixie wishes she could find a way of knowing it for sure."

Leinad face turned dark as though he'd lost all the tastes in life.

"Do you think he was…?"

He began abruptly, but he was afraid of hearing the answer.

"Don't worry, Leinad, Vixie is sure he must have been struck with something trivial," said the Finixie, grimacing.

"And this," said the girl, pushing a small pale green parchment toward him, she added, "is from your father. You should figure out what has written on it."

Leinad's face lit up with thrill. *Something from my father!*

"Now, you must leave, Leinad," cried the Finixie.

"And take these with you. Vixie prepared for Hasyn, but did not make it."

"Thanks, but what are they?"

"Special plant granule cubes from this land or powder bombs, if you like. They might come in handy especially when you are in a critical situation. But, open the jars only when you have to use the contents. Both the black and red chunks will effectively burst in a second out of the jars. Remember, though, these are not bombs, and they do not kill anything."

Leinad looked at her eyes with a gentle smile, but he was not listening to her explanation. His mind was filled with speculation for the parchment that his father had left for him.

Finally, I have something from my father.

"If you go straight out of the gate, you will see the diamond statue as before. Holler the words, and you are out of this land. With peace, you are always welcome, Leinad!"

Waving his hands at the Finixie, Leinad rushed toward the giant gate. It was only after her figure disappeared when he realized that he did not even say thank-you for all.

Next time, Vixie!

Yes, if I come again, it would be with my father for sure.

It was so bright that Leinad felt it was a blackout. Then, the view changed again. He was back in the hidden dungeon of the giant cliff. It was almost like jumping out of a dream by design, and throwing to reality. He moved his steps up the spiral stairs, and the dungeon graveyard gradually obscured into darkness. He stepped up fast, and shortly the gate unbolted on its own accord. And out of the gate, he sensed a cool puff of air under the bright sky. Then he suddenly felt that he was away for a long time and he grew a lot.

Chapter 8
ALONE

To his relief the Dark Choppers were not home and the cliff was still empty. Leinad beheld the peaceful sky and wondered if they really vanished with the wild beasts for good.

Master, you would not believe what I have gone through.

He rushed down the cliff, speculating if Cobah saw him returning. When he was near the ground he heard a growl from somewhere. He stepped back in alert. And there came a wild animal, threatening with needle-sharp fangs. A few more showed up in the next moment. And shortly the entire ground was filled with hungry beasts. As Leinad moved back further up, now the beasts hesitantly but steadily followed him one by one, growling one another, as if arguing their turns or possession.

Leinad knew that he would be completely trapped in the end, but he climbed back to the top of the cliff hurriedly. Now the beasts cornered him with confidence, yet grumbling one another. As he understood no way of running off from the beasts anymore, he looked down the cliff hopelessly. Then, he saw Cobah running toward the cliff. He yelled out loudly for her immediate attention. In the very next second the beasts took off to attack, and he had to jump off the cliff, calling out Cobah one more time.

Cobah also jumped high toward Leinad right on time. Amazingly she jumped so high that Leinad's fear lasted barely two seconds before he caught the saddle and landed on her back in mid-air. Then the next seconds Cobah touched the beast-free ground safely with a soft thud. And the instant she settled, she raced down the hill and dashed into the forest. She must have still remembered the order of the master. There were many wild animals barking fiercely along the way. But Cobah ran stunningly fast to shun the chasers. It was an order. They were wild and tough, but they were no match for Cobah at all.

Leinad, you must make it for tomorrow.

Leinad woke up in the morning by the sound of neighing from Cobah. At first he thought it was Rhodin with master Rupidd, but it was only the alarm call of Cobah to wake him up.

Time to wake up and get ready for the journey to the castle, Leinad.

The truth was Rupidd did not return home until morning. Leinad remembered what had happened to the archeologist. He attempted to shake off the memory. *Master Rupidd is, of course, different.* He decided. But the concern constantly haunted his mind, gnawing his resolution bit by bit.

He will come back and see me if I wait just a little longer…

No, I must go now! He fought back.

"No matter what happened." Leinad cried, imitating his master.

Now, if I stay here any longer, even I will blame myself.

"Cobah is waiting. I must go now," he assured himself.

Father is waiting. He knows I am coming.

Chapter 9
FATHER'S MESSAGE

Leinad nearly forgot about the parchment from the Finixie. His mind has been preoccupied by the concern about his master. He decided that his master had returned home only late, and he settled with an idea of letting his master know that he arrived in the castle safely. Thus, once the reception with the king was over that night, he wrote a note for his master. Then, the following morning before even others woke up, he went straight to Cobah.

"Cobah, you will need to go and see your friend, Rhodin," said Leinad cheerfully. "You have worried about him, too, haven't you?" Leinad soothed Cobah's neck with a mild smile. "Happy now?"

The horse neighed cheerfully once, his tail wagging for a moment.

"And can you do me a favor, Cobah?" asked Leinad, showing a small parchment to his horse. "It's for master Rupidd. I am sure he returned home by now with Rhodin, and if you can deliver it for me, please, Cobah," said Leinad sincerely.

He threw his hand into the saddle pocket and took out the case containing the parchment and the jars from the Finixie. He then removed the parchment from the case and rested his note in it. He showed the case to Cobah and placed it back into the saddle pocket.

"Cobah, please, don't mind the saddle on your back."

The horse neighed once again and trotted out of the stall. Leinad led her toward the main entrance gate. When the gigantic gate opened widely, Cobah dashed straight out toward the passageway as though she would need to run away from the deadly prison. While watching Cobah disappearing into the morning mist, Leinad had to press hard to stifle a sudden desire to run home with her.

Yet, it was too early for the first event to start. Back in his room he sat on the bedside and unrolled the parchment quietly. For a brief second Leinad thought it was for someone else. But next second he knew it was his father's because it was a riddle from his father in his own way. As far as he knew only his father would do that. Brief and mysterious as it read:

D A N I E L,

Congratulations at last you made it.

Sure I knew you would without help.

You are strong and wise as always be.

Trust power and wisdom in you.

Believe no scales in your ability.

I hope you find joys and meaning in your life.

Always with you on this land my only son.

D654321 Y1Y2C3I2 Y8Y5 T1A8Y1 I4T2B3 S7A6

A sudden wave of sorrow surged upon Leinad's mind with his father's handwriting. It's been many years ever since his father first taught him with his own hands and voice. And here in his hand were words that his father had written for him five years ago. Hoping to understand what was in his father's mind he tried to sense the words rather than reading them. He felt his father's words standing out brightly among the jumbled letters. Then, it seemed that the words on the parchment were turning into a voice, and he felt that he was hearing his father right beside him. And now they were more than just a few brief and concise words. They were sweet and encouraging words out of his father's mouth. Then, his father asked him to do something serious, yet his voice appealing.

"Go find the power, son, and save the world."

Leinad face turned dark as the words of his father touched his senses. He suddenly felt that he was the only dependable person on the land.

"But, father, I do not understand. What power and why we need to save the world? And for any reasons my urgent matter is you. I just have to find out what had happened to you, father. I can't think of anything else now." Leinad mumbled faintly, feeling ever low.

"My lad, are you all right?"

A friendly voice revived the air of grief in the room, drawing Leinad's awareness. There was a man stood by the door with a concerned expression. Leinad at once recognized that he was one of the servants for the king.

"Hello, sir, just a little...," managed Leinad politely, clearing his throat. He attempted to hide his dark face with a smile. "Is it already the time?" He asked, standing up.

"Well, almost. As the head general, I am just checking if everyone's ready," said the man proudly, emphasizing 'head general.'

"My lad, you miss your home already, I presume," uttered the general, shooting a glance at the parchment in Leinad's hand.

"Miss my home? Oh, no, sir."

Leinad noticed the general looking at the parchment seriously.

"Just wrote a few things to be done, sir, while I am waiting," said Leinad brightly, tapping the parchment on his leg.

"You did, indeed," exclaimed the general in a similar tone.

"Well, you must get moving now," he said with a tedious expression, stepping back toward the door.

"Ah," he said, narrowing his eyes, "you haven't seen a little mouse, have you?"

"A mouse, sir…, head general?" asked Leinad.

"Something like that," replied the general unsurely.

"No, head general," said Leinad, looking around room. "Are you –."

"No, I am not playing with animals. Animals are not for playing," uttered the general dully.

"There has been a disturbing little animal around this area," declared the general, his eyes surveying Leinad's eyes thoughtfully. "And I am sure you did not bring anything dangerous."

"No, no, head general," replied Leinad abruptly.

The general nodded, looking satisfied. Then he disappeared without any further comments. On seeing the door closed, Leinad hid the parchment under the drawer of the bedside table at once, and stood up to leave for the launching hall. However, his mind held him with the thought of 'anything dangerous' that the general had referred. He gazed at the bedside table vaguely as though he was waiting for any dangerous words to be discharged from the parchment, if any.

"A dangerous game…," murmured Leinad faintly.

The real game would start soon, he knew, but whatever it was, he was not interested for the moment. The urgent matter for him now was to find any information about his father. To begin with, he would figure out whether his father was really there in the castle. Then, he would definitely need to find someone to ask about his father first. For a brief moment he weighed up his father's words seriously once more, but saving the world was far beyond his thoughts.

"Sorry, father. Whatever the world you meant, you are the world for me, and I will have to work on it, first."

He set off to the launching hall to join the first game. "Let's begin."

Chapter 10
DANGEROUS GAME

"Sir, excuse me." Leinad called the man who was about to disappear behind the door of the launching hall. "Can I...have a moment with you, sir?" asked Leinad, smiling ineptly.

"Yes?" said the man, turning his head to Leinad. "Ah, what an honor it is! I didn't dare to meet one of the best riders personally." He cried with an exaggerate sense of a smile. "Fast and brave! I have been a gamekeeper for years, but never seen anyone like you ever since...," said the man cheerfully.

"So, what brought you to draw my mind today? Nad..., Leinad, I believe."

"Oh, yes, sir. That is my name," said Leinad thankfully.

"Why, you want to complain about your victory, Leinad?"

No, no, absolutely not, sir. It was an exciting game, regardless of the result," said Leinad openly. "Well, I just wanted to say hello, sir."

"Ah, that's nice of you, Leinad," said the gamekeeper, beaming.

"Well," the gamekeeper began thoughtfully now, "what can be the most likely matter stuck in your mind, stopping my way?"

"Oh, no, sir. Please don't get me wrong. Seriously, I am happy with everything as it is," said Leinad hastily, his eyes bulging as though being frightened by the question of the man.

"Yes, the next game. A wise one always prepares in advance," said the man caringly, ignoring Leinad's innocent gesture. "Yes, better to know certain dangers this time," he added, nodding. "Whether you enjoyed the first game or not, I would say, it was only the practice for this game. Certainly there are some unavoidable serious dangers that you will have to deal with during the game," said the man with intent.

Leinad decided to be a good listener now, with visible interest on his face.

"But," he began again, his finger pointing at Leinad's eyes, "they could be nothing at all to you. B.A.S.! That's all you need for this game. Brave, Astute and Swift!" He exclaimed eagerly.

"Well," he said encouragingly, "that's exactly what YOU have."

"Oh, thank you, sir." Leinad acknowledged sincerely, but his mind was not exactly following the man because a question came out of his mind when the man said, 'unavoidable serious dangers' in the next game.

"In the past was there anyone –."

"Missing?" The man speculated. "Certainly, there has always been anyone lacking the content for such a game ever since the game became part of the events."

"Five…," began Leinad hesitantly, "I am suddenly curious to know, sir… Was there anyone missing during the game five years ago?" Leinad managed to ask a question, trying to hide his intension.

With this question, however, the gamekeeper gazed at Leinad's eyes seriously for a few seconds before turning his head toward the hallway.

"Five years ago…," said the man, his voice went down quite a bit. "Well, I assume you have any specific reason for that."

Leinad thought fast if he could tell the man about his father for any useful pieces of advice. Who else otherwise? He seemed to be the most appropriate person to ask such a question in the castle.

"I am just curious to know if there was anyone missing five years ago. That's all, sir," said Leinad plainly as though it was unimportant.

"Anyone… Do you know his name by any chance?"

"…Hasyn, sir," replied Leinad cautiously, surveying the man's face carefully. "I only thought that he might have been here for the games five years ago, sir."

With these words the gamekeeper's eyes traveled awkwardly up and down the corridor at once before settling down on the hallway.

"Hmmm." He released a faint sigh.

"I am not sure if I can answer to that, Leinad," he said regretfully. "The game was introduced only recently, I am afraid." His eyes now returned back to Leinad with an unnatural smile.

"I am sorry, if I troubled you with the question, sir," said Leinad sincerely.

Leinad was quite surprised by the unexpected response from the man. Then he made an effort to change the subjects with intent.

"You are right, sir, the game sounds very dangerous."

"Yes, Leinad," replied the man, "but again, BAS! He exclaimed brightly.

"Well, guessing from the way you play, I daresay you are on the safe side, and it is nothing to worry for you. You will be in the real hunting pretty soon."

His expression turned into cheers now, smacking Leinad's shoulder.

"That much I can tell you for sure," added the man conclusively.

His voice was bright, but Leinad did not miss to see him sighing deeply.

"…the beginning…," muttered the man in a barely audible voice.

"Norrikee!"

An aggressive voice came from the doorway. It was the 'head' general.

"You mustn't let Your Highness wait, my dear," he cried edgily.

Leinad was about to say a word of greeting, but could not find a room for it.

"Well, I must run fast now to report, my boy, good luck to you tomorrow."

"Thanks a lot, sir," yelled Leinad spiritedly toward the man who, following the general, was already stepping down the hallway.

Leinad stood there, watching them for a while. But his mind was held by the thought of what the gamekeeper tried to say in a muffled voice. Was that something about the happening five years ago? He wondered. *Something maybe related to the mystery of my father?* He considered. Then, he felt a tiny bit of encouragement growing inside. He would look for another time to talk to the gamekeeper for sure, and he could not wait too long.

Chapter 11
NORRIKEE'S ADVICE

Although his mind was preoccupied with the thoughts of his father, Leinad managed the danger well in the second game. However, an opportunity to talk to the gamekeeper never came to him throughout the day.

Leinad looked for such an opportunity when the game was first introduced by the gamekeeper in the morning. But he had to give it up because unexpectedly the general was along side like monitoring participants. Ever since the morning of the first day, Leinad had a bad impression on the general. It was a poor feeling. The general maybe a helpful person, but there was something that kept pushing Leinad's mind away from him. Moreover, the way he talked to the gamekeeper was certainly annoying.

Then again, Leinad hoped for a chance after the game. However, when he returned to the castle after the game, he was unable to find any chance to talk to the gamekeeper, because he darted away immediately from the throng for a mysterious reason. Leinad only presumed that the gamekeeper went to report to the king about the game.

Feeling pressed, Leinad came out of the hall and looked over the quiet corridor which curved down the silvery walls. Then he stepped along the hallway quite blankly. Just then, there came a familiar sweet voice behind him.

"My lad."

Startled, Leinad turned around to face the general.

"Sir. Hello, sir."

"Is there any trouble that I can help you out now?"

"No, no. Thank you, sir..., head general," Leinad managed to thank him with difficulty.

"Indeed," cried the general, nodding lightly. "You must be now too excited with all that. Well, in that case, why don't you go back to your room and rest for the next event?" suggested the general, smiling considerately. "And I blame your excitement to suffer the loss of your sense of direction. See, your room is on the other side of the hall, right?"

"Ah, you are right, head general. I must have been out of my mind," replied Leinad with a clumsy grin. "Then, I must return now," said Leinad, stepping back to the door.

"Were you...by any chance, looking for Norrikee?" asked the general tenderly behind Leinad.

The gamekeeper? Leinad recalled the name in the next second. "No, no, head general," he replied promptly, trying to sound genuine.

"I see," declared the general courteously. "Well, whatever the results I am achieving, I won't forget my reason in here with this precious opportunity, if I were you, my lad."

"I won't, head general." said Leinad before sliding into the gap of the door.

Leinad returned to his room immediately, but his mind was held up tightly with the view beyond the hallway. The interest grew, overwhelming the anxiety inside. There must be something very important for any reason, he decided. But apparently things would not be that easy at all.

"I will have to go find out," he ensured himself.

"Master Rupidd, what should I do now?" He mumbled faintly, his mind set on the moments he had spent with his master in Blue Forest. It seemed like years since he had left his master. Then he suddenly realized that he went through quite an adventure without his master. He did it all independently.

Yes, I am twelve, and I am independent! I must carry through whatever impediment to my way. Go, Leinad!

Leinad went to the launching hall again with a hope to see the gamekeeper once in private. It was not even close to midnight, but the hall was completely deserted. It was so quiet that he wondered if there was a specific reason for the night or even an announcement after the game. He lingered around the hall for a while, yet hoping to see the gamekeeper come back from the king.

The gamekeeper did not show up after all. Leinad beheld the door which seemed bolted so tight. Forbidden area… *Why?* He questioned. *Maybe it's because the king's palace is there?* He considered once. But then, when he speculated from the way the general had reacted, it did not sound right. He gazed at the door, pressing the temptation growing fast inside. No risk, no fruit.

Now, out of the hall, he moved his steps cautiously to the curved hallway, hoping to meet no one but the gamekeeper. As he bravely kept on walking, he met a big silver door at the end of the hallway. He opened the door very carefully, his mind already gone to the hidden place with full of clues for his father.

The first things he saw were five giant silver statues of what looked like flying animals in a spacious round hall. And there were five big identical silver doors evenly spaced around the wall. Each one of the statues of the flying animals was pointing to one of the doors in some way. Apparently one of the figures was a hemaby, but the remaining four were new to Leinad. Right in the center there was a tall slim silvery coral tree surrounded by the statues. There were illuminating letters brightly spread horizontally on a huge glittering ball on the top of the coral tree. It read PENTADIA.

Feeling dumfounded, Leinad stood there for a while. Then he concluded that there might be many undiscovered places within the castle, and the answer to the mystery of his father was hidden somewhere in one of these places. He surveyed the surrounding briefly once more and silently moved his steps to the door facing the statue of a hemaby.

The door cracked open into two pieces smoothly as Leinad touched it. He walked out of the hall and saw, first, a few stairs, and beyond, a curved corridor. He stepped up the stairway nervously. Looking at the curved corridor, suddenly he felt very cold, his footsteps sounded so loud, and the light unpleasant. There he heard voices. He advanced very quietly along the corridor until he could spy a hall with a huge silver door and two soldiers by the door, talking to the general.

"…didn't show up, head general."

"Indeed, he didn't," uttered the general, snorting. "That fool, I warned once already… Must be completely out of his mind now."

Then, his eyes shifted abruptly to the corridor, sniffing grossly. Leinad quickly threw himself behind the curved wall. It was almost an automatic response that he did not think a thing before the action.

"Don't you smell anything?"

"Smell?" asked one of the guards. "What smell, head general?"

"Never mind," replied the general, resuming his attention back to the soldiers. "I will go see Your Highness. And you both, if this fool appears, report to me right away, understood?"

"Understood, head general," replied the soldiers in one voice.

"Is that it?" Leinad muttered, stepping back out of the curved wall.

Just then, someone pulled him from the back without warning, and Leinad nearly screamed out by shock. To his pleasant surprise, though, it was Norrikee, the gamekeeper.

"What are you doing here, Leinad?" hissed Norrikee alertly, looking very frightened. "Come quickly this way," breathed Norrikee anxiously, directing back to the stairway.

As Leinad was down the stairs, he swiftly jumped up to the corner and peeked if anyone (probably the general) was coming.

"I was just –." Leinad tried to explain.

"Listen, Leinad," said Norrikee, promptly returning to Leinad with a big sigh. "You should not be here for any reasons. I thought I had announced it."

Leinad knew it, but he could not tell the real reason for now.

"I am sorry, sir, I was not sure for real," said Leinad politely. "I, uh, did not mean to come this far, but I just wanted to…," added Leinad hesitantly, trying to find a better excuse, "I just hoped to thank you for the advice you had given me before the game…"

The gamekeeper was not listening to Leinad's poor excuse. His mind seemed still with the present concern. He restlessly peeked over the wall, and suggested, "Come with me."

Norrikee led Leinad to the door next to the statue of a hemaby. Behind the door there was a long corridor with several silvery doors on both sides. Norrikee pulled Leinad into the nearest door at once. Then he checked the corridor briefly and closed the door cautiously behind. He released a sigh quietly. Meanwhile, Leinad tried to get a glimpse of the room they just entered. The immediate impression for him was that it was a museum of marine life. There was a large collection of various items from the ocean.

Norrikee stepped to the items displayed in a glass container. Then he cast a glance at Leinad like he just noticed Leinad was there. His face was dark and serious. His eyes were unusually cold, but Leinad was not sure if it was fear or anger. He seemed working hard to be unnoticed. Certainly he was not the usual gamekeeper.

"This room is called Marineum, housing various substances in this ocean world. Samples of leaves of ocean plants, bones of marine animals, and unique minerals from ocean floor are well stored and preserved in here," explained Norrikee, looking around the display.

Leinad put down the emerging questions inside for now and decided to hear. He hoped that the gamekeeper could keep talking. For the moment whatever subjects he talked about, it could be helpful for both, he thought.

"Many items here are unique and rare, and you would never see anywhere else," said Norrikee, opening one of the glass boxes before him.

He gazed at the contents for a few seconds.

"This," picking up a semi-transparent oval-shaped object, he said, "is absolutely beautiful. Don't you think so, Leinad?"

Smaller than a fist, shiny like an opal, nearly transparent, it was a unique mineral for sure.

"It is a mineral stone, sir," said Leinad at last, smiling confidently.

"Mineral!" exclaimed Norrikee, turning his head to Leinad, his face forming a faint smile for the first time. "Naturally... Well, a good guess, though," said Norrikee encouragingly. "You will have to believe me, Leinad, it is an egg," he said friendly now. "Of course, not just an ordinary one, though."

It certainly looked unique, but Leinad still doubted it.

"Are you sure...if that is an egg of a bird or something?"

"Yes. Well, if you say it's a seed, that's correct, too."

"A seed, sir?" asked Leinad, his face forming a silly smile.

"Exactly," exclaimed Norrikee. "Of course, I wouldn't believe until I hear a story about it," he added.

"You mean there is a story of a seed or an egg or something?" Leinad asked.

"Close. Precisely, it's a story of a bird called Bullaby," Norrikee said. "Ah, remember the statue facing this way in PENTADIA? I can only guess, but yes, that's how it looks."

"Have you seen one for real, sir?" Leinad asked.

"Have I seen one?" Norrikee asked him back, chuckling a bit. "I don't have time to tell you the full story now,

Leinad. In short, Bullaby in fact is nearly an imaginary creature. It is an invisible bird that lays an egg in her life time. A new-laid egg which is also invisible is earthed at once. By the time it is visible it is more like a seed that grows into a visible tree or plant, which is unknown. Once it grows fully in such a form, it burns of its own accord, turning into an invisible bird again."

Norrikee finished his story by adding, "Bullabies live in an afar land and never come back unless they lay eggs."

"Wow, for real, sir," said Leinad brightly.

"Yes, indeed. But, I conveyed you only a bit of it, Leinad," cried Norrikee.

Leinad looked at Norrikee's eyes, wondering where he learned it.

"It seems someone told you about it." He said cautiously.

"Someone…" Norrikee recited, his voice faint, his expression suddenly darkened. In a moment he brightened up his face a bit, and said, "Yes, there was someone just like you."

Norrikee placed the egg back into the container silently. Leinad noticed a faint sigh subdued inside.

"You have a good friend, sir, sharing stories and all that," Leinad tried to cheer him up.

"A friend… Yes, you are right…," said Norrikee, his words unfinished. He read Leinad's face silently for a few seconds. "Leinad," he began now with a look of anxiety, "you are an eager and intelligent fellow, I have no doubt about it, but then again, that's my concern. If you ever have any other reason why you are here, you must let go.

83

While you are here, you really need to work on your duty just like others," advised Norrikee genuinely.

"But, sir, I am just…" Leinad attempted at once, but he could not find proper words to argue with Norrikee. It was very much unexpected.

"Be careful with everyone in the castle, and be cautious with the words of rules and regulations. I hate to say, but don't try to understand things based on your standard or scale in here. You are invited as a rider, and you wouldn't need to have unrelated questions or even curiosity. They are trivial, but can be crucial here. You will only run into a trouble, Leinad, a serious trouble."

"I don't understand. What's wrong with having a question, sir?"

Norrikee did not answer to this promptly. Instead, he looked at Leinad's eyes worriedly for a few seconds and shook his head gently.

"The king wouldn't detain you for that. But, it doesn't matter. Don't forget, he is the ruler of this land, and he can do anything bad with no reason," declared Norrikee pitifully.

"But, such a nice king wouldn't do that," cried Leinad innocently.

"He may be a nice king, but an order must be obeyed."

Norrikee stepped toward the back of the room and Leinad followed.

"I am sure you will understand what I mean," said Norrikee conclusively.

He led Leinad to an open area at the end of the room. There were an oval-shaped table and a few chairs surrounded by rows of shelves. The table was shiny as though being made up of pieces of marble.

"Leinad," called Norrikee, halting his steps by the table, turning to Leinad. "I know it's hard, but please, disregard your other reason for your own safety." His words were sincere and beseeching.

Leinad saw Norrikee's face hardening, but he was not sure whether it was because he knew that Leinad would not listen or something else started to disturb his mind.

My own safety... If that was more important, I would not have come this far.

Chapter 12
LOOMING DANGER

"Now, I must go…, and you," said Norrikee, pointing to the door, "must leave now through that door."

Leinad nodded, looking at the door without a word. After all, he was not able to find a second to ask about his father. Conversely, he was more or less happy, because at least he had someone now whom he could talk to. *Maybe next time.*

"If you go out, you will see a bigger door which is the back door of the whole section. I am sure no one will be there. Now, if you open that door…"

Norrikee suddenly turned his head to the front door, his eyes sharpened.

"Wait!" he hissed, pulling Leinad down behind the shelves. "Someone's coming!" He said sharply with an alert, his finger placed across his lips.

Sure enough, lumbering footsteps came close, stirring up the silence, and the door swung open. After two seconds of quiet moments objects in the room were vibrated by a vigorous yell.

"Aha! At long last, I caught your tail, indeed!"

It was such an obvious voice. Leinad looked for Norrikee's eyes, feeling his chest tightening. Norrikee squeezed Leinad's shoulder gently once as if he saw the fear inside.

"Show yourself before I go cut your throat!" shouted the general impatiently, sniffing coarsely.

Leinad's heart started to thump fast, his eyes wandering between Norrikee to the general restlessly. Norrikee held up a small pebble in his hand for Leinad to notice. And in the next quiet second he threw it toward the other side of the shelves. The pebble bounced on the floor, cracking lively, and rolled over to the other side of the shelves. Norrikee swiftly followed the pebble without making any additional noise. The general's head turned to the direction at once.

"There you are! That's better," exclaimed the general contentedly.

Leinad's eyes tried to spot Norrikee who now crawled over to a corner. In the next moment Leinad was shocked nearly to death because of yelling of the gamekeeper.

"Ouch, I missed it!

Norrikee sprang up straight to his feet with a loud unnecessary thud.

"Oh, head general, it was you!" Norrikee cried, sounding unexpected.

The gamekeeper's voice was calm and natural, but it was even more frightening than the general's.

"Sorry, head general, I knew I had to go, but as I caught a sight of a little animal on my way, I could not let it go. And, and I did not realize where I came until now, head general," declared Norrikee regretfully. "I am so –."

"Out of your mind!" shouted the general furiously.

"You idiot! I saved your neck all these years, and now you thank me bravely like that!" He yelled impatiently, steaming hot air on his head.

"Sorry, head general, but I thought you were looking for the little animal badly, and so, I wanted to –," said Norrikee cautiously.

"Damn it! Who cares about that little mouse?" shouted the general, pulling his glaring eyes out toward Norrikee as much as he could.

"What did I say to you to do, you stupid thing? I told you to report me everything without delay. I asked you to monitor that little annoying boy, didn't I? You brainless dupe, haven't I, indeed?"

His brain seemed boiling up mechanically with the words he spat out.

"On top of all that, you dared ignore my warning! Who told you come and play in here? No one ever can come in this room without my permission!" yelled the general scornfully.

"Now, move! I must not leave you unharmed this time."

Norrikee opened the door, but the general stood there, sniffing grossly, surveying shelves and showcases across the room.

"That little mouse still in this room, you did say."

"NO, NO, head general. It's already gone! I think it's in the launching hall now. It is very clever and I can assure you that it sneaks out of the back door and climbs up the stairs to the observatory porch, the king's favorite sky lounge. Then, it runs across the porch to the other entrance and through the door down to the launching hall –."

"Shut up, at once! You useless thing, I know it's somewhere. My eyes may fail, but my nose never. The

brainless boy must be looking for it, too, I can tell...
Stupid thing, move!"

Leinad stayed there frozen, keeping quiet until there
was no audible bit of sound. His mind began to settle with
the fear fading. However, as the fear inside grew fainter,
frustration arose and filled in.

*Now, Norrikee is in danger because of me. This time the
gamekeeper...*

He was frustrated because he had no idea what to do
for the gamekeeper. He was depressed because he had no
one to discuss about the hidden fangs of the general in
the castle, anymore.

Who should I trust, father? What should I do, master?

Minutes later, following Norrikee's thankful last
second hint, through the back door and the stairs Leinad
went up to the observatory porch. The fresh air rushed in
through his throat, but it did not refresh his mind. It was
only cold and painful. While looking down the scenery
beyond the dark ocean, he felt the gamekeeper stand right
beside him, yet beseeching him sincerely.

"I urge you, Leinad, please, let it go by."

His voice echoed clearly in his mind repeatedly, but
gradually ebbed away. It was only a farewell before a long
journey into the mist of the ocean. He sighed deeply.
Then, again following the hint from Norrikee, he walked
to the door across the porch and climbed down the stairs.
And when he safely entered the launching hall, he felt a
bit better. However, along the way to his room there was
one thing remained, aching his mind. It was a hope to see
the gamekeeper with the same smile at the same time in
the following morning.

Chapter 13
MOHZAKE

Leinad woke up restlessly in the morning and rushed to the gathering at the launching hall. Everything remained the same except one fact. Norrikee was not there. The instruction for the daily events was described by a substitute with the general right beside. Leinad peeped at the throng and every corner in the hall, but Norrikee was not seen anywhere.

As the main event was about to start at last, everyone looked very keen on taking off to the sky, and thus, no one bothered with a missing man. Leinad kept peeking at the door every time it opened, but until the last seconds Norrikee did not show up. He once considered asking the general about the absence of the gamekeeper. But, that would be the silliest idea now.

Maybe Norrikee is assigned for other duty, which seems not unusual. Leinad deemed. *Just today, maybe. Otherwise, I will see him around, anyway.* He decided.

Now, everyone was dismissed and prepared for the race. When Leinad was nearly reconciled with the race, there was someone calling his awareness.

"My lad."

Sweet and friendly, but gross and sinister. He could tell who that was without even a glance. Leinad's senses were frozen again by the sudden recall of the memory over the night.

"Is everything all right with you, my dear?"

"Yes, head general. Everything is fine. Thank you," replied Leinad politely.

"Be honored. Best regards from Your Majesty, I must tell you now," said the general, sounding very proud. "And now, it's your turn to show your exceptional talent."

"Thank you, head general, and I will do my best for sure," said Leinad brightly, but his voice shivered. "Then, if you please excuse me, head general," he added, forcing a smile.

After looking around the hall briefly one last time, he departed the launching hall along with others. And up in the sky his troubled mind was soon washed away by the magnificent view of the sky. He enjoyed the ride for a while, but only until the warning of Norrikee returned to his mind again. Then, he struggled with distress that went on even deeper. Meanwhile, he tried hard to mull over a sound way to check and inspect every corner in the castle safely.

If Norrikee is still around, it can be much easier. He regretted.

Leinad's hope to see Norrikee after the ride was only a hope. Norrikee was not amid the throng in the hall. Instead, Leinad spotted the general rummaging around with his bulging eyes. Leinad had totally forgotten about the conversation he had with the general earlier. By instinct he pretended not knowing the presence of the general, turning his awareness to someone right beside.

"Hey, my friend, how was your flight?" asked Leinad friendly, grinning.

"Not bad, thank you," said the boy, his expression bewildered. "And yours?"

"Yeah, it was good, but, er, feeling a bit dizzy after hours of flying...," said Leinad, sounding somewhat sleepy.

"Dizzy, did you say, because of the long flight?" cried the boy sarcastically.

"You are asking me to believe it? Everyone already knows you are the craziest guy here," he uttered, sneering. "Besides, you did not fly at all today. I saw you go up there only to get lost," he added contemptuously.

He was right about it, but apparently Leinad's mind was busy with something else at the moment.

"Yeah, the dazzling views! It made me dizzy obviously," said Leinad lightly, his eyes peeping at the general.

"Hey, listen," said Leinad, looking at the cap. "May I?" asked Leinad courteously with a smile. "Come with me now, please. I have something to tell you," whispered Leinad, pulling his sleeve gently toward the door.

He walked along the boy, blocking his face with the cap, his eyes still stealing at the general.

"That was close," muttered Leinad when they were out of the hall.

The boy glared at Leinad suspiciously.

"Hey!" exclaimed Leinad, attempting to quench the cold stare of the boy. "Don't worry, my friend. It's nothing."

"Of course, it is nothing," he snapped scornfully, snatching his cap from Leinad. "That's for sure," he added, stepping to the door. "And I can easily ask the general about it," said the boy sarcastically, trying to open the door.

"Oh, no, no!" Leinad dashed at once to him, and grabbed his arm.

As the boy halted, Leinad released a soft sigh.

"OK, come with me now, my friend," cried Leinad, hitting his shoulder once, "and I will tell you something then."

Leinad pulled his arm and directed him toward the residential unit.

"I am Leinad, I should have told you first. Sorry," said Leinad as they came into the lounge of the residential unit.

"Mohzake," he replied with a barely visible smile.

"Well, Mohzake, How is it going?" asked Leinad ingenuously.

"…can't complain," said Mohzake hesitantly. "Thrilling and challenging…what else you can say?"

"That is right. And this is the moment only once in your life," said Leinad.

"So?" asked Mohzake, his expression yet flummoxed.

"Yes. So, we'd better enjoy all these moments," said Leinad favorably.

"I am listening, Leinad."

"Hey, er, how about we go to your room now?" asked Leinad, beaming.

"To my room? What's so special?" Mohzake asked casually.

"Nothing…, but I don't want to be interrupted by anyone in the middle of our conversation, if you know what I mean," uttered Leinad with a grimace.

Mohzake studied Leinad's face briefly and brightened his face.

"All right. I hope it's worth showing my private space," said Mohzake.

"Mohzake, what do you think about this place?" asked Leinad as they entered the room.

"This castle?" asked Mohzake.

Leinad nodded.

"It's…not too bad." Mohzake said, sounding unsure.

"Are you going to tell me your story today?" Mohzake asked edgily.

"It sounds strange, but I think the general has been watching all of us," said Leinad anxiously.

"Everyone? I thought it was you," said Mohzake carelessly.

"Well, it seems, but…," said Leinad without conviction.

Mohzake inspected Leinad's eyes for a few seconds.

"I don't believe your conclusion, Leinad. Both the king and the general deserve more than your suspicion," said Mohzake decisively.

"You are right, Mohzake. But I changed my mind yesterday when…," Leinad began eagerly, but his voice diminished like he decided to take it back.

"What happened?" asked Mohzake, lightening his face now.

"You know," Leinad began, "I thought he was looking for something, but actually that was the way of checking us all."

"So, what happened yesterday?" asked Mohzake again.

"I just happened to overhear a conversation…"

"You heard his private conversation?" asked Mohzake, sounding hurt.

"Well, I didn't mean to, but…anyway, to me it sounded like a blaming."

"Blaming? Who was there with the general?" asked Mohzake nosily.

"It was the gamekeeper. The general had ordered him to monitor us, but obviously he did not follow the order. So, the general yelled at him very badly and took him to the king."

Mohzake gazed at Leinad for a while with a look of suspicion. "You must have gone somewhere else, if you heard that."

"Yes, I was...," said Leinad timidly, his voice tailed off again.

"I was curious about the castle, and, and last night I went to the other unit."

"What? You mean you went to the king's palace or something?" asked Mohzake, his eyes widened.

"Not exactly, but...," said Leinad.

"We are not allowed to go there, didn't you know that?" cried Mohzake anxiously. "Besides, it's dangerous."

"Dangerous?" copied Leinad doubtfully. "Why?"

"The general expressed something the other day. Didn't you hear that?"

"Not really. What was that about, anyway?

"The Goddess created five formidable mythical animals to protect the king's palace in the beginning. These animals have been in deep sleep like rocks ever since the first day. However, they are vigilant and always ready to wake up promptly for any intruders to the palace," explained Mohzake realistically.

"He really said that?" asked Leinad, making a silly face in disbelief.

"Well, sort of, but it sounded for real," replied Mohzake defensively.

"So..., nothing happened? I mean you haven't seen anything unusual there?" asked Mohzake vigilantly.

"Nothing particular," said Leinad at once.

Then, he remembered the statues like flying creatures. Yes, there were five statues of some kinds of imaginary animals. Maybe that's what he meant.

"Nothing?" recited Mohzake with a look of disappointment.

"Come on, Mohzake. You silly," said Leinad, grinning broadly.

"Well, I guess I should leave you alone now."

"You still did not answer precisely why the general was after you, Leinad," said Mohzake discontentedly.

"He believes I have something that he has been looking for."

"What is it?" demanded Mohzake.

"I am not sure because I don't have. But it sounded like an animal, something like a mouse, maybe," replied Leinad uncertainly.

"An animal… He has been after an animal?" asked Mohzake faintly.

"Now, listen, Mohzake, this is something else, but, I haven't seen Norrikee since last night, and I have a bad feeling about that. I think now we all have to be very careful with the general."

"Norrikee?" asked Mohzake.

"Yes, that's the gamekeeper I mentioned." Leinad replied bitterly. "He has been taken away only because he was merciful and friendly to us."

Mohzake looked at Leinad with a dark expression, but Leinad could not tell it was due to worries or suspicion over his statement.

"Leinad, what are you doing to do?" He asked worriedly.

"I want to make the general happy with the animal, but at the same time I have to figure out what happened to Norrikee," said Leinad brightly.

Although he said it optimistically, Leinad could not avoid a sigh coming out of his mind. He had no idea where to start and he had no way of protecting himself from the danger.

"Can you help me, Mohzake?" asked Leinad sincerely.

"Help you…, how?" asked Mohzake seriously.

"I am planning to sneak into the palace to see if they kept Norrikee somewhere…, can you go with me?" asked Leinad cautiously.

"Are you crazy? I told you what's in there," exclaimed Mohzake abruptly.

"Oh, come on, that's just a story, Mohzake. I have seen those things. They were only statues."

"What? You actually saw them!" cried Mohzake in astonishment.

"They are in a hall called PENTADIA, not far away from the launching hall," said Leinad courageously. "But, don't worry about the danger of being exposed in the hallway. I know a safer way to get there."

"Safer way? What is it?" asked Mohzake, yet with a cynical look.

"If you decide, I will tell you."

Mohzake looked at Leinad thoughtfully for a few seconds.

"Do you think we can find the animal somewhere at the palace?" he asked.

"Don't know, but probably," said Leinad, nodding. "If we don't see it around here, it could be there in the palace."

"OK, I will go with you," said Mohzake brightly, but his voice wobbled.

"Great!" cried Leinad in gladness with a sudden courage growing inside.

"So, where is the safer way?" asked Mohzake nervously.

"I will tell you where it starts when I see you tonight. It's one of the doors at the launching hall," said Leinad resolutely.

"At the launching hall?" Mohzake asked back with a perplexed look.

Leinad nodded, grinning.

"And once we get to the secret room, we will make a plan."

"Secret room?" asked Mohzake.

"It's a museum. Well, it's not secret, but I think it's safer there."

Leinad examined Mohzake's confused face for a moment.

"You will be all right, Mohzake," said Leinad cheerfully, "and thanks."

"Then, I will see you there, Mohzake," he added, looking around the room for the first time.

The room was very tidy except the table which was messed up with many small identical pieces. On the wall were clearly visible letters which read ZENIA. Before Leinad asked him anything, the door was closed.

As expected, the launching hall was very quiet, and no one was inside when Leinad opened the door. Apparently the general swept everyone away as night fell, and the entire hall was in peace without any turbulence.

Where is Mohzake? Leinad walked from side to side twitchily, his eyes kept sneaking at the door. He would need to disappear from the site before the general would smell anything. Now he was not sure if Mohzake would really show up. *Maybe not tonight.* Then he decided to go alone.

He opened the door which would lead to the observatory porch, and he stepped out of the hall. When the door behind him was nearly closed, through the gap he saw the main door of the launching hall open quietly. Leinad's face instantly formed a bright smile which then congealed in barely a second. It was the general.

Leinad let the door close tight very quietly and ran up the stairs at once. He almost forgot to breathe until he reached the porch, and fresh air urgently rushed in. After soothing his lung a bit, he hurried his steps down the stairs to the back door of Marineum. His mind was quite blank until he entered the room safely. But then, he was struck with the thought of Mohzake who might have been in trouble now. Conversely, the general would not do anything bad, because Mohzake has done nothing seriously wrong, he thought. In spite of that, Leinad only hoped that Mohzake had really changed his mind for now and did not even show up.

Leinad thought over the plan which he had considered to do with Mohzake. He made sure that he would need to check every room to trace Norrikee. *But first, I will sneak in PENTADIA, and from there...* At that moment his attention was distracted by a door slam shut and a faint voice coming from somewhere. In alert he immediately retreated, his eyes looking for a hideout. Then he found himself in a room which was completely different from Marineum. Folding other thoughts aside, he approached to a wall quietly and pressed his ear hard on the wall. There were at least two voices.

"…please, I will never be around here again."

"Well, if you tell me why you sneaked into the palace."

"I was just curious, believe me, please, head general."

Leinad was nearly shocked. For sure it was Mohzake and the general.

"Indeed, you were curious. So, you didn't believe the story. Well then, I can wake them up for you to believe at least in the last minutes," said the general with an obnoxious snort.

"Please, head general, I will help you find the animal," cried Mohzake.

"The animal?" said the general, his voice turned tender. "What do you know about it?"

"I saw her once near the residential unit, but until now I did not know you were looking for her, head general," said Mohzake regretfully. "But I know someone who was also looking for her, head general."

"Someone was looking for the animal?" said the general, his voice sharpened stiffly.

"Spit it out at once!" yelled the general impatiently.

"Leinad, head general. I thought you knew it already."

"A ha! That boy, indeed," said the general, chuckling. "Yes, yes, I knew. I smelled something from him, indeed," he added, nodding contentedly.

"Well, I can offer you a chance to clean your wrong, if you wish."

"Please, kindly," cried Mohzake keenly.

"Go and be the shadow of the boy. And report everything to me," ordered the general firmly. "And find out why he is after that little mouse."

"I will, head general," said Mohzake affirmatively.

"Go prove yourself at once."

Leinad stepped out of the room quietly. Now he noticed that there were a few more identical doors along the way, and it was the second door he happened to enter. He cautiously opened the third door from the end. As he entered, his senses directly told him that it was Marineum.

Chapter 14
REAL FACE OF THE GENERAL

While Leinad was immersed with thoughts, he had a strange feeling that something was watching over him. He turned his head toward the shelves before him, but there was nothing particular. This time he heard a weird slithering sound from the back of the shelves. In fact he now saw something dark amongst the display of the marine creatures. Then he spotted two eyes glaring at him. He promptly stepped backward in surprise, but it did not move at all.

"Who, who's there?" asked Leinad vigilantly.

The creature slowly came out of the shadow, and at some point it sprang up swiftly and landed on a shelf near Leinad. *The animal!* Leinad's face brightened up at once. Apparently it was much bigger than a 'little mouse' that the general had referred. It was much like a kitten except the bright eyes with circled dark blue iris. Its hairs were pointy like spiky little pine tree leaves. It was only a little creature but brave enough to approach Leinad very close. It stood in front of him, keeping firm and quiet. Leinad had no idea why it came to his awareness. By all means now he was not sure whether he had to try to capture it or help it to escape from the general.

"Leinad!"

A sudden call from behind made Leinad quite startled in that instant. Thankfully, it was not the general's.

"Sorry, I am late," said Mohzake, smiling nervously.

Leinad did not care about what he said for the moment, he hastily turned his head back, but the animal was not there on the shelf anymore. He briefly surveyed other shelves, but there was no trace of it at all. It was gone.

"You found something in here, Leinad?" asked Mohzake cautiously, his eyes momentarily followed Leinad's eyes.

"No, no, nothing, Mohzake. So, what happened? What took you so long?" asked Leinad, turning his interest to Mohzake with a concerned look. "I thought you changed your mind."

"My apologies. So, what's the plan?" asked Mohzake lively.

"I think we will look for the animal," said Leinad.

"What about the gamekeeper?" asked Mohzake.

"We will think about that later. Why?"

"I don't know. I thought it's more important. That's all," said Mohzake.

"It is. But, better to know reasons why he is after the animal," said Leinad.

"All right, then. Where are we starting from?"

"Don't know," replied Leinad unsurely. "Maybe, we can try the rooms further down the hallway for now."

"Down the hallway?" asked Mohzake, sounding interested.

With that, Mohzake's eyes traveled around shelves with interest like he just noticed that he was surrounded by a large number of strange animals.

"Is this place –?" Mohzake asked.

"Yes, the museum I mentioned earlier. It's a museum for marine life or maybe those unique stuffs in the ocean," said Leinad, his eyes following Mohzake's. "Anyway, nothing much of our interest," added Leinad.

"Shall we?" Leinad asked politely, now walking toward the front door.

"We are going out through the front door?" asked Mohzake anxiously.

"Yeah, it could be dangerous, but I don't know much about other rooms; they don't seem to have back doors like here," said Leinad uncertainly. "OK, ready now?" asked Leinad, holding the door knob.

He opened the door cautiously and peeped at both sides. Then he retrieved his head quickly and closed the door again.

"Good. It's clear," Leinad hissed, casting a glance at Mohzake who now sat beside Leinad nervously.

"I don't know why he is looking for that particular animal," uttered Leinad.

Mohzake's mind seemed somewhere else. His eyes blinked momentarily.

"Mohzake," called Leinad, his eyes looking for Mohzake's, "we will start from the room across the corridor."

By this, Mohzake's attention came back to the matter at stake.

"Can you go check the rooms across the corridor yourself? Then I will check those on this side myself," suggested Mohzake considerately.

"Oh, you want to go alone? OK, that's fine with me," said Leinad.

"I will come back here once it's done," said Mohzake.

"Here? No, I think better meeting in the residential lounge. It's safer there. You never know. He's got a very good sensor," said Leinad anxiously.

"OK, then. I'm ready now."

Leinad opened the door cautiously. Checking both ways again, he gestured for Mohzake to go ahead. Mohzake swiftly ran out to his first destination. Now Leinad, too, stepped out of the door quietly. Just then, he heard some voices coming from PENTADIA. Being alert, he jumped quickly back to the room and closed the door. Throwing himself into a corner against the wall, he pressed his ear on the wall as close as possible.

"...very brave...play the fool with me."

"Please, head general, believe me. I didn't do that!"

"You just wanted to follow Norrikee. I know that's what you wanted. I must show you now how he ended, or you will never know the price for disregarding my order."

"I am innocent, head general, plea –!"

"Shut it up at once or I will rip it off first!"

Their voices grew less. When they were out of earshot, Leinad opened the door carefully. The corridor was quiet and clear again. As he found himself in such an empty space alone, in his mind developed a reckless craving of following them without reflecting on any possible danger. Then he ran bravely all the way to the door at the end of the corridor.

The door cracked open as he placed his hand onto the handle. And there appeared a stairway down under dim light. For a moment Leinad had to fight with his mind if he really wanted to go further down the stairs.

"Move on! The game already began..." he cried.

And he moved down the stairs as he was told.

It was a long way down. When he landed on what looked like the bottom of the whole castle, he found himself in front of another door. He tried hard to listen in any voices from inside, but he heard nothing. He opened the door bit by bit until he could see all walls and entered the room. The ceiling was high in a circle. It was beautiful with colorful drawings of various marine creatures in combination with large numbers of shiny balls. The room was wide, but nothing was on the floor except a water pool in the center. The pool was large and filled up with light blue water. It was empty.

Chapter 15
ZENIA

Leinad came back to Marineum where his investigation began. He would need to start it over now. Obviously the general seized the gamekeeper in one of the rooms, and he took the man there. Then, they might have come across Mohzake. It may be no big deal for Mohzake to stumble upon the general in the middle of his search. But, he would have to prove himself with a stimulating piece of new information about Leinad. And that was why the general gave a freedom to him, Leinad thought. Then, suddenly a simple question about Mohzake came up. Why he wanted to go alone when he had an order to shadow someone? Leinad speculated if Mohzake was also interested in the little animal regardless of the order.

In fact, it was Leinad himself who became interested in this little animal. This peculiar creature had really approached him without fear. It was only a short time to face the creature, but Leinad still remembered its appearance quite well. Now, being eager to meet it again, he surveyed the shelves and beyond for any hints of its presence. Nothing particular. Perceptibly, he believed that it was there in the room, its two brave eyes watching over him. But even so, it was not a bad feeling at all. By all means he would never do any harm to it, and of course, no intention of capturing it for any reason. He was only a liar to Mohzake.

"Hello!" cried Leinad friendly, his eyes scrutinizing every corner keenly. "I know you are here, my little friend… Can you come out once again…, please?" begged Leinad sincerely.

No response. Not even a wee bit of sound. Leinad moved to the back of the room where the animal had once shown up, and he called it again from there. It was still silent. Just then, the front door opened with a gentle crack which stringently stole Leinad's breath without warning. A hot wave of electricity penetrated through his spine. Leinad quickly threw himself behind a shelf nearby. He even felt his brain stop functioning momentarily. *The general! He must have smelled.* He held himself squeezed tight, working hard on a best excuse. Loud gross yelling immediately came out of his memory; the general had said, "Show yourself before I go cut your throat!"

However, the actual voice that stirred the moment was completely different.

"Are you there?"

It was a soft and anxious voice. Leinad instantaneously knew to whom it belonged. *Mohzake! He came to see me!* In delight he was about to stand up, but the next word halted him.

"Zenia?"

Leinad instinctively shrank back on the same spot without any sound.

Zenia? What is that?

"Can you come out at once, please?" begged Mohzake sincerely. "I know what happened to you, and you don't have to feel bad about it, Zenia," added Mohzake seriously, trying to catch a glimpse of anything particular behind the shelves.

"It's me, I know. It's my fault, and that's why you are so mad at me," said Mohzake faintly, his repentant eyes set on the display before him like he was only talking to it.

"See, here I came back you, and I will to fix it somehow. So, please, Zenia."

Leinad began to feel uncomfortable now as Mohzake's motive unexpectedly turned inexplicable. *Zenia? Is that the reason why he came to the castle?* Leinad could not stop speculating the story behind the secrecy. Now, as things moved to an unanticipated direction, Leinad was not sure how to handle the situation. But at least he would have to quit eavesdropping Mohzake's secrete life. It was Leinad's turn to show up and apologize. He determined. At that moment, Mohzake bade Zenia farewell with an interesting comment.

"Please, open your mind for me, Zenia. I cannot do anything until I see you are well," exclaimed Mohzake sincerely. "I have to go see the general now... See, at least I can go anywhere in the castle at the present," he said optimistically.

"He knows something about you, Zenia, and I have to make sure he will not find you someway...," said Mohzake, his voice turned nervous. "Zenia, something very odd happened to the gamekeeper. I saw him. I think it's the general who did it... Zenia, please, be careful. He is not normal."

After another glance over the shelves, Mohzake opened the door and left the room silently. Leinad attempted to reflect on what Mohzake would tell about to the general. There was at least one thing he was sure; Mohzake would tell a lie for Zenia.

Leinad stood up to his feet, his eyes looking over the shelves absentmindedly. Of course, there was no one else in the room. Then he thought about the gamekeeper who, according to Mohzake, must have been treated very badly by the general. So, it was the general who played an evil all this time. He decided. *And that was exactly what happened to my father.*

Leinad's mind raced fast to the room where his father might have been locked up just like the gamekeeper. He wanted to go and check the situation of the gamekeeper. *The general should be with Mohzake, so it is safe now.* He convinced himself. While he was walking toward the front door, from the corner of his eyes he saw something move in the blink of an eye. His memory worked faster than senses, telling him that it was the little animal. He turned around, looking at the suspicious spot. Nothing disturbed.

"Hello there," called Leinad brightly. His spirit was slightly elevated with expectation. "I know you are here, and I am sure you will come and greet me, my dear friend," exclaimed Leinad happily.

Sure enough, in the next moment a familiar figure came out of a shadowed area slowly and swiftly jumped onto an open space of a shelf. Of course, Leinad would not forget to welcome it with cheers.

"There you are!" exclaimed Leinad in delight.

Leinad came close to the animal cautiously while it kept unmoved. He had no idea why it ran away in the first place, but apparently it was fearless now. He could draw near the animal, close enough to feel its fur, but he was a bit nervous to do so. It might run away again.

Chapter 16
KITTOUSE

It was very pretty with bright and clever-looking blue eyes. Its body color occasionally changed from white to black, back and forth, with the waves of the hairs. It simply was a charming unimaginable creature. Leinad looked at its eyes with a soft natural smile for a while. Somehow, they were very familiar.

"Do you have any name, my dear friend?" asked Leinad friendly.

"Well," he said, grinning brightly, "maybe, I will call you…Kittouse. You are very much like a cute kitten, but with a little bit of others as well. So…"

He just made it up with a thought of a kitten and a little mouse; 'kitt' from kitten and 'ouse' from mouse.

"Kittouse… How does that sound to you?" asked Leinad innocently.

"I don't know if you like it," he continued, examining its reaction, "but until I find your real name, you know."

The little animal stayed calm a bit, then, it stood up and moved to the other side of the shelf, its eyes yet remained on Leinad.

"Where are you going, my friend? Don't you want to know my name?" asked Leinad, following the animal absentmindedly.

But it ignored Leinad's claim as though it was unable to hear.

Seeing Leinad following, it jumped down onto shadowed floor. Now, Leinad questioned its intension and decided to follow it.

"Where are you taking me, my friend? A hidden home?" asked Leinad.

The animal, occasionally peeking at the follower, passed a few more shelves loaded up with fossilized marine creatures. Leinad realized that the room was much bigger than he thought. He looked back, and for the first time with the animal he felt serious. And he suddenly remembered the name, Zenia.

Maybe it is taking me to Zenia.

The aisle now turned brighter along the way. And there, it stopped. In a corner was a huge semi-transparent pot with piles of balls filled in it. The balls, which were bigger than an apple, brightly emitted, lighting up the area.

It sat on the rim of the pot, amusingly looking down Leinad.

"What now?" he muttered.

But before a moment to weigh up the situation, it swiftly dived into the pot.

"Wait!" yelled Leinad, dashing to the pot.

The pot was taller than he. With a bit of effort he climbed up the rim and tried to see where it vanished. He pushed and smashed some of the balls away to see any further. It seemed simply bottomless.

"Hey! Where are you now?" he called out in irritation.

"Well, it is only a pot, anyway." He decided. "Besides, it's fun to dive into a pool of balls!"

Now he sat on the rim and stretched out his legs toward the center of the pot. Then, he cautiously dropped his legs down onto the stack of balls as if to measure the depth of the pool. The next moment he had a strange feeling around his legs. He abruptly pulled out his legs, causing to lose his control, and falling into the mass of the balls. His weight delivered him at once into the swamp of balls. A sudden thrill twisted his spine, but it lasted only for a few seconds. He was already at the bottom. In fact it was not the bottom of the pot. It was now quite a spacious room. Above him there were balls floated like clouds, forming a bright ceiling. On one side of a round wall there was a small door.

"An exit?" He muttered in confusion.

The door, which was slightly curved to fit the wall of the space, opened smoothly in two ways when he pushed one side. Leinad quickly walked out through the open gap of the door. It closed by itself as he let it go.

Now Leinad found himself on one end of a narrow ascending path shaped like a circular tube, its diameter larger than his height. There were some numbers of lighted balls floated on the ceiling. On the other end of the path was Kittouse, the creature, standing up motionlessly like a stuffed animal; or maybe like Rupidd waiting for his apprentice, gazing at Leinad as if to say, 'What's the matter, Leinad? You are so slow today.' Behind Kittouse there was another door shaped like a large silver coin. As he advanced, the door cracked into halves, and Kittouse crossed the threshold.

"Hey, wait!" shouted Leinad, but the door already closed.

With a feeling of annoyance Leinad pushed the door to open. It undid almost naturally and sealed as he crossed over. Now what he saw was almost like a huge sphere with no significant edges of ceiling, wall, or even floor although much of the top part of the room was filled with small lighted balls. When he surveyed the surface around his height level once more, he noted that there were a lot of circular cracks which could be considered as doors (or exits). Around mid-space there were many semi-transparent compound lines, resembling overpasses.

Kittouse was not anywhere. Leinad guessed that it must have gone through one of the doors. Before any further speculation, Kittouse for sure showed up and jumped down on an overpass right in front of Leinad.

Kittouse looked at Leinad amusingly, making him feel weird than delightful.

"Hey…," began Leinad nervously, his eyes moving around room again, "is this place… Are you with Zenia?" asked Leinad cautiously.

Kittouse only stared at Leinad without motion or sound like it was yet in the process of measuring the so-far performance of its apprentice.

"What's up, my friend?" asked Leinad, still politely. "Where is Zenia? Mohzake is looking for her badly, she must know that," he added.

Leinad only said the fact, but now he really worried about Mohzake who came with a reason just like Leinad himself. It was something that made him feel not alone. However, Mohzake already gave a handle to the general, and he could be in danger with any nonsense reason.

"Please, make me understand why I am here, my dear friend."

Kittouse stood up with an envelope in its front paws. Until then Leinad did not notice it had brought something. It smartly showed the front of the envelope. There was a word that read MOHZAKE. The letters comprised many small pieces of shiny green coral glued neatly on the envelope.

"Mohzake?" he questioned unsurely.

Leinad's eyes shifted to Kittouse with a lost look.

"You are asking me to deliver it to…Mohzake?"

Kittouse nodded in reply. For half a second Leinad took it as a normal reaction, but in the next half he was surprised to realize that Kittouse actually communicated with him.

Now, that's better. Leinad could not help smiling.

Kittouse jumped off the overpass at once and approached to Leinad bravely. Then it stood up to its hind legs and lifted up the envelope with its forelegs. Leinad bent down carefully and took the envelope from Kittouse. His eyes still remained in the sparkling eyes of Kittouse. *A message…from Zenia.*

"So, this is it?" Leinad asked lightly.

"And you are not taking me to Zenia?"

Kittouse did not respond to his question. Leinad's eyes moved around and stopped at a door nearby as if he found the hideout of the mysterious girl by chance. After a moment or two, Kittouse jumped up to the overpass and darted to the door that Leinad had gazed. It pushed the door to open. Leinad did not actually expect that it would do so for real. Then he thought that Kittouse would take him to Zenia. *At last!* Feeling thrilled Leinad followed Kittouse without a word.

Chapter 17
TRAP

The passageway was similar to the previous one except that there were also some lighted balls on the ground. Kittouse moved fast, occasionally its body was obscured by lighted balls on the floor. It stood up by the circular door located at the end of the passageway, looking back at Leinad following. Leinad's mind was quite blank until he passed through the door and saw large numbers of shiny balls. And the instant he faced the balls, he doubted that Kittouse meant to take him to Zenia. When he thought about calling it for a question, he heard someone talking from somewhere down below the lighted balls. He held his breath for the moment, his steps frozen on the spot at once. The actual voices were slightly buried with vibrations through the waves of the balls. However, it was not hard to recognize the voice of the infamous general.

"Indeed, he has been after Norrikee...."

"Yes. But I don't know the reason, head general."

"That little boy outsmarted... Just pretended to be after the little mouse," said the general obnoxiously. "Well, then you will find that out now. Take him to Nokilleum and show the man to the boy," he added scornfully.

"You mean I take him to the gamekeeper..., head general?"

"Right. Then, you will know the reason."

"But, but, sir, what about the little mouse?" asked Mohzake anxiously.

"No worries, my boy. I have already taken care of that matter with a brilliant scheme," said the general happily. "Dead or alive, I will probably see her at Marineum shortly, indeed," he added proudly.

"Poor little thing. Her life should be no more by now," said the general under his breath contemptuously. "The question still remained is where this thing hid the atlas…"

Then it was quiet for a while. Leinad thought that their conversation was over. But the general manifested what was going on there.

"Something is wrong, my boy? Why are you looking at me like that?"

"No, no, head general. I am just –."

"Just what, impressed by my brilliant scheme?" he asked mockingly.

"Ye, yes, of course, head general, it's sh, shocking," cried Mohzake brightly, but his voice shuddered.

"But, I don't understand until you tell me what you did, head general."

"YOU don't need to know that!" snorted the general at once, "you just do whatever I order!"

"Of, of course, I do, head general. That's how I have been –."

"Smart boy. I know you are not dumb like the all others. So, be quick and bring me some keen information, indeed," hissed the general coldly.

"Yes, yes, I will, head general. He will be shadowed from now on until I have a firm piece of information," said Mohzake confidently.

"Good," said the general, sounding satisfied.

"Well, recently I figured out that this little mouse had a regular path in this castle… I knew this castle had some sort of hidden passages, but the big pot… Damn it! I never guessed this thing found a way of striding all over the castle. Right under my nose! I should have done something when this thing first had followed us," cried the general annoyingly. "A terrible headache from the first day…," he added bitterly.

"Anyway," began the general in his normal way now, "I ordered to place a lethal trap in the passage pot at Marineum," he said pleasingly.

"Thankfully, this little thing passes there everyday around this time. Now, one step in, this thing will be dead or trapped for good," declared the general amusingly. "Well, she dared play with me, and that's only the price for that, anyway," said the general, chuckling.

It was quiet again for a while. Leinad peeped at Kittouse, wondering if it also heard what the general had said. Of course Leinad knew well about the pot passage, and thankful to Kittouse, too, for not going back there.

"Ve, very well, head general, then I should get going." Mohzake's voice was very unstable now. "I, I must go shadow him at once…"

"Good. Now, calm down, my boy. That's really no big deal at all," he said pompously. "Well, then, I will go enjoy myself."

"Thank you, head general," said Mohzake hurriedly.

Now the back door cracked open and clicked shut. It was suddenly so quiet that Leinad had to breathe very slowly until the general walked out of the front door. Now both of them were gone in the same manner, but with different emotions and reasons at the end of the conversation; the general was happy and excited while

Mohzake frightened and nervous. Leinad pondered what might have been going on with Mohzake. He was sure that it was beyond the general's usual threat this time. Maybe Mohzake figured out that the little animal was with Zenia, he considered.

Apparently the general was right about the passageway through the big pot, and maybe also right about its regular traveling route. But, it was unfortunate for him that his so-called 'brilliant scheme' did not work as expected. Pretty soon he would be very disappointed and fuming dreadfully. On the other hand, it was very fortunate for both Kittouse and Leinad. Naturally Leinad was happier and more excited (than the general), and he wanted to give cheers to Kittouse for the critical decision of taking a detour. Whatever the reasons Kittouse saved two lives from an awful trouble. Now feeling happy, Leinad looked at Kittouse' eyes with a broad grin. Momentarily Kittouse widened its eyes as big as plums, and all of a sudden, it scurried across the beam of the ceiling. Then it darted away through the passageway as if it just realized Leinad was a ghastly monster.

"Hey, Kittouse!" yelled Leinad at Kittouse who already had vanished into the tube with lighting balls in its way.

A few soft thuds came along and ebbed in a few seconds. Then it was very quiet again. No sounds from down below, either. He pushed away the balls that blocked his view beneath his steps. Certainly he was on the ceiling of a room. Presumably it was the secret den of the general. In fact, he was on top of a wall between two rooms. Over the other side of the wall he spotted another room which must be the room that he had discovered earlier while overhearing the private conversation of the general.

Leinad spied a few short metal pieces which stood out perpendicularly in a line on the upper part of the wall. He then placed his steps cautiously and climbed down the wall. On landing he right away headed to the hallway where he might see Mohzake. He would be happy for now if Mohzake could take him to the gamekeeper. Leinad could not wait to see the man who was for sure under a serious condition. And he would not think of what to tell to his shadow until seeing the gamekeeper.

"Nokilleum?" muttered Leinad, peeking over the silent corridor. The general must have left Marineun by now, Leinad thought. The general should be in a terrible mood now, and encountering him anywhere would be the worst thing to imagine at this moment.

"All right, then. Let's be quick," said Leinad encouragingly, walking out of the corner. At that point, he heard a gross voice echo in the corridor. Leinad automatically returned, throwing himself into a corner.

"I knew he was out of his mind when I had first discovered some funny glass plate in his room. Of course, I smashed it at once, but I saw words clearly written on it. It was something about finding out the story of Safrah and Ripper," exclaimed the general with assent.

"Quiet! Don't ever say my name in public," yelled the king angrily, "if you still need that mouth! And don't tell me you learned how to read before. If you keep spitting out garbage, I will trust what you say no more."

"But, this boy, Your Highness, I spared his life generously, and he dared play with us," complained the general with loathing.

"Shut up! It's you, not us. And never put me in any form of your stupid schemes. What I mean by this is to imply as long as I am the king here, understood?"

"You mean forever," uttered the general apprehensively.

"Ripper!" shouted the king angrily, stopping his steps at once.

"OK, understood, Your Highness."

"So, where is he now?" asked the king, resuming his steps.

"I held him in Nokilleum for now along with Norrikee," said Ripper arrogantly. "But if you allow me, I will get rid of them both this time," added Ripper rather carefully, "Your Highness."

"Let me see him, first, and I will decide how to dispose," replied the king plainly. "What do you think the reason why this boy troubled you with the little mouse?" asked the king in his normal voice.

"Don't know… Well, I don't think there was any important reason for this brainless boy. I doubt it," said Ripper idly. "I just asked him to watch the boy, and he was like a good listener. But then, the next second he jumped into a trouble right in front of me. Stupid. Why would he risk his life for a little animal?"

"What boy?" asked the king, snubbing Ripper's question.

"It's, er, Leinad."

"Leinad?" asked the king with interest.

"I smell something from this boy, but still…," said Ripper discontentedly. "I was hoping this brainless boy would bring me something interesting. But until now I only know this boy has been after Norrikee."

"He is a smart boy, general, and make sure you know what you are doing," declared the king softly. "Now, no one yet noticed why you have been after this little animal, I suppose," said the king suspiciously.

"No, for sure. But, what about this boy? Like you said, if he is not that dumb, he may know this little mouse hid the atlas of this –."

"Shut up at once! Are you trying to broadcast that aloud?" shouted the king angrily. "I should never let you do something imperative, anymore."

"Come on, no one is around," protested Ripper imprudently. "And no one dare come this far."

With this, Leinad shrunk down in the corner like a little mouse, his eyes looking for a door to run in any case. He sensed the general sniffing intensely to verify the scent around the area.

"Stop fooling yourself no more and open the door at once!" shouted the king exasperatingly. "And think how to catch that little thing!"

"Understood, Your Highness, but, please," cried Ripper, sounding discontented. "You never look at my…" he added demandingly.

The rest of his words could not be heard as the door clicked shut. They must have entered the room called Nokilleum where Norrikee and Mohzake were detained now, Leinad concluded.

Chapter 18
NO MERCY

Leinad sat with his back against the wall in the corner. He was in the dark helplessly again. There were three things that came up to his mind now. First, it was the king who played the evil in the castle. After all, the general has been only a puppet. Second, Mohzake really knew that Kittouse was with Zenia. And that was why he was very shocked and raced to save Kittouse although he only ended up being a miserable captive of the general. And third, the king believed that Kittouse had something important.

Leinad thought about the envelope which he had to deliver to Mohzake on behalf of Kittouse. He could not imagine how happy Mohzake would be to see a message from Zenia, but it seemed a little late for that. Chances to meet Mohzake were very little now. Besides, the king might have decided to 'dispose him' by now. There would be no way of rescuing Mohzake. Leinad's ears ached as the word 'dispose' hit his eardrums repeatedly. He wondered if Zenia ever knew all this happening.

Leinad thought that he would go and see what might be happening in the room or at least he would find a way of meeting Zenia. He decided to take one of the hidden passageways on the ceiling as he believed that there was a connection to Nokilleum as well although he was not sure which one.

He considered starting from the big pot at Marineum once, but it could be still dangerous. *Now I will have to start from the ceiling of the general's den. From there I can go to the sphere, the center of all passageways. Then I will pick the one that leads to the ceiling of Nokilleum... If I ever meet Kittouse somewhere there...*

"Move, you rubbish!"

A sudden yell stirred up Leinad's musing. It was the general, and he was very close. Leinad was shocked by the unexpected emergence of the general out of nowhere. He ran to a door nearby and threw himself in right away. He was pretty sure that the general sensed or at least heard the door open and shut. He pressed his ear on the door and tried to see the situation outside. Fortunately, the general was quite spirited. It seemed that his elevated mood disabled his sensors.

"Wow, it's perfect! He is in a good shape as well this time. And what's more, you spared his life, indeed! Excellent work, Your Highness!" exclaimed the general excitedly.

"Nothing to be so excited about, General, for such an effortless thing," said the king self-righteously, sounding very contented.

"Ever since your first mistake, your skills have been improved tremendously, Your Highness," said the general joyfully.

"Quiet! It was not a mistake, you fool. An accident!"

"Yes, yes, an accident you had told me, Your Highness," said the general playfully. "You tried to make a little hemaby, but something bothered you, I remember now."

"It was that stupid necklace she had. Otherwise, it could have been a perfect little hemaby," said the king.

"Otherwise, we don't have a headache now, Your Highness," said the general in a similar tone, his eyes stealing a glace at the king. "But, it is a perfect little thing to me, indeed," he added.

Now returning his interest to the matter in hand, the general said amusingly, "OK. Then I will take this, this hemaby to the others…"

"And Your Highness, I have this man to –."

"Dispose as you wish," said the king stiffly.

"To the –."

"That's fine, general," said the king, cutting off his words promptly.

"Well, he is already rubbish, anyway, and hard to drag all the way there…"

"Damn it! Don't you see a good transportation you have here now?" barked the king exasperatedly.

"A ha! That's a good option, Your Highness."

"And don't forget to clean the mess."

"I did not make a mess, Your Highness, did I?" he asked unsurely.

Spotless around the pool!" hissed the king condemningly.

"If you ever go hunting without my authorization, at least you should respect one thing."

"OK, Your Highness, understood. I will make sure –."

"I will return to my palace now, and you will report to me for any progress with the little thing," uttered the king thoughtlessly. "And watch the boy. Don't try any stupid trap thing to him or you will be trapped. By now you should know that he is smarter than you."

Then, it was quiet except the footsteps which eventually died as the door clicked shut. The king must have gone. Now, the general breathed coarsely, trying to place someone on the hemaby. Leinad was sure that it was the gamekeeper; a man barely able to move, unable to talk, and thus treated as rubbish...

"...that's it. Very good. Yes, yes, that's my boy," said the general happily.

"OK, stay there. I will open the door for you." His voice was ever friendly.

"Now, you know where we are going. Excellent! It suits you better, yes, for sire."

With a click from the door the general's cheerful voice was gone. Leinad gave another minute to make sure. Then, he opened the door and stepped out of the room, hoping that every door on the corridor bolted tight for now. It was still very quiet and no one was around. He took a deep breath once and stepped fast toward Nokilleum. While his mind was flying fast to rescue Mohzake who might have been treated badly, Leinad opened the door cautiously and entered the room. In a few seconds, however, he figured out that there was no one to set free.

The room was like a big rectangular storage that housed a large number of diverse farming tools and equipments on shelves along the walls. They were made out of woods or metals in a variety of colors and sizes. Amazingly there was a colorful painting that covered up the entire floor. It was like a map of Bubble Land. It depicted from the castle to the ocean over the land which included cities, villages, fields, mountains, meadows, and rivers... It was indeed an enchanting miniature land under the bright light from the ceiling. Leinad stood on a mountain like a lost giant troll. The charming view was partially spoiled by a few grey metal beams placed horizontally across the ceiling, and some numbers of chains and ropes, hanging in a line along the metal beam.

Then again, the room was empty; Mohzake was not anywhere. Maybe the general had already taken Mohzake before he came, Leinad considered. Or the mysterious girl came down from the ceiling and rescued him fast… Looking at the bright balls on the ceiling, he thought that he could have been somewhere there eavesdropping the king's scheme and deed. His eyes traveled around as if to spot any trace of Mohzake being vanished. Then, he spied something moving. He did not hear anything, but some of the light balls were glinted once or twice. Something must have been there. Leinad was pretty sure that it was Kittouse who had been there, listening what they were talking.

"Hello." Leinad called softly, his eyes trying to catch any glimpse.

"Kittouse?" he called friendly. "Are you there?"

The silence remained, and there was no hint of any moving creatures. Leinad yet wanted to believe his senses.

"Just wanted to say sorry, Kittouse, because…"

As he suddenly remembered that it all happened because of Kittouse, he could not say anything about Mohzake.

"I still have your letter," said Leinad regretfully.

"But, don't worry. I will find and, and deliver it to him…" He said optimistically, but then he could not promise.

"Kittouse, did you see what happened to the gamekeeper? I think the general has taken him to the pool, but not sure why…," he said timidly like talking alone.

"I am going back to my room now, but I will come back later…"

After surveying the room briefly once more, Leinad opened the door with vigilance. And on seeing the corridor lying in enchanting peace, he sneaked out of the door and vanished in the twinkling of an eye.

Chapter 19
UNFINISHED STORY

Leinad sat back on a sofa in the lounge and attempted to relax for any seconds with the peace that befell in the residential unit. However, he was not able to fight with the negative side of his mind. *Peace? Wake up, Leinad! There is no such thing as peace anywhere in the castle. It is only a fake. You should know that by now.* He had to admit it. Norrikee had failed, and probably Mohzake, as well just like him. There was no doubt that the whole castle has been doomed by the play of the evils.

Leinad opened the door quietly. If ever possible, he thought, he would be very happy to hear Mohzake's scornful yell for entering his room without permission. Although the room, as expected, was only silent and empty, Leinad could feel full of distress and sorrow in the room. After his devoted efforts, Mohzake could not keep the promise. He could not finish his assignment.

ZENIA... The name was still there on the wall and the broken pieces of something like thin opaque glass plate yet left on the table. Obviously, it was the general who smashed it on the floor. The general had said that there were words on it, Leinad remembered that now. He sat down to examine the pieces. Then, in a moment he recognized that they were only blank broken glass pieces. There were no words at all on any of the pieces for real. The general might be illiterate as the king had said, but 'blank' sounded strange. Now it would be silly, but Leinad decided to believe at least a bit of what the general had said. Besides, the general did not have guts to make it up for his pride before the king. Nevertheless, if there was anything that Leinad could do for Mohzake now, it would be to help his unfinished work such as this.

Leinad pushed the jumbled pieces to a corner and started to assemble into something that could make sense. And after some time he made them into a rectangular plate. Then, something happened to the assembled pieces. Now every piece began to bind to the neighboring pieces, and in a brief moment the pieces turned into a thin glass plate with very faint traces of cracks remained like stitches. Then, words appeared enchantingly on the plain surface. The words arranged in such a way that one sentence on one stitched piece. His eyes widened with interest. And once there was no further change on the plate, he started to read.

"After you disappeared with the two beasts, I drowned to death with grief on my way back home alone."

"It was absolutely my fault."

"I was so stupid to take you to the forest, or it would have never happened."

"I have regretted a hundred times, but it never helped."

"Now I passed the qualification test and shortly I will be in the castle."

"Zenia, please, show me where you are now."

"I know you will not see me whatever I say, but it won't change my reason."

"It is my second day, and I figured out that the general could do something extraordinary."

"Please, be careful, Zenia, the general is very dangerous."

"Zenia, it would be much easier if you show up…"

It was the unfinished story of Mohzake. The words on every piece were written handsomely by hand. But more than two third of the whole space was empty, yet to be filled.

Interestingly it was very light for a glass plate. Having the plate under his arm Leinad opened the door cautiously. After checking both ways, he darted toward his room without fear or favor. He thought that he should deliver it to Zenia. And that would be another thing he could do on behalf of Mohzake. Now, once he returned to his room, he wrapped up the plate with a cloth and placed it under his shirts. Then his steps enthrallingly took him to Marineum through his usual route.

It was silent as usual or even more in Marineum. Without disturbing the stillness Leinad strode directly toward the big pot, the hidden passageway. He wondered if the general disarmed the 'lethal' trap. He plunged a few lighting balls nearby. Nothing happened. Then he called out Kittouse once and twice. The next moment over the corner of his eyes he saw something jump up a shelf.

"Who, who's there?" cried Leinad mindlessly.

It was something small and fast. It was obvious.

"Kittouse, my friend?"

The figure showed up, stepping out to a brighter area. It was Kittouse.

"There you are! I knew I would see you here," exclaimed Leinad, beaming.

Then he felt regretful with the memory of the unpleasant moments that Kittouse had experienced earlier. He decided to move on.

"Listen, Kittouse, I have something…," he began, but hesitated for a second as Kittouse stared at him quite seriously.

Leinad was not sure now whether it was a normal behavior of it.

"Do you think I can meet Zenia by any chance?" asked Leinad with curiosity.

He knew that Kittouse would not answer verbally, but at least it would respond by nodding, and there was a chance it might take him to Zenia this time.

"Can you please take me to her, Kittouse? I need to apologize to her and, and I have something from Mohzake."

Kittouse was still motionless, but Leinad did not miss the moment to see its eyes flicker with the last few words. *Is that really normal for an animal?* He was not sure. Then, he had a strange hunch that there was no such thing as Zenia. And he had a sudden belief that Kittouse was not an animal but something unexplainable, and it was she who might have an incredible story of her life.

"I have this," said Leinad, pulling the thin glass plate out of his shirts, "for you, Kittouse. Not sure how you will handle it, but I leave it here for now."

Leinad placed the plate on one of the shelves nearby and stepped back. "And please accept my apologies," said Leinad regretfully.

He picked out the envelope from his pocket to place it by the plate. Unexpectedly, Kittouse came close enough and handed it over from Leinad with her front paws. Then she clumsily but carefully opened the envelope and took out the content.

It was a piece of ivory-colored cloth folded to the size of the envelope. Kittouse placed it on the floor and unfolded. It was something like a diagram of certain place at first. Then, Leinad spotted words on top of the figure.

"Atlas of Silver Castle," he read, his eyes returning to Kittouse.

"Atlas?" he repeated once more, thinking momentarily.

"Wait! Isn't it what the king has been looking for... Kittouse?" asked Leinad, his eyes still firm on Kittouse, his face brightened a bit.

Obviously, this was the reason why they have been after Kittouse. Leinad's interest went back to the Atlas now. Knowing that it was the atlas of the castle, he began to appreciate the appealing features of it.

There were four separate squares with subtitles; The Ground, The Basement, The Passageways, and The Hidden Land. And below the subtitle was a square box with descriptive diagrams.

The Atlas of The Ground showed rooms, halls and hallways in details. The Atlas of The Basement showed similarly except for a certain trail into the ocean. The Passageways must be the hidden routes that Kittouse used. Leinad was amazed by the complexity in connection between rooms and halls, not to mention the king's palace. No wonder why the general had been so annoyed.

"The Hidden Land?" recited Leinad with interest for the remaining subtitle.

The diagram was much simpler than the others. It was more like an actual field map with guiding trails. Within the square box there were two oval-shaped circles with dotted lines connecting each other. 'Light-Devils Home' was the words written in the circle on the left and 'The Silver Castle' on the right.

Somehow Kittouse had obtained this Atlas and wanted to give it to Mohzake in a way of helping him, Leinad thought. For a split second Leinad held his breath by the thought that Zenia was in such a place like Hidden Land on the Atlas. But he withdrew it at once. *Zenia is not for real.*

"So, you wanted to help Mohzake with this?" asked Leinad thoughtfully, folding the Atlas and putting back into the envelope.

"I, er, would like to inspect it, if you don't mind," he said carefully.

It could be very handy for any reason in the castle. Kittouse gazed at Leinad for a bit like she was considering. Then, she nodded softly, her eyes looking even clever with the permission. Leinad gave her a thankful grin.

"Well, I must leave you alone now if you don't mind. I suddenly feel that I have a lot of work to do, Kittouse," said Leinad, throwing the envelope back into his pocket. "Yeah, I think so. I should get going now, Kittouse," said Leinad decisively, walking toward the back door.

"Zenia!" yelled Leinad abruptly, turning back to Kittouse.

By that, Kittouse was quite troubled, standing up straight at once. Leinad saw her eyes shimmering with the light over her face. She was right in front of the glass plate that he had brought. *Kittouse can read?* She must have been looking at the unfinished letter of Mohzake. *Is she crying now?*

"Sorry, my friend, I just wanted to tell you that I would not look for anyone by that name. I am fine with just you, Kittouse. You are my friend. Maybe we can inspect this castle together from now," said Leinad brightly.

"Bye for now," said Leinad, closing the door behind him.

Chapter 20
HOME OF THE GENERAL

Leinad was returning to his room through his usual route via the king's favorite sky lounge. On his way he pondered what to do with the Atlas in hand now. He climbed up the stairs, came out to the sky lounge. Just then, he heard a loud thud from the other side of the lounge. Leinad quickly hid behind a towering beam nearby, peeking.

Leinad was not sure that it was the general until the figure was near the door. The general did not seem to sense Leinad nearby. He opened the door and rushed down the stairs without inkling. Leinad hesitated for a moment, but he decided to be brave.

Despite of his remarkable nose, the general was not aware of someone following. He kept walking quietly until he reached to a room in the basement. Leinad recognized the room quite promptly; he had happened to be there once while chasing the general earlier. This time he was sure that the general went to the room. He still had a good picture of the room inside.

Leinad very cautiously opened the door a bit to peep inside. There was no indication of anyone as far as he could see from there. He wanted to go check inside, but his nerves seized his legs so tight. He sat, leaning against the door, trying to hear anything coming from the other side of the door. He still believed that the general was there inside. He waited and waited patiently, and then, all of a sudden he heard water flooding over the pool, followed by someone complaining under his breath. Through a tiny gap he peeked again. There was a man walking out of the pool, who held some fish in his hands. Leinad was only able to see the fish, but he was sure that it was the general.

Now by the sound Leinad guessed that this man started to eat the fish from the pool. But he must have finished it all in a minute because Leinad saw him move around, mumbling words of satisfaction, followed by complaints.

"Don't forget to clean up the mess on the floor! Ha! Do I ever leave a mess? Why he always treats me like that? I am the HEAD general, haven't you forgotten that?"

Leinad reckoned that this greedy man was now busy cleaning up the area while complaining excessively to the king.

"Nobody ever cleans up like me to tell you the truth, Safrah, understood?" cried the man sarcastically. "And see who's actually caring about debris like this," he added discontentedly.

After that, there were noises from splashing and flooding. He must have dived again. But this time he came out of the pool only in a few minutes. And when he did, Leinad saw the face of the man for half a second. It was for sure the general, whose wet face was handsome and shiny by the reflection of the cheerful light from the ceiling.

Now by instinct, Leinad knew that this man would go to somewhere for a long sweet sleep. And there was no reason for Leinad to stick around the dangerous place. He ran out of the location immediately and raced all the way up to his room. And as soon as he returned, he fell on the bed, hoping for a long sweet sleep as well.

Meanwhile, he tried to review the real story he had experienced over the long day, but it was very difficult to fight with the physical desire. One thing for sure was that he now began to feel a glimpse of evidence for his father's disappearance. Whatever danger might lie upon his way, he would look into the activities of the king, Safrah and his man, Ripper. The very last thing he remembered before falling asleep was that he wished to see Mohzake in the morning out of nowhere like nothing had happened to him.

Leinad woke up in the morning brightly and joined the gathering in the launching hall. He decided to do his duty just like the rest of the participants for the time being. Now it was most likely that he would have his own investigation only at night when everyone was gone for the day. Thus, regardless of the fact that he has been monitored, he worked on his duty, waiting for the night for another beginning.

While he was studying on the atlas of the castle at night, Leinad noticed that there was a passage out of the castle building in a basement room. He believed that this strange water pool had something to do with it. So, he wanted to check the truth of the information of the atlas in line with his belief. Then, he decided to go to the pool and dive into it for real.

Leinad was engrossed by the thought of the king and his man until he entered the basement room. Mohzake in his note had indicated that the general had extraordinary power. But until now, Leinad has never seen anything extraordinary from the general. Not even close. Likewise, he was only a servant for the king. And the king would not spat out words of humiliation thoughtlessly to an extraordinary man. Maybe if Mohzake was somewhere in the castle, he would want to correct his note, Leinad thought. He considered that the king might have such evil power. But again, he has never seen anything extraordinary from the king yet. Now, with the atlas in hand he would be able to sneak into the king's palace to discover anything that the king has been hiding...

"Damn it! Fish again?"

Leinad caught a disgruntled voice from outside when he was about to dive into the pool. *Someone's coming!* The room was entirely open and nowhere to hide. He quickly thought to dive and disappear, but then he would leave noises and ripples as a good hint for an intruder.

The ceiling was the only hideout. He thought fast. It was covered with lighted balls and the view was well obscured behind the light. Above his height on the wall by the door there were small metal pieces stuck out in a horizontal line. He dashed to the wall and jumped up. He caught the metal pieces with two hands, simultaneously pulling his body up. Then he climbed like a frightened spider and darted into the mass of bright balls at once. They came in right that moment. Without a doubt, they were the king and the general.

"I am tired of seafood!" said the king, annoyingly, yet his voice was mild.

"But, today we will catch something special for a change...," said the general convincingly. "I spotted something very delicious last..."

"Last night! Ha! Now you are telling me the truth, Ripper," said the king softly. "And that's why I smell something here now, you hopeless fool. Why don't you admit that you had a feast with some good meat for a change, my dear general?"

"I, I didn't eat any meat for sure, Safrah," declared Ripper.

"What smell is this, then? You think I was out for hunting secretly?"

"No, but, it wasn't me, Safrah. Believe me," cried Ripper.

"All right, general, easy, I don't kill you for that, easy," said Safrah nicely.

"So, the fish that I spotted –."

"Damn it! Can't you just forget about that fish at once?" snapped Safrah. "Don't you see that I am sick without something really fresh?"

"Well, then, shall we go," said Ripper submissively. "In a few minutes we will be home," added Ripper delightfully, opening the door, "Your Highness."

Then, together out they went and marched up the stairs. By the time Leinad carefully climbed down and went up the stairs, they were nowhere.

In a few minutes to home… Leinad could hardly know their destination. It had to be somewhere within the castle, he thought, but even with the atlas of the castle, he could hardly guess anywhere that those two greedy men could call home. In the end he decided to go and meet Kittouse in Marineum instead of wandering around the castle dangerously to find their mysterious home.

Kittouse did not appear even he called several times. Then he waited for a while, attempting to be absorbed by the historical display in Marineum. After some time he called her once more and waited again, yet she did not show up. Suddenly he felt very lonely. He walked out of the room and headed back to his room, wondering if the general ever set a 'silly' trap in the entrance pot again.

When he entered his room absentmindedly, something fell down from the ceiling and landed on the table, making him almost jump in surprise.

"Kittouse!" he called out loud in delight.

He felt that he at long last met an old friend (not the little peculiar cat he knew), and he would tell her everything about what he has gone through until now; for sure he would ask her neither about Zenia nor the notes written by Mohzake on the thin glass plate.

"Kittouse," he called friendly, sitting on the edge of his bed.

"I haven't seen anything extraordinary, but I think it is the king who did all the foul things," said Leinad conclusively.

"You already knew it, didn't you?" he asked. "I guessed it some time ago, but now I begin to believe it for real," he added.

"Well, I hoped to discover something more critical this night, but they've just gone to somewhere to eat something like meat. They called it home, but I have no idea where they meant."

Kittouse suddenly stood up and scurried to the door. Leinad opened the door for her, and she ran out hurriedly. Leinad did not bother to ask anything. It was not the first time to follow her. Soon he knew that they were going to the king's favorite sky lounge. There again, Leinad opened the door for her, but Kittouse remained solid. Leinad stood still beside her without knowing the reason. But in a few minutes he knew the precise reason. There were two loud thuds on the lounge. Leinad was surprised and closed the door spontaneously.

"What was that?" asked Leinad in a whisper.

He leaned himself against the door quietly, pressing his ear as close as possible. There was a rough dragging sound, and then it was silent again. Leinad opened the door a bit, but Kittouse pushed and slipped out of it. Then, she ran all the way toward the door on the other side of the lounge. Leinad followed her again.

Running down the stairs, Leinad yet followed Kittouse. He now questioned if Kittouse also had a sensitive nose to follow any trace of smell like the general. In effect, he realized that he could also smell something. It certainly smelled fresh flesh which must have been disseminated only a moment ago. Kittouse strode straight to the end of the corridor, down the stairs. By then, Leinad knew the destination of this little chaser.

Chapter 21
IDENTITY OF LEINAD

Here we go again. Quietly sitting by the door outside, Leinad tried hard to eavesdrop. Their conversation sounded ever pleasant this time as far as the way the king said to the general.

"...but, er, can we try barbeque this time?" said Ripper hesitantly.

"Well, go ahead with your feeling, but I only like fresh one," Safrah said.

"And can I borrow your flame, please?" asked Ripper politely.

A sudden rumble echoed the room. And soon after, an invisible current carried an irritating smell out of the door to Leinad. With a curious look he turned his head to Kittouse, but he realized that she was gone already.

"Ha, look at this!" exclaimed Ripper, excitedly.

The aroma of sizzling meat must be tickling Ripper's nostrils. By now, Leinad knew the taste of Ripper; without doubt this man would prefer anything from ocean. Nevertheless, Ripper seemed really in appreciation of the barbeque of the flesh as well.

"Ha, this one is really good, indeed. Sooo tasty!" cried Ripper, munching greedily. "Do you want some, too?" asked Ripper clumsily with full of stuff in his mouth.

"Damn it! Put that away? How many hell lots of times should I tell you that I hate cooked meat? Especially when it's burnt!" shouted Safrah annoyingly.

His voice was cold with a rage, but Ripper simply disregarded.

"Oh, yeah," uttered Ripper playfully in an Oops-tone. "Sorry, my bad. I have forgotten…you have a bad reaction to black powder or something ever since we came here, but, er…," Ripper stopped for a moment, swallowing the stuff in his mouth. "Well, I think I am OK with anything except for red dust. It's just burning me to death."

"Shut up!! Don't ever talk about such things in public!" snapped Safrah angrily in a warning tone.

Ripper protested exasperatedly, "I am not that dumb. Don't you worry about it?"

Now, both were engaged quietly in filling up their empty stomachs for a few minutes until Ripper pulled up an account of his own.

"Oh, I saw that little mouse the other day, you know," said Ripper. "Funny. This thing was bravely sitting in front of the aquarium, watching the hemabies amusingly," added Ripper carelessly.

"You missed it, anyway," said Safrah scornfully.

"Well, it was frantically running away for life, so…"

"So what? Don't you ever feel shameful? Why don't you NOT telling me anything that you failed. I really doubt you ever care about being dummy, at all."

It was quiet for a while again, Ripper seemed OK with the humiliating advice from Safrah this time. At the same time they were busy eating without any further comments on their meal. This amusing time lasted in silence until Ripper brought up another account.

"Oh, by the way," said Ripper, swallowing, "that boy, I mean, Leinad, I think I have seen him before…in the forest I just remembered recently."

"When?" asked Safrah, munching loudly.

"Yesterday, probably," replied Ripper plainly.

"When did you SEE him, I asked," said Safrah annoyingly.

"Oh, that…well, I don't remember," said Ripper in an as-a-matter-of-fact tone.

After thinking hard for a moment, he stopped chewing, and said, "Yeah, actually it was only a few days ago. I think it was one or two days before these kids came here. Yes, I was checking the watchers at that time and –."

"You mean hunting," interrupted Safrah sarcastically.

"No, seriously, Safrah, I was just on my duty patrolling around, and then I saw this boy with an old man coming to the forest… Well, to be generous I let them go into the forest. But then, they overlooked my generosity and dared cross the threshold of our home. You can't believe they just came into Arch Cliff fearlessly," explained Ripper, sounding very upset at that time.

"And so," putting some stuff into his mouth again, he continued, "I let the watchers attack the old man," said Ripper bossily.

"Stupid dogs! They couldn't even ingest an old man like him who came right into their throats," he yelled in dismay.

"You couldn't finish him, either, I presume," said Safrah mockingly.

"Oh yeah, I attacked him right on, and in one shot he was dead," said Ripper arrogantly. "Master, yes, this boy called him master, but he was no match for me, you know," he added.

"Master?" recited Safrah in curiosity.

"Yeah, I think he called this man Master Rupidd or something like that, I remember now."

"Rupidd, did you say?" asked Safrah keenly.

"I think that was it," replied Ripper.

"Indeed, that was Rupidd...," said Safrah, forming a thin smile in his expression.

"But I killed him right at –."

"Shut up! You are no match for him. Stupid. Don't tell me you saw him dead," snapped Safrah scornfully.

"Well, no. But he was –."

"Quiet, then!" shouted Safrah, ignoring his protest.

"He must have died by –."

"Ripper!" shouted Safrah again, sounding very annoyed.

"OK, OK, easy, please," cried Ripper, laughing impractically.

Packing his mouth with another piece of meat, he refreshed, "Who is that man, anyway?"

"I knew this boy was different...," said Safrah pensively. "And what happened to the boy?" he asked.

'Well, of course, he tried to run away at once, and I ordered the watchers to go finish him... Damn idiots! They disappointed me again with that. Until now, I have never thought this little boy was still alive," said Ripper, fuming.

"He was riding a white horse, I presume," said Safrah.

"Yeah. A coward. Seized with fear for sure. They could have knocked 'em down in a flash and filled their stomachs happily in that instant."

"Shut it up once," yelled Safrah, "if you don't know about Cobah."

"I am just telling you…," said Ripper, swallowing the stuff in his mouth.

"What is Cobah, anyway?" Ripper asked carelessly.

"What did you discover about this boy so far?" asked Safrah interrogatively now.

"He was looking for Norrikee for a while as I had locked this man in… Well, not much since I disposed him," said Ripper decisively. "Certainly Norrikee had said something to him, but…," he added unsurely.

"Did you find out what Norrikee had said to him?"

"No, not a chance," replied Ripper promptly, "but what's the worry? I can drag and finish him any time, can't I?"

"Can't you just shut that up for one second, please, Ripper? You are always going much too far brainlessly. NEVER kill him without my permission, understood?"

"Well, if you say so," said Ripper and added at once, "OK, understood."

"It's obvious, but, I want to know precisely why Rupidd sent him here," said Safrah musingly, forming a bitter smile across his lips.

Turning his awareness back to Ripper, he yelled, "Can't you stop eating that at once! And go find out now what he is up to!"

"Almost –."

"I said NOW!" shouted Safrah angrily.

Leinad left the location without beating about the bush. He was pretty sure that, if he stayed there any longer, he would either break the silence with an unstoppable laugher, or be solidified by the surprising information.

Chapter 22
FROZEN MAN

Leinad could not sleep well. All night long he was by himself in a dark ocean, swimming down and down to reach the bottom that seemingly never existed. And eventually he woke up very early in the morning with a poor feeling. It was all too much to handle now in reality. He could breathe well at this moment, yet, he was no better than a mouse in a trap. Whether it would be disposed or spared, his life depended totally on the decision of Safrah now. He tried to soothe his anxious mind with the fact that at least they would not kill him yet. Then he reminded himself of his unfinished investigation.

Yes, I will have to carry it on while I am still useful to them.

And he decided to go check the mysterious pool in the morning.

Surprisingly, Leinad was not the earliest bird who came to the pool. His breath halted by the familiar voices coming from inside when he was about to open the door. He recognized that they were Safrah and Ripper right away. For the first few seconds he wondered why they were there in such an early morning. Then he speculated that they came for a breakfast, and if there was a passageway, they would disappear pretty soon. Leinad was positive. Now, it was quiet for a few minutes. They must have dived into the pool. Then, almost unconsciously he decided to follow them wherever the destination lay.

Leinad dived into the uncanny pool bravely, and soon he confirmed that it really was a passage. As he forwarded, the passage led to a dark ocean valley full of debris and lifeless forms of bones and skeletons of fish and animals. It was a grave yard. And there, for the first time Leinad saw two monstrous figures swimming ahead in the distance. The two handsome men were not anywhere. They were the real figures of the king and the general without a doubt.

As they advanced, soon they were out of the graveyard. Now they were so busy catching fish. In fact any moving creature before them simply turned lifeless. Creatures were immobilized powerlessly in front of the hungry monsters. They devoured the preys in two shakes. There was another excursion for them after the meal. They seemed yet unsatisfied. They moved over to another valley full of activities of marine creatures. Then they were engaged again in searching for preys.

Unexpectedly, one of the monsters turned his head to Leinad while hunting. Leinad hid quite promptly underneath a big rock shaped like a huge ball. It was heavily loaded with sea plants, shells and coral which covered up the entire surface.

Now, the other monster moved over to the area, scrutinizing around intensely. But he failed to spot Leinad who was attached to the big rock and well covered with plentiful marine life. In addition, with a stomach full of stuff and a mouth full of blood still left after his meal, the monster's nose seemed futile to identify the existence of a human nearby. He returned to his companion, and together they went on their joyful excursion of the second round hunting.

As they were out of sight, Leinad emerged from the hideout. When he looked back at the big rock thankfully, he had a weird feeling with the rock full of sea creatures on its round surface. He drew near and carefully rooted out the weeds and coral on a spot. Then, he wiped out a small area of the surface to examine inside.

Interestingly there was a shiny surface that he could feel with his hands. It was certainly not a rock. For half a second he thought that it was a huge marble or a giant egg, but it was not even close; it was a huge ball with some figures visible vaguely inside. Then, he had a strange belief that there was a human inside. Now with a burning desire to see the entire bodies of the figures he hurriedly cleaned up wider area of the surface.

It took him only a moment before confirming that there was really a human inside. A man on a hemaby was visible almost like real. And the man in there was none other than his father. Undeniably, it was the face that he has missed for many long years. Waves of uncontrollable grief came upon him, breaking down his heart into million pieces.

Now what?

After all the remorseful moments and painful efforts, he now found his father who has been left on the ocean floor, being petrified like a fossil. It was not the lack of air that gave him an irresistible pain inside, but it was the rage that tortured him with a wild anguish. He came out of the water and shouted over and over until his throat ached so much. He cried out so loud until he surrendered to think a thing.

Some time later when he got over, and all became quiet again, he submerged back to his father. He removed all the sea creatures from the surface and cleaned as much as he felt satisfied. He hoped his father could get some light. Plenty of light. At least he could enjoy the light.

Leinad went back to the castle, but he was not able to join the race for the day. He stayed in his room all day long without doing a thing. His mind was occupied only by his father, the fossilized man. A new gamekeeper once came to bother him with what was going on. Later the gamekeeper came back again and informed that he would have a new hemaby from the day. Leinad ignored him with an excuse of feeling very sick. He endeavored to get some sleep to no avail. He only pretended with his eyes locked tight. In his mind there was no room for anything other than finding out what had happened to his father. Now he had a firm belief that the death of his father has been hidden behind the smile of the monstrous king.

When Leinad unlocked his eyes, he saw Kittouse sit beside him, watching him sorrowfully. Leinad wondered if she had already known everything about his father. He wished that his father could have turned into an animal just like Kittouse, if ever possible. Then at least he could talk to his father now.

"Kittouse," said Leinad, sitting up, "I understand now how dreadful it is for you to be in this horrible place," said Leinad, his face hardened with grief. "I feel so sorry, Kittouse. I wish I have supernatural power so that I can set you free," said Leinad pitifully. *And so that I will do some magic on my father to return…*

"I finally saw my father, Kittouse… He was fossilized down in the ocean…," said Leinad, swallowing the lumps of pain that came along with the memory of his father.

"You are not too bad…, at least you are not like that, Kittouse."

Leinad had to stop for now. He buried his face between his knees and tried to consume the sorrow quietly. Then, he felt something touching his arm smoothly. It was Kittouse who came close enough, brushing his arm with her forelegs as though trying to help soothe the pain in his heart. He gently placed his hand on her fur in appreciation of her effort. She seemed happy with that and rested on his arm peacefully for some time.

"Kittouse…, do you think we can revenge the evil men?" asked Leinad, attempting to sound cheerful. "In any case…if I fail, please don't do anything silly…for Mohzake…and me. Can you promise, Kittouse?" asked Leinad calmly.

Kittouse lifted up her head and looked him straight in the eyes for a few seconds. Then, she closed her mournful eyes hard and shook her head painfully. Leinad knew what it meant, but he had no words to appease her sorrow in return.

"Safrah knew my master pretty well somehow…," said Leinad painfully.

"For any reason, Kittouse, if you leave the castle, can you please find him? His name is Rupidd. I feel that he is the only one who can be helpful to you, Kittouse. I will keep the atlas of the castle here in the bedside drawer," said Leinad, pointing, "and also the letter from my father, if you can bring them it to my master…"

The memory with his master suddenly brought another lump to his throat unbearably, and he had to swallow hard again.

"Remember Rupidd in a small village near Humington," he said.

"This night I will sneak in the palace and listen in more of their talks. This evil man knows a lot of me now, and I don't have much time before...," he said, swallowing again. "I just want to make sure, Kittouse, you don't try anything new or dangerous from now on. And please, don't go anywhere else, Kittouse."

Leinad knew that she was not sleeping, but she remained only still. He lifted her up gently and placed on his bed. Kittouse curled up her body smoothly without making noise. He soothed her neck a few times and left his room silently.

"I wish I could take you wherever I go," he said, but the words only stayed in his mouth and never came out.

Chapter 23
SEARCHING FOR THE POWER

After checking the hidden passageway on the atlas once more, Leinad went to the palace directly and sneaked in the king's hall quietly. It was quite late, but the king and the general were still in a secretive conversation. Their voice tones were coarse. They were talking about the races and something about power in a bubble ball. The king was complaining about the situation exasperatingly.

"…if things are going this way, I doubt anyone will ever bring the remaining power to me."

"Well, why don't we just go find it ourselves?" cried the servant plainly.

"No, we can't! Stupid, you asked me to repeat that again. If Neptess smells anything, she won't leave us alone. We have to get the power before she finds out our plan. Don't you ever make me repeat that again, idiot!"

"Well," Safrah began, cooling down his steaming head, "one day, I will be the most powerful being in the whole world…only once I have the rest of the power in my hands," he said, shaking his firm grip.

"Now, we have to put more efforts on this. Add more rewards and make them work hard and seriously on this!" Safrah said grimly, his eyes shifting to Ripper's.

"OK," cried Ripper promptly. "But, please, don't call me idiot. I'm not –."

"AND," Safrah continued, pointing at Ripper, "make sure no one notices our plan. From now on, don't come back to the castle until all dummies return. You will monitor them seriously and report precisely to me what's going on up there. Disguise yourself and don't get spotted!" yelled Safrah warningly. "And once you are done up there, come back straight to the castle. DON'T even think about the forest. Don't ever linger around the forest without my okay!" declared Safrah firmly. "Your job continues here at the castle if you know what I mean," he added, dropping his voice back to normal.

"Anything new about the boy?" asked Safrah gently now.

"Well, not much. He stayed in his room for a whole day. He said he's been sick, but I can smell something out of his mind," uttered Ripper skeptically.

"Smell something? I would trust that dummy nose of yours by no means," said Safrah sarcastically. "Have you really ever done anything other than eating and sleeping ever since you landed here? I doubt you are really doing your job up there, to be honest," added Safrah under his breath with a look of disbelief.

"What are you talking about, Safrah? I am –."

"That's fine without an excuse. Now, go and get sleep at once. That will suit you better," retorted Safrah coldly.

Leinad quietly moved his steps back to the door on the ceiling. But his mind was totally bemused by their conversation. He came back to his room hurriedly.

Kittouse was not there anymore. He wondered if she had gone somewhere only momentarily. Soon, his mind was loaded with the possible dark scheme of the two evil men. Now it appeared that their intention was to get a ball containing some kind of power. It has been all planned by these two monsters with the bad will. His father was only a small obstacle that they could easily dump into the ocean just like that.

He was right. We all have been only dumb, helping their plots eagerly.

Leinad wanted to revenge badly. He struggled to find any possible way, but only ended up with a simple question. *How in the world a powerless boy like me can go for such revenge?* He mulled the question over and over with no definite solution. If there was, it should be whatever they were after, he thought. The power… They were doing anything to get the power.

Power? Leinad suddenly remembered his father's cheerful message. He pulled out the parchment which he had obtained from the Finixie on behalf of his father. Now, his father's encouraging words were right before him, but his eyes firm on the word 'power' as if to absorb any hidden power for real.

DANIEL,

Congratulations at last you made it.

Sure I knew you would without help.

You are strong and wise as always be.

Trust power and wisdom in you.

Believe no scales in your ability.

I hope you find joys and meaning in your life.

Always with you on this land my only son.

D654321 Y1Y2C3I2 Y8Y5 T1A8Y1 I4T2B3 S7A6

Leinad's main interest was the last line containing letters combined with numbers. It did not take too long before he figured out that the first letter of each line was different as D, C, S, Y, T, B, I, and A, and the last line was a riddle.

Based on that information, he learned that every letter in the line of the riddle represented the first letter of a specific line. The accompanied numbers simply indicated the location of the specific word (or letter) within the line. When he extracted out the core words in this way, it read as follows:

Leinad

you are last hope

be wise

trust only you

find power scales

help land

"Find power scales!"

They were only the hidden words of his father on the parchment, but he felt his father yelling to remind him of finding the power scales.

"They are looking for the hidden power scales! That's it!"

It could be the only thing for Safrah to become the most powerful being. Conversely, it could have been the only hope for his father and even for the whole world. Leinad began to see what his father had meant by 'Saving the world.'

Following morning Leinad joined the race brightly. There was no reason to chew over the evil scheme of Safrah anymore. And he did not need to concern about the hidden eyes of Ripper. He raced to the sky in search of the hope, the power scales. And up in the sky he (just like Safrah) only thought about the power in his hand until he dragged his tired body back to his room. Although there was no luck or success at the end of the day, he was yet spirited for he still had the hope.

However, when another day passed by without even a single clue, he could not help feeling down. His efforts only delivered him sighs and frustration. The power and the hope were now even farther away, and he began to believe that there would be no way of grabbing them soon or later. Then, his mind came back to where all had begun, and he wondered if this was all for real. *This is pointless...*

"What should I do now? Father, please...," he called his father aloud.

In the late afternoon Leinad dived to his father again. He knew it would not make any difference, but he polished the surface of the ball excessively well, pressing down an irresistible sorrow. Now, when he was about to return to the castle, he spotted some words written on the sleeve of his father's shirts. He nearly pumped out a bucket of tears by the sight of his father's familiar handwriting.

"L25G29?"

Leinad questioned, but at once he decided that it was an important note for what his father was looking for. Then, he considered it being an imperative hint left for his son because it appeared very similar to the riddle in his father's message; L and G were the first letters of two words, leading two numbers, 25 and 29, respectively.

Leinad speculated that something had happened to his father while he was up in the sky because his father was yet on his hemaby. He came out of the water and looked at the late afternoon sky which was brightened with the light from above. Leinad opened his mind eyes and tried to revisit the bubble ball forest. He saw endless bubble balls spread in clusters horizontally and in layers over layers like sheets of paper.

Layers and clusters of bubble balls... His eyes lit up with inspiration. He never thought that they were in layers and clusters until now. Days of his efforts in the midst of the bubble ball forest were not in vain after all. He was very confident with his interpretation. Then, the numbers (25 and 29) must indicate certain layer and clustered group numbers, he thought.

"That's what it is!" he exclaimed in thrill.

He felt that the power was already in his hand now.

"The first thing I have to check tomorrow for sure," he assured himself pleasingly, and he hurried to the castle with an exceptional feeling.

I can't wait to see the hope come true.

Chapter 24
TRUTH OF THE LIAR

The moment he returned, Leinad wanted to see Kittouse to share his discovery. He came back to his room straight, hoping to see her there. He called her aloud, but she did not show up. He waited until late night, then, he decided to go to Marineum.

The whole castle seemed in deep sleep when he stepped out of his room. This time he did not take his usual route through the back door. It was very late that even the two evil men must have gone to sleep. And momentarily, he was not afraid of them at all. He entered the room through the front door, pressing down the growing enthusiasm and the cheers to deliver to her.

"Kittouse!" Leinad called out pleasantly.

"Kittouse, are you here?" he called again. "I've got good news now, Kittouse," he said brightly.

"Kittous?" There came another voice like an echo from the back of the room.

Leinad's hairs erect instantaneously with the familiar gross voice. There could be no mistaking what he saw in the room now. It was Safrah. Behind him was Ripper, the bighearted general. Their hidden monstrous figures were almost visible now.

"My dear boy came here to see someone, general," said Safrah softly.

"Yes, indeed, Your Highness," replied Ripper. "It was Key-toss."

"Key-toss?" copied Safrah, turning his head toward Ripper whose mouth twisted awkwardly with a soundless word of who-knows.

"Well, general, don't you feel strange when you see one of our dear riders in my collection room in the middle of a dead night?" exclaimed Safrah cheerfully, his lips curved into a mean smile with the last few words.

"I do, indeed, Your Highness," replied Ripper, his mood elevated.

Leinad felt sudden chill penetrating his chest but for barely two seconds before he flew into a rage which he had curbed over days and nights. He could not stop it. His mind was soon filled up with fuming anger against the deed of the evil man. For the moment he forgot everything; even the power scales which he needed to challenge the evil. They seemed to have evaporated into thin air with the steam out of his boiling mind.

"You killed my father!" Leinad exploded his anger at last.

"Kill your father?" asked Safrah, turning his bewildered face to Ripper.

"General, by any chance…?" he asked, but he did not wait for a reply.

"My dear fellow, I don't even know your father. Besides, why do I ever kill innocent people?"

"You liar!" shouted Leinad with full of detestation in his eyes. "Don't give me bullshit! Don't tell me you didn't dump my father down there! You killed all the innocent people just like that, you evil monster!" His deafening voice echoed in the room.

Safrah eyed Leinad now very seriously and laughed out loud atrociously. Then he said brightly to Ripper, yet his eyes firm on Leinad, "Finally, my dear boy has discovered something, right, Ripper?"

"Indeed, he has, Your Highness." replied Ripper promptly.

"All right, then," began Safrah, turning his notice to Ripper, "we will have a small sideshow for a change," he added, walking toward the door.

"Now, if you kindly follow me, my boy," said Safrah.

The boy reluctantly moved his steps after Safrah as Ripper pushed him. They entered the deserted launching hall.

Safrah stopped near the aquarium, turning to Leinad, he asked, "So, Rupidd sent you here to challenge me?"

"Don't insult my master with your evil tongue! I came to kill you with my own will!" shouted Leinad.

"Brave, my boy, brave, just like your father. What a pity! Rupidd tried with Hasyn, and now he sent Hasyn's son for another go. Poor Rupidd, he failed to defeat me three times already. I guess he is too old now to mend the fatal mistake in his life," said Safrah with sympathy.

"My boy, do you want to know how Rupidd and I were linked together?" asked Safrah. Looking at the ceiling once, he continued, "He was my master, well, precisely, I was only his pet. He thankfully raised me for all those years, traveling troublesome worlds until we, well, I settled down on this land. In spite of this, he attempted to kill me when I was such an adorable pet long ago only because I was a potential threat to his beloved horses. And now, he even on the sly followed me to this peaceful land for another shot. Have I become too strong for him? You see, I never did any harm to him and I will never, because he is yet my master and yet like my father. Well, of course, without his care and training I wouldn't be here today. And I can't thank him enough for letting me filch a bit of mystic power of Silane Land, which dramatically changed my life. Poor old man, whatever he tries, it only helps my life better," exclaimed Safrah morosely.

"Your humble master didn't tell you a thing, did he?" asked Safrah.

Jumping out of the rage, Leinad could not believe what he just heard. It was simply out of the question to have a connection between his noble master and this evil monster.

"You liar! I don't care what you were! Don't ever connect my master to your stinking life, you monster!" shouted Leinad in agony.

"Lair, you are saying?" asked Safrah, chuckling impractically. "Well, then, let me tell you how I LIED to your father, my boy. He was smart and stupid," said Safrah, his face forming a malicious smile.

"At least in his opinion, I believe, I was once a good friend of him back in the forest. I told him that I came to help him save animals from dangers, and he believed it. Unfortunately I only lied to him because I needed to use him. I wanted to know about Bubble Land, the castle, the king or anything. I pretended to be useful, taking care of animals and their shelters with him. Of course, as long as he was with me he was always safe. Once he told me about a strange vision for an animal land, and he wanted to make it for real. I promised to help him as a good friend. Later, he told me about an opportunity to become a king and his decision to go for it to bring the vision to reality. I knew what it meant to me. I begged and I insisted, and he arranged for me to go with him. He was obviously the most likely person to win the competition. So, I stuck around him in the final race. Naturally, he excavated a ball containing power scales up in the sky. Then, our relationship and his role were all done. I snatched the ball from him at once, and our brave general here finished your father. Well, it was very unfortunate for your father, but, thanks to him, I won the crown of this land happily after."

"No! That's not true! You stinking monster, I will chop your head off!"

"That's a nice one," said Safrah spiritedly, "for a change."

"Well, if you have no more appreciable words, Ripper, shall we begin?" asked Safrah gently, disregarding Leinad's furious cry.

Safrah's eyes stopped at the aquarium for a few seconds, and the instant a hemaby appeared, he continued. "Now, I presume you also want to see the power of the scales."

"Poor boy, you think you are clever enough to find it out, but you are only dumb to push yourself into danger with all that," said Safrah firmly.

"Now, I want to give you a chance. Yes, I should, in appreciation of your master's love and care for me. We can give him at least one last chance, right, Ripper?" asked Safrah with full of pride in his voice.

"Indeed, we can, Your Highness" replied Ripper in the same way.

"I will let you join the race unless you want to join your father. How does that sound?"

Safrah was noticeably enjoying the moment with his sarcastic expressions.

"All right, Ripper, can you show us something?"

As Safrah gave a signal, the hemaby in the aquarium kicked out of the water, and flew in mid-air, gyrating.

"So," began Ripper, "this thing used to be yours, I believe. But, you don't need it anymore," said Ripper.

Turning his attention to Safrah, he begged, "Please. Your Highness."

"Certainly, general," Safrah replied friendly.

Now, Safrah swung his hands toward the hemaby as though cutting off the air before him. In a moment a thick line of steam came out from the back of the hemaby, covering the entire body of its own accord. Shortly, the hemaby was completely wrapped up with white milky clouds. Safrah watched the sinister scene amusingly for a few seconds before he blew the clouds away. As the white clouds dissolved in the air, a half comatose boy revealed, falling down to the floor. Leinad was shocked by the appearance of a boy. What's more, the boy was Mohzake.

"Well, well, well. Welcome back, my dear boy!" exclaimed Ripper delightfully. "But, not for long," added Ripper.

With a grim expression he was swiftly transformed into a monstrous figure. Then he inhaled deeply and blew out damp wind over Mohzake. In a brief moment, a large amount of clear viscous liquid came out of his mouth, covering up the entire body of Mohzake. And in seconds it formed a large clear ball with Mohzake stood lifelessly inside. He was only a human fossil in a rock now.

"Your Highness?" said Ripper delightedly, and he was transformed back into a handsome general again.

"No, no, Ripper," exclaimed the king, "that's not what he wants, Can't you see that?" asked Safrah ever spiritedly.

"OK, then, he wants to stay alive," said Ripper gracefully.

He looked very happy because there was no yelling from Safrah.

"There you go," added Safrah with a pleasant smile.

Now Safrah took out a silver scale and drew Leinad's attention.

"The power of this little thing, you probably have never seen before," said Safrah doubtfully. "Well, no need now. Experiencing is better than seeing."

Safrah threw the scale up in the air, and he was transformed into a monstrous figure in a tick. When the scale fell half way down to the floor, he growled out loudly. Then he spat out a wisp of blue flame which instantaneously transferred to the scale before it touched the floor. In the next second a shaft of light was created within the scale, and in a flash it drove into Leinad's chest. Without a moment to resist, Leinad was thrown up to the air and fell down into the empty aquarium with a big splash. White foam filled up the entire aquarium, and nothing was visible for now. Ripper bolted his mouth tight, casting stealthy glances at Safrah who only kept staring at the aquarium as though to appraise the result of his experiment. The aquarium steadily settled in peace and it was crystal clear again. However, the furious boy was gone with the white foam and the ripples. He vanished like he never existed. Instead, there was a hemaby on the aquarium floor motionlessly.

"Well, well, there he is!" exclaimed Safrah, chuckling happily. "But, he still looks pretty charming to me. What do you think, Ripper?"

"Yes, he indeed does," replied Ripper in his usual way.

"Get him out!" ordered Safrah carelessly. "And remove all the scales!"

"Right away, Your Highness."

"Well, leave just one scale for the memory of my beloved master. Otherwise, no one will notice that it is a hemaby and no one will ask him for a ride," uttered Safrah brightly.

"If you ever find a rider, my boy, you are very welcome to be free! And I can share all the power with you," yelled Safrah happily.

"Hmmm… Now I wonder whom my dear master will send next!" exclaimed Safrah joyfully. "Well, instead of giving another shot, if he comes to me in person, at least I can give him many sincere thanks for teaching me how to walk off with all the remarkable things. Otherwise, I would have been a poor pet forever!" yelled Safrah with a big happy laughter.

It was quiet again after the two handsome men happily walked away. Maybe it was too quiet for those creatures left in the hall. In the aquarium lay one hemaby lifelessly with two most sorrowful eyes. And yet, there was a little creature sat silently far up on the ceiling with full of tears in her eyes.

Chapter 25
WORDS OF THE GODDESS

The ball in the ocean floor was shiny like a crystal as light came through the water. It was such bright light that could visualize merrily dancing small living things in the water. The light went through the surface of the ball and reached the frozen man. How long he has been there in the darkness, he was not sure.

For umpteenth years he waited to see light, but it had never happened until this very moment when his son came and wiped out the surface for him. However, it was only a moment for him to feel the joy. He was so sad. He saw his son's sorrow, anger and fear over his face. He knew that there was nothing he could do for his son. He was only a fossilized man. He struggled with thousands of emotional words constantly coiling up in his brain.

"My son is in a great danger. He needs help. I must get out of this. Let me get out, let me, please! I can't let the evil man kill my son. I can't leave the evil man rule the world!"

The soundless words left his heart and traveled through the ball and beyond.

"Mighty Goddess, spare me a hope. Please, let me have the strength!"

His silent voice traveled with the waves of light over the ocean depth. It seemed the Goddess was able to see the man underwater through the bright light over the crystal clear surface.

The frozen man heard a voice from somewhere far and wide.

"Trust your son, Hasyn! It is only he who will have to do it. The future of this land, not to mention your life, only depends on him. You must now believe the wisdom and the courage in him."

PART 2 UGLEY

Once there was a formidable man called Harfhas who was known to be the scariest among the forest animals. He was believed to be a lion with remarkable power. He was convinced that his power would grow by the numbers and the kinds of animals he killed. Therefore, he killed any animal in sight to become even more powerful. As his killing continued, his power also grew indeed.

He never knew how many animals he killed, but somehow, he gained so much power that no animals could run before him. And then, something remarkable happened to him; he could have wings when he wanted to catch birds, and he could hide his paws and tails when he was willing to disguise himself for any reason.

It was now the time when he thought that there were no more animals attracting him. He smiled at the endless span of the ocean. With webbed feet it was an easy job for him to play underwater.

Once there was a shark called Ripper who was known to be the most violent in the ocean. Ripper believed that one day he would walk out of the water to catch inland animals if he killed fish of all kinds in the ocean. Indeed, as his killing went on, his physical shape changed significantly. He grew webbed legs and arms. However, Ripper underestimated the power of the Goddess of the ocean. His life was detained in an ice cube before even having the first step on land with his own feet.

It had been so long for Ripper before Harfhas discovered and brought him out of the frozen cube to be free. Ripper was so grateful and thankful to Harfhas to let him resurrect. Thus Ripper decided to serve Harfhas forever beside him...

Chapter 1
BIRTHDAY PRESENT

Gosh, I almost forgot!

I needed to buy some school stuff at a store near my home. I entered the store and moved to the stationary aisle which was at a corner far end of the store. I purposely passed through the gaming section to see if any new fancy items were released. Of course, there were all sorts of attractive toys, dolls, and games of characters of new movies and books. On the other side were various puzzles of the characters displayed on a shelf.

"Puzzles!"

I could not just pass by the section. Ever since my mother had brought me a box of jigsaw puzzle when I was a toddler, puzzle games of all kinds became one of my favorite things. Especially, I was taken with jigsaw puzzles.

Of all jigsaw puzzles on display there was a particular puzzle game which keenly enchanted my eyes. I picked up the box in curiosity. It was a 3 dimensional jigsaw puzzle with a thousand pieces. There was a cover picture of a brilliant silver castle. On top of the picture was a title: Sand Castle. The castle on the picture was bright white and so pretty as if it was made up of real silver.

"Sand Castle? Nonsense!" I cried in disbelief.

Obviously, it was a silver castle. I briefly checked the area to see if any other boxes of the same kind left, but that was the only one there.

"Well, what's the big deal about it, anyway?"

In fact, I had never cared much about cover pictures when I did puzzles. But, the complexity with a thousand pieces... I could not imagine doing it without a glimpse at an actual picture. And that would be really a big deal for me. *It may take days, or maybe I can never make it... Moreover, it's three dimensional! Impossible.*

My thought and steps moved to the stationary section now. I should find all the items before too late. I was already hearing my mother yelling at me. I placed the items in a basket and paced toward the cashier. Then again, I walked through the gaming section. Maybe I wanted to see those games one last time. I knew I would not have any other opportunity to visit any stores for a while.

For some reasons I automatically stopped by the corner of piece puzzles. I was not sure why, but I was gazing at the puzzle, entitled Sand Castle, quite absentmindedly until someone called.

"Hello, there."

There was an old man who stood beside me with a peculiar smile. I could tell at once that he was one of the staffs by looking at his blue uniform with a company logo on it. He looked pretty old for a sales staff with short grey hairs and a mustache.

"How may I help you, Mr. handsome?" He asked, looking mildly at my eyes over his glasses.

"Oh, I am OK. Thank you, sir." I said sincerely. I stepped back from the display and walked out of the section.

"Ah, I know what you are interested in, Mr. handsome," said the man joyfully.

I stopped on the spot and looked back. Surely no one was around, and he was talking to me. He was holding a box of a puzzle game, and I spied a silver castle on the cover. He must have watched me over in the first place.

Tapping the box gently with a big smile, he said, "Silver castle!"

I had already dropped the matter, but it still irked me. Obviously, something was not correct, either the title or the picture.

"That's Sand Castle, it says," I argued. "Anyway, I was not interested in it. Just a bit curious, that's all."

After taking a look at the cover of the box, the old man declared friendly, "Aha! Yes, you are right. Yes, it indeed says Sand Castle."

The man shrugged with an uncoordinated smile.

"People always make mistakes. Supposed to be Silver Castle, I believe. Well, in that case," he paused for a moment, looking at my eyes straight as though the next words could be found only in there. And after some time he found words to follow, "I can offer it to you, so you will figure out whether it is silver or sand. How does that sound?"

That sounded perfectly good to me, and I would be delighted with that.

"You mean it's free?" I asked.

"That's what meant."

He pushed the box toward me, his face full of happiness.

"Thank you, but are you sure?" I questioned again with a shred of doubt.

"Yes, of course, yes. I will be so glad if you accept it," he said with a broad grin.

He noticed that I was still hesitating, my eyes looking around.

"No worries. You are not stealing anything, Mr. Hands –."

"Ryan, sir." I interrupted to correct my name.

I was still not sure if I had to take it, but he forced me to take it. He already pulled out a plastic bag and placed the box in it.

Handing it over to me, he said, "Oh, by the way, Ryan, for this game, there is an interesting rule that I want to tell you now."

With this, he smiled mildly, but it sounded more like a warning to me.

"You like challenging games, don't you?" asked the man lightly.

"Yes." I said, nodding at the same time.

"Yes, yes, that is good then," said the man, breathing a negligible sigh of relief. "Let's say, you will complete this puzzle before the bed time tonight." He assumed tentatively, his eyes fixed on my face like forcing me to say, 'Yes, I will.'

Of course, I will. As far as I remembered I'd never stopped once I started. Whatever rule he talked about, this has been my rule. *But, why is he saying that, anyway? Anything will happen if undone by then?*

He must have read my mind.

"Nothing will happen to you, Ryan. However, if you have such a rule that you must follow, you will try hard to make it on time," said the man. "Let's say, this is very important for everyone, but no one could have done it. Imagine it all depends on you, Ryan," added the man, striving to be convincing.

It made no sense to me. But, whatever he meant, no problem to me.

"I will make it." I said confidently. *It will be challenging, for sure. But what's the big deal with some additional pieces. And I have a good cover picture as well.*

"I am so glad to see your confidence. I am sure you will be able to make it, and I believe in you, Ryan," he said, looking very delighted by my positive answer.

I was about to ask if there were any other rules, but he let me go and deal with it. With visible satisfaction he cheerfully marched away, his hand waving several times. That was a strange man and a strange puzzle game with a strange rule. His voice echoed in my eardrums.

"But please, think twice before you open the box!"

"There you are!" exclaimed my mother the moment she saw me entering the house.

She was doing the dishes in the kitchen.

"Hi, mom." I said merrily, putting the plastic bags on the sofa.

"What took you so long?" She complained, making a face worriedly.

"Ask me about it, mom. The shop was jam-packed with people all over the places… Mom, next time I should buy these stuffs earlier. I don't want to wait in queue just to buy a few items like this." I uttered, trying to look as frustrated as possible.

"Well, you ask me about it," she said, imitating my complaint. "Now you get the point. Every summer you are so busy doing nothing but playing around the beach. And every summer I recited a hundred times to buy your stuff before the last week of summer vacation. See, you always say, 'Later, mom,' 'Still have a plenty of time, mom,' or

'No need to hurry, mom.' And now you are complaining about it. It makes perfect sense, doesn't it?" she yelled at me cheerfully, but her face full of sarcasm.

I could not find words to quarrel with her. That was only true. I still had loads of work to be done before going back to school. At least I should have my homework done as soon as possible before she would ask me again.

Feeling guilty, I pulled out the note, listing the items that I had to buy.

"I think I bought everything in the list." I said cautiously, my eyes following the list, my mind hoping she would drop the matter.

"Are you ready?" asked my mother, casting a curious glance at me.

She seemed happy to leave it at that.

"Yeah, I think so, mom. I have everything I need now. But I will double check tonight or tomorrow to make sure." I replied, my voice slightly restless by the thought of meeting friends and classmates again.

I noticed that my mother suddenly stopped doing the dishes, staring at me. I must have done something wrong again or maybe forgotten, I guessed. And I was right. She breathed a sigh of disappointment.

"Have you already forgotten it, young man?" She asked annoyingly.

"I asked if you were ready to go to your grandma's house," explained my mother calmly. "Didn't you tell me that you wanted to pick up some minerals for your project, young man?"

Oops. I totally forgot about that. I did not know where to look. My eyes eventually settled on her furious eyes. I smiled awkwardly at her, expecting another heavy nagging from her. I had to manage to say something before she began.

"Yeah, the project... Of course, I am ready, mom. I was thinking later today or early morning tomorrow." I said lightly, pretending to be perfectly normal.

"Always like that. Always. You have to change it, Ryan."

Probably she wanted to say more, maybe about the homework, but she seemed to decide not to. She shook her head, resuming her work.

"Don't worry, mom. I have been there thousands times, and no need to be ready."

It was partially true because I have been there many times already on my own, and I knew how to get there well. Luckily, my grandma lived in a small village in countryside, not far away from my home, and I could get there easily by bus. She lived by herself now, but I was told that she became alone ever since my grandpa (along with his two horses and a little pet) had disappeared when a great storm swiped Blue Forest near her home. I had asked grandma many times about it, but she had never said a thing.

I used to visit my grandma every summer once or twice for a few days. It was very good for me, firstly, to have a grandma like her who always treated me so well, and secondly, another home in a rural area was a superb advantage for me because I liked natural science. I could discover all sorts of things which were only available in countryside. Thus, it would be the most favorable part of my summer vacation this year as well. And I planned to do the research project on minerals. *How could I have forgotten?* I blamed myself.

"If you are ready, Ryan, then I will –."

"Please, mom, don't!" I cut off her words immediately, because I knew what she was going to say. "Please, skip that, mom. I am not going there for a month." I cried innocently. But I knew nothing would convince her.

"What are those hands for, Ryan?" She sighed again. "You lazy boy, you never want to carry a thing. Soon or later, you will feel sorry for that, and after all you will hate yourself when you have to go on your own, I am telling you now."

What else I could expect from her other than that. I just hoped that she was wrong about it.

"Your grandma is very old now, and don't you ever think that it is that easy for her to feed you so well? I told you many times already, in case you have forgotten again, that she became abnormally quiet ever since the great storm. Now, young man, this is your opportunity to help and comfort her, not the other way around."

She was right about it again. I knew she always has been. But I would never mind her nagging if it was for my grandma. And I have never been as a bad grandson as my mother thought.

"OK, mom. I get your point. But, don't pack too much foodstuff, though. It won't be long this time, and while I am there, I will do my serving for her. Happy?" I grinned clumsily, the shopping bags in my hand, my steps already on their way to the stairs. And as soon as I saw a smile of her permission, I raced to my room.

It was the 30th of August, one day after my birthday when I had this puzzle game. Back in my room, I placed the shopping items on the table straight away and removed the plastic bag to reveal the puzzle box. With an attractive cover picture, it was definitely an ordinary jigsaw puzzle. *As long as I keep track of cover picture on my work, I will never go wrong. I will soon or later see the same picture out of my work.* The old man treated me like a little child with a stupid idea of 'Rule' thing, I decided. Whatever the reason, it did not matter for me now. Then I speculated to see grandma sometime in the afternoon.

When I undid the cover, to my surprise, there was a birthday card with it. I knew it was silly, but I wanted to check inside first if there was anything like rules or warnings. I opened the puzzle box and I saw what looked like millions of big fat worms hibernating in a square shelter for a season. What else have I expected to reveal? Yes, it certainly was a jigsaw puzzle with a thousand pieces in it. But, no rules, no warnings.

In truth I was a little bit disappointed by this normality. I turned my interest to the birthday card. Interestingly it showed a picture of a sand castle instead of a silver castle. It was composed of simple sand, yet it was a magnificent piece of work. Then I noticed that there was a story under the picture, entitled Sand Castle in silver letters. It was a story of the castle. My eyes instantaneously followed the lines silently.

SAND CASTLE

Long, long time ago far away in the ocean down came a Goddess called Neptess. She was so happy to see beautiful sea creatures in the ocean. However, soon she saw the darkness in the deep ocean floor. This made her feel so sad that she could not enjoy the journey anymore...

Far underneath the ocean floor, there were compact layers of various pressurized unusual minerals. It was the mineral layers that kept substances with remarkable potentials to generate essential gases for living organisms. However, they were hidden and had never been useful.

Finally, the power of the Goddess triggered them out, and a vast number of gaseous substances in huge bubble balls were released from the minerals underneath the ocean floor. As bubble balls were constantly produced for so long, the mineral layers of the ocean floor were pushed up at once in one piece. Accordingly, a whole new land appeared beneath the hemisphere mineral layers. The layers of crystal-clear mineral films were well supported by countless bubble balls. Then, the sky was filled with groups and layers of gleaming bubble balls in a spiral.

From the world above the ocean, invisible rays out of the sun light passed through the surface of the ocean and traveled all the way down to the millions of bubble balls beneath the hemisphere mineral layers. As soon as the rays touched the bubble balls, they become brighter like recharged light bulbs. The light was amassed during days, and nights fell under dim light. Thus, the bubble balls in groups and layers glittered all year long.

After many years the land became beautiful and rich for living. Then, Neptess invited many humans and animals from other worlds to live on this remarkable new land with peace and joys. She built a magnificent castle made up of pure silver that could last forever.

Neptess was very happy to look back what she had done for the land which she called now Bubble Land. It had been great for her to see humans living happily. However, on the other side of her mind there was always a concern. She needed to return to her own world. Thus, she opted for a man with W.E.L. (Wisdom, Equality, and Love) and gave him three-hundred sixty-five pieces of power portions out of a thousand to rule the land every day wisely and equally with love. Then, she selected one bubble ball in the sky and stored the remaining force to give off the most brilliant light. Now, she saw the bright light cheerfully reach every corner of Bubble Land, and finally she was very happy to leave.

Without the direct care of the Goddess, everything remained in peace for many years. But there were two things that were changed recently without knowing the reasons. The silver castle which meant to last forever has gradually turned into a sand castle, and the bubble ball which used to give off the brilliant light could be spotted nowhere in the sky.

That was the end of the story of Sand Castle. *Nice try.* I turned the page over and I saw a birthday greeting:

> Happy birthday, Ryan Baker.
> It may bring joys.
> May bring challenges.
> May bring fears.
> Challenge fears for joys.
> Or fears challenge you.

How in the world was my name there? I had no idea. For a moment I considered that the old man in the store knew me somehow. But, I withdrew it at once. It was just an incident that my name happened to be there. There might be thousands of Ryan Baker in the world.

Nevertheless, it was not a bad feeling to see my name there.

My interest moved back to the puzzle game. I stared at the puzzle pieces blankly. *A thousand pieces...* I began to feel sick with the word, 'thousand' already. I sighed. I enticed myself to start it. *Yes, Ryan, you like challenges...* I looked at the character pictures hung on the wall. They were all jumbled pieces to begin with. But, once they were done and framed, they were simply perfect pieces of art. I sighed again. Then I began to search for the first piece to be sorted while imagining a magnificent silver castle built on my table.

Soon I was absorbed in my work. I was eager to see the castle out of my hand. I concentrated like I was building a real castle. Depression came upon me with sighs, but every moment when I saw part of the castle being built, motivation grew over it.

I was not sure how long, but I made it. Well, almost. Only one last piece on the gate of the castle left to be placed, but it was missing.

"Darn it!" I shouted in disappointment.

"Wow, that was something!"

I was not so happy about the missing piece, but still quite excited to complete the whole thing. Yes, for the first time in my life! The entire box was empty now. It seemed that the thousand big fat worms were transformed nicely into a beautiful castle. And I proved that the cover picture was wrong; it was only a sand castle. But, in my mind there was no difference at all. The point was I made it... almost. I looked at the sand castle out of the puzzle pieces in appreciation of my work. Then suddenly, I wanted to see real sand. I needed to feel fresh smell of sand. That was not a bad idea, because I still had some time before catching the bus to grandma's house. I collected the things that I might need.

"OK, now I have some clothes, a cap, books to read, textbooks and references for homework, stationary…"

I looked around the room to find any items to pile up in my bag. My mind kept fighting with myself. *I will have to do the homework, the project and…* In the end, I removed everything for my homework. *I will come back and do it all HERE in my room!* No more fighting for that, I decided. With the bag on my back, I rushed straight out of the house and raced down to the beach which my mother referred to 'my playground for the whole summer vacation.'

I stood on the sandy beach and endeavored to touch the memory of the castle. I could still see the sand castle clearly through my mind eyes. Then I had an instant yearning to reproduce it out of real sand. The sand, which was as shiny as pure silver granules after being washed by surf, was right before me, waiting for my touch. I put down the bag and gathered the sand as much as I could to build a castle.

I was totally engrossed. My hands and my mind were ever busy working on an art with the real sand. I must have forgotten the existence of the space and the time. While the waves produced fresh sand and enchanting sounds constantly, I was near to the final touch for the castle. Now I needed more wet sand after another wave ran down. Then I noticed a shiny object glittering amongst the wet sand. I picked it up and washed it with water. It was a silver metal piece. I threw it into my pocket and resumed my work. But, all of sudden, it rained.

"What the?" I cried, looking at the sky in frustration.

I knew that the rain would eventually wash down the castle, but still, I could not stop my work. Soon, the rain became a shower, pouring down over me as if the sky was so mad at me. There was no choice now. I had to find a shelter to dodge the rain until the sky would calm down. I picked up my bag, my eyes searching for a shelter absentmindedly. Of course I knew there was nothing.

"Darn it! I should have included an umbrella."

I looked around again and I noticed that there was a phone booth by the beach.

"Huh?" I exclaimed in confusion.

I knew more than well around the beach. It was kind of weird to see a phone booth that I had never seen before.

Well, it is a big deal for me now. Maybe they placed one for visitors.

"Cool. Now I can call mom to bring me an umbrella."

I dashed to the booth to get away from the rain.

Certainly, there was a phone, too. But then again, I cried. "Darn it! No coin!"

Out of the blue, I remembered the metal piece which I had found in the sand. I put down the bag and pulled out the metal piece from my pocket. Disappointingly, though, it was far from a quarter which I could use for the phone. It was shiny, but very light for a piece of metal. On both sides were several delicate fine lines engraved in a pattern. There was no chance to substitute a quarter because, first, it was bigger and thinner than a quarter, and second, it was slightly oval-shaped. Feeling down, I blankly looked at the rain drops heavily smashing onto the booth. I brought the metal piece to the phone and inserted it into the slot. In reality I was not aware of what I was doing until I heard a cheerful sound.

"Clink!"

For a moment or two I thought it worked. But after three seconds, the metal piece popped out of the machine. I picked up the metal piece, and in frustration I almost smacked the phone before noticing a message on the screen.

"Hello, Ryan Baker.
Bubble Buth welcomes you!
Bubble Land is near.
Be brave.
Be strong.
Your challenge begins."

"Huh?" I was thrilled.
My name again? Bubble Buth? Bubble Land?
Feeling weird, I looked outside anxiously. But there was nothing particular except for the rain. Perceptibly, there was something unusual about the rain. I now noticed that there were so many bubbles produced from the rain around the phone booth. And shortly, I could not even see a thing outside through the booth windows. Panic began to seize me. I strived to open the booth door, but it was bolted tight. Screams came out of my mouth. I felt I would be frozen to death any minute. To make matters worse, now bubbles, which resembled huge marbles, began to fill up the booth from the sandy floor, threatening my life every second.

"Help! Somebody help!!" I banged the walls and the door hysterically, shouting over and over even though I knew it was all useless.

The booth was now completely filled up with gleaming marbles. Then, the game was over. The last thing I remembered was the feeling of sinking down somewhere in the dark.

The flood must be washing the phone booth with me all the way down into the ocean depth. I must be dying...

Chapter 2
INVITATION KEY

Am I still alive? The rain and the bubbles were all gone now. The door swung open almost automatically when I touched it. I rubbed my eyes and stepped out of the booth, feeling exhausted. The first thing in my mind was to run home at once. But, there was a little bit of memory of the sand castle that held my steps regretfully. Of course, it was washed away long ago. However, in half a second the regret turned into an unmistakable thrill. I could not believe my eyes. In the distance on the ocean there was a real castle, captivating my eyes irresistibly every moment.

Am I in a dream? I looked around again as though to find an exit to reality, but I only found myself standing on a beach. At first, I thought I was in my usual beach, but by and by, I recognized it was different. It was not just a different beach. In some way, it was a totally different place; the castle, the trees, the sand, the ocean, and even the sky were not the same. *Where in the world am I now?* I failed to find a way of going home, but I had no worries for now. My mind was strongly impelled by the curiosity, forcing my steps toward the castle.

The castle from the distance was brightly shiny with the reflection of light. As I saw a real castle, the first thing I recalled was the silver castle illustrated on the cover of the puzzle box. However, as I walked toward the castle, I began to believe that it was a castle only made out of sand. Observably, there was no mark of such magnificence in this real castle. Yet, it was genuine beauty of a perfect sand castle. While I was looking at the castle, I recognized that this was already the third castle in a day, and they were all sand castles; the first one, which came out of the puzzle pieces, was incomplete with a missing piece. The second one, out of real sand, was unfinished due to the rain. And now, I was standing in front of the third one, a complete real sand castle!

The castle was surrounded by the ocean water except the passageway toward the beach. Occasionally, some colorful fish jumped out of the water as if trying to tease me with soundless words. The castle was one thing. The sky was another thing that made me gape at it for long. It was not blue, but bright with so many balls of light all over the sky as if the sun was broken down into millions of small suns, resembling stars. The sky touched the ocean on one side and far away to the dark green forests on the other side. As far as my eyes could reach, I spotted villages scattered here and there over green meadows. The villages looked ever peaceful from the distance, partly hidden by deep green and brown trees.

Even for a dream it was strange. *I must have died in the phone booth, and now I must be in heaven.* I decided to blame the phone booth for all this, while letting my feet carry me toward the gate. Yes, the gate to heaven.

Is this how you feel…after death? Maybe dying is not too bad, after all.

As I came near the castle, I smelled salty sea water through an ocean breeze. And I found myself standing in front of the gate of the castle. The gate was made up with fine white sand. It was very big, but looked so fragile. I wondered that it would collapse if I sneezed; it would turn into sand dust at once if I ever touched it. Nonetheless, it stood in front of me like an invulnerable wall, being bolted solidly for any reason. Now without knowing what to do, I looked around the gate blankly. Then, I heard a friendly voice drawing my awareness.

"Hello there."

I was not sure where he suddenly sprang from, but there was an old man standing beside me with a big smile. Then, he looked at a small chart in his hand.

"Your name is…"

"Oh, sorry, sir, it's Ryan. Ryan Baker, sir." I answered almost naturally.

"Ryan…" He mumbled my name a few times while checking the list on the chart. "Hmmm, I don't seem to have…" He said faintly. Then, he dropped the chart, drawing his attention to me.

"Well, if you have an invitation card, Ryan?" asked the man.

What invitation? I had nothing in my pocket, anyway.

"I don't have anything like that, sir." I said, throwing my hands into the pockets mindlessly.

The only thing that I fished out was, of course, the silver metal piece which was still in my pocket. I shrugged my shoulders with the metal piece in my hand.

"Oh, you don't… Well, in that case," said the man plainly, his eyes narrowed with a bit of sympathy. "I am afraid there is no way I can let you in, Ryan," declared the man piteously.

He then looked at my hand which was still holding the metal piece.

"Is that…"

His eyes began to light up with curiosity.

"Is that a silver…key?" He managed to ask, his eyes focusing on the metal piece in my hand. "May I?" asked the man without even looking at me.

He carefully picked up the metal piece from my hand and studied it very seriously for a while before waking up to see me in a more or less normal way.

"Tell you what," said the man, glancing at the metal piece once more, "if this is one of those real keys, I should, well, actually this castle will accept you happily," cried the man, sounding half excited. "I am not sure if this one is real, though. Haven't seen one myself…," mumbled the man absentmindedly. A smile lit up his face again, and he added joyfully, "Well then, what am I waiting for?"

He stepped toward the big gate and examined around the gate handle, his hand still holding the metal piece. I did not recognize that there was a small slit by the gate handle until then. The man inserted the metal piece very cautiously into it. Surprisingly, in two seconds the gigantic gate cracked open mechanically without a speck of sand before me.

"Wow! It worked for real!" exclaimed the man animatedly.

I stepped back in surprise, calling out just like him.

"Well, the gate is now open for you, Ryan." He said brightly, his hand pointing to the way beyond the gate. "Absolutely, it is my honor to have you here, Ryan. And now, you can go enjoy no limit!" cried the man, his cheerful eyes settled on mine. "One rule!" declared the man, his index finger pointing at me, his face yet full of joy. "You won't be able to leave until you have another key."

His voice was still soft, but I took it as a warning. Then, his hand directed to the porch behind the gate. I thanked him and nervously stepped toward the porch.

The first particular thing I met was a long corridor stretched down to a big silvery door. The floor was well paved with off-white pebble stones. From one side of the corridor wall to the ceiling there was a long aquarium inhabited with various small living creatures under bright light from the top of the ceiling. On the other side were chambers of galleries also visible through transparent glass windows. In fact, it was like a large aquarium partitioned into many chambers. But, there was no fish.

In the first chamber I perceived stones and various marine creatures such as coral and shells as well as skeletal bones in unique shapes. I was not sure if they were of fish or birds. The effect of the display was significantly multiplied by mineral stones in various sizes, forms and colors. Small bubbles were escaped constantly from the floor around the mineral stones.

I felt that I was in a unique marine museum as I moved to the next chamber. Even more variety of items was put on view in the chamber. A large number of huge bubbles like beach balls filled the entire ceiling above the water level. There were also bubble balls in various sizes across the floor. They were like marine plants, attached to the ground through thin tubes. They swayed gently with the current flow over the ground which was filled with plume-sized pebble stones in various colors. There were also pebble stones in pale grey among them. I noticed that seven of those pebble stones were arranged in a row. And each one of them, except the middle one, had a letter or a number carved as L, 2, 9 and G, 2, 9. While looking at the pretty scene presented, I tried to guess the meaning.

"Lovely 29 and Glorious 29!"

I grinned awkwardly as I recalled my birthday, August 29 which was just yesterday.

The next gallery was also an aquarium filled with sea creatures. There were various sea plants, bopping lively along with anemones and coral leaves. The particular things in this chamber were the anemones. They were so huge that they could snatch any fish nearby.

A magnificent view in the next chamber drew my attention immediately. It was a beautiful miniature world. The sky was entirely filled with small glittering bubble balls. They were like thousands of mini-light bulbs casting soft light cheerfully over the whole land. Down below the bright sky there were people around villages and fields, and there were animals on meadows, by rivers, and around mountains. It was a peaceful world.

The last chamber showed another miniature world in which, however, there was only a small castle on a sandy ground. Small identical bubble balls covered up the ceiling as before. They gleamed like stars with dim light. One noticeable difference was that the bubble balls in this chamber were much well organized. They seemed arranged spirally toward the center. The castle on the ground was a beautiful silver castle.

I had no idea what all these were about, but I decided to pass over the questions for now. Now, pushing away the feeling on the exhibition, I reached the big silver door before me.

As the door cracked open, suddenly a compound of noises poured over me. My immediate impression was that there were many people in a hall, talking to one another without even noticing me. My next impression was that most people were pretty young, maybe around my age.

The hall was very big and spacious. The ceiling, more than half of which was covered up with bright balls, was very high and narrowed in the center into a cylinder. It was like a big chimney, but it only reminded me of a dark well or maybe a passage to heaven (real one). The ceiling ran down to an oval-shaped wall and to a floor without any significant division between the wall and the ceiling.

Particularly noticeable was a great aquarium filled with a large number of big blue fish swimming around under dim light. Mostly they all looked the same. In fact, I was not sure if they were fish at all. Significant parts of their bodies were the shapes of head, fins and tails. Two huge pectoral fins were like front legs with webbed feet, behind which were even bigger fins, but unmoved. They were like a pair of folded muscular legs. There were also four smaller dorsal fins on their back; two were between two front pectoral fins and two were between two hind pectoral fins. Across their bodies were shiny silver scales which disappeared around the top of the head, down the abdomen and before the tail and the fins. Their tails were short and fat with two or more separate soft ends like a normal fish tail. Their head looked far from fish, but resembled mammals' with distinctive sensory organs around their grey faces. It was separated from the main body through a short neck. At first, I thought they had all the same appearance, but after another look I concluded that they all appeared different; first, there was a certain unique pattern in arrangement of scales on every fish; second, the shape and the location of their sensory organs on the faces were somewhat different for every fish. As far as I could see, there were no gills. And as honest as I could be, they were very bizarre fish.

What is this place? Where in the world were all these kids from?

The new scene with people of my age triggered my latent curiosity to awake.

The opposite side to the aquarium was the origin of a hullabaloo. I stepped toward the throng with a wondrous mind. Soon, I became aware that boys and girls were giggling excitedly, standing in the center of a big circled area. As they were moving their steps, their bodies shook awkwardly up and down. The floor in the circled area was particularly soft and elastic. Certainly, it was a generous consideration for those playful young visitors like them.

Now, some playful fellows bravely started to bounce off the ground. And shortly, screams of excitement flew everywhere up in the air as they jumped high above the top of their cheerers. A smile came across the corner of my mouth, but I quickly hid as I felt silly. I just stood there against the wall, my mind vague, but still watching the people and hearing them yelling for the time being. Then, someone awoke me from the reverie.

"Hey…"

I looked at the direction blankly.

"Hey, how are you doing, there?"

That was a girl of probably, again, my age, looking at me with a playful smile. She had big eyes with deep blue irises under dark brown thick eyebrows. Her hair was dark brown with a very short pony tail smartly tied up with a black rubber band.

"You know, you look silly, standing there doing nothing," said the girl with a grimace, surveying my eyes. "Look at the people, enjoying the party," she cried, grinning clumsily.

"Party? What party?" I asked, sounding stupid.

The question came out of my mouth mindlessly, although I wanted to say something else for a better impression than 'silly' like she said.

"Well, precisely…," she tailed off her words, "I am not sure, but I understood tomorrow is an anniversary for the king since…"

"An anniversary?" I asked back promptly with interest.

"Yeah. Well, I don't know much about it, but…," said the girl, then she abruptly changed her tone, "hey, it's not so important, is it?"

With that, she pulled my sleeve toward the crowd.

"Come on, we can just play, can't we?"

She brightened up her eyes like she remembered something crucial.

"Oh, by the way, I'm Ella and –?"

"Ryan." I quickly added my name.

She smiled, copying my name.

"OK, Ryan, come on, let's get spoiled."

This time she pulled my hand over toward the crowd. I hesitated, my steps barely moved. She dropped my hand and began to talk again.

"You know, Ryan, like I said, tomorrow is an anniversary for the king, but more importantly and especially to me, it is my birthday! Now I am turning twelve, and you know what, I feel that all this is just for me!"

Her excitement seemed on top of her mind by the way she showed.

"Oh, that's very good for you," I said briefly, "and my congratulations as well." Then I paused for few seconds, thinking my own birthday. "Actually, mine is August 29 which was –." Remembering what I did and my birthday presents, I was going to add 'yesterday,' but she interrupted me.

"Yours is the 29th of August, too?" She asked delightedly. "Wow, that's great! But, didn't you know that it is tomorrow?"

Her face was lighted by a pleasant smile around her marble-like eyes.

I felt weird about the date. *Wasn't yesterday the 29th of August and my birthday?* No doubt. I could re-open and see my birthday presents through my mind eyes. I was going to argue with her about the date, but, she broke into my thoughts with a different subject.

"Do you know," she began amiably, looking at my baffled eyes, "why we are here?"

Obviously that was exactly I wanted to know. She must have read my vague mind.

"Of course we are invited because we are qualified," she said naturally. "And we are certainly the selected riders for the games and the races," she added proudly as if to find herself know-it-all.

"Gosh, don't you feel just excited?" exclaimed Ella amusingly, her expression was self-enthralled.

She momentarily examined my face which undoubtedly indicated that I was a know-nothing. She then altered her interest to my appearance. I was perfectly normal with a pair of dark brown jean and a bright blue T-shirt with a big logo of a baseball team on it.

Her gaze came back to my eyes again, and she asked, "You, er…, actually, you don't look normal, Ryan. You aren't from around here, are you?"

Feeling insulted, I glanced at her outfit quickly (but not offensively). I noticed that she wore a green shirt with lots of unusual animal drawings. In fact, it appeared to me that it was she who was not normal, wearing something like four shirts; a long sleeve shirt in blue, a little shorter sleeve shirt in light blue over it, then another even shorter sleeve shirt in light green over it and to finish, a very short sleeve shirt – almost like a tank top – in green over it. Her pants were light blue also with lots of drawings of symbols and letters in various colors. They were loose and looked more like a pair of pajamas to me.

No wonder why she said I was not normal. She must have concluded that I was an alien because I did not wear a pair of pajamas.

Nonetheless, I considered myself from somewhere in space. With this perception in mind when I looked at the people at the hall, they all looked different, one way or another, from me. Their outfits simply did not match for those people at my school. Their skin color looked paler (brighter), and apparently they have different styles of clothes in some unique colors. No one wore a pair of jeans like me, and no one was in a shirt like mine with a baseball team logo.

Seriously now I reconsidered myself being in some kind of undiscovered land or country, and I happened to enter through a secrete passageway – yes, the peculiar phone booth (or Bubble Buth) was one thing like that.

"Hey, uh, Ella, yes, I am not from around here, but where am I, anyway?" I managed to answer with a question in return. But then, the answer to my question was partially explained by someone else.

"Hello!"

A loud cheerful voice echoed in the hall, zipping up all the noisy mouths. Roughly half of the screams and yells were gone.

"Welcome, everyone, to the home of Bubble Land!"

I now caught sight of a man who was standing by the aquarium, whose hands up in the air to draw attention from the throng. From his elegant outfit, I was quite immediately able to guess who he was.

"That's the king, whose name is Safrah," said Ella brightly, her eyes trying to catch any expression on his face.

"On behalf of the people in Bubble Land, I would like to welcome all of you to this event. I have waited for this day so long. And now, it at long last has come with you all in this very moment. See, how lucky I am to meet you all who have been well selected and invited to this event." His voice boomed out cheerfully in the hall.

Now I understood what Ella had proudly said about herself being selected. Then I wondered how they all have been qualified. Apparently, they all have been invited by the king.

"I am so thrilled to begin this celebration today, and I am so pleased that all of you accepted my invitation to this event. I announce proudly now, it is the very first official celebration which I hope to be an on-going event every year. See, how important your presence is!" exclaimed the king energetically, showing his fist up in the air.

"That sounds great! Gosh, I can't imagine another birthday party in this castle, if I ever have a chance again," cried Ella joyfully.

I was about to ask how she has been selected, but the king continued.

"I know we are all eager to begin the exciting events which you may be already aware of. The events will include a few stimulating games as well before the actual competitions start." He paused for a moment, looking around like he intended to assure himself that they were really aware of it. Forcing his lips into a smile, he continued, "Yes, the competition. It is challenging, but much the same or even more you will enjoy it."

The king looked thoroughly at the audience once more. My impression was that with a pleasant eye contact he kept trying to induce everyone to smile.

"Yes, Your Majesty. We surely know the fantastic games and stuff. So, please, move on," said Ella, her eyes turning to mine, her voice rigid with impatience, but it was only a fake. Her face failed to hide her joyful smile at me.

"Well, you might have experienced riding horses or birds whichever you preferred. But we don't fancy such rides here. We have a special friendly transportation only available here for those who have been selected. Now, just imagine yourself flying on a fish! You will enjoy the rides for the better! I ensured that everyone would have one of these attractive and intelligent fish. Now, unlike other fish, they have wings to fly with you and fins to swim with you. Hemabies…that's what they are called. You will soon discover how wonderful creatures they are!"

"Nonsense," I mumbled, disapprovingly "Fish use gills to breathe in water, at least I know that much."

Ella heard me talking in disbelief.

"I know. But it's true, Ryan. They call it fish, but, precisely, you know, they are like mammals living in water," cried Ella, trying to convince me.

She was almost a know-it-all already. *Sure. She is not an alien like me, and she should know it all.* The king was of a kind, and he must have read the alien's suspicion for sure.

"You might ask how fish can stay out of water," explained the king, sounding smart. "Well, I wouldn't estimate their capability until you experience with them."

He pointed to the fish lively swimming in the aquarium.

"And finally, I can't skip the best part of this event. Great PRIZES!" exclaimed the king cheerfully, emphasizing the last word in an exaggerate sense of expression.

By that, some playful boys screamed excitedly.

And surely Ella did not leave them alone. "Bravo!" She called out loud.

Cheerful applauses filled the entire hall for a long minute.

"Yes, yes," resumed the king again, "you are all very special in this kingdom, and this is an exceptional event to all of you. Definitely, I will make sure whoever stands out in the games and races will receive invaluable prizes. Of course, best one for the winners!"

This brought even more screams, cheers, and applauses into the hall, which lasted until the king hoisted his hands up in the air again.

The king seemed to leave it at that with what he wanted to say.

"Now, in the mean time, you will just enjoy the fun tonight with food or play whichever you prefer," cried the king.

Now his mood was elevated. He looked around and spoke out even loudly.

"All my guests and fellows, what are you waiting for! Let's begin!"

And out came cheerful music from somewhere, filling up the hall.

Shortly, to my amazement, the fish jumped out of the aquarium one by one and started to fly synchronously. And in a few seconds there were full of merrily dancing fish, gyrating in mid-air to allure everyone in the hall.

"Whoa!" I exclaimed without knowing it, but I was not alone for sure.

"Wow!" cried the throng all at the same time. "Supper!"

I saw Ella gaping at them soundlessly. She already looked half hallucinated. Probably my jaws fell open, looking even worse. Undeniably, I was seeing fish flying right in front of me. Their wings were not like birds (with something like leather instead of feather). Their tails and fins were moving like fish's in water.

My skepticism collapsed at once. They were unquestionably unique creatures as the king had said. I only had underestimated the capability of the flying fish. *Hemaby…is that it?*

As the music went faster, some of the excited boys attempted to catch the hemabies. But they did not need to, because the hemabies came down right in front of them when they waved. They already knew their own riders and all the hemabies were ready to serve.

In a while, some people were yet struggling with their rides, and others already managed to stick onto their hemabies up in the air. Screams began to rumble frighteningly. But, of course I knew what they meant. Their mind must be filled with only the thrill and the excitement.

"Ellaxia!" called out a boy in the crowd.

"Laxan! Over here!" Ella waved her hands vigorously. "That's my brother, Laxan." She grinned at me, still waving.

"You were here, I thought you have evaporated...," said Laxan as he approached to us, his words unfinished as he realized that she was not alone.

"This is Ryan," she said to her brother, "and Ryan, this is my brother –,"

"Laxan." I said his name on behalf of her, with a bright smile.

"Ellaxan, if you prefer to call him more formally, but he likes Laxan," uttered Ella, making an ugly face to her brother.

"You guys are..."

"Good guess. Yes, we are twin. Lucky. We both are selected for this event," said Ella eagerly, peeking at her brother with a smile.

As I have expected, Laxan, after stealing a glance over me, also treated me as an alien. He started with a typical question, "Precisely, where are you from?"

"Come on, Ryan! What are you waiting for?"

Thankfully, Ella ignored her brother's question and pulled my arm toward the center, her eyes were up in the air, presumably looking for her hemaby.

"Wait, Ella, I think I will join you a little later."

She caught my smile and let go my arm, and said, "Well, then I catch you later, but don't miss the fun."

With an eye contact with her brother, they both marched toward the center.

"Don't forget! It's OUR birthdays!" shouted Ella before vanishing into the crowd.

I stood there alone again, vaguely watching them playing with their hemabies. But, soon, I had to fight with a different thought while everyone else was enjoying the time with riding, playing or chatting. *What am I doing here? What the heck am I doing in a strange place with strange people for a strange event?*

Then, suddenly I felt homesick. *I should go back home by some means. Well, I don't even have any hemaby for a ride, anyway.*

I looked around to find the way out. Incidentally, my eyes passed by the aquarium before locating the exit door. Unless my eyes tricked me, I saw something in the aquarium. I had to take another look at it to confirm. Maybe I also wanted a hemaby, and thus I needed to check once more if there was any hemaby waiting for a rider.

No one seemed to have noticed (or cared), but certainly there was one more hemaby staying far inside of the shadow without moving. Curiosity arose. I walked toward the aquarium to verify my observation, wondering why this one was there in the dark without any motion.

But I could not tell anything even from there. It simply sat there, unmoved. For some time I tried to allure with gestures to make it mobilized, but in the end I gave it up without any hint of success.

Darn it! Who cares about a hemaby or whatever not moving around, anyway?

Frustrated, without another glance or thought, I walked away from the aquarium. I did not want to add another annoyance to my troubled mind. I already had a growing pain with homesick, and I had nothing but despair without any idea about the key the gatekeeper had mentioned.

If I had gone straight to my grandma after the jigsaw puzzle game, I could have been treated as a price long ago.

I could feel my grandma smiling at me, but she was simply million miles away.

Chapter 3
UGLY HEMABY

The evening passed just like that. In the end, everyone except me enjoyed 'the party' very well until they could only drag their bodies to their rooms. It was then a quiet night. Everyone must have dived into the deep ocean of sleep. However, sleeping sounded none of my business. And there was no reason of swimming in the ocean of sleep for me. I had done nothing but watching the show. Well, in spite of everything, riding on a flying fish looked quite fun. If I had a hemaby to ride, maybe I would have tried.

If I only had any hemaby other than the dummy in the shadow...

"Why, is this dumb hemaby still sleeping in the shadow?" I asked to myself.

The curiosity in my mind won over the annoyance, and I decided to go and check it.

I went to the aquarium in the hall again. It was so quiet that even all the hemabies were gone to the ocean of sleep. The aquarium was empty. Well, almost empty, I noticed now, because the dummy was still there, sitting on a dark spot like a statue. I knew it would not move whatever I would do. But I decided to try again. *Maybe it is now so tired sitting there for hours, wanting to be called out.*

I went onto the jumping zone and started bouncing, and shouted.

"Come on, buddy! I am waiting to see you out of that boring aquarium. I want you to give me a ride. Come on out!"

That was silliest thing I ever did, I knew. It was such a dumb hemaby, after all. Now I was getting kind of excited as my jumping progressed ever high. I set my eyes straight on the aquarium, and continued yelling.

"Please, just one ride. It's not gong to damage your feeling, is it?"

Then I waited for about ten seconds, my eyes still fixed on the aquarium.

No response.

"You need music, buddy? I can sing a song for you."

And that was a terrible idea. My mother had reminded me at least a thousand times already, "Never ever sing in public, Ryan."

I would only make it worse, but I decided. Whatever I might try, I would not make it better, anyway.

"Here we go!" I exclaimed cheerfully.

And I started singing one of my own versions of a fast silly song.

"Alice Abel Albert is her name
But bold brave if you call her
Crazy cranky coward or
Dummy dumb dupe
Everyone ever eagerly exclaims
For sure we love you for you are
Gorgeous glorious and
Hearty hilarious
I ingenuously identify but it is only true
Just like that

Kind knowledgeable is one thing
Lovely lively and more
Mysteriously mighty is she
Nobody nixes nobler."

"Once on odd occasion
Phantom perished panicked people powerlessly
Quickly queer quaint she came
Righteously retaliated remarkable revenge
Swiftly splendidly skillfully she solved
Tremendously toughly to the threatening terrible target
Unmistakably unsurpassed she brought
Vivacious viva victory
Which we welcome with witty wonder
Xtra cheers xtra bravos
Yahoo yodels years
Zippy zealous we are no zany
Yahoo yodels years
Zippy zealous we are no zany."

"Zippy zealous we are no zany
Yahoo yodels years
Zippy zealous we are no zany
Yahoo yodels years
Xtra cheers xtra bravos
Which we welcome with witty wonder
Vivacious viva victory
Unmistakably unsurpassed she brought
Tremendously toughly to the threatening terrible target
Swiftly splendidly skillfully she solved
Righteously retaliated remarkable revenge
Quickly queer quaint she came

Phantom perished panicked people powerlessly
Once on odd occasion."

"Nobody nixes nobler
Mysteriously mighty is she
Lovely lively and more
Kind knowledgeable is one thing
Just like that
I ingenuously identify but it is only true
Hearty hilarious
Gorgeous glorious and
For sure we love you for you are
Everyone ever eagerly exclaims
Dummy dumb dupe
Crazy cranky coward or
But bold brave if you call her
Alice Abel Albert is her name."

I kept singing merrily. But I hated to remind myself it was horrible. In fact, it was worse than that. Singing and jumping would never go together at least in my case. While singing, I only laughed at myself stupidly. Then suddenly, my mouth and my legs were frozen by the sight before me. After a long wait, there the hemaby was! It was not that dumb, on balance. I was so excited to see it out of the shadow. I resumed jumping, this time, screaming.

However, that was only the beginning of another wonder. The excitement lasted barely a minute before turning into remorse. I saw the hemaby, and my eyes promptly moved away from the sight of it. But my stomach was fast in response, turning by the memory of the contour of the hemaby. I swallowed hard, struggling to keep the stuff down. So sickening. I only wished that I did not call it and never ever saw it at all.

What a miserable curiosity.

Having no scales (well, there was one scale which I doubted its normality) was one thing. There were so many nasty spots of something like pimples, humps almost everywhere around the body. *Can animals be leprous or something?* I asked to myself.

Yes, this one must have been very sick and waiting to die. That was why it was there in the shadow. I was positive. *No, I wouldn't care for a ride.*

"No. Not a chance!" I shook my head.

Losing the taste for a ride and the interest in jumping, I stepped out of the jumping zone and moved a heavy gait toward the aquarium. I just wanted to say bye and disappear as soon as possible. I stood in front of the aquarium, but I was not sure where to look until my eyes found two spots. It was only the two eyes that I could stand.

Then, I wanted to say sorry because I could not keep my words. However, I could not say any word of it when I saw its eyes. I was not sure it was normal for such species, but somehow, they looked so sad as though it has been crying all this time. Sympathy grew.

The eyes seemed sincerely asking me for a rescue from the sea of sorrow. I felt strangely sorry to the hemaby. And out of the blue, I wanted to see happy eyes of the hemaby, daring to touch the hemaby, which would cost more than my mental capacity.

"Ride! Yes, I need a ride!" I yelled out loud.

And that was the craziest decision I ever made. I shouted eagerly again like I just recharged the battery in me.

"Come on, buddy. I said I wanted a ride, didn't I? Come on, you have my words!"

I started to sing again, but quietly this time, as though casting a spell to hypnotize myself and the hemaby. Yes, it was working (at least for the hemaby). It started to move more lively. I could tell that it was preparing for a hilarious launch by accumulating its energy. Then, right after another joyful cheer out of my mouth, the hemaby's wings flapped half open on both sides and pushed the water sturdily. In a flash with a massive splash it jumped up out of the water as if to push away tons of grief amassed in its mind for years.

"There!! There you are!" I shouted excitedly and quickly moved over to the jumping zone. After circling around in mid-air several times the hemaby approached to me hesitantly. Meanwhile, I had to force my senses ever hard to accept the hemaby.

"Come on, Ryan, you made the decision, and you will keep the promise!"

I urged myself over and over, but it simply took a long time before my mind settled with the hemaby. Now, once I was on the hemaby with my mind seemingly in peace, the hemaby did not give me a second to find myself right on its repulsive back skin. Without warning, it sharply sped up. By shock, I grasped its fins and neck so tight, forgetting all about the nasty things, and by thrills, in the next seconds I shouted out deafeningly to the hemaby.

"Go! Go! Faster!"

And that was the only request that I challenged to ask.

Now, after making several circles in mid-air, unexpectedly the hemaby dashed up toward the center of the cylindrical ceiling. I looked up the fast approaching ceiling which was so high under the dim light from the top. Anxiety grew regretfully. But, the hemaby raced toward the top yet fast like it knew well about its destination. Soon the ceiling narrowed significantly and turned into a roof with a silvery top. Surprisingly, there was an open gate on the very top. And the hemaby shot out of the open roof fearlessly. It was amazing to fly all the way out of the castle like a launching rocket.

It was a charming night. The surrounding was so quiet under the dim light from the sky. It was so beautiful, looking down the glittering ocean stretched beyond the castle. I just had to shout out any words. For a moment I must have forgotten that I was on a flying hemaby (and for the first time). While shaking up my hands in the air vigorously, I screamed out loud over and over. This eventually caused me to slip off from the hemaby, and I fell down into the dark ocean water with a tremendous splash. Fear came up on me instantly with pain, but only until I heard another splash by the hemaby. Then, I was back high into the sky again.

We had another expedition in the night sky over the castle before coming back to the hall. Now I wondered how this hemaby would feel after the excursion. I climbed down from its back and glimpsed at its eyes. They looked much better by hook or by crook.

Was that a smile? I could not tell.

"Thank you, buddy, for the awesome ride. And don't even think you are alone." I said cheerfully with a forced smile, yet swallowing the lumps still left in my throat.

That was it. I felt much better to begin with. My reaction to the sight of the hemaby was improved substantially.

"Well, impressive, my dear fellow..." Unexpectedly, that was the king who stopped my way back to my room.

"Ryan, sir." I promptly reminded him of my name.

"Yes, Ryan. After all, he has found his rider now," said the king cheerfully.

He must have watched everything.

"I've never seen such a happy face ever since..." He discontinued and gazed at my eyes for three seconds. "Well, in fact, I've never thought that he would find anyone asking for a ride. He was almost like a wrecked piece of wood lying on the dark shadowy floor in the aquarium," explained the king with interest.

Knowing he was a king, I was not sure how to begin in the first place. I just managed to ask a question, hoping not offensive.

"Sir, do you know what happened to this hemaby?"

"Well," said the king decisively, "I have no idea about that. And I have even no knowledge on how he ended up in the aquarium."

And after hearing two noes, I was not able to ask him any further.

Chapter 4
GAME NUMBER ONE

Now it was the morning of the first game. I instantaneously recalled the pleasant event with the nauseating hemaby. It was not so bad to advance one step to the clue of the mystery. It seemed that even the king did not know anything except it was a he-hemaby. Nonetheless, calling the hemaby 'him' sounded perfectly right to me now.

I knew that the hemaby was so ugly that for sure no one would like to see him, and naturally they would point at us. Nervous feeling grew inside, but I was already determined. The memory of the remarkable night excursion span around in my mind. I might be able to see a glimpse of happiness out of his eyes soon.

I opened the door to the launching hall. My mind was vague in thought until I found a hullabaloo among groups of people jammed in the hall. Apparently, everyone was quite animated, talking hectically, and no one even noticed me coming in. I simply looked around blankly as I had no one particularly close enough to approach for a chat. Then, there came a familiar voice out of the throng.

"There you are, Ry..."

"Ryan, if you wish to call me formally," I said, imitating her way and accent, then I recalled her name, "...Ella." I added friendly, hoping to sound not silly.

"So, what's up, Ry, you had fun last night by any chance? I didn't get to see you after that. Did you go anywhere else?" asked Ella cheerfully without waiting for my reply.

"Oh, tell you about it now. Awesome! Gosh, you should have done it, Ry," she exclaimed, her face was bright, still highly spirited with the memory of the fun and everything.

She surveyed my eyes once and found a small hint of happiness out of my mind.

"You had fun, too, didn't you?" asked Ella suspiciously, trying to press her own elevated emotion.

"Well, sort of." I said reluctantly.

I was not ready yet to tell the detail of my first experience to anyone. Besides, it was about the ugly hemaby whom they have probably never seen before.

"What is it? Come on, tell me about it now," insisted Ella playfully with a grimace.

"It was…"

I was going to tell the story about the excursion with the ugly hemaby. However, gazing at the aquarium over the throng, I changed my mind. Everyone would see him shortly, anyway. And through my mind eyes, I was almost able to see them turning their heads in repugnance.

"It was awesome, too." I said that much. And I tried to find other thing to talk about for a change. Then, one of the servants in the castle entered the hall for an announcement regarding the first event to be held. Ella did not wait for the man to start first. She nudged me, stealing my interest from the man. I thought there was something urgent for her to make sure before start, but that was only a cute gesture.

"Hey, Ry, I will be in your team," whispered Ella, her eyes on the man who was now waving to draw attention from the people around.

"Do you know about the game?" I asked her plainly.

"My brother does," said Ella, lowering her voice, her eyes traveling around the hall. "He likes games and stuff," added Ella, now her eyes fixed on something.

"Gee, I have to go, Ry. Catch you later!"

She darted away into the throng. I rubbernecked and tried to trace what she was looking at. Nothing significant I could spot. *She is only a funny girl, weirdo.* When my attention came back to the announcer, he already finished some of the introduction.

"…and thanks to Your Highness. This game has been created for you people to enjoy the events… The rules are pretty simple. 28 players. Two teams: red or blue. 14 players for each team. All players of a team wear a red vest which has a large white sticker with a number in blue on the back. And a blue vest with a red number for the other team, vice versa. The number on a sticker can be any from 2 to 14. And two stickers have a drawing of either a tiger or an eagle instead of a number. And whoever gets this vest will be the captain of their team. You are given a special pole called Safrah's Sitting Duck, you can call SSD, if you wish. You will see that in a minute, but this one has a small ball with attractive tentacles on both ends. Players will try to steal the stickers from their rivals, but only Safrah's Sitting Duck is used throughout the game. Any team extracting all stickers from the opponent, or simply obtaining the captain's symbolic sticker will win the game. Disqualification will be given to any player, using hands or falling off." The man explained without stopping like he was reading an invisible manual.

"And now, anyone knows how to decide which team you are in?"

No response. No one seemed to have any clue.

"Well, you will start with a race, necessarily as part of the game. If you go straight up, you won't miss a cluster containing a black ball surrounded by a large number of white balls. All you do is to run to it and get one of those white balls using your SSD. On taking one white ball out of the cluster, you will see the black ball being released and falling down. Now, on your way down, you need to break off your white ball and get a vest out of it. The vest should be either blue or red. Then, you go straight to the designated area of your team of red or blue. Since the main game will start as soon as the black ball touches the water, you do not have much time to maneuver with your team members. You will need to protect your captain, not to mention yourself from the attack of your enemy. Any question?"

When he finished, a group of helpers brought Safrah's Sitting Ducks and distributed to individual riders. Now I began to worry about Ella.

Will she ever return before the game starts?

I stretched out my neck and checked around, but I could not spot her or even her brother.

The game will be starting soon, and we must get ready by now, but…

"Oh, well," I sighed. "None of my business. I already have plenty of stuff on my own plate." I dropped the thought, shooting one last glance at the door.

The people were dismissed, mostly with an excited look, swinging their SSD playfully. Apparently, some diligent fellows were already warming up for the rides. Now the man announced that the game would start with music soon. Then there came the hemabies out of the aquarium one by one. They circled around the hall lively, looking for their riders.

"OK, let's get started, Ryan," I encouraged myself.

While trying to squash the nervousness that just began to grow, I approached to the aquarium and smiled intentionally at the hemaby in the dark shade before words of cheers.

"Come on, buddy, let's get going!"

The hemaby heard me. Soon it swam out of the dark shade and swiftly jumped out of the aquarium. And sure enough, someone shouted out loud right away.

"Ugh! Look at that!"

Riders looked at the hemaby. As expected, some frowned at him while others turned their faces away. As the hemaby approached to me, by design I showed a big smile, petting his sticky back with my hand.

"Ryan!" shouted Ella, coming close to me from behind.

She tried to say something, but at once she closed her mouth with her both hands. *Sure, I expected it.* I said quickly to her with an artificial smile.

"Hey, Ella. This is," I introduced, looking into the eyes of the hemaby, "my hemaby, I was going to tell you."

And of course, he became my friend now.

"He is," I began to feel embarrassed for not knowing what to say next, "he is, uh, Ugl…. Yes, Ugley. Euugley or Euuu-glei, if you like."

Then, I attempted to erase the first impression on the hemaby from her memory.

"Hey, check his eyes!"

Still her hands over her mouth, her unfocused eyes were wandering around the hemaby like she could not find the big eyes of the hemaby.

"He's got awesome eyes! And he is very fast, believe me!"

My excited voice waked her up from the hypnotism.

"Oh, sure... So, you also have a hemaby. That's great!"

She managed to say, her hands still covering her mouth.

"OK then, good luck, Ryan, I need to go."

With that, she vanished into the crowd without a second glance. I began to wonder if she still wanted to be in the same team.

"Hey, listen, buddy, don't worry about others. OK? I am with you, you know that, Ugl-...uh, Ugley." I said to his eyes with a smile as if to confirm, 'That's your name, buddy.'

I jumped up on his back, getting ready for the ride. Then I realized that the music was already on, and the riders were out of sight. Ugley must have realized that, too. He shot out of the site as soon as I patted his back neck. In a flash we were exposed to the bright light from above.

Surely we were late. I spotted riders, coming down fast. They turned into red or blue with their vests, screaming ever excitedly. The black ball was falling already half way down to the water. Yes, there was one last ball, wagging back and forth as if it was exasperated by our delay. I snatched, breaking it off, and raced down to the battle field.

It was a blue vest. Whichever team I belonged to, I was quite excited. My only hope was that there would not be any cause to damage our team only because of the appearance of Ugley. The black ball touched the water, and in no time, players shuffled each other, struggling for survival. I spotted Ella was in my team, making me smile at once. And soon, I realized that she was the captain of our team. She had a blue head of a tiger on her back. The opposite team was quite aggressive from the beginning. Interestingly, the captain with an eagle symbol was actively attacking our team, rather than being protected by his teammates.

"Ry!" shouted Ella toward me as soon as I was near the blue team area.

"Told you!" said Ella proudly, smiling at me for one second.

She looked very nervous, her eyes now traveling around every second. A player beside her saw me and then Ugley. Ouch! He scowled almost immediately.

"What the hell! Get that away, man!" shouted the player near hysterically.

"Don't worry, Ruth, that hemaby, Ugley is very useful, you will see," said Ella, smiling awkwardly over her nervous mind.

I thanked briefly and ran away from them as though either Ella or Ruth was the one actually disgusting, not Ugley. I was relieved that Ella was in my team. Then I wondered her brother Laxan was also in our team, but he was not seen anywhere in the game field. I did not have any chance yet to ask Ella about her brother.

The game was excitingly fast, but dizzy and hurly-burly with too many players mingled in every spot, hurling themselves upon their opponents. The bad news was everyone (including my own teammates) was very upset when I approached to them to attack or even trying to save their necks. But, the good news was they were reluctant to attack me. It was all because of one obvious reason; ugly Ugley.

Over all, my judgment was that our team was doing better. Then I decided to back up to protect the captain. Ella was significantly getting better as a captain. She seemed even remembering names of all players in her team. Being vigilant with every enemy approaching to her, she was very busy shouting commandingly.

"There! Over here! Up there, 9! Behind you, 5!"

And occasionally, she cried, "Get that guy! Knock him down! Yes, yes, that's it!"

She looked proud of herself by the time when I returned to protect her. And noticeably she was happy to see me and even Ugley. She only smiled at him.

Now, Ruth was up in the front line, yelling at his teammates bossily. His skill was surprisingly outstanding. Many of opponents already went down by his fast and effective attack. He occasionally shot a glance to Ella, yet deciding promptly on next target enemy.

"Everyone, to Chrom, the captain!" Ruth shouted to riders around him.

But Chrom only showed a thin smile, which then turned into a devilish snarl.

"Well, then, come on and try me, dupes, if you want to see your head falling down into the water!"

For sure, he was invincible. He was only showing off his skills by knocking off one or two foes at a time. It was only a matter of time for him to bring all huddles down before winning the game. I urgently dashed to Chrom to be of help, but two of Chrom's cronies appeared from thin air and blocked my way, attacking me aggressively. In fact, they did not try to snatch my sticker, instead, they violently beat and smashed Ugley with their SSDs.

Ruth spotted it, rushing toward us, and immediately swung his SSD over them, causing them out of their positions, falling down into the water. Meanwhile, I had an instant problem with my ride. Ugley vigorously twisted his body in pain and moved abruptly up and down, and in the end throwing me into the air.

I was almost finished with the game. Now, before I touched the water, Ella called me out, stretching her SSD toward me like an angel. And I managed to hold her SSD tight until Ugley came back to bus me up again. My neck, my sticker, and my hemaby, all were still there with me, and I did not touch the water. I was not disqualified yet.

Chrom was now with Ruth, fighting like knights with SSDs instead of swords. I darted toward them to help Ruth. Chrom noticed it. With a desperate desire of winning the dual, he abruptly smashed the head of the hemaby of Ruth. Then the hemaby yowled sharply, coiling its body in agony. Throwing Ruth into the air, it swooped out of the site with a loud flapping noise.

"You tricked me, you bastard!"

Ruth went down into the water in no time. I was already facing Chrom.

"Ha! You again! Such a long life with that thing, UGLY," snarled Chrom, tapping his SSD gently, as if trying to find the best spot to cause me and Ugley to death.

Ugley seemed to know well about Chrom who would do a trick any time. He drew near Chrom, his eyes fixed on Chrom intently, getting ready for any dirty trick. For Chrom, apparently Ugley was a target of more interest. He was looking for any chance to attack Ugley.

"So, what happened to you, Ry's dear ugly?" asked Chrom contemptuously, giving a malicious smile at Ugley.

"Deadly disease upon you? From where? Out of this world? Well, I can help you out, ugly," added Chrom sincerely.

He then keenly aimed to strike Ugley on the head with his SSD, but Ugley was fast, jerking himself two feet back right before his reach. Then, he promptly swooped down a few feet below Chrom's hemaby, his eyes aiming the eagle face on the back of Chrom.

Just then, Ruth's voice sharply rumbled. "Ryan, Watch out!"

There was a rider's pole heading toward us from below. One of Chrom's teammates aimed it at us. It flew right toward my face. I was not able to think any other way. I whacked the pole with my SSD as hard as possible. The pole spun around like a propeller, moving like a boomerang toward Chrom's hemaby. By this unexpected attack, flapping its wings loudly, the hemaby abruptly turned its back, its body almost upside down. Sure enough, this caused Chrom to slip off from his hemaby.

I quickly approached to Chrom who was now dangling on the tail of his hemaby. As I stretched out my arm, my SSD touched his back for the captain's symbol. But he was still fast, snatching my SSD at once, trying to save his life. Next, Ella was available to finish it off. She swiftly came close to Chrom without much hassle and stole Chrom's final identification of the symbolic eagle of the red team. Then, I would not need to fight for my precious SSD anymore, and I would be very happy to give it to him.

"Well, then, you can keep it, Chrom."

I let go of it. Chrom's wailing sound merrily echoed in my eardrums. I saw Ella waving the sticker of the red eagle excitedly. The game was over. I patted Ugley's neck in appreciation of his wonderful job.

"Well done, Ugley. You deserve it all, buddy." I cheered him up wildly.

And then I said to him silently, "See that, people accept you now."

In the distance I saw two figures standing on the terrace of the castle tower. I could tell one of them was the king, but not sure if the other one was the announcer. The king waved his hand once toward us, then, I noticed that he did it only because Ella waved excitedly.

Chapter 5
INVESTIGATOR LAXAN

"Ry!"

It was Ella, her face was pinky with excitement. She was still panting heavily like she just ran away from a monster.

"Hey, that was excellent! You did...you and your Ugley did a wonderful job!" exclaimed Ella, casting a quick slant at the aquarium.

She did not give me a second for a question.

"Oh, man. What a thrill!" She cried, her face turned to scarlet.

With a playful grin, she whispered, "Did you see his face when I snatched his captain sticker? He just gawked at me so blank almost like...a moron. No, actually, he was like chewing mouthful of, excuse me, of muck, and begging, 'Please, Ella, don't torture me like this!'" said Ella playfully.

She burst her sides with laughing at once.

"Wasn't that the best part or what?" She asked animatedly, her voice full of pride, sounding self-esteemed.

I thought it was not bad, but it seemed more than exciting to Ella. It appeared to me that her spirit was very high, not because of winning the game, but only because of her excellent job to defeat Chrom who did all malicious tricks during the game. Certainly it was such sarcastic fun to see Chrom falling off helplessly, but for me the fun was mainly because of Ugley. Under the circumstance he simply worked it out so well to begin with. I vaguely looked at the imaginary hemaby, Ugley in the aquarium, forgetting Ella was still there.

"Gosh. Can't wait till tomorrow!" Ella drew my attention again. I only looked at her like a good listener, expecting her to explain all that.

"I don't fancy playing underwater too much, but it should be fun and I won't miss it!" declare Ella decisively, her voice still in high spirit.

"It seems you know it all already." I uttered, sounding flummoxed.

"Well, my brother does," cried Ella proudly.

I suddenly remembered the absence of Laxan in the game.

"Oh, yes, I was going to ask about him. What happened? He did not join the game, did he?"

"No. Not really. Actually, he doesn't like such thing. But he likes underwater stuff, though. Yeah, we are totally opposite, to tell the truth. He likes the water and I like the sky. Sometimes, confusing we are related," said Ella almost to herself, her eyes unfocussed for a moment.

She looked at me in the eyes and remembered my question.

"Well," she began, "he said he urgently had to go somewhere right before the game, which I am still not sure."

Then her eyes brightened up with something.

"Remember I was running from the gathering before the game? Someone called me, and I had to go see my brother. But...," she hesitated a bit, and then, she went on decisively, "anyway, I already knew the game rules and stuff."

I thought she was going to say something rather important, but she only withdrew it.

"Weird. I mean, my brother. He is always like that... He likes investigating things. See that's how I knew about the next game stuff."

Apparently now, she only gave me more questions.

"What's up to him now?" I asked her interrogatingly like a detective.

"I don't know. He only told me that..."

She hesitated again, like trying to pull out something more interesting than that. I felt that I just kept driving her into a corner. It was Laxan's business, anyway.

"So, what are we doing tomorrow?" I asked cheerfully, my eyes turning to the aquarium, my mind slightly elevated with the picture of Ugley delivering the race underwater tomorrow. Ella saw me looking at the aquarium tentatively.

"Yes, you will need to corporate well with him tomorrow. And of course, he will do his best," said Ella enviously, sounding thankful to change the subjects.

"Well, actually it could be more dangerous than exciting."

She looked at me in the eyes seriously for a few seconds like attempting to find a hint of fear in there. I only grimaced dully and nodded in reply without saying anything.

"Down on the sea floor there will be 14 white boxes. Which means, of course, only 14 runners will be qualified out of 28. Anyway, each box contains a backpack in either red or blue. And so, there are seven red backpacks and seven blue. Again whichever color you have, that will be the color of you and your team. Now the dangerous part is this." Ella paused to make sure of my reaction again.

"Go on, Ella, you don't have to check my nerves every second." I barked playfully.

"Of course, you will have to kick out of the water, if you can't hold on long enough without air to breathe. Otherwise, you will have to move on as fast as you can to the actual field for the game. I think you will see the light from there, so you just go straight and," breathed Ella, looking at my eyes briefly. "OK, this is it. This light is in fact from bubble balls called air-pockets attached to the floor through tubing, and that's what you need to survive. HOWEVER, that's what you need to be careful. You won't see anything much on the actual floor because of the light above, but behind the light there are hundreds or more small creatures. It is like a devil fish, but better to call it a sea monster, I presume. These little monsters attract preys with light of air-pockets and catch the preys when they approach. And you know what? They can camouflage before preys."

Ella sighed momentarily as though the best part of her story was over and the remainder was boring.

"OK, the game. So, once you have an air-pocket in your hand, put that in your backpack and breathe through the tubing while playing. If you are lucky or corporate well with your hemaby, you will still have seven teammates. Ah, especially you, Ry, have to keep an eye on Chrom. For sure he will revenge you regardless of team. I guess he can attempt to steal your air-pocket."

"No worries, Ella, Ugley will be faster." I declared proudly.

"Each one of us will be given a pole called SAC. I think it stands for Safrah's Arrow Catcher or something like that. Anyway, on one end it has a small metal o-ring with an invisible net. Now, you need to open your eyes wide enough to see any objects moving other than the players. There are seven soft balls shaped like eggs, that is, six white balls called White Arrows and a black ball called Black Arrow. In some way they have invisible fins and tails and stuff, and so they move very fast within the game field. The black one is there all through the game, but white one comes one after another. Now, our duty is to catch them all using SACs. Black Arrow is extremely fast and very hard to catch. The game will end when the scores are obvious. Now, score means each White Arrow is equal to one point and three for Black Arrow."

Ella gazed at my eyes expressionlessly and breathed a sigh.

"I think that's it." She said, her eyes unfocused, thinking hard.

Apparently, one would be disqualified if running to the surface, I thought.

"We can get more than one air-pocket, I guess." I said unsurely.

"I think so, 'cause it might take a while before the game ends... Oh, I MUST be in your team, Ry, in some way," cried Ella nervously, sounding more important.

Suddenly she looked very funny when I thought about her face with the color of the opposite team tomorrow.

"Let me tell you, Ella," I began with a grin, "firstly, you will have to get to the boxes before the 14th runner, and secondly, in any case if you ever pick the opposite color, I suggest you check with Chrom. I guess he might be happy with that unless you both already in the same team, which will be the most unfortunate event for you."

Then I added with a playful smile. "In that case, that will be a good chance for you to consider building up a better relationship with him."

And as soon as I saw her eyes grow to sparkling marbles, I ran away from the site, waving my hand pleasantly behind.

Chapter 6
LIGHT-DEVILS

I thought it was earlier when I woke up in the following day morning, but I was already hearing people talking outside. They must have been too excited to sleep tight before the next game. I loaded up cheers for Ugley in my mind and I opened my eyes. In the very next moment I almost jumped to see something in my room. There was a small animal on the table, watching over me bravely.

At first, I thought it was a cat, but it was too weird for a cat. Then I decided it was another strange animal on this strange place. *Why is it in my room, anyway? And where did it spring from?* I looked around the room and the ceiling. Then, for the first time I noticed that there were a lot of light balls on the ceiling. I drew my attention back to the animal who was yet gazing at me like it was seriously trying to find anything normal from me.

"Do I look like an alien to you, too?" I asked friendly, clearing my throat quietly. "Do you live up there, buddy?" I asked gently, taking a crack at being warm.

The animal did not show any motion, its eyes yet firm on mine. I began to feel annoyed by its helpless stare and the ignorance of my friendly words. Moreover I had to go and get ready with Ugley before the game.

"Well, whatever the reason you may have, I have to go now, buddy."

Now the animal stood up as if it understood what I just said. Then it swiftly jumped down to the floor. There, to my surprise, was an envelope right in front of the animal. On seeing my notice to the envelope, the little animal returned back to the table in a flash. There was a word on the envelope. With difficulty I read it out.

"Moh…zake?"

My eyes shifted to the table with a bemused expression, but the table was empty. I looked up the bubble ball-filled ceiling, but it was only quiet.

I picked up the envelope and opened it with interest delivered by an animal. It was an atlas of the castle.

"An atlas from Mohzake?"

I examined the atlas briefly, speculating once if I would ever need it. I put it back into the envelope and threw the envelope into my pocket. Then I went to the hall, and stepped straight away to the aquarium, hoping to give Ugley some cheers. But, he seemed already in an elevated mood when I saw him. He must be confident in front of people now, I guessed. Good news was at least he would not cause any screaming or yelling anymore.

"A smart hemaby you have."

It was Ruth, stopping by to cheer up the victory of the first game.

"Ugley, right? He did a terrific job yesterday," applauded Ruth, his eyes fixed on Ugley's. Then, pointing at Ugley, he said, "I am watching you today, Ugley."

He then went on his way, showing his thumb up. I took it as a sign for 'Let's go and knock him down!' Hopefully he would be in the same team. Tough, but nice, I thought.

"Ry!"

Ella spotted me first as usual. I noticed that she was with her brother.

"Hey!" I yelled brightly, ignoring Ella. "You are a busy guy, Laxan."

I did not ask what he has been investigating about. Instead, I asked, "You are coming for the game today, aren't you?"

At least that was what Ella had said for sure, and he'd liked activities in water.

"Well, yes, of course, I will," replied Laxan, sounding unsure.

"That's great! We can play together. Hopefully, not roaring each other furiously."

"No, don't bother, Ry, he's no enemy to…," said Ella, resentfully, but her brother interrupted her, making an ugly face.

"But, an awful enemy to you, sis," said Laxan, turning his attention to me.

"I heard you did an awesome job, Ryan, with your grateful teammate…Ugley, right?" said Laxan, looking at the aquarium briefly to spot the imaginary Ugley. "Good for you, Ryan," he added enviously, turning his attention back to me.

I believed that he has never seen Ugley before. And I doubted that he had spotted Ugley who was now swimming merrily along with other hemabies. I could easily anticipate his reaction if he really saw Ugley.

"Yeah, I am lucky. Let me tell you about it, he certainly got the better of it." I said cheerfully, hoping not to be boasted about.

"He won't believe until you prove it, Ry. Told you he is an investigator," said Ella, peeking at her brother's reaction promptly.

And her brother rolled his eyes, looking around at once. "Stop it, sis!" he hissed.

"Don't worry, brother, no one else knows you are an –."

"I said stop it," cried Laxan, dropping his voice quite a bit.

Laxan looked around once more and breathed a sigh. He then made an angry face for her, but Ella only crashed it with a playful smile. And her awkward smile only made me think that her brother has been engaged in a secret investigation.

Something unlawful, maybe? No, then why is Ella not taking it seriously?

"Sorry, Ryan, my sis must have made up some stories for you. She is always like that, I can tell you now. For one thing, yes, she is right. I like investigating, but what are you going to find here? Gaming things? What's the big deal about knowing it beforehand? You will know it all soon or later anyway, right?"

As Laxan's voice turned persuasive, Ella suddenly became a good listener now. She looked very serious while listening. It was quite unusual for Ella, but only cute.

"I am enjoying the time here, you know. Nice castle, wise and cheerful king and his royal men, and remarkable riders, games and stuff," said Laxan approvingly, his eyes looking at mine all along.

I nodded. And I suddenly realized that I have been enjoying it as well ever since I had entered this castle. Then I mused if I was still an alien to them.

"Isn't this simply awesome?" exclaimed Laxan cheerfully.

Certainly his positive reaction made me convinced, but one way or another I still felt that I was not convinced completely. Yet the missing point was that he has been engaged in a secret investigation.

"Brother, do you think we can be in the same team, me and Ry?" asked Ella anxiously, her serious face turning into a grin with the question.

"Well, I can tell you now that you have more than 50 percentage probability," said Laxan brightly, his eyes looking at his sister's as though to appease her heartache.

Why is that for sure? I only wondered.

"So, cross your fingers, sis. But, I think it is better if you both are not in the same team this time…for a change, maybe," said Laxan with a mild smile which turned into smirking when he said, "Then, I don't have to roar furiously at anyone of you."

He laughed pleasantly, but it appeared rather uncoordinated.

"Honestly," he began again, "I am not interest in the game that much, if you ask me. But I wouldn't try to catch the black guy until the end, if I was in," said Laxan plainly like losing interest in conversation. "Waste of my time and energy for such a tricky thing. I would rather research on light-devils, instead," declared Laxan affirmatively, but his face suddenly appeared so dark.

"Light-devils?" I questioned timidly.

"Oh, they are those little monsters I told you, you know, hiding behind air-pockets…," said Ella scholarly on behalf of her brother.

I already guessed that little monsters she had said were light devils. I recited the name only because it sounded familiar. By a sudden supposition I pulled out the envelope from my pocket. I have almost forgotten about the little cat.

"What is it, Ry?" asked Ella, her eyes following my hands.

"Oh, I think it's an atlas of this castle." I said blankly while unfolding the cloth out of the envelope. "Sorry, I just need to check something here…."

After a quick inspection, I said, "Yeah, I was right. It IS something to do with light devils. Home of Light-Devils, it says…" I said proudly like I discovered the hidden location of the treasures on the map.

"Home of Light-Devils?" recited Laxan, his voice sounding very curious. "Can I see it for a second, please?" asked Laxan politely, his hand already snatching the atlas from me.

"Wow! It's…it's awesome!" cried Laxan excitedly, his voice lowered significantly.

Ella joined him promptly with a pair of marble-like eyes.

"Look, sis! It has everything…," hissed Laxan in disbelief, yet gawking at the diagrams. "How in the world could you get it, Ryan?" asked Laxan perplexedly, his eyes still inspecting the atlas.

"Well, I got it from Mohzake, but…" I said unsurely. In fact, I was not sure if I had to explain about the strange cat which might belong to whoever called Mohzake.

"My gosh! Did you say Mohzake?" asked Ella spontaneously.

The marbles in her eyes grew even bigger now with the name, Mohzake. Her attention altered to her brother.

"Did you hear that, brother?" asked Ella, looking very excited. "Ryan knows –."

"Quiet, sis!" hissed Laxan coldly, his eyes briefly looking into other people nearby.

He turned his attention to me seriously.

"First, Ryan, how do you know our cousin, I mean, Mohzake?" asked Laxan, dropping his voice to a whisper.

I was quite surprised by their reaction and now I have to say it all.

"I didn't…. Well, I don't know him at all, to tell the truth." I said honestly.

"You don't know him? How…," asked Laxan, sounding quite unexpected.

"How did you get this atlas from him?" asked Ella on behalf of her brother.

"Well, if you ask me that, the only thing I can tell you is that somehow a little animal sneaked into my room and dropped off an envelope with the name Mohzake on it."

I said genially, but I began to feel annoyed by the interrogative questions for something which was nothing to do with my bidding.

"So, obviously now, it belongs to your cousin, and there is no reason for it hanging around my pocket."

I put the atlas back into the envelope and handed it over to Laxan.

"It's yours, Laxan. You are the best and the right person to deal with it."

"Are you sure?" asked Laxan, taking the envelope hesitantly, his eyes checking Ella.

Looking at his sister shrugging, he also did the same with an awkward expression.

"I don't know where it came from, but I guess this little animal was smart enough to deliver the atlas to you, Laxan, but confused with me in the end." I said approvingly.

"It's an animal, anyway. Well, thanks a bunch, and –"

Laxan had to stop the remainder of his talk because the gamekeeper started to describe the rules of the game.

"I get to go now, Ryan," managed Laxan hurriedly, then seeing his sister's eyes grow with his departure, he added, "No worries, sis, I am coming for the game."

With a teasing smile to both Ella and me, Laxan darted into the throng.

Ella did not say anything this time, but only shook her head in disbelief while her attention joining to the gamekeeper who only repeated what Ella had said except for the beginning.

"…once you are out of the castle, you will see a hemaby soaring up into the sky. It carries a bundle of air-pockets attached to a hoop. There are 28 air-pockets so that all of you will get one of them. Then, you will go straight down to the sea floor. Now, as soon as you touch one of 14 white boxes, you will be qualified, and that's the end of the race. I am telling you now again, the air-pocket you get from the hoop is the only source of air before you actually obtain one in the game field."

The gamekeeper looked around once to check if there was anyone with a question. My eyes were also traveling around as if to make sure he would not miss anyone. Then, I noticed that Chrom was staring at me with the furious steam still left over from the previous day. Ella must have seen him as well.

"Ignore him, such a jerk," advised Ella, sounding full of loathing. "We just have fun, watching him being silly, that's all."

With a good luck from the gamekeeper, the race began. Visibly they knew the importance of speed for this game. Everyone shot out of the site at top speed. Ella also has gone with her brother who joined in the last minutes. It was our turn now. But, no need to rush. Ugley always had the strength to catch them up.

Ugley kicked out of the tower and soared into the sky. I could see the group of riders heading toward the broad spacious sky where a hemaby was flying high to run away from the chasers. But the chasers were faster. All the hemabies flapped their wings ever energetically while the riders gaily shouting words of excitement.

Moments later, one by one, they picked an air-pocket. Then they passed through the hoop, and swooped down toward the water. Their faces were now so serious as though their life was totally depending on this race. I reached to the hoop only last, but there was no air-pocket waiting for me. They were all gone or never existed. I surrendered with the missing air-pocket at once. Then, passing through the hoop, Ugley raced down toward the water. He caught up the group inch by inch in every second.

After some time, like cascade bombing on an invisible target, they started to dive into the designated area on the water with consecutive splashes. After a deep breath in, I dived roughly along with a few others.

Ugley swam ever fast, his wings half folded, moving his tail gently, spinning his whole body smoothly, toward the target floor. I could assure myself that we were at least in the middle of the racing group which stretched behind us like a long tail of a giant eel. And the head, of course, was led by Ruth and Chrom. I spotted Ella and her brother somewhere ahead of me. Knowing they were at the front part of the group, they were relaxed. Ella kept looking back, waving her hand as if to make certain I was within the cutoff.

I was relieved to see a few boxes before me. But, of course I only needed one, and I must hurry. I still had some air left in my lung. I opened the box, finding out that I had a red one. Looking around, I instantaneously spotted the possible location of the game field. I patted Ugley's back, pointing to the location. Ugley knew the urgency. He shot like a torpedo toward the light. Pressure started to develop in my chest while my eyes were getting foggy. Now I must hold on Ugley's back tight, I decided. Otherwise I might like to go up to the surface every second.

Now, the surrounding was suddenly so bright, but I only wanted to give it up at once. I felt something touching my feet. Then, something nasty creeping up my legs, more than one, I could feel it. Ugley made a big jerk with a sharp screeching sound. And then, he moved his body very vigorously as if to shake me off. I held so tight on Ugley's back with all my remaining strength. I wouldn't lose him for sure. Then I lost the things on my legs, I could feel it. Next moment Ugley shrieked piercingly once and screamed over and over hysterically. I opened my eyes, but I could only see a blurry picture of surrounding. My eyes wandered and spotted a light ball swaying in a blurry scene. I stretched out my arm to reach it. With my last strength I acquired a thin tube which was held in Ugley's mouth. It came with the glittering light ball. I placed the tube into my mouth and breathed in deeply. Yes, it was air. The most delicious substance in the whole world! My eyes automatically shut tight while I lay on my face down on Ugley's back, filling my empty lung with air constantly.

Someone tapped my back, but I could barely turn myself to see, feeling still faint. It was Ella who came to ensure me. She soothed my back gently, placing the air-pocket into my red backpack, then, helped me putting the backpack on my back. I only smiled at her to thank and smiled again when I realized she also had a red backpack. Seeing that I was getting better, she pointed to the ground where gleaming light was dancing about. Yes, she needed one for herself. I tapped her shoulder gently with my pole, and she raced down below.

My view was still unclear, but I was now feeling much better. I looked at Ugley's eyes with an effort. He looked ever cheerful. Maybe, it was because I made it. He has done it for me. I could not estimate how much more he could do for me. Now I began to resume my mental strength.

"OK, Ugley, I am back."

I smoothed his neck in appreciation of his job to save my life for real, not to mention for the game. I looked around and figured out that we were far up from the light on the floor. With my tapping signal, Ugley swooped down to the field. I saw some riders hurry toward the opposite direction. They must have given up the game due to an urgent need of air. My air-pocket was already getting low as well. I would need another one pretty soon.

When we were around the game field, Ugley stopped without warning. Then I saw something swiftly passing across my sight. It was one of those arrow things. It was white, small and fast. Ella approached to us with an air-pocket in her hand. I smiled, pointing to the White Arrow. She looked at my eyes worriedly. I nodded for her. Then, she shot out of the site in a flash after the White Arrow. As I joined the game now I spotted only four players with red backpacks. Ella and two others were in our team, engaged in chasing the White Arrow. Ruth was again in our team as well, gyrating smoothly around the midfield, his eyes traveling over the field seriously. He was trying to spy Black Arrow.

The blue team also had five players. With Chrom in the center, they were very active in the game. After all, Chrom returned as an evil foe again. I could tell that he already began to accumulate his tamper now. He was quite irritated, pointing to the moving object for his teammates.

The White Arrow was much faster and smarter than I imagined. It already started to turn my nerve upside down. My chasing was only fruitless so far, but Ella and two others were still in high spirit. Now they cornered the White Arrow, which in the last second made a fast and prompt move to get out of the spot. A blue team member swiftly raced to it and swung his SAC which missed the target by inches. The White Arrow jerked backward immediately, but that was only a mistake. One of our teammates snatched it at once with his o-ring. Then the White Arrow stuck in the center of the o-ring. The red team now captured the first one.

Shortly after that, another one came into view. This time it was Black Arrow, moving radically around us. Both Chrom and Ruth spotted it at once and dashed toward it, their eyes brightened with excitement. Just then, another White Arrow came out of nowhere, alluring Ruth and then Chrom, interrupting his way to Black Arrow. Now Chrom was annoyed by this. He gave a jerk to his hemaby abruptly, stopping at the spot, his eyes still chasing his main target. Then he tricked the White Arrow by pretending to change his course, almost spontaneously he swung his SAC, smashing his aim, the White Arrow on his left.

An echo of a sudden strike was fast spread with waves across the field. The White Arrow shot out of the spot piercingly. It flew down toward one of Chrom's teammates and landed on the net of his SAC. I could see Chrom swinging his furious fist up in the blank water. Then, he turned his head to Ruth and hurried toward where there might be his main target. Other people were already busy with another White Arrow, but I had an urgent matter now. I needed to go and get an air-pocket before Ugley would take another risk of his life.

In just a moment we were near the ground. Ugley stopped at a distance of about ten feet. I could see nothing but cheerful light from air-pockets. It was hard to believe that devilish creatures were watching us behind the awesome brightness. I stretched my SAC with my firm grip on the ring side. Yet it was too far to reach. I hesitated for a moment, but I knew I did not have much time and I should take a risk a bit.

I tapped Ugley's neck gently to go further down. Ugley also hesitated, keeping on the spot. Then he reluctantly moved down very cautiously. A thin lamenting wail came out of his mouth. If I was only able to see the things, it would be much easier. I only needed one air-pocket out of thousands which were right in front within my reach, but such a hard thing to get. *Not much time. I must do something.* I urged again.

Ugley approached about two feet, but immediately jerked back about double. For a moment I thought he was very scared, turning paranoid. And I totally understood his reaction; one horrible experience with those creatures must have been surely enough for him. Next moment Ugley turned around and raced all the way almost to the end of the field. He then halted there for a moment, facing the ground with the alluring light ahead. Then he dashed back to the deadly devil ground. Keeping the distance to the light as close as I could reach, he sped up, causing all the air-pockets on his way dancing around. I stretched my arm now without a moment of fear. I tried to grab any one of them, but it was unsuccessful. They just slipped out of my hand. I pulled out my SAC, holding the handle, and stretched out the o-ring end deep into the light forest. I saw some of air-pockets being liberated, flying out of the devils' home. And I snatched one of them.

I pulled my SAC back, but it was somehow heavy. For a split second I thought it was tangled with something, but shortly I knew what that was. A nasty creature slinking up my arm, then jumped onto my leg. It was virtually invisible. My hairs erected instantaneously in horror. I tried to shake it off, but failed. Something like tentacles held my leg so tight, giving me so much pain. I could feel something sharp, coming through my pants. I smashed the spot on my leg with the SAC as hard as I could. Yet, it did not work. I beat it even harder and constantly until I actually felt piercing pain with that. Then, with a dull yowling sound, it was gone. I looked back at the ground once again and I only saw peace bath the glittering sea floor. Ugley raced up fast back to the field where the brave knights were actively engaged in a battle with the never-seems-useful weapons called SACs. Yes, it was a battle between the riders and the light-devils.

Black Arrow was still at large under no control even by the mighty general, Chrom. Now Ruth also looked so annoyed by his fruitless effort. Ella saw me approaching and brightened up her face. With a clumsy smile she showed her fingers to indicate numbers. It was three to one. The red team was leading the game.

Now I could tell the situation by looking at the blue team with such a tension. Only two more White Arrows and Black Arrow were left now. And the blue team would need at least one more White as well as Black Arrow. Therefore, Black Arrow was a must for both teams. By now Chrom looked very distracted, chasing the target almost hysterically. Black Arrow stood yet confidently in front of Chrom like it knew how to play with him so well now. For our team in fact there was no need to get Black Arrow at all if we could get the remaining two White Arrows. Then the game would end automatically.

However, my assumption soon collapsed with the next news in favor of the blue team. Another White Arrow was caught in the net of their SACs. Their intensive effort worked out well. Now the scores were three to two. I could even hear Chrom screaming for they were by an inch close to victory.

Everyone now set out hunting Black Arrow. I also poured my effort as much as I could. Once we tried to trap it with all our team together, but it never helped. It was just around us, but way too fast. The White Arrow was also within our reach, but no one bothered much anymore.

I decided to set myself back. Ugley also looked tired of such a fruitless chasing job. Ella approached to me, pointing her backpack. Apparently her air was low now, which meant another battle with the light-devils. I noticed some riders had the same situation as Ella; a few of them already raced down for another air supply. I caught sight of Chrom who was yet energetic, but annoyed by his hemaby who looked very fatigued. I wondered how long it could carry Chrom under such a condition.

Ella now decided to run for another air-pocket, and I resolved to go with her. I tailgated Ella, thinking hard to find a way of finishing the game with Black Arrow in hand. I thought about Laxan, the investigator. He indeed did not join the game. If he was in the game, he could have found the solution long ago. For sure he was one of the fourteen riders and thus qualified, but absent again. *Another urgent matter to explore?*

Then I suddenly remembered what he had said before the game. Yes, he had mentioned something about the game. *It was something about catching the black guy... No, it was something about NOT catching the black guy.* I confirmed. *Then, by all means do we have to catch all White Arrows first?* I doubted it would make any difference, but I decided to see the positive side, first. Anyway, he was an investigator, and currently we seemed to have no other options.

Ella was quite brave in an attempt to steal an air-pocket. With her SAC in her hand, she stretched her arms all the way down until the o-ring part of her SAC touched something. Then she pulled it back steadily. I prepared to dash to Ella. I narrowed my eyes, expecting to see something nasty out of her SAC in any second. And I breathed in deeply as a repulsive feeling already started to grow inside. Ella's eyes fixed tensely on her SAC while her hemaby moved backward very gently. Now more than half of her SAC was out of the depth.

Sure enough, I could tell that Ella fished out something other than an air-pocket. I noted she felt some weight on her SAC. Then I saw an air-pocket coming along with it. Ella tapped her hemaby who gradually sped its way up from the location.

I set to follow her quietly, but I was pretty sure that I caused to disturb her elaborated work. Ugley and I must have scared the creature on her SAC. All of a sudden, Ella made a jerk, shaking her body frantically. I promptly dashed to her, my eyes attempting to locate the devil. Now she was struggling to push something off her leg with her SAC, but it did not seem to work. She looked at me restlessly, her eyes horrorstricken.

"OK, easy, Ella!"

Ugley approached as close as he could. I aimed at the suspicious spot on her leg, and smashed with my SAC exactly the way I did before. With a dull wail it came off, I sensed. Now the air-pocket came free going down along with it. I raced down and snatched the air-pocket. There was nothing attached to it. I returned to Ella with the air-pocket. I felt guilty, but I was not sure how to say sorry. Then I thought it was good to be underwater for the moment, because all I could do was smiling. Ella's eyes glittered again with full of energy and confidence in about a minute. A brave girl she was.

When we returned back to the game zone, I realized that a few riders were gone. They must have failed with air supply. The blue team now had three players who had to face four of the red team. I presumed Chrom still did not get another air-pocket and began to wonder how he was managing it. By looking, I could tell that he was almost running out of air. He nervously gazed at Black Arrow before him, but he quite frequently looked down toward the floor as though constantly measuring the time to get there before sprinting to it.

I gave a signal to Ruth who just came back with another air-pocket. When four of us were all together, I gestured to Ruth to go chase Black Arrow again while the rest of us three going for hunting the last White Arrow. There was no better way of maneuvering within the team underwater, but explaining only briefly with hands.

As we suddenly started to pay attention to the White Arrow, Chrom and his teammates looked at one anther, the expressions on their faces bewildered. Three of us dispersed in three directions while our eyes remained firmly on the moving target. We then attempted to corner the target by approaching it all together. Ugley was very much ready to jump any direction, if needed. The White Arrow was enjoying every moment being cornered. It waited until we were close enough. The moment when both Ella and the other player swung their SACs, it lurched upwards. Ugley threw himself spontaneously toward it almost at the same time. Now for a split second the target was within my reach. I swung my SAC as fast as

I could. Then I heard a bang sound and a jagged vibration transferred to my hand through the pole. I must have hit it with my pole instead of capturing it on the o-ring.

The White Arrow flew sharply toward Ruth on his left, but about three feet beyond his reach. Ruth swiftly moved toward it, stretching his arm with his SAC ready. Then, the White Arrow came to rest right in the center of the o-ring of his SAC. I shook my SAC enthusiastically, my eyes searching for the location of Black Arrow instinctively.

No! Chrom spotted first. It was about ten feet away from him. Ruth was even farther away after jumping to catch the last White Arrow. Somehow Black Arrow moved very slowly now. The best chance was for Chrom. In desperate, Chrom demanded his hemaby to move promptly. The hemaby sped up to the target as requested. Yet, Chrom was unsatisfied. His tamper rose up ahead. He smashed the neck of his hemaby with his SAC. By shock, his hemaby shot out to the target. Chrom's lips formed a wicked thin smile. As he suddenly came close, Black Arrow jerked away, but he was faster. He stretched his whole body, almost standing up on the hemaby, and there, he swung his SAC.

Chrom at long last grasped the target with his SAC. He nearly forgot everything for the moment. His mind was occupied only by the happiness and the thrill until he realized that his hemaby was gone, and he was there alone. He tried to swim up to get out of the water, but it was very hard. Instead, he was sinking down. He screwed his face in pain. He had no air left for his dear life.

Ugley kicked the spot immediate with my signal. Chrom was now near the deadly air-pocket forest. *I must hurry.* I saw Ruth was on his way as well. I stretched my SAC all the way to him. He was almost within my reach, but his legs were already into the depth behind the light. *No!* I panicked.

I stretched my arm and snatched his backpack, holding it tight in my grip. I signaled Ugley to pull up, but it did not work. Too heavy. Ruth came along on his hemaby, trying to reach me. He held my SAC and ready to pull me up at the same time. Now, two hemabies tried to haul us all. With a great difficulty, Chrom came free from the ground.

It was now easier, but he was still heavy, and I knew why. As Ruth backed off, Ugley rushed with acceleration, soaring up all the way toward the surface. I attempted to push the tubing of my air-pocket into his mouth, but his jaws were bolted tight. It was useless. After a long moment, Ugley broke through the surface and soared up to the sky.

I was tired with my grip, holding the backpack with Chrom. While switching my hands, to my surprise, I saw the nasty creatures which were now visible out of the water. There were ten or more dangling on Chrom's bloodstained legs. As Ugley soared up, they fell off one by one from Chrom's body, yowling miserably.

Right that moment, all other riders also flew out of the water. And as soon as they saw the creatures in the air, they aimed, and smashed them with their SACs as hard as they could, as if it was still part of the game, but at last the best part of it. Everyone was enjoying this unexpected part of the game. Only hoorays and yahoos were echoed merrily in the air.

The game number two was such a nightmare from the very beginning for me. Even Ella did not say much about the game. She only mentioned how she caught one of the White Arrows, and then she said about how many devils she knocked down in the sky.

"That should be counted as scored," cried Ella disappointedly, but her face half satisfied. "He got Black Arrow after all, but he missed the best part of the game."

She said contentedly, but I could tell she was feeling bitter. I knew Chrom became the worst person for her to face ever since the first game.

"Well, such fun doesn't suit him. Only wining, victory, or triumph, that sort of things, maybe. That's his fun." I said plainly.

And that sounded perfectly right. For the whole evening Chrom did not wake up, but through the time of unconsciousness, he looked very happy. I witnessed that his face was so peaceful after the deadly moments only because he brought the victory, the glorious achievement. Even his SAC was still in his grip as though it, together with the victory, became now part of his body. Ella must have seen Chrom, lying down with such a happy face.

"Yeah, I think he has forgotten to wake up after all that happiness," she said.

"But, I doubt if he really knows he is still alive," added Ella askance. "So stupid. I wonder he would really know that his life is at least more worth than such a victory." She uttered sarcastically, shaking her head a bit.

"Actually, Ry," she said with a gawky grin now, "I was in blue team, but I switched with my brother." She smiled a guilty smile.

"You really did!" I responded promptly. "Darn it! I just missed the chance to smack you," I exclaimed in disappointment.

"You are right," cried Ella, grimacing. "Yeah, then you missed the chance to drag my half dead body on top of Chrom's." She cackled.

Then again, what happened to Laxan? My awareness shifted to Ella's brother.

"So, Laxan was in…" I said musingly, looking at her eyes to draw her attention.

"But, you didn't see him after, did you?" I asked interrogatively, but then I regretted to ask about her brother.

"I guess he needed some fresh air." I tried to mend it.

Surely, something's up to him underwater, but what could that be? I wondered.

"I doubt it," said Ella with poise. "Haven't seen him after that…" Her face darkened. "I hope he is not doing anything with light-devils."

Suddenly she looked very anxious. She might be right. Laxan had said about light-devils before the game. I began to feel bad now, and I really hoped that his business was nothing to do with the devils whatever the reasons.

Chapter 7
SEARCHING FOR THE BUBBLE BALL

Another day began. I woke up early again with a lot more noises from outside. I guessed why; at last, it was the first day for the actual races to the sky. All the riders must have been excited as their minds were already on the way to the charming bubble balls up in the sky. Moreover, finding the prettiest bubble ball sounded much easier, compared to fighting with maddening little Arrows or awfully devilish creatures. In addition, no rules or no disqualification was another reason for them to be excited about. Ella would not need to tell me about what to do for this.

I sat on the edge of my bed, feeling jagged as I remembered the conversation with Ella about her brother the previous night. I had a strange feeling that the cause of the disappearance of Laxan was the atlas of the castle that I had given him. An atlas of the castle and the hidden land… It was an invaluable piece of information to an investigator like Laxan. I remembered his thrilled face with the atlas in his hand. Laxan must have been engaged in something very dangerous with the atlas now, I decided.

If I did not give him the atlas, I would not feel this bad, at least. I blamed myself, and the little animal who brought the atlas in the first place. For a moment, I stared at the bubble ball-filled ceiling as if to condemn the little animal who might have been watching over me all this time. Attempting briefly to spot any trace of it, I wondered if there was a passage for such an animal. I decided to call it.

"Hello, my little buddy! Are you there?"

It was quiet. I felt silly, but I continued.

"Would you like to come down for a little chat with me, buddy?"

I felt stupid of myself now and gave it up. With an awkward smile across my lips I cast one last glance at the ceiling, and I stood up to leave my room. Then I saw something scampering behind the light of the balls.

"Come on, buddy, I am waiting!" I requested cheerfully, my eyes yet trying to locate the animal. Then, it showed up.

"There you are!" I exclaimed in glee.

It came down cautiously along the wall behind the table. Then, it rested on the table quietly. For sure it was the little animal who delivered the atlas of the castle. Now I began to believe that it was really an errand animal because it brought down something again.

"Another deliver from Mohzake?" I questioned, sounding surprised.

"Are you sure that's for me?" I asked mildly, making a face.

Now I had no doubt that the animal was quite smart to understand what I said.

"Seriously, buddy, I don't expect anything... Well, precisely speaking, I don't know anyone here, I mean, on this land."

The animal did not respond. Standing up on its hind legs, it gazed at me intently as if to reproach me for what happened to Laxan with the atlas.

"The atlas of the castle from Mohzake..." I began, feeling guilty. "I thought it was for Laxan because he is Mohzake's cousin... I am sorry, buddy, but, I had to give it to him."

The animal let its forelegs go steadily on the table, its head down, resting for some time. Then it stood up quietly as though to make a hard decision. Now it pushed the delivering items toward me, its eyes back on mine. I could see its eyes narrowed for a brief second, but I was not sure it could be considered as a smile of such an animal. It seemed its business was done now. After casting a fleeting look at the ceiling, in a half second it swiftly jumped up toward the bright ceiling.

"Hey! Wait! I haven't finished!" I yelled at the animal, but it was already gone.

Another delivery... The animal was not that dumb. But the question yet remained unanswered. *Who would ever send me something on this land when I had no acquaintance at all?* And it was already second time.

The delivered items were two small jars connected together with a short string. The content of one of the jars was perceptibly black chunks, and there was a letter S written on the jar. The other jar was filled with red chunks and a letter R was visible. I had no idea what they were, and of course, again why they were delivered to me. Putting the items aside on the table I shot a glimpse at the ceiling and I hurried to the launching hall.

As usual I walked straight toward the aquarium, feeling regretful to Ugley for losing the game after all his remarkable effort for the game, let alone saving my life. If it were not for Ugley, I could have ended up much worse than Chrom by now.

"Hey!"

I was not sure if anyone was talking to me. I looked at the direction quite blankly. Unexpectedly, it was Chrom who came close to talk to me.

"What's up?" asked Chrom lightly.

"You…, OK?" I was not sure what to say, but only a few words which sounded like a question.

"Yeah, I guess," breathed Chrom, smiling awkwardly, his hand pointing to his legs which were still wrapped up tight.

Evidently, his reply did not seem right.

"Man, such a long time you were…" I began worriedly, but then I couldn't find any words to follow; there was nothing much to talk about with him in my mind, and of course I wouldn't talk about how happy he had looked after winning the game and all through the night.

"So, ready to be off?" Chrom asked, disregarding my worries.

"Uh, yes. It's the first day of the races, and…" I answered promptly, then, I realized that he wouldn't be able to join the races for a while.

"Actually, it's not a race. Wandering around the sky for hours in search of some kind of bubble balls… It would be boring, anyway." I said openly, my eyes glimpsing at his legs once again, and I added, "Don't bother about it, Chrom."

He seemed to see my point. "I'll be OK by tomorrow," he declared.

"Oh, that's good!" I exclaimed gaily.

"Well then, I should leave you alone now," said Chrom. His expression was dull and plain like he did not hear my cheers for him.

"Listen, Ryan. I, er...," he hesitated for a bit, but he only said a greeting, "catch you later."

After that, he walked toward the door with a limp.

"Hey, by the way, congratulations!" I cried out toward him who was about to disappear. I saw him waving in reply.

By tomorrow... Such a fast guy, even the recovery is fast, too. Maybe Ella was right about it; he thinks that his life is not worth than a victory. He can't just leave us alone.

Now taking up my attention to Ugley again I walked to the aquarium, my eyes were traveling around the hall. Then I spotted Ruth in conversation with others, waving his hand. He showed his big thumb up. I did the same in reply, grinning.

Now, what happened to Ella? I questioned. She should have been here long ago, greeting me first, but there was no sign of her around yet.

The same gamekeeper came for a brief message for the riders. There was nothing particular except for the main duty which, of course, Ella already had told me; we would need to deliver the most charming bubble ball. Once the message was announced, they were all dismissed in preparation for the departure. Then, they launched after the signal with the music. Without much hassle this time, everyone flew up steadily in peace to the way out, yet full of energy. In a few seconds, only Ugley and I were left alone in the broad launching hall.

"OK, Ugley. Ready?"

I smoothed his neck with a mild smile and mounted on his back gently. Then with my signal, Ugley spontaneously flew out of the castle and soared up to the sky. He gained speed radically fast, trying to catch up other riders ahead.

However, when we were near bubble ball clouds, he abruptly changed his courses, turning back to the castle.

Feeling baffled, I yelled at him to resume the race, but he simply did not listen. He swooped all the way down and dived into the water. Then he jumped out of the water, spinning and wagging his body in any possible angles vigorously until he shook me off. Once I was thrown away, he smashed himself onto the water furiously over and over. Then, it was quiet. He was gone to the depth of the ocean. I endeavored to reason whatever I could have done wrong, or whichever could cause him uncontrollable, but I could not find anything to reason it. Such a smart hemaby. He should have his own reasons for the agony, I concluded.

I was determined to wait for him. I knew he would come back. I submerged my head to resolve my thirst for the curiosity and the concern. Down below it was extremely calm as though no one ever furiously disturbed the peace. I waited and waited patiently, and after what seemed like hours, ultimately he came out of the water.

Seeing my dear buddy in one piece, I released a huge sigh of relief. However, even before a word of cheer out of my mouth, Ugley kicked out of the water, soaring up into the air without leaving a hint of his recovery. Being unable to guess what was going on in his mind, I gazed at the running away mate blankly. I pressed down the feeling of annoyance that grew inside.

In some way Ugley looked quite happy this time, I now noticed. Speculating what possibly made him spirited, I eyed his possible destination ahead. Then, I just noted that something was actually flying toward him as well. Obviously it was much smaller than Ugley, but I could not confirm anything of the UFO.

Now Ugley was in proximity, slowing down his pace gradually. And there, they rendezvoused. Ugley flapped his wings lively, spinning his body merrily around over and over with the unidentified flying creature. Then, Ugley, with his wings widely opened, swooped down along with the little creature toward me. Whatever that was, it made Ugley's spirit dramatically change to normal or better. It was more than thankful for me, too. I began to feel happy now, yet there was a question remained.

What is that little cheer-maker?

Ugley approached to me with his tail waggling enjoyably, his wings folded in. He landed on the water smoothly without generating too many undulations before me. And the little animal, who now appeared quite like a baby hemaby, gently settled on Ugley's back, wagging its tail as if to copy Ugley's action. Ephemerally, I had an instant delusion that this little creature was only Ugley, the mysterious hemaby's missing child.

The image of this delightful relationship subsided in the next few seconds. The grey skin of this little creature gradually formed spiky hairs. Interestingly, the color of the hairs shifted between white and black, back and forth, as the hairs moved like waves. With the wings waned, it was now totally a different animal. And that was no one but the little messenger animal to my pleasing surprise.

My mouth fell open speechlessly, and for a long moment I gaped at the animal in astonishment. Now it could even change its shape into a little hemaby, flying like a bird, and probably of course swimming like fish. After all the wonders that this little creature had brought, it still seemed to have more surprises to deliver. But, above all, my mind hovered with one simple question.

How does it know Ugley?

Coming close, Ugley produced a thin melody toward the sky as if to exclaim, 'Sorry to keep you waiting so long.' I accepted his apology with an agreeable smile. Then I carried the same smile to the little animal.

"Hello, my little buddy." I greeted softly. "Man, you are amazing, really." I added convincingly. "And I should respect you from now on." I said and I meant it.

The little animal lifted its head and attempted to make a sound like Ugley as if to exclaim, 'Thanks a lot, but you don't have to.'

"So, any more delivery from Mohzake?" I asked mildly, remembering the two jars. "I still have to figure out what to do with the black and red chunks you brought to me the other day. I just kept them aside on my table for now."

Ugley groaned faintly with this, his head turned, his eyes moved to the little creature who was yet resting on Ugley's back. I was not sure if Ugley asked or complained to the animal for something. Now this animal stood up quietly, its color changed to grey. Then, in the blink of an eye it vanished into the water, leaving only a few small ripples behind.

Ugley, like nothing happened, now came closer and rolled over at once. I took it as a gesture for 'Ready to go.' I climbed on his back, and he shot off the site in a flash into the ocean depth. While Ugley was fast catching up the little hemaby, my mind raced to the gleaming bubble ball clouds up in the sky.

The first place Ugley and his companion took me was like a death valley which was completely bathed with dark grey clouds. It was a graveyard for animals with piles of debris and bones of small and big mammals and fish all around the valley. No moving creatures were visible. Not even any sea plants seemed to have ever existed in the dark grey valley. I had an air-pocket in my hand, but I was barely able to breathe. *How can all the animal bones be here?* It seemed that a whole city had enjoyed a feast with animals and dumped all the leftovers into the water. I felt horrible, but I could not even speculate the reason why Ugley brought me there in the first place.

Ugley passed through the valley, taking me to the next place with plenty of moving creatures. Now, my body cells were back in action, letting me breathe normally. Small fish, coral, sea plants were all in their places, busy for living. When Ugley stopped at an area which was particularly rich with living organisms, for a moment, I thought Ugley meant to show me the beauty of the underwater nature. But there was more imperative reason for him to stop there.

There was a grey rock shaped like a huge ball in front of us. I slipped off Ugley's back to examine it more precisely. There were sea plants and coral on the surface, but it was relatively clean, compared to the surrounding. I carefully removed them from the surface of an area with my hands. To my surprise, the surface was very smooth, and a clean shiny spot was revealed.

It was certainly not a rock, but some kind of huge ball. I cleaned more areas quickly. The next moment I was nearly shocked. There was a human on a flying hemaby petrified right in the center of the ball. I immediately turned my head to Ugley as if to share my horror. He and the little hemaby were not in the location where they used to be. I tracked the current waves Ugley had left. *He must have gone crazy again.* I wiped out the surface as much as I could before joining Ugley.

Ugley was up in the sky again flying uneasily and even spat sharp screams toward the empty sky. His little friend was beside for any way of soothing him, but only fruitless. Ugley must have known something about him, I guessed.

Who is this man? And why did he end up like that? Questions loaded up in my mind.

"Can we go see him again?" I asked Ugley when he eventually returned with his little friend. He looked better now.

The man must have been a rider just like us. I concluded after a brief inspection. *What horrible thing had happened to this rider?* I struggled to deduce how a rider could bring Ugley such an uncontrollable agony, my eyes yet surveying the man.

L25G29? I just perceived that there was a note on his sleeve.

Perplexed, I looked at Ugley, hoping to see an interpretation from him. It occurred to me that Ugley was now trying to show somewhat different expression on his face. And I decided to take it as a smile.

So, this is something important. Maybe some kind of key word... And this man was killed for some enigmatic reason?

Now Ugley came close to me and rolled his body over once. He was ready to take me somewhere again. I climbed on his back, and as soon as I was aboard, Ugley shot out of the spot. I made sure that our little pal would not lose us.

Ugley did not stop at the surface. He extended his journey all the way to the sky. Amazingly, our little hemaby was right beside us, soaring up fast. With a cheerful smile I stretched my hand toward it.

"Hey, buddy, come on, I have some room for you!"

I gestured again with an even bigger smile, yelling.

"We still have quite a long way up, buddy!"

Now the little hemaby was quite close, flying smoothly right above us. The decision seemed near to be made now.

"And Ugley will be very happy!" I yelled once more to seal its mind.

Ugley opened up his wings as wide as he could, slowing down significantly. There, the little friend landed gently on Ugley's back right in front of me.

"Wow!" I screamed excitedly.

I then cautiously stretched my arm around its neck to cuddle it securely. Resting now in my arm, it was only a grey baby hemaby.

Ugley resumed his usual speed, escalating us ever dynamically up to the sky. Meanwhile, the answer to the question of L25G29 was still delayed in my mind. When Ugley initially flew straight up to the sky, I doubted that I could find the answer from anywhere with only bubble balls around. Nevertheless, I was quite excited because I was at last going up to the forest of bubble balls for the first time ever since I came to Bubble Land, and I could work on my original goal; searching for the most charming bubble ball. I began to believe that Ugley now came back to normal and decided to join the races as well.

Chapter 8
SILVER SCALE

It was not so long before we reached layers of bubble balls. While Ugley flew through the forest of bubble balls, I opened my eyes wide like I was scared of missing any single bubble ball ahead. Every bubble ball looked so beautiful that I could hardly tell which one would mean to be the most charming. I thought that air-pockets found down underwater were so pretty, but they could not be compared. They looked as soft as feathers and as shiny as crystals, yet all empty. How could this simple transparent bubble ball give off such light? I wondered. Even with real crystals it would not make any better.

While I was fascinated with the beauty and engrossed in the thought of the wondrous nature of Bubble Land, Ugley stopped by a group of bubble balls for a moment. I gazed at the group, pondering why Ugley stopped there for my attention. But I only found that they were bright and cheerful just like others. Ugley smoothly advanced toward the group, and I attempted to study every one of them specifically. Then I figured out that a few bubble balls amongst them appeared different. In a sense they were rather dull and boring like aged bulbs.

Maybe they have lived long enough and now they are running on the downhill.

Ugley drew nearer. I was not sure it was because of the dirt covered on the surface, or the less brightness of the light inside, but there was the fact that they were not charming bubble balls. *Then, why do we need to spare time here?*

"Move on, Ugley." I demanded plainly.

And without another thought, I turned my attention to other groups ahead. Ugley smoothly glided away from the group. But strangely, far back of my mind seemed still clung to the previous bubble balls, and I had an annoying desire to go check them again.

"Ugl –"

I was going to ask Ugley to revisit them, but brilliantly, he was already returning. Now this time, I wiped out the dirt on the surface of one of the bubble balls within the group. My mind was vague, expecting to see nothing special or something like others. However, the moment I saw inside, I was simply wordless by the unexpected picture revealed before me.

"What the…!"

All of sudden, bright light escaped from the bubble ball through the cleaned spot. For a millisecond I thought that unmistakably there was a crystal in it. What made me amazed was, though, the scene of a silver scale that vividly emitted bright light from within.

"Whoa! Awesome!" I hissed. "Did you see that?" I asked to the little buddy tactlessly. "Ugley, super! This is remarkable!"

I shouted out loud with irresistible excitement.

I quickly snatched out the ball from the group, my mind already delivering the joy to the kingdom. The next moment, however, my joy turned into a grief as the brightness soon ebbed away. The silver scale, the core of the beauty was gone.

"What have I done wrong, Ugley?" I asked faintly like talking to myself, my eyes blankly wandering between Ugley and the little hemaby.

My attention jumped to the other bubble balls along side. They lay quietly without knowing what had happened to one of the family members. *OK, try again.* I approached another one and cleaned the surface cautiously. A silver scale was shooting cheerful light over my face just like the previous one. And the third one was exactly the same. With an extra caution I grabbed one and took it out of the group, my eyes permanently fixed on the scale inside. However, it happened again. I only witnessed that the light faded and disappeared with the scale just like that.

"Illusion. It's a trick!" I uttered disappointedly.

But, my mind still held it as real.

"Darn it! What the heck was wrong?" I cried, feeling dejected.

All I did was cleaning the surface and observing inside...

I gazed at the third bubble ball which I had already cleaned. It was shooting out light yet cheerfully.

"Guys, what do you think?"

I examined Ugley's eyes momentarily, then, the little mate's as though to find the missing scale from one of them.

"It seems these balls have life in it, but only within the group," I said decisively, pondering the mysterious nature of bubble balls in this world. "Out of the family they are like powerless light bulbs, if you know what I mean." I declared. I wished they could talk just for now.

"But," I said, staring at the shiny ball, "if that's the case, it is useless."

I looked at Ugley's eyes again. They seemed to have a disagreement with me.

"Unless it is some kind of hint or clue…" I considered now for Ugley.

But, my mind only landed on a question against the consideration.

How can such an illusive thing be a hint? An illusion can be simple, but various. It can occur anywhere in any form.

"Ugley." I called him to move on, tapping his neck.

Feeling disappointed, I absentmindedly touched the clean surface of the remaining bubble ball with my open hand. Maybe I just wanted to feel the warmth of the light from the fake silver scale before moving away from the illusion. Unexpectedly, there was no heat on the surface at all. Instead, I felt a small sensation through my fingers. It was like a small bug on my palm, jittering desperately for life. Now, with my hand still on the bubble ball, I closed my eyes, trying to, sort of, appreciate the delicate feeling of it. No more sensation I felt through my fingers. *The bug's dead?* Then, suddenly I saw something moving in the bubble ball beyond the brightness.

"Holy cow!"

I immediately withdrew my hand and unbolted my eyes.

"Something's in there!"

I looked at the surrounding like I expected to see a new world. But, what I saw was nothing but the endless span of bubble balls. Weird.

Is this some kind of trick, too? Another illusion? I could not tell anything from Ugley's eyes or our little friend's. I would need to take another look at it before jumping into a conclusion.

I cleaned the surface widely. Then I closed my eyes and gently placed my hands on the surface, both hands this time. I could feel the light suddenly touching my eye lids through my fingers. I was not sure whether it was because of the light or the sudden eeriness, I felt painful heat on my hands fleetingly. At that juncture, a motion picture appeared in my sight. It was not the fake scale I had seen before, but what I saw now was a small fish. Its skin was shinny, but there were no scales. It was not in a bubble ball anymore. It was somewhere in the sky, yet swimming merrily.

The fish moved toward a bubble ball layer, and accordingly my eyes followed. Shortly, it reached to a layer full of shiny bubble balls. The fish ignored them, passing cheerfully over. After another layer, it slowed in front of a group of identical bubble balls which were exceptionally bright and shinny. The moment the fish approached, the brightness of some of them disappeared. The fish advanced vigilantly and touched one of them gently with its tail. Then, all of a sudden, three bubble balls moved forcefully. They bounced up and down against the group aggressively, trying to run off from the family. And eventually, the three bubble balls escaped from the group. In the next seconds they were transformed into three monstrous creatures which were very much like light-devils. With their enormously healthy legs they dashed toward the fish, their mouths opened grossly. The fish responded spontaneously. It ran straight down to the previous layer and jumped into a bubble ball cluster. The monstrous chasers burst and vanished right before they reached the cluster.

Now the fish set off to the next layer again with vigilance. When it neared the layer, it hesitated a bit. Then it wheeled around a few times, constantly peeking at the bubble balls ahead like it was waiting for something to happen. A moment later it rushed to the bubble balls ahead. Until then, I did not notice that there was a small empty space amongst the bubble balls within the group. Again, my eyes followed as it dived straight into it. The gap was small but the fish passed through without disturbing any one of the bubble balls around. There was no trace of nasty monsters following. The fish merrily ran to the next bubble ball layer.

This layer was identical to the previous one, except for two balls which were much brighter. I guessed that the source of the brightness was silver scales stored inside. Now, the fish circled a few times and then dived again, but this time, right into one of the two bright bubble balls there. The bubble ball burst, and the bright light was gone in that instant. However, the fish was there unharmed; its skin now glittered with silver scales. It danced around cheerfully as if to express that it possessed the whole world now. The fish then swooped straight down, passing all the layers of bubble balls, and dived into the water. I attempted to follow the fish underwater, but I was only able to see it racing toward dazzling brightness behind swaying sea plants before the scene became blurry.

What is this all about?

I drew my hands back from the bubble ball which was yet gleaming.

"Guess what I have just seen, guys?" I asked to the two hemabies.

It was neither a dream nor an imagination for sure. It was like a short excursion that I have just experienced with a little guide fish. *They wouldn't believe me.*

I explained to them exactly what I had seen in there. And I just wished they could give me their opinion, or at least a word or two.

"Yes, it's a silver scale we need to find." I declared when I finished my story.

"And yes, it must be somewhere near here." I said tentatively, my eyes now moving around the area.

The small fish flew up only a few layers of bubble balls.

"Maybe four layers apart…," I said unsurely, trying to replay the vision with the little fish, "or five, maybe…"

It occurred to me now that there could be some kind of order or arrangement.

Then I suddenly remembered the unexplained numbers that the petrified man had on his sleeve. *The numbers!*

"That numbers we saw earlier, Ugley… Is that anything to do with all this?" I asked Ugley quietly, but almost inquiring to myself, meditating a possible connection.

With that, Ugley, for the first time, tried to communicate with me by nodding vigorously.

"It is?" My eyes lit up with thrill.

Now my little buddy flew up lively to share the thrill.

"And that's why you brought me up here?" I cried spiritedly in amazement.

"You knew it!" I exclaimed delightedly in response to his first body expression. Looking at the dancing little hemaby, I yelled, "Darn it! You both knew it all!"

In elation I had a sudden impulse to fool around with Ugley and our little friend, but I reined in for now. I had to deal with the first thing first.

"So, it was L25G29, and which means…"

I attempted but only able to guess.

"Is this kind of what…layer or group or something?" I said without confidence, my eyes inspecting the surrounding.

That brought an instant nodding from Ugley, and a shriek from our little buddy.

"Then, it is layer number 25, and…we are on what… group 29, maybe?"

That was a very good guess. I could tell by a scream, this time, from Ugley.

"We are sitting on group 29 and layer 25…" I mumbled quietly while looking at the surrounding.

Certainly, after knowing all that, everything looked different. They were not just clouds or forest of bubble balls. They were all in an order of groups and layers in a certain pattern. I suddenly felt that I grasped something that has never been touched before. And I wondered if it was really anything to do with all these hustle and bustle competitions.

We slowly moved up across the layers. We passed two identical groups in the next two layers. Now Ugley stopped by a group with bright bubble balls in the following layer. Definitely, I sensed an atrocious attraction toward it. The bubble balls there appeared so beautiful, yet never meant to be touched.

Thank goodness, I saw it happen in the vision. I shuddered with a feeling of horror.

"Move on, Ugley."

Our little hemaby instantly flapped over it, and Ugley followed as requested.

"Don't we have to check the groups as well? I mean, starting from group one or something…" I asked, sounding uncertain.

No response. I could tell Ugley was ignoring me with that.

"I am not sure which one is G29," I muttered, looking at the two bright bubble balls right ahead of us now.

Ugley and the little hemaby stopped there momentarily, gazing at the balls as though it was the answer to my question. Then, they both quietly advanced to the balls. My eyes stopped at Ugley's eyes once and moved over to the bubble balls. Interestingly, they were as bright as others even though the surface was covered with dirt. I stretched my arm halfheartedly to one of them and carefully wiped out the surface of it. Unmistakably, there was a bright scale within. Wild sensation ran through my vein.

"See that?" I cried, pressing down the feeling of exhilaration.

It surely looked so real, but I still could not trust it. I hesitated a moment, but I could not withstand the temptation. I took it out of the group very carefully, my eyes fixed on the glittering light. Yes, out of the group, the scale was still alive with the vivid light.

"This is it!" I boomed with thrill.

"We got it, Ugley! See this, buddy!"

This must be the one! The most charming bubble ball! We at last got it!

My mind raced fast to the castle with an uncontrollable thrill. Fastening the precious bubble ball firmly on my chest, I gave a playful smack on Ugley's neck. Then, he plunged like a bullet down to castle, the most pleasant destination for sure. I looked back to make sure our little mate was following, but then I realized it was already ahead of us. It was faster than my mind.

My joy and happiness lasted only a while; only until I figured out that the destination of my dear hemabies was not the castle. What's more, I had to wake up from the daydream by a big deafening splash in the next moment. I wanted to shout at Ugley for his insane action. By all means, there was no reason or excuse for diving into the water after a wonderful discovery. Meanwhile, I recalled what happened to the small fish in the vision. The fish had definitely jumped into the water just like us. But then, that was only a vision. Besides, we discovered what we wanted.

The silver scale!

I looked around, but there was no indication of our invaluable bubble ball. The bubble ball seemed to have melted like a cotton candy and the precious silver scale was gone with the waves of the water. And Ugley and the little hemaby were gone as well.

"What now?"

In frustration, I pushed my head into the water like a hungry duck looking for fish, my eyes widely opened to see any trace of the disappearance of the scale. Then I saw two hemabies swimming fast toward me from the depth.

Popping out of the water, Ugley flapped his wings cheerfully, taking no notice of my mood. Out came the little hemaby. Flapping its wings in the air briefly, it gently landed on the back of Ugley who was already at ease. The little hemaby bragged with a reason. Its wings fluttering, its tail danced as if to draw a full attention from the imaginary spectators. Then I spied a silver scale held in its mouth. My anger simply melted away with a clumsy smile. I carefully picked it up from its mouth. And looking at the small cold scale in my hand, for the first time I appreciated the subtle joy of being on Bubble Land.

Chapter 9
INVISIBLE TRAIL

As I placed the scale safely in my pocket, the two hemabies stretched their wings and flapped wildly like preparing for a long journey. Naturally they should know our destination, I decided. I grabbed the tip of Ugley's tail this time, and the tail hauled me to the ocean floor. Meanwhile, in a forest of marine plants and coral I acquired a few air-pockets. I swallowed a lung-full of air, wondering if this little hemaby ever needed air supply without gills just like Ugley.

In a little while, Ugley and our little companion stopped. As they rested on a quiet floor, temporarily, I thought that they only took a break. But then, it occurred to me that the two hemabies were looking for something, circling around me who was glimpsing at the surrounding without a hint. We were in some place where the vision ended, I decided, and they were struggling to find the direction afterward.

In the meantime, I pulled out the scale and gazed at it, my mind clueless. Yet, nothing seemed to convince me why we were not going back to the castle. Now looking at my companions absentmindedly, I wished they could just take me to the castle to finish the race and all, forgetting any further snag such as this. Then I could easily make an awesome story for our discovery, followed by the awards, cheers and stuff...

I drew my attention back to the scale in my hand. In effect, it was so clear in water, and I thought that it was transparent. But in a moment, I realized that the view was different through the scale. What I saw on the scale were various sea creatures, but they were those living things which I never saw in anywhere else. Apparently, the scale showed some place where I have never been before.

I removed the scale from my eyes and waved my hand for Ugley and the little hemaby. Then I noticed that there was something opaque, resembling a cloud, nearing to us. By the time the object was in close proximity to us, its shape was like a large fish. My two companions were also aware of it. They came near me. The figure stopped right in font of us, its head facing us. Until then I did not realize that the opaque cloudy figure was indeed fish. To my amazement, it was a swarm of tiny flying fish gathered together making a shape like a huge fish. Each one was so busy keeping its position, playing its role in a remarkably ordered fashion. For minutes I gaped at the creatures which were moving so synchronized as one. It was simply astonishing.

I must have been lost until they were moving around us broadly.

So, they came to lead us somewhere, I thought. Now, my mind already started racing ahead of us, speculating the destination. I hopped onto Ugley's back right away to set off the journey with them. However, it was only another daydream. In the next moment Ugley, without warning, flipped over and threw me away mercilessly. Right then, in the twinkling of an eye, the swarm of fish scattered everywhere as though it was exploded by an invisible bomb. Next, the individual fish slowly reoriented and formed what looked like a big flattened snake, mobilizing toward me. As soon as it approached close enough to touch my body, it started to wrap up my whole body enchantingly, coiling over me. The last thing I saw, before it completely covered up my face, was the gratifying faces of the two hemabies who stood in the distance, watching over me with their wings and fins gently swaying.

I must have been captivated, because I stood there without resistance, watching their elaborate work on me without fear. Only when they lifted me up, I felt a wondrous fear momentarily. It was very soft, but so dark that I felt I was in a cylindrical cell which was filled up with snow-white cotton. I felt my body move gently as though I was lying on ocean waves. For a brief second I was surprised to know that I was breathing without any air-pocket. I began to doubt that I was alive.

They place my body in a very comfy coffin, and they take me to an unsung land.

Where am I now? When I opened my eyes because of sudden brightness, I was free from the coffin, sitting on Ugley's back again. I briefly looked around, wondering what had happened to me and the swarm of fish. I discovered that I was now on a sea floor with plenty of living organisms. The area was bright with the light from air-pockets on the floor. In mid-water here and there, tiny semi-transparent particles (or maybe, life forms) were cheerfully sparkled by the reflection of the light from the air-pockets. Now I felt tight on my chest by the sight of the air-pockets. Ugley bent down his neck and quickly snatched one of them with his mouth like he saw the pain in my chest. I enjoyed as much air as I could, and I decided that I now came back to reality.

I tapped Ugley's neck gently, wanting to know where we were. Suddenly Ugley opened his wings about half and revolved around me as if to celebrate my return from the death. Our little companion was not around any more. Near by a sea knoll was a dark figure of fish, gently wagging its tail alluringly. For sure the swarm of fish was still with us. I surveyed the surrounding again and figured out that the scene was not totally new to me somehow. Yes, it was the place which I had seen on the scale earlier.

Ugley moved over to the sea knoll. Noticeably now, there were even more living creatures which were all unusually big. The most striking species were anemones which were so huge that they could swallow a few animals at the same time. Then, my question was why the swarm of fish bravely lingered around right in front of them. However, it was only the beginning.

"Yikes!"

Shockingly, the swarm of fish dived right into the horrifying mouth of an anemone. In just seconds, the swarm of fish disappeared without any trace. At a loss, I gaped at the monstrous anemone and then Ugley for any explanation. They were only mindless fish after all, I thought. By now the giant anemone must be very happy with its stomach full of a crunchy fresh snack, I was pretty sure.

Now Ugley's eyes were firmly fixed on the anemone as though he was enthralled. It was certainly not a good sign at all. I could surely tell what Ugley was thinking. My stomach started turning and my hair erect. *No way!*

"No! Ugley, No!" I shouted frantically. Lumps of water drove into my throat.

He already made up his mind. Without giving me a second or two to prepare, Ugley dashed straight into what seemed like a revolting gate to a hell. I screamed with my eyes bolted tight. I felt miserable for dying in the stupidest way I could ever imagine. And I just hoped that it would not take too long.

I was not sure why I could still think. With a weird feeling I unbolted my eyes. *What the heck is going on?* I found myself in a damp descending path under dim light. The swarm of fish was not there. Clearly, the worst part did not come yet, I thought. We would get to its burning stomach or something very hot and dark pretty soon, I decided. Then again, I thought that the path was quite wide and long even for a gorge of a giant marine creature. Ugley was even flying in it! As he moved on, now it was getting brighter due to the light coming from what was visible like a full moon.

OK, here comes the worst part!

"Ugley, dead-end!" I called out, pointing at the bright circular wall ahead of us.

Of course Ugley noticed it, but he did not slow down. In fact, the moment I called him, he started to speed up until he was near to the end. Then, his wings folding in, he fearlessly dashed right into it.

"Whoa!" I screamed while my body was glued to Ugley's back as tight as possible.

Something soft swiftly touched my head, and then, my back for a brief second. I felt like being scanned by a certain hospital device; there was a faint sensation that fleetingly passed through my body from head to toes. It was cool and white. Then it was quiet. I opened my eyes cautiously with a weird feeling.

Chapter 10
HIDDEN LAND

It was not the burning stomach of the giant anemone. Yet, the dead-end led us to another opening. We were in a huge clearing. For a split second I thought that we ended up in heaven. Then I considered that we just happened to be out of the ocean and landed on somewhere hidden in remote mountains of Bubble Land. But I doubted it at once, because there was a ceiling of the clearing.

The space was so big that it reminded me of a huge sports dome of one of my favorite baseball teams. There were a large number of bubble balls beneath the ceiling, casting pleasant light constantly to the surroundings. Down below the bubble balls in mid-air was the swarm of flying fish, merrily gyrating with a vivid motion as though they were performing an air show to celebrate the most memorable visit of The Ryan and Ugley Squad. In the center of the ground was a silver castle, magnificently glittering with the light from above. The ground around the castle was covered with bean-sized silvery pebble stones, and beyond was filled with snow-white sand. Further down half way towards walls lay water. The walls of the dome were made up of circular stones, which stood firmly like giant flat mountain rocks. The water was so clear that I thought it was waterless until I saw more flying fish playing around there. They formed different shapes and sizes of swarms, jumping out of the water and somersaulted cheerfully in the air before diving back into the water. It was a fascinating show in a marine land.

Unable to act, I gazed at the distant objects aimlessly. My brain was tangled with the sense, the memories, and even the knowledge of Bubble Land. I narrowed my eyes to reevaluate pieces of information, ideas and observation.

Another bubble land… Yes, it is the unseen land of the bubble ball world.

Meanwhile, Ugley took me to the castle on the ground. The castle was an awesome work of art. The wall outside indicated that it was made up of silver bricks all around. Small, but together with a tower, it was a perfect silver castle. However, it was sealed completely, and virtually there was no way of viewing inside.

I landed on the ground in front of the gate. While I was scrutinizing the surface of the gate, I found a small slit-like gap around the center, which was nearly undetectable.

"It doesn't look like…a crack or something, does it, Ugley?" I said, still examining the break eagerly.

"Yes!" I blurted. "The coin!"

I remembered the metal piece that had let me enter the gate of the main castle when I first arrived in Bubble Land. It was now much like a silver scale, but then, it had been a coin for the phone booth, and a key to the castle gate.

I threw my hand into the pocket and picked out the silver scale. A mild smile lit up my face. I looked at Ugley, my mind full of expectation.

"This should do it, Ugley."

I brought it to the slit and inserted very cautiously like handling a dangerous material. Yes, it fitted perfectly.

"There!" I exclaimed in delight.

The gate cracked open promptly. I released a pleasing sigh.

As I nervously stepped in, dim light streams poured on my face. Then, the gate automatically slid to close behind me, leaving Ugley outside. I felt a sudden pressure in my chest as the gate separated me from Ugley.

Although it was only the size of a house, there was a spacious oval-shaped hall without many things. In fact, it was empty except the stairs which led to the upper level in the center of the hall. There were no windows on the walls, comprising only gigantic silvery brick pieces.

"Hang on! Isn't there something on the brick?" I questioned, stretching out my neck toward the wall.

In just a second I was amazed to notice fish drawings engraved on every silver brick. And they were all different!

"Wow! Ugley, buddy..." I yelled at the imaginary Ugley.

Next, I realized the silver bricks around me were quite alike, yet all different in shapes.

"Holy cow! They are jigsaw puzzle pieces!"

The entire castle building was made up of huge silver puzzle pieces with fish drawings on every piece. It could be more than a thousand, to my amazement. I took another look at the brick wall all around as if to appreciate the far-fetched work of art. Bricks with fish drawings continued to the upper floor, including the flat ceiling and the stairs located in the center. The stairs should lead to the tower, but it was blocked by the bricks on the ceiling.

"This is it?" I cried in disappointment. "Nothing but a hallow space?"

I suddenly felt that I was in detention. I felt that I have been charmed to come all the way from another world only to be detained, in the hidden castle of Bubble Land; in the beautiful silver castle with a thousand or more fish drawings.

I looked around the wall again and wondered how many fish drawings there were; how many silver bricks were needed to build the entire castle.

"The lower level alone can be five hundreds or more..," I estimated roughly. Now, it was silly to attempt to count them all, but I could not defy the temptation. So I decided to count.

I went down to the lower level to start possibly from any piece by the gate. Then, I discovered something stimulating on a brick by the gate; there was no fish drawing on the brick. Instead, there were words on it with letters deeply engraved on the surface. It was entitled SILVER SCALES.

SILVER SCALES

The most beautiful bubble ball. It is this bubble ball that contains the silver scales. The Goddess collects a thousand silver scales from a thousand kinds of fish living in the ocean. The Goddess gives three-hundreds sixty-five to the ruler. The remaining silver scales are concealed unseen. It is about the power of the silver scales when they are all together. Therefore it is not intended that any human possesses all the scales. Peace remains only when it is controlled or never.

"Wow! A thousand silver scales…, Ugley!" I called out the imaginary Ugley again.

Thousand… The word alone already sounded extremely powerful, regardless of the actual power in hand. My heart raced fast. I suddenly felt that the hall was full of mind-boggling treasures that I would never be able to handle.

"So, that's everything," I exclaimed, feeling recovered from the damage done to my emotion.

I touched the cold fish of the next brick gently like I found the right reason for counting them all now. And I began. On I went counting steadily with patience. When I counted near six hundreds, my steps were on the upper level. A moment later, while I was counting six-hundred thirty, I suddenly recalled the figures other than a thousand written on the brick. "Yes, the king… He has 365 silver scales." I nearly forgot about it because my mind was momentarily overwhelmed by the power of the two words; thousand scales.

"Now, 635 silver scales are yet to be found. And all are in one bubble ball!"

Trying to find a single ball out of millions out there?

I shook my head. And just like that, I felt the hall was so big and I could not reach the gleaming treasures which were visible on the ceiling. *It's impossible to find it unless…* I gazed at the fish drawing on the silver brick that I counted six-hundred thirty. *…unless there are clues in here or elsewhere.*

"Six-hundred thirty-one," I resumed counting, thinking hard on finding possible clues, "…six-hundred thirty-four, six-hundred thirty-five."

When I said six-hundred thirty-five, I felt a small agitation inside. It was the number that was attracting me now.

"Six-hundred thirty-five silver scales!"

I lay my hand on the cold fish of the 635th brick gently as though to avoid disturbing its peaceful sleep. Then, something happened to the brick. The thick silver brick suddenly slid out toward me about a foot from the main structure of the wall.

"Whoa!" I abruptly jerked by surprise. "What was that?"

Nothing further happened. I vigilantly zoomed in and confirmed that it was only a storage drawer. There was a cubic-shaped silvery chest in it. My mind quickly filled up with booming curiosity. I took out the chest cautiously, expecting to reveal something very important. Then I spotted words engraved on the lid of the chest.

Do not dare to open it unless you challenge your life.

Should you do, be prepared before you do. You only have time to breathe.

Chill rose upon my spine immediately. *Do I have any other option?*

I breathed in the air as much as my lung allowed, and I gently placed my hand on the lid of the chest. I briefly gazed at my hands which were already getting moisture. I undid the chest to see large numbers of metal pieces all in shiny white. For half a second I thought that I found the remaining 635 silver scales. Then, next half a second I considered that I just opened a chest full of priceless treasures.

Feeling amazed, I picked up a few pieces as if to appreciate the treasure that I just discovered in the long run. The pieces were quite thick and bright, and the shapes of the pieces were all odd and different. Then I figured out that they were actually pieces of a jigsaw puzzle just like the castle. And they promptly reminded me of the puzzle of a sand castle that I had done at home right before coming to Bubble Land. Although the pieces here were real silver, both puzzles looked very similar.

I felt a bit of joyous commotion inside by the memory. But then, the memory also brought me the pain that I had experienced while working on it. I sighed.

Now I am back again with thousands or more pieces to sort out.

Looking at the pieces all in silver, I doubted that I would ever be able to distinguish them all. The gate must be bolted tightly now. Evidently, I had no other option.

I spread out the puzzle pieces on the floor and stared at them seriously as if to find the first piece out of what seemed like millions. I breathed in the air deeply and began to sort out the shiny silver pieces one by one. With the memory of one missing piece for the previous puzzle, I hoped that it included the last piece for sure this time.

The air was running out, I only sensed, and I wondered if I would ever have enough oxygen until I could place the last piece. While my mouth was desiccated, every part of my body ran with chill water as though the sweat gland was ruptured. My ear was detecting hundreds of flies wailing, and my eyes were getting blurry and itching with the salty water rolled down my forehead. My fingers... I felt them shaking as I tried intensely to focus on my job. And two sides of my mind began to fight each other, yet to be optimistic.

It is not so bad to breathe my last breath in a beautiful real silver castle. It is cool to die in a magnificent hidden world. It is much better than being killed by nasty light-devils or a horrendous giant anemone…

But I still want to live. I am only twelve. I still have millions of things to do…

At long last, the floor was empty. The last piece, which I had worried, must have been placed as well. It was grey and cold. I felt I was squashed and compressed to fit into the chest box in return.

Maybe I have been thrown into a deep ocean floor where you only feel the darkness, chill, extreme pressure…

Then somehow, I began to feel happy. It was very strange because now I embarked on seeing something wondrous and hearing sweet melodies. I released my eyes with irresistible curiosity. And I could not believe myself to see thousands of glowing fish filling up the entire room. While they were constantly generating melodious sounds enchantingly, they moved on in one direction in harmony as though they were following a paranormal current within. They were those fish on the bricks.

Death… Yes, I am almost there. And they came out of the bricks now to welcome me.

Compassion grew sorrowfully. I closed my eyes. It was dark and quiet again.

"Mom…"

I only sensed my husky voice, instead of hearing. She seemed light years away. I would never able to see her…

I wanted to take one last breath of carbon dioxide while my brain was still functioning. With my eyes yet forced shut tight, I breathed in deeply, which was only a torture. Then strangely, I heard a flapping sound from somewhere far away. Another flapping sound echoed. This time I was hearing the sound more precisely.

Something must be near…

Now I considered that my ears were actually receiving sounds. And my eyes behind the shutter were detecting light that came from the other side of the shutter.

I slowly unbolted my eyes with fixed doubt. There was light that came and touch my sense like a cool white fog. But it was for real. And there was delicious warm air. I narrowed my eyes as though I was mesmerized by a hallucination. It was Ugley, cheerfully wiggling his tail in the air. Behind him the ceiling was left widely open around the stairs. A cool breeze blew over me with bright light. Ugley made a cheerful melody as if to say, 'For real, Ryan! You have done it for real!'

I looked at Ugley, forcing a smile.

"Am I…I made it, didn't I, Ugley?"

I looked around the hall, still in disbelief until my eyes set on the silver castle out of the jigsaw puzzle pieces. Yet, I could not believe that I actually built such a magnificent castle with my own hand.

"Yes, you did, or who else?" said the other side of my mind on behalf of Ugley.

"I did it, Ugley!"

Ugley mobilized himself abnormally up and down in the air like dancing for me. I understood. He must have been chocked to death, waiting for the gate to open. Another fresh breeze came upon me through the open ceiling and drew my attention to the stairs. I felt dizzy, but I managed to stand up, eager to see anything important and straightforward.

My steps slowly moved up the stairs and to the tower level. My eyes were soon filled with the scenery of the world under the dome once again. Ugley was already playing actively in the air, dancing synchronously with the swarm of little flying fish. Momentarily, I stood on the porch of the tower, watching them dance under the pleasing light from above. It was so bright that the swarm of little fish was like dust of diamonds scattered in the air.

"Was it this bright before?" I murmured unsurely.

No doubt. There was a great deal of visible changes now. The bubble balls on the ceiling of the dome were yet shiny, but, quite a lot of them had turned brighter. And amid these bright bubble balls, there was a particular one, whose brightness dominated over all others. Furthermore, all these brighter bubble balls were in a certain pattern; they were distributed to the space in a spiral shape. And it was in the very center of the spiral where this brightest bubble ball located. Overall, its arrangement was like a spiral constellation; a charming mini spiral galaxy, maybe.

Despite of this appealing change, I was yet in the dark. I had only hoped that I could see an answer or any clue to the power silver scales. But it seemed that after one dangerous game, I had only brought another puzzling game; my precious life could have ended only for such a thing. Then I thought about a scenario of what if I failed; it could have been a miserable ending that no one would care in this world. I would be discovered (if lucky enough) dead. Then, they could take it as the first lesson of how anyone in search of the forbidden power would end.

Depression grew inside, and another internal fight began.

"Come on, Ryan, you did a great job. You discovered something remarkable. And you are almost there. Just keep it up, buddy!" said the positive side of my mind.

"Darn it! Who cares about the silver scales? Drop it, Ryan. Don't you see that you have done so much for nothing? Wake up, buddy, it's not worth your life! And you don't even belong to this world!" criticized the negative side.

I felt sick. My brain must have been damaged and not cooperating with my mind anymore. I gazed at Ugley who was yet animatedly enjoying the moment with the swarm of flying fish.

"Ugley, what's up, buddy?" I called out loud, cupping my hands around my mouth.

Ugley flew up high together with the swarm of fish, but it was not clear if they were trying to run away from Ugley. Maybe they were taking Ugley somewhere, I thought. They were heading to the bubble balls on the ceiling. In fact, they directed straight toward the center of the spiral galaxy. The bubble ball in the center was like a sun, looking sizzling hot. They approached to it dangerously fast.

"Ugley!" I shouted in alarm, trying to see them through the beaming light.

It was only a split second when the light was completely covered by a grey cloud before beaming again. Ugley abruptly made a u-turn, swooping down toward me. *What happened to them?* They disappeared as if they were melted and vaporized instantly by the sizzling sun.

"Ugley!" I called him out loud like he was half deaf. "You all right?" I bellowed at him, shifting my eyes to the center again.

Ugley stopped by me and rolled over his body once, his tail gently wiggling.

"Are you OK, buddy?" I asked worriedly, casting a glance at the ceiling.

Ugley made a cheerful sound at once, flapping his wings playfully.

"So," I said, looking back at Ugley now, "we are leaving without anything, ah?" I questioned bitterly.

With that, my chest suddenly ached. Yes, I really have done enough that could last for a whole year, I decided. The negative side won regardless of the situation.

As I stepped out of the castle, the gate closed behind me automatically. Then, quite promptly the silver scale popped out of the slit. Then, the bright light on the ceiling faded away; the galaxy disappeared into the clusters of dim light.

I hopped on Ugley's back after stealing another glance at the sky. And I tried to dig any indication out of what has been discovered so far.

A silver scale, hidden gate, dome, silver castle, silver bricks, 635th silver brick, chest box, jigsaw puzzle, and a spiral galaxy...

The galaxy was the most important part of the story so far because it almost took my precious life... Conversely, maybe I saved more than a thousand lives with that puzzle game, I thought. If it was worth that much, it must have led us to the final answer or at least the final clue. I hoped that it was really the last, whatever it meant.

The passageway was very long on our way back. I anticipated seeing the anemone mouth any minute, but it was never likely to appear. Only dim yellow light from the shiny wall of the passage lighted up our way. When I began to doubt that it was really the way out, I saw a dead-end ahead of us. It was not the anemone gorge or mouth. It was like a permeable wall which we had passed through to get into the dome world earlier. Nevertheless, it was a good sign. As expected, Ugley dashed straight to the wall without hesitation. And we were through with no damage done. However, the passageway yet continued. It was now much damper with a greasy wall like a real gorge of a giant anemone. I was convinced that we were about to come out of the mouth. Then again, the gorge continued tediously for what seemed like hours before it curved down stiffly. Unexpectedly, the passageway from there was filled up with water.

"Whoa!" I screamed by a sudden jolt.

Ugley of his own accord dived into the water without much splash, but it was a disaster for me. Unwanted lumps of water pumped into my throat. No oxygen was in my lung, no air-pockets in my hand. Once again, it all depended on Ugley. Irritated, I tapped Ugley's neck uneasily, trying to gesture with my mouth full of water rather than oxygen. Ugley sensed the urgency once more and shot down toward the bottom in no time.

The floor was widely spanned, smoothening down horizontally. While I was trying to hold my breath, I let my eyes go search for any air-pocket nearby. Nothing. Then I spied that there was dim light coming from the other side. Ugley rushed over at once, but there was nothing like a life saver. Meanwhile, I felt an invisible turbulence around the area. Shortly, Ugley moved fast along with a current, yet his wings, fins, and tail wagged gently. In a moment with the speed gained, Ugley withdrew his wings completely, his tail swaying gently, trying to keep himself under control. Now the current delivered us upwards, and that was where the light coming from. It was a good sign again.

"Up, up!" I wailed almost hysterically.

Ugley opened his wings half now, gently push down the current until we were out of the path. We were thrown onto a broad sea floor. The current was gone. I thanked the Goddess that I had spotted the source of the light. There were air-pockets waving cheerfully to me. I dashed straight to one of the life-savers. For the second time in a day I appreciated air, the tastiest substance of all. Once I was saturated with air, I awkwardly smiled at Ugley who was circling around me peacefully.

"So, where are we, Ugley. Any idea?"

I sent a message to him with my hands, shrugging.
Somehow, this place is quite familiar.

Over the other side of us, I saw now gloriously dazzling light spread around the area like a city in a festive. A thousand or more of brightly lighted air-pockets…

"Wait!"

I looked at Ugley, my eyes grew bigger than Ella's.
That's the field for the game number two!

A sudden fear seized upon me. I quickly jumped on Ugley's back, while my eyes wandering around the ground where I stood like I accidentally dropped the precious silver scale. On the contrary, the sea floor beneath us was ever peaceful except for the light of air-pockets that waggled gently here and there with the current flow out of the dark exit nearby.

I released a sigh. And, for the first time in my life, I missed my room in the castle so much; the only space on Bubble Land...

Such a long day. I petted Ugley's neck gently, while my eyes turning back to the alluringly tempting light from the field, wondering how those light-devils would survive if living creatures never came within their reach. All the same, it was their home.

While Ugley set off to the castle merrily, I looked at the dark exit once more, but strangely it was not there anymore. Even the air-pockets in the surrounding stopped dancing. They were now resting quietly as if to pretend that there was no such thing as an exit.

Maybe we were in a giant anemone's excretory passage and we were really lucky to be there on time, and discharged.

Chapter 11
HARFHAS AND RIPPER

I could not rest right away even though I felt my shoulders getting heavy. It was a bizarre incident that gave another burden on me. The castle was aired with an invisible panic; several riders were missing, but no one knew what had happened. Meanwhile the king only cheered them up without any comments on the happening. I was not sure why the king did not say anything about it. But I decided that such a great king should have a convincing reason. Probably he has been endeavoring to cope with the current situation. *He is a wise king.*

Momentarily sitting on a sofa in the residential lounge, I wondered how a wise king like him could have been chosen on Bubble Land when there was nothing like an election in my world. Then, my thought suddenly jumped into the world where I was born and raised; my own world where I enjoyed for twelve years with a lot of familiar fun games around. Of course, one of my choices was puzzle games such as jigsaw puzzles. Certainly, the one with thousand pieces that I had completed could (proudly now) be an example although it had oddly happened to throw me to this land, yet mysteriously.

As a matter of fact, there has been something really weird about all the incidents happened around me recently. First, if it was not the first jigsaw puzzle I did at home, I probably was not able to complete the one in the silver castle. Next, the fact that the silver metal coin (or scale), which I had picked up at the beach was nicely used as a key to this land, also came so real. Now it occurred to me that anything that brought me over to this land seemed related. I would say it had turned helpful, or at least useful.

"Anything else that might be helpful in the future?" I questioned.

Maybe the birthday card... Yes, the sand castle, I just remembered. I reopened the page of the story in my memory. *Sand Castle...* It had described that how the bubble world was created by the Goddess. There was something about a spiral arrangement of groups and layers of bubble balls as well. It had also mentioned about storing the force, selecting a king, and giving the power to the king... I only wished that I could have recalled all this just a bit earlier.

As he may have been depressed, the king stood outside of the castle balcony, looking at the dark ocean. I did not have a precise reason why I would dare to see him in private, but I decided to discuss anything with him. He noticed me approaching with intent. I stood beside him with a greeting. I told him that I had been depressed because of my hemaby. I said that I had hoped to go and try to figure out what had happened out there, and that I had wanted to get a glimpse of bubble balls up in the sky. But it was only a white lie.

"But, my hemaby is doing better now, sir. I think I can join the race tomorrow."

I waited for a moment, casting a stealthy glance at him. He looked truly down.

"It's really terrible. But, I am sure it'll all turn out nicely, sir." I tried like an adviser.

The king still kept silent, looking at the distant view. Now I decided to tell him a little bit of my finding. Maybe I could see his awareness of the power scales or his intention.

"I happened to know a bit of the history of this castle..., sir, and something like silver metal pieces... Do you know anything about that, sir, Your Highness?"

The king narrowed his eyes, yet gazing at the distant view.

"Bad will," said the king, finally.

I traced his diminishing voice, mumbling the words several times.

"Bad will?" I responded promptly, but not rudely. "What do you mean, sir?"

The king now looked at me in the eyes briefly. "No, you don't want to hear about it," said the king, shaking his head a bit.

He turned his head away to the sky which was poured mild light ever innocently, and he sighed deeply as if to blame the heaven for the bad will.

"It's a scary story, my dear fellow, very scary," cried the king very seriously, his eyes still set on the sky.

I now seemed to get an opportunity to discover the king and his will.

"Yes, yes, Your Highness. Please. I am so curious." I said, exaggeratedly demanding.

"Curious... Well, you may not believe me, but it is more than that, my dear fellow."

Obviously, I had chosen wrong words.

"I meant, sir, I really wanted to hear about it. Can you, please?" I begged.

In response, the king, after another big sigh, began his story.

"Once there was a formidable man called Harfhas who was known to be the scariest among the forest animals. He was believed to be a lion with remarkable power. He was convinced that his power would grow by the numbers and the kinds of animals he killed. Therefore, he killed any animal in sight to become even more powerful. As his killing continued, his power also grew indeed.

He never knew how many animals he killed, but somehow, he gained so much power that no animals could run before him. And then, something remarkable happened to him; he could have wings when he wanted to catch birds, and he could hide his paws and tails when he was willing to disguise himself for any reason.

It was now the time when he thought that there were no more animals attracting him. He smiled at the endless span of the ocean. With webbed feet it was an easy job for him to play underwater.

Once there was a shark called Ripper who was known to be the most violent in the ocean. Ripper believed that one day he would walk out of the water to catch inland animals if he killed fish of all kinds in the ocean. Indeed, as his killing went on, his physical shape changed significantly. He grew webbed legs and arms. However, Ripper underestimated the power of the Goddess of the ocean. His life was detained in an ice cube before even having the first step on land with his own feet.

It had been so long for Ripper before Harfhas discovered and brought him out of the frozen cube to be free. Ripper was so grateful and thankful to Harfhas to let him resurrect. Thus Ripper decided to serve Harfhas forever beside him.

Since then, they did everything together. Ripper was able to eat real animals beyond the ocean. And now Ripper, too, developed an ability to shift his shape for his desire. They could navigate for preys with their webbed feet in the ocean, and they could search for targets in the sky with their own wings when they needed.

Ripper told Harfhas a great deal of his story about the Goddess who once detained Ripper for thousands of years in a freezing cube only because she had created the world for humans, and not for any other innocent creatures like Ripper. Meanwhile, they learned of great power given to the king to rule all humans and animals, and even greater power that she reserved somewhere. Harfhas has been waiting for a better opportunity to change his life with this power. The precise location of the hidden power has not been discovered yet, but it is only a matter of time for Harfhas."

The king finished the story with words that sounded like a conclusion.

"No one dared challenge his invincible power."

To me the overall story was like a fairy tale of Bubble Land, but only the beginning part and the creepiest.

"So, they have been after the power of the silver metal pieces hidden somewhere…" I said pensively as if to find the actual location of the hidden power from the words.

The king had his own supposition of the story.

"Yes, we have to find them as soon as possible before they do."

Chapter 12
SAFRAH'S INTEREST

Another day started. I woke up early in the morning again. But it was not the noise from the people outside that disturbed me this time. Without knowing, I was already absorbed by the thought of my inexplicable experience which came like a morning brightness to wake me up. The instant I heard voices of the people from outside, my mind was busy mulling over my current situation and the prospect of the forthcoming hours. Although there was a growing danger, I would need to get started properly today as I had told the king.

My physical condition returned perfectly normal since the deadly puzzle game. At the same time I was pretty happy with Ugley who brilliantly cooperated well with me after such a wild mental pain that had tortured him. Certainly he had managed the pain well. Ever since the little hemaby had shown up, Ugley seemed to decide to be a good boy, curbing his anguish well. *Cheers and happiness...* Yes, that was what this little buddy had delivered to me and Ugley this time.

I looked up the ceiling quite blankly, questioning what the little messenger has been up to. Whether it was a weird little hemaby or a peculiar cat, there was no difference for me now. It became my favorite friend, and with this friend, we were an invincible team.

"Hello, my little teammate!" I called out to the ceiling, my voice quite animated. "Are you there, my little buddy?" I cried again, my eyes still searching for any visible hint.

I would be very happy to take it to the excursion if it only appeared.

"Ugley and I will be very happy if you join our trip today…, my friend."

My friend… Remembering now how I have been calling it all this time, I suddenly felt ashamed. I could have given it a good name long ago. Then, I had a sudden bid from my mind to call it Kittous from 'Kitten To Us' (like a little messenger).

"Hello, my little buddy, can I call you…Kittous now?"

Yet, there was no sign of any activity on the ceiling.

Maybe it has gone somewhere for another delivery.

Chances were, my little teammate, Kittous, would join us any time up in the sky. We both would be very much looking forward to seeing our new teammate, Kittous again. And I decided Kittous was a girl; Kittous was cute and smart, and besides, I already had a boy (Ugley) in my team.

While I was walking toward the launching hall, I was wrapped up with the scenery of the galaxy under the dome. *The power scales…* I thought that I knew a lot now, but things were yet vague like I just arrived from another world. I was not sure if I or Ugley could do anything up there yet. And there was a new question now irking me. *What the heck happened to those missing people?*

Maybe I should discuss with the king about our discovery and all. I felt a bit regretful for not telling him the truth yesterday. *He is a wise man after all. He may have better thoughts or even solutions if I only tell him about our discovery.* Then again, if the king's fairy tale was really true, it would be very dangerous for all of us. Of course, there would be no hope for those missing riders. They must have been killed by those monsters out there for sure. Or perhaps, they were petrified, just like the man I had seen underwater. Obviously now, this petrified man was only one of the victims of the evil power. What were their names, Harfhas and Ripper?

I entered the hall and walked toward the aquarium, making an effort to ignore the massive noises from the throng. Then I heard someone calling me from behind.

"Ry!"

It was Ella, running toward me. She looked a bit nervous for some reason. I suddenly felt full of life to see her with tons of matters to discuss.

"Hey, Ella, right on time." I did not wait for her to say anything first. "Listen, Ella, can I have a moment with you? It's very important." I demanded, trying to sound very serious.

"Sure, what is it? Well, actually I have something to tell you, too," said Ella, her expression was anxious, which was unusual for her.

I looked around to find any possible spot for that matter, but people were everywhere at the hall. Another busy morning for everyone in the castle.

"Wait, maybe we can talk…over there."

I found an appropriate spot, and I pulled her over. I determined to tell her everything I had discovered. I started first.

"I heard something from the king last night, but uh, you didn't hear anything serious from him yet, I guess."

She shook her head quietly. I gazed at her eyes worriedly.

"You are not planning to go up there today, are you?" I asked.

"Was going to, but… what did he say about, anyway?" she questioned in return.

"Bad will." I said, sounding depressed, attempting to duplicate the king's voice.

"What's that?" She demanded.

"There are two evil men watching over us." I said modestly in a way of making a scary story simple.

But that was silly. She knew more about it.

"Evil man…," recited Ella breaking into my thought. "Actually, I was too scared to tell anyone, But I saw something out there," said Ella, her voice went down dramatically. For a moment she looked around nervously. I could almost hear her eyes rolling.

"Evil man? No, this one was like a shark, but with wings, legs, arms, and creepy stuffs… No, it was a horrible monster. Even my hemaby has been in panic ever since being chased by that thing…"

She undoubtedly looked appalled even now with the memory.

"You know what, Ry? That thing can even speak. He shouted, 'You thank my lord for saving your neck! Save not for long!'"

"That must be Ripper, according to the king. How about the other one, you didn't see him, did you?" I asked doubtfully, screwing my face. "This one must be like a…a winged lion, if you ask me."

"No, none other than that…," said Ella timidly, evoking me another question.

"Why did he chase you, anyway?" I asked.

"Don't know, really...," she said, sounding uncertain.

Then, she suddenly covered up her mouth with her hands and cried, "Horrible, that monster was!" Her eyes grew bigger, her voice destabilized. "Spat out something huge, and, and it was like, like a bucket of glue, and, and I saw someone falling down," said Ella recklessly as if she was obsessed by the monster just now.

"By any chance, Ella, you know what they are after, I mean, what they really want?" I asked thoughtfully when she recuperated her soul a moment later.

Naturally, she looked very confused with my question.

"Silver metal pieces, Ella. Well, precisely, silver scales." I said neatly. "You haven't heard about them, have you?" I guessed.

"Listen, Ella," I began again with a genuine look, "you need to know why we are here, first, I mean really why." I said seriously.

Certainly it sounded very important. Maybe it sounded like something more than the prizes from the races and stuff. She understood my point, but she only shrugged her shoulders. Now, without an explanation about the power scales, it would only bring her more shrugs, I thought. And I decided to tell her. When I was just about to enlighten the power scales for her, I heard an urgent voice calling me out.

"Ryan! There you are, my dear fellow!" With a big artificial smile the king approached to us. "How are you and your friend, Ug?" asked the king softly.

"He is fine, and I am, too. Thank you, sir..., Your Highness." I answered in a similar soft tone, but sincerely.

"Well," said the king, smiling at Ella, "I just hoped to see you Ryan before you fly."

By that, Ella smiled at me and awkwardly at the king.

"I think I should get going, Ryan, catch you later," said Ella, waving her hands.

Both the king and I replied with a smile behind her. I was still looking at her disappearing into the crowd when the king recited the question once more.

"So, you both are doing OK?"

"Yes, yes, we are doing great, sir." I answered submissively like a soldier.

"I worried actually about you, Ryan," said the king, his voice sounded serious. "I should have not told you about the story of the horrible men out there yesterday..."

He scrutinized my face for two seconds. "I am sure you had a nightmare last night," he said with a concerned air.

That was unexpectedly kind of him to worry about me.

"No, sir. No, I slept tight. Thank you." I declared jovially.

Really, I had a good sleep all through till morning. I must have been so tired after the weird journey underwater, of which I had no words yet to the king.

"I am glad to hear that," said the king friendly. Pausing for a second, he looked at me with a serious expression before he continued.

"Ryan, I slept over the current situation out there…, and decided to send a few armed men to patrol around and protect you riders. Now, with that, my only hope is you people can find the silver scales as soon as possible, of course, before the evil men."

"That's great, sir. Very good news for…," I said hesitantly. I was going to include me and Ugley, but I changed my mind. "Definitely we all should be very happy with that, sir."

The king looked quite happy as well to see me smile.

"Yes, I guess that was what I wanted to say… Oh, did you by any chance tell anyone about it?" asked the king considerately.

"About…?" I asked him back.

"Harfhas and Ripper," said the king promptly.

"No, sir, no." I said confirmatively.

Then, I remembered what Ella had said to me.

"Well, only a little bit…" I tried to fix, feeling rather guilty.

"Hmmm. I just don't want them to have nightmares by any chance." He said, sounding quite worried, but he refreshed himself, forcing a smile.

"OK, that's that."

He then pulled out an unexpected topic.

"And…, by the way, Ryan, you mentioned about the power silver scales… I was just curious…," said the king openly, "about what you know."

He said he was curious, but it sounded more or less like a serious question. I was almost determined, anyway, to discuss with the king about the power silver scales. With the wisdom and the power of the silver scales of 365 he may have, the king would be the only person who could handle the situation. The king should be the only reliable person now.

I shivered by a sudden thought of the two unseen figures of the evil men based on Ella's description, overlapping with their hideous faces with the remaining 635 pieces in their hands.

The game is over. Harfhas wins, Neptess loses. We all lose.

The king was quite right.

We will have to find the power scales before they do.

"Yes, the power scales, sir. I was going to tell you about…," I paused for a second as my eyes met the king's which looked so intense for simple curiosity, "…about what we discovered with a silver scale." Now I began to solve the mystery for the king.

"A silver scale?" He copied.

"Yes, it was in a bubble ball which we found amongst bubble ball clusters. I thought we unearthed the prettiest one which we all have been looking for. So, we were coming back to the castle happily, but…" Another pause to confirm myself how much detail I should tell him.

"But?" He demanded impatiently.

"We just fell into the water, sir." I smiled, feeling uncomfortable with his stare. He read my expression and tried to cheer me up.

"Aha, you were too excited with the beauty, weren't you?"

He was right, but not completely. I did not say anything about the vision with the small fish.

"Probably, we were. But then, the bubble ball in my hand was gone and we only found," I showed the scale out of my pocket, "this, sir." I shook it gently as if to show off the feeling of pride.

The king seemed so impressed by that, licking a thin smile across his lips.

"That looks quite familiar to me…I mean fascinating!"

He narrowed his eyes at the scale which sparkled between my fingers.

"May I?"

He stretched his hand toward me. "Are you sure this is from the bubble ball?" asked the king, carefully picking up the scale from my hand, his eyes focusing on the scale. "So, what did you find with this little thing, Ryan?"

"Nothing or a lot…, sir." I said timidly, tailing my voice.

"And what does that mean, my dear fellow?" requested the king impatiently.

"With this scale we were able to see a trail which actually led us to a hidden land." I made it up, but I felt there was really a trail.

"It was almost like this land here with bubble balls, but smaller…, and a small silver castle. And then, I was able to enter the castle with that scale…"

I gazed at the scale in his hand, but the king looked at me very intently.

"Go on, my friend, what was there?"

"But the scale only locked me in, sir. The gate opened only when I was almost chocked to death. When I recovered, I saw bright bubble balls outside…"

I breathed a sigh like I said the worst part of the story.

"That's it? Nothing else was there, my friend?" asked the king demandingly.

"Well, yes, except for the…the jigsaw puzzle game that I had to do."

"What is that? You played a game in there?" asked the king with a thin snarl across his lips.

"It wasn't just a game. I would have been killed, if I didn't do it, sir."

The king did not seem convinced at all. He returned the scale to me like it had no more interest left for him.

"Well, that sounds quite an adventure, but I am not sure about that at all," said the king, moving a step back.

He looked very disappointed. Surely, he must have expected to hear more than just rubbish.

"But, I thought it could be a clue to the rest of the silver scales. And if we put our heads together…." I said carefully, hoping to read his mind.

"Well, my dear fellow, we can do that, but I doubt that would lead us anywhere before the evil men," uttered the king cynically.

"Anyway, you keep it up with me for any news, and I will see what I can do to protect you all from the danger," added the king decisively.

Losing interest in the conversation, the king was about to go when I held his steps with another matter.

"Sir, one of the evil men you mentioned, Ripper," I said.

"What about him?" He asked dully.

"I think he is the one who killed the riders. He is like a flying shark or something. He spat out some kind of sticky glue over the riders." I said gloomily.

"Is that right? That sounds horrible already. Did you see him, though?"

"Well, I haven't actually seen him, sir. I only heard it, but I think that's what happened, sir," I said confidently.

"Hmmm. Indeed, someone did see him..." He said anxiously.

After looking at the ceiling vaguely for a few seconds, he brightened up his face.

"Well, I must get going now, my dear fellow. And I will have to order my men to patrol as soon as possible," said the king, stepping toward the door.

When he was opening the door, I suddenly remembered something that might be related.

"Oh, actually, sir, I found a man underwater, petrified badly..."

By that, the king held his steps on the spot as if he, too, was petrified. I must have said something pretty interesting to him.

"He and his hemaby were there in a big transparent rock, just like a big bubble ball. From my observation, they were there for years. And that means, the evil man, Ripper has been around here for a long time." I said conclusively like an investigator.

The king closed the door before him and smiled at me.

"That's nice to know, Ryan. Yes, glad to have a clever boy like you here. Any other discovery with that man? Did he leave any clue for us?"

I took his question rather sarcastic than in appreciation.

"No, not much, sir. There was only this L25G29 written on his sleeve." I said hesitantly.

"L25G29…and you figured that out, I suppose?" He asked me, still holding the door knob with his hand.

"I had no idea at first, but Ugley took me somewhere up there. And then, I figured out that L25G29 meant bubble ball layer 25 and group 29."

"Ha! That's where you discovered that little thing! Quite impressive, your Ug!"

I was not sure if he really meant it. Nonetheless, it was not too bad to learn that the king appreciated our discovery.

"A good lesson for everyone. Surely, your discovery is worth winning a great prize. That is an achievement, my dear fellow. I will have that informed right away. Well said and done. Now I must leave you alone, and you give a plenty of cheers to your friend Ug on my behalf."

He smiled at me, and while opening the door, he added a few words almost undertone, which I could barely hear it. "…outsmart…just like…"

I was going to ask him about the other evil man, Harfhas, but he was already out of sight.

Chapter 13
ELLA'S SECRET

I noticed that people were already ready to leap off. They looked quite excited before the flight began. Apparently the king did not inform them anything about the silver scales, not to mention Harfhas and Ripper.

As I walked to the aquarium, Ugley jumped out of the water at once like complaining about my delay and the itchiness on his wings while waiting. Even so, he looked quite happy, wagging his tail steadily. I appeased his neck and whispered cheerfully.

"We are almost there, Ugley, almost."

Now I tapped his neck a few times and hopped on his back. My eyes caught other riders who were leaving the hall bravely. Ugley started to warm up, wheeling around the empty space, his wings open wide, flapping energetically up and down. Then I noticed that the king was there by the door watching us anxiously. I looked at the king once and at Ugley.

"Come on, Ugley. You know why we have to keep flying." I said quietly.

It occurred to me that it was very unusual for Ugley spending such a long time on warming up.

"Say, our biggest chance is yet to come. And now, we have one good reason to go there." I whispered again, striving to ease his neck gently in a way of cheering him up.

Ugley flew almost like swimming in mid-air without changing the courses. I discerned that Ugley was not

312

looking at me even when I was talking to him. His eyes were only fixed on the sight of the king. I looked at the king who was waving his hand reluctantly with a forced smile.

"Tell you what. The king gave you a huge cheer for your wonderful and smart job, Ugley. Great achievement in finding the scale and all!"

Ugley only blew a thin noise out of his nose. I knew he understood. Ugley was exceptionally smart. But at the same time he was ugly, which sounded never suitable for a hemaby in any way. Why, I wondered, such an exceptional hemaby happened to be in the aquarium in the first place.

"Maybe you remember what happened to you before."

Ugley ignored me. I felt sympathy grow inside.

"OK, once we are done with all this, we can figure that out, Ugley. Well, I can even talk to the king, I promise." I whispered convincingly, my eyes stealing another glance at the king who was still looking at us worriedly.

"But first, we need to deal with the bad guys out there; two evil monsters called Harfhas and Ripper, the king had said."

When I was trying to trace any hint of emotional change in his eyes, Ugley, without warning, shot out of the site toward the exit on the ceiling as though he was shocked by an unexpected attack of hundreds of light-devils. I barely had time to seize him around the neck and fins before he was transformed into a launching rocket.

With the speed he gained, in a few minutes, he caught up the herd of the hemabies. My mind began to float with enthusiasm as soon as I saw them. In fact, it was the first time for me to be up there along with other riders. When I became part of the racing group, I felt a sudden impulse to discuss about the situation with them up in the sky in the absence of the king. However, Ugley sped up even faster from there, and soon we were ahead of them.

"Hey, Ugley! Need to talk to the people." I yelled.

I turned my head back to the riders who were now behind us.

"Slow down, Ugley!" I yelled again.

I was sure that he heard me. But, there was no sign of any change. He seemed very angry with something.

Did I hurt him with anything by any chance?

"Ugley, stop it at once! You heard about Harfhas and Ripper! Want to offer them another smile?" I bellowed. My voice was very coarse.

Ugley abruptly stopped, just about throwing me off into the air.

"Ugley, I am sorry," I breathed, "if you are mad at me, I apologize, but please, this is not the right time. I just need to warn them!"

As Ugley turned around, I saw the people fast approaching. Waving both hands vigorously to draw their attentions, I shouted.

"Halt!"

I saw some of them pointing at me.

"There! There!" I said wittily, looking at Ugley, breathing a sigh of relief.

I thanked him, patting his neck. They slowed, and in due course all came to a halt.

"It's you, Ryan. I thought we had to prepare for a battle," said the rider in front.

"Sorry to disappoint you, Ruth, but, I meant to cheer you up!"

I looked at the people around nervously with an awkward smile. They were staring at me frighteningly, but they all looked half nervous and half baffled.

"Sorry to bother you like this, guys, but I just wanted to discuss with you about something."

Temporarily, I had to think hard how to tell. I could already feel their obvious reaction with the words of the two evil monsters and the power scales which the monsters have been after.

I knew that I would make it only worse by stimulating their angers with the story.

But, if I don't, it can go even worse. They all have to know before too late.

I decided now. I hoped to make it simple and appreciable.

"Well, regardless of the situation, I think it's wonderful to be up here." I cried calmly, trying to avoid misunderstanding of my position.

"There is something important I happened to know…"

My mind was still weighing between telling and not telling the power scales to them.

But, what else I can do to convince them, otherwise?

"Do you know that there are two evil men up there?" I asked anxiously, but their plain expression only looked to say, 'Sure. That's what I guessed.'

I made up my mind now. "And," I continued lively, "they have been after the power scales which were hidden somewhere in the forest of bubble balls?"

By this, apparently the air around throng turned hot. I could see the people now frowning or grimacing with one another as if they found something in the air to quarrel about.

"Man, what the heck are you talking about? You stopped us in the middle of nowhere, and suddenly telling us what, power scales? Anyone knows what the heck he is talking about?"

It was one of the cronies of Chrom who argued in a sort of sarcastic way. I had expected such a reaction, anyway.

"Well, he seems to know something...worth hearing, I think," snapped Chrom plainly, to my pleasant surprise.

"They are the silver scales that once the Goddess had collected from a thousand different fish in the ocean. Now, be aware that we are not just hunting one of the pretty bubble balls. We are looking for the one that contains these silver scales. And that's what the two evil men are after. I should point out that it is not just a single silver scale, but as many as six-hundred thirty five silver scales in a single bubble ball!"

"So what? They can do any wicked magic tricks or something?" Someone argued again.

Magic... Maybe that can be part of the power.

I eyed him for a few seconds, dreaming to convince him wordlessly. But then, I only managed to say, "Well, my guess is that it could be even worse. But, not quite sure as I have never seen them."

That was a very stupid answer, letting people smirk for a moment.

I wanted to avoid a miserable feeling with an embarrassing laughter. I quickly pulled out the silver scale from my pocket and lifted it up in the air so that everyone could see.

"This is a real scale I discovered from one of those bubble balls."

I showed the scale to them, but I regretted at once.

"That thing, the scale you have, is that, did it show you anything powerful? Something like making your Ugley a little less ugly?"

Yikes! I quickly checked Ugley with a secretive slant. To my relief he disregarded the big laughter. He was simply cool, calm and collected at this point. *Good boy.*

"It can make you a little less smart, if that's what you meant." I replied wittily. "And that much I can guarantee with one piece. However, it empowers great deal with numbers." I said tentatively, but it sounded quite right in my second thought.

"Now, guess what? Three-hundred sixty-five pieces of silver scales! That much power was already given to the king."

The throng waved with chatters again. Now I told them pretty much everything; the king possessed the power scales as many as 365, and the two evil men were looking for the rest (635). So, I decided to leave it to them.

"Listen up, everyone." I called out roughly. "Again, sorry for stopping you up here, but I thought it was important, and I hoped to share the ideas with you guys."

No one said anything for a while, and everyone looked quite serious now.

"Obviously," said Ruth critically, breaking the silence, "the king has been badly after the power scales, too, then.

What are we all doing this for? He's been using us just like that. Well, what is then the difference between the monsters up there and the king down there?"

For sure that sounded pretty aggressive. Silence followed oddly for a few seconds until I broke it with a comment for Ruth.

"Actually, Ruth, I asked the king about the power scales last night."

Then I suddenly realized that no one asked me about how I had known the power scales in the first place. So, I moved on hurriedly.

"He told me about the two evil men, Harfhas and Ripper, who were actually the awful monsters desperately looking for the power scales. And that was why the king himself decided to find the scales. He said that ever since he had discovered all that, he tried to find the scales, yet secretly." I explained, trying to sound truthful.

Meanwhile, my mind began to weigh what the king had said regarding the power scales. In spite of the good reason why he had to find the power scales, maybe he really has been dreaming of possessing the absolute power with a thousand silver scales. In fact, it seemed very natural to crave the power when someone was in such a position.

"But uh," I said hesitantly, "yeah, to be honest, I don't totally believe that he has been after the power scales only because of that reason. Maybe we should keep that in mind until we find out more."

I saw people nodding now. Approved. No argument or yelling.

"Now, up there," I changed the topics, rather cheerfully this time, "be careful with the one called Ripper, whose appearance is like a shark, but nasty looking, really."

I gave a quick smile at Ugley, hoping he did not feel offended with my expression.

"If you ever encounter this one, I suggest you run away as quickly as possible and never challenge face to face with him. You need to stay away at least, say, a hundred feet or more from him, and watch anything out of his mouth."

I just spotted Ella far at the back. Giving a barely discernable eye smile to her for the credit of the last piece of information, I looked around one more time.

"Well, I think that's all for me now."

"How about the other one?" A question came from the back when people were about to resume their flight.

"Yes, Harfhas is yet unknown, but I presume it's even worse, because this Ripper calls him my lord." I explained to the crowd as a warning, but rather lightly.

Then, after five seconds of a bustling moment, without leaving a trace, everyone parted, racing toward the bubble clouds up ahead.

"So, how did it go?" Ella asked me, coming near after watching them all vanish into the bubble ball forest.

She smiled at me briefly, but I could see a hint of anxiety on her face.

"I thought you would come, Ella." I said with a pleasant smile which then turned into a grimace to answer her question. "Well, sort of trouble with this silver scale, but otherwise…"

I showed her the scale held in my fingers.

"That's a scale?" She gazed at the scale with full of longing to snatch.

With a clumsy smile across her lips, she stretched out her neck like a turtle at a sight of a bug somersaulting in front of it.

"This is a silver scale hidden in a bubble ball up there. We, actually, Ugley found the bubble ball containing this." I said while tapping Ugley's neck approvingly with a proud smile for him.

"Hey, Ella," I began, remembering the moment at the castle, "I was going to tell you about the power scales and stuff, but didn't get a chance. Sorry. If you have time later today…" I said regretfully.

"Sure, I should be OK." Ella said, turning her attention back to the scale in my hand. "So, that's one of the power scales you were talking about?"

"Yeah. This one is only a key, though, for the remaining…"

"A key?" She asked, her eyes moving on to mine.

They looked dark and grim. I glimpsed her eyes for a few seconds as I realized that I was about to begin a long story.

"Listen, Ella, I promise I will tell you everything when I see you later. I might need your thoughts with this as well. So…, would you mind?"

"No, no, not at all," uttered Ella. She suddenly looked very nervous. Forcing a smile, she managed to say brightly.

"Well, then off we go!"

"Catch you later at the hall!" I shouted animatedly.

Then she, too, vanished into thin air in a few minutes. I looked blankly at the imaginary trail left behind her. *She is unusual.* She wasn't like herself. Talkative and cheerful…, and that was what I wanted to see.

Is that because of her brother?

I had not seen her brother ever since the beginning of the second game. Precisely, it was after I gave him the atlas of the castle, delivered from his cousin.

Has he been really up to some dangerous stuff in his investigation? I had decided not to ask Ella about her brother, but I could not help wondering about him.

"What do you think, Ugley? Don't you feel that Ella has been hiding something?"

With a tapping signal, Ugley flew up the way they had vanished. Until several layers passed by, I kept quiet, letting Ugley bus me anywhere. But, perceptibly I assumed that Ugley would be taking me to the bubble ball layer twenty-nine. Then I had a strange feeling that today was not the day hanging around the layer twenty-nine. A different thought came up to my mind.

"Ugley," I divulged, "can we go somewhere else today?"

I requested, but I had no idea where else we could go.

Maybe somewhere we can find the home of the evil monsters.

"How about…going further up?"

It wasn't precisely a charming plan, but it was accepted by Ugley. Without bothering checking around, he drove straight to what seemed like an endless forest with densely populated bubble balls.

Now, we must have come very deep. It was eerie and silent. I began to hear my heart thumping. I gently patted Ugley's neck a few times, and he forwarded hesitantly. I wondered if anyone ever dared come this far. No one would suppose that the treasure could be hidden anywhere here, I thought. I looked around, my mind was quite blank. Then I heard something. I was pretty positive. But I was not sure if I saw anything passing by. Ugley smoothly glided very quietly, now toward the direction of the sound. Just then, I spied something barely half a second before it disappeared into bubble ball clouds again. It was a hemaby, but were there two? I was not sure. Ugley cautiously circled around over several layers, but we could not find a trace of them.

After a while, we renounced and moved over to other area. Right then, someone stirred up the silence with a malicious yell, and I almost screamed by shock.

"Hurry up, Miss! Can't let him wait!"

We quickly hid behind the bubble balls nearby, yet, trying to see who that was. I was only able to take a glimpse of the figures, but for sure this time I did not miss to see two people with their hemabies. One of them was a man, and he should be the one who just yelled because the other one was a girl.

"Huh!"

I suddenly thought that the girl was Ella.

My breath stopped, my eyes yet searching for the girl, wanting to make sure it was not Ella. But there was no visible or audible trace of them. Ugley remained on the spot for a while until I signaled to forward to the way they went. He set off again very quietly.

Until we ultimately reached layers where we could smell fresh air and hear familiar noises, I kept silent, lost in thought. That was Ella, I decided now. But, who was that man? Of course, that wasn't her brother Laxan. And definitely that was not one of the riders, either. Then, there was another question. What the heck was she doing there with a creepy man? *Come on, Ella, what are you up to?*

Now the only thing I could think of was either to ask her or wait for her explanation. Then I wondered if I could ever wait until she would come to tell me all about it.

We did not go to the bubble ball layer twenty-nine. Instead, we cruised several bubble ball layers broadly like we were on duty by the order of the king for any suspicious phenomena. Meanwhile, I decided that Ella had found something strange up in the bubble forest and she had needed to ask help from one of the guards, and then they were rushing back to the castle to report to the king.

Chapter 14
FAKE GALAXY

Many riders were already home. I thought it was quite unusual for them to come back so early. They were rather enjoying time over conversations here and there or playing in the launching hall. My conclusion was that no one was missing today. Maybe they listened to my warning well.

Ugley went back to the aquarium, and I returned to my room without delay. I sat on the bedside to relax for a little while. Then I noticed the small jars on the table by the wall. *Kittous!* I had forgotten about our teammate, Kittous. She did not show up for any reason today. Maybe she did not know where we were because we had changed our destination in the last minutes, I considered. At least I could have told Ugley about the name, Kittous, if I had only remembered. I blamed myself.

I looked up the ceiling and wondered how she would react with her name. I believed that she had a lot more reasons to come down to see me now instead of quietly peeping from her hiding place behind the light. *She will show up again when we really need to see her.*

My thought moved to Ella whom I was supposed to meet at the launching hall. However, I was not able to make a quick decision whether I would go and find her or wait for her at the hall. After minutes of long fighting, I at length made up my mind to wait for her at the hall. *She knows that I will come, and whatever the reason she is coming.* I felt itching inside to ask her if I could help her with anything.

There were still quite a lot of people talking and playing at the hall, but Ella was not there. My favorite ally, Ruth was not in the hall. I approached to one of Ruth's friends to ask if he saw Ella. A rider in other chatting group nearby must have overheard me.

"There comes your girlfriend, Ry!" He yelled at me sarcastically.

"Ouch!" I cried, making a painful face for him for the thankful piece of information before turning to see Ella who just entered the hall.

"Hey, Ella!" I waved first.

Without doubt, she must have seen me first, but again, she waved only in return. She looked very tired or maybe horrorstricken based on my perception. She smiled at me without a word. Her marble eyes looked slim down to half.

"You just got back?" I asked, but it was not the question I had intended.

"Yes. Well, actually a while ago." She said, sounding a bit down.

"You, uh, OK?" I checked her expression on her face for a second. "Hey, if it isn't good time for you, then…" I tailed off my voice, trying to examine her mood.

She replied quite spontaneously with a whole-hearted smile.

"Oh, yes, yes. This is a perfect time for me…, Ryan."

That sounded much better.

"Well, then…"

I looked around to find a setting for a good long conversation. There was no secret, but I just did not want to be interrupted by the king or others this time. And she seemed to have the same thought. She pulled my arms toward the main gate of the hall. And we ended up throwing ourselves outside the big gate of the launching hall. It was the corridor with the large aquarium and the exhibition gallery of marine life.

I stood by the gallery and scanned Ella's eyes briefly. They seemed recharged and ready to muse upon my fairy tale now. Suddenly, a small thrill was developed in my mind by the thought that it was Ella who was now an alien, and I was not, anymore.

"I was going to tell you about the power silver scales. But, I think you should listen to this story, first. It's my own version of a fairy tale of Bubble Land, if you ask me." I said proudly, sounding to be an egghead (just like Ella when I had been an alien). I traced a smile that lasted only half a second on her face with what I said.

At last, I began the story in a usual way for a fairy tale.

"Long ago, a Goddess called Neptess created Bubble Land. Then, she invited many humans and animals from other worlds. Once all settled in peace, she selected a king with a will of W.E.L., that is, Wisdom, Equality, and Love. Neptess collected a thousand pieces of silver scales from a thousand different kinds of fish in the ocean. She gave three-hundred sixty-five pieces to empower the king to rule the land with W.E.L. The silver scales were the sources of the power that the king could use for peace on the land. The Goddess left Bubble Land, and the remaining six-hundred thirty-five scales were hidden securely somewhere."

My story was stopped there momentarily both by the memory of the accomplishment I had already made with

Ugley, and by the view of the bubble balls displayed in the gallery right beside me. It reminded me of the pain and the joy. *The gallery…* I remembered now, but it seemed so long ago. Yes, the gallery was the first thing I saw when I had entered the castle. Mineral stones on the ground and bubble balls on the sea floor and…

I spied the letters and the numbers which were engraved on the pebble stones now in such an easy way to understand: L29 G29. And there were revolting anemones which eventually had led us to the hidden land. The gleaming castle in the next column of the gallery was the silver castle under the dome…

"Ha!" I exclaimed, my eyes briefly reviewing the entire gallery once more.

"Huh? What's going on, Ry?" she asked, her lips half way forming an inept smile.

I must have looked very funny to make her smile out of her intricate mind. I was totally lost for a few seconds.

"Oh, sorry, I'm sorry, Ella… I was –."

"Talking about somewhere…the silver scales were hidden securely." She refreshed my memory rather cheerfully.

"Yeah. Look, Ella!" I cried. My mouth fell open again.

"So stupid. I can't believe that I had forgotten all this." I said painfully, looking back at the gallery.

"This will tell you a great deal, Ella."

It would be easier and more convincing with visible evidence now. I animatedly described her everything based on the display in the gallery from the first column to the last. With great interest Ella turned much brighter when I talked about how we ended up discovering the silver castle under the dome from the discovery of one silver scale. She over time covered up her mouth with her hands when I said all about the fish drawings and the hidden jigsaw puzzle of a thousand silver metal pieces which had almost killed me. And at last, the view of the brightest bubble ball located in the spiral center.

"After risking my life, I should deserve more than another puzzle, but, only the view of something like a fake galaxy..." I said resentfully while looking at the last column of the gallery.

The bubble balls in the spiral were sparkly, and I could almost hear them yelling at me all in one voice, 'You stupid! I am not a fake!'

I remembered where I was talking about with the fairy tale now.

"Yes, six-hundred thirty-five silver scales were hidden somewhere." I said sourly. "And we must find them before..., before the monsters out there."

Certainly the king was right. It would be very dangerous if the power scales ever landed on the hands of the evil men. However, my mind was not yet fully supportive to the king. *Does he really have a fair will with this? Or, it is just a game?* I could not tell after all.

It is not intended, however, that any human possesses all the scales. Peace remains only when it is controlled or never.

The Goddess' words piercingly banged my eardrums.

"Oh, Ry, you said that it is one bubble ball that contains all the remaining silver scales..." Ella said, sounding to be useful, looking at the bubble balls in the last column of the gallery.

The bubble ball at the very heart of the cluster was casting dazzling light.

"If you have that many power scales in one bubble ball, somehow, wouldn't it be so hot, or so bright, and, or energetic, maybe, just like that?"

She pointed to the brightest bubble ball in the center. I stared at it almost blankly. Then, I began to feel hot inside as if the heat of the brightest bubble ball has been transferred to my heart. *Yes, all these are giving the same message for sure.* In spite of everything, the deadly jigsaw puzzle wasn't useless.

In fact, when I was amongst the bubble balls back in the sky, I had never noticed such a thing as a spiral. However, all the bubble balls might have been in a pattern like a spiral. And the one containing the power scales were hidden right in the center of a group of a certain layer. Now I remembered a description about it in the story of the sand castle written on my birthday card.

Neptess selected one bubble ball and stored the remaining force to give off the most brilliant light...

I felt hot on my face. The heat now came up to my face from my chest.

"Ella, I think you are right. That should be the answer. Yes, I am positive!"

I hurried to the door, waving. "I must see Ugley now, thanks a bunch, Ella."

A big smile ran through my face mindlessly. "I will catch you shortly."

And I added just a few words of pride before disappearing behind the door.

"Oh, by the way, Ella, I just wanted to tell you that ugly Ugley is the smartest and most charming hemaby in the whole world." I exclaimed playfully.

She knew what I meant only so well, but I just hoped that she could forget about whatever was troubling her badly, at least for a few seconds.

Chapter 15
UNDERWATER GRAVEYARD

I had a firm belief that the power scales lay at the heart of the group 29. In truth, they were not hidden, but just lay there untouched. My steps were suddenly very light – lighter than a feather. I even felt that I could fly fast myself to the galaxy without Ugley! Now I suffered from the pain inside with a frenzied desire to check the location. Tomorrow seemed a century away, and I could not wait that long.

In the mean time, two sides of my mind were engaged in making a pleasant decision. *What should I do, first? Report the information to the king, or checking the location myself?* In the end, I could not prevail over the madcap desire with the latter – being the first human to touch the real thing!

I have to see Ugley, now. If I ask, he will fly, right away.

My elevated mood was destructed by a sudden scream, followed by a thud when I was just about to call Ugley. I instantly noted that it was Chrom who had fallen off to the floor. A few people rushed to him for any usefulness. However, while Chrom lay unconsciously on the floor, no one seemed to have any idea of what to do. Knowing it was Chrom, I hesitated for a bit, but my legs threw me to the site.

"That stupid thing!" One of Chrom's friends yelled, pointing to a hemaby.

"It threw Chrom to death! We have to kill it!" He shouted furiously, looking at the people around.

But I rather believed that it was Chrom who accidentally slipped off from the hemaby. I knew that Chrom had a bad tamper. His manner to his hemaby had almost killed him last time during the game. One thing, though, I was not so sure about was the hemaby. Still up in mid-air, it twisted its body hysterically nonstop. That was way abnormal whatever the reason.

"That's not Chrom's!" Someone yelled, frowning at the hemaby.

"I know that, mister!" barked the other boy angrily. "He rode mine yesterday, and he got that stupid thing just today," said Chrom's friend coldly. Then, he drew his attention to Chrom who was lying on the floor unconsciously.

His own hemaby ran away, and his new hemaby kicked him off. What a bad temper and a bad luck for Chrom all these days!

"Chrom!" I shook him on the arm anxiously. He did not seem aware of my effort. He was still breathing ever quietly, and I could feel his pulse peacefully tickling my finger. He must be only in deep faint (once again), I concluded. Some water might help, I thought.

"Anyone, get some water for him, please!" I shouted to the observers.

Someone scurried away at once. And without protest, I followed my legs carrying me toward the door to see the king.

"You guys watch him. Give him some water, somehow. I will go report to the king."

I said that, but it was only an inducement to persuade the other side of my mind. I'd better report the location of the unseen power scales, I thought. Surely the king would have to be the first person to know. I should not play a game for my own joy in this critical situation. Instead, let him fast handle the jumpy situation with the two evil monsters for the sake of everyone on this land. I decided now.

I came out of the launching hall, and for the first time I entered the hall located at the end of the corridor. The hall was colossal with five silvery sculptures in the central area. With additional four doors distributed along the walls, I had an immediate impression that the hall was in the center of the castle, connecting five separate units, including the king's palace.

"PENTADIA?"

I read the illuminating word written on a huge scintillating ball on top of the coral tree which stood right behind the sculptures. The figures of the sculptures appeared to be only imaginary animals, but very unique to draw my attention constantly. However, there was not much room in my stolen mind to contemplate them.

Pressing the curiosity and the anxiety down, I rushed toward the speculated hallway to the king's palace. Then, I momentarily saw two people disappeared at the corner of the hall. I was not sure who they were, but my mind suddenly picked up a scene like a snap shot.

"Wait! Was that…Ella?"

Now I remembered Ella with an unknown man in the deep bubble forest.

Another incident to report to the king? But, now where are they going?

I promptly decided to follow them. I would not lose them this time.

I scurried over at once, but, the hallway was quiet without a trace. There was a long deserted hallway with several silvery doors along the way on both sides. And at the end of the hallway was another door which stood alluringly with glittery brightness. I instinctively experienced a queer feeling about the door and quietly sprinted to it. The instant I pushed the door, my four senses told me that it was not a pleasant place to go further.

A sinister breeze touched my bare skin with a salty smell. The sound from my own body echoed under the eerily dim light that stretched all the way down the stony stairs.

Be brave. Be strong, Ryan. Your challenge began. I mesmerized myself with the words, of which I was not able to recall the origin. Making barely a sound, I stepped down the stairs bravely. The salty smell irritated my nose ever strongly along the way down.

Eventually I reached the bottom of what felt like a thousand stairs. At the end of the stairs were two big metal pieces, vertically standing before me, indicative of an uncanny gate. I heard my heart thumping now. I pushed one side of the gate with extreme caution, but instantaneously let it close again as bright light carried a coarse voice of a man through the open gap. It was the same man, and I knew it without looking at him. I shoved the gate as little as I could peek or hear them talk, but it was only after they disappeared into nowhere.

Behind the gate was a round hall with nothing but a pool in the center. They must have dived into the pool unless vanished into thin air. The surface of the pool was glittered with the light coming from the bubble balls on the ceiling. The water waving with gentle ripples was an evidence of their disappearance.

I waited outside in case they would poke out of the pool, but only moments of silence piled up the minutes. There was something weird about the pool. *Is that a passage to somewhere underwater?* An urgent surge came up to my mind to follow wherever they were up to. Then I dared to dive into the pool.

It certainly was not a normal pool, but a passage tunnel underwater. It was so deep that I almost decided to return for air before touching the bottom. The floor was so broad, full of little air-pockets wagging with current amongst small marine lives such as coral, shells, mussels, and abalones. After feeding myself with oxygen from an air-pocket, I eyed the passageway that progressed to an L shape along the broad sea floor. The whole space and the passageway were gleaming with the light of the bubble balls dangling on the ground. Being alone there was rather amusing than fearful when I was watching it. I nearly forgot why I was there for the time being, watching the scenery ahead of me.

I moved forward, my eyes fixed on the view in my direction. There was no trace of anyone gone through. As the broad passageway stretched straight ahead, I advanced myself freely fast. I needed to draw near to them or return to the castle. The passageway gradually bent downward, then, I began to see a dark view in the distance through the overcast water.

Soon, the passageway ended. Now, as I came out of the way, I found myself at the edge of a cliff facing a large ocean valley. The surrounding was very gray with the light coming from far away. I began to feel chilly. I returned to the passageway and acquired a few bubble balls in my grip. I swallowed enough oxygen and dived down toward the valley.

With the light from the air-pockets in my hand, I focused on the view ahead. There was something peculiar about the place; it was like a ghostly graveyard which certainly was not new to me at all. Yes, I came here before with Ugley, I remembered. I had seen nothing but heaps of bones, skeletons, and the like.

While I was studying the surrounding thoroughly for any hint that they had left, I spied a dark figure along with something under the dim light. I positioned myself near to the sea floor and approached to the figure slowly until I was close enough to watch them safely. From there, now I could see two figures under the diffused bubble ball light. Yes, one of them was certainly Ella. For a moment I thought that they were just Ella and her hemaby. But, that was only my hope. In the next moment I confirmed the identity of the other figure. It was the horrible monster that Ella had described once. I swallowed the fear along with another lung-full of oxygen, my eyes kept on the spot. I felt the vicious jaws of the shark monster being ever close to me.

Come on, Ryan, Don't you have guts? Don't you see Ella is in danger?

I attempted to cut back the growing hesitation to follow them. I waited until the vague view of the figures ebbed into the grey water. Then, with the remaining air-pockets on my back, I advanced toward the direction. While I was passing the location where they had been, beneath the grey water I spotted a few round objects scattered on the sea floor. I thought that they were rocks, but then, I saw humans inside. Their faces, with swelled eyes, were yet vivid; horrorstruck. Brave and innocent they must have been, but only lifeless now. There was nothing I could do for them.

I forwarded until the surrounding turned normal. I sensed augmentation of marine life under the dispersed light in the distance. But there was no vestige of their way. *I lost them again.* I had an instant vision of where they might have gone to, but I had no urgent mean to get there.

Feeling down I remained there vacantly for a moment, unable to decide if I would go back to the castle. Then, out of the blue my eyes lit up with stimulation.

"Holy cow!" I swallowed a bucket of salty water happily.

I had no idea how he knew that I was here, but, yes, it was my handsome teammate approaching peacefully toward me.

"Ugley!"

By an impetuous thrill I could not breathe properly at the sight of him.

"You genius buddy, how the heck did you know I was here, waiting for you?"

I shouted soundlessly, but I knew he heard me, because I saw him waggling his tails and fins ever merrily. The next second, I had to saturate myself with another bucket of water.

"Kittous!"

I just spotted my little teammate behind Ugley. But even that was not the end of the surprise. There was another hemaby following them. *My gosh!* It was the hemaby who shook off Chrom. At a loss, I gazed at Ugley disapprovingly, but he reacted perfectly normal to my suspicious glare. Two hemabies (precisely three including Kittous) flew out of the castle without riders? I understood a hemaby would never do anything without an order... I was not sure about that now.

Did the king send them to me? I considered, but I could hardly see any chance for him to know where I was. Maybe, it was just Ugley who had sensed my call; the truth was I could never measure the real capability of Ugley until now. Nevertheless, now I had an immediate mean to activate myself.

As I settled comfortably on his back, Ugley smoothly slid down into the depth with Kittous along side. I naturally deemed that Ugley and Kittous knew where to go, and they would direct the way. However, to my surprise, the companion of Ugley was ahead of us, swaying its tail quietly. I could not make myself believe that it was the same hemaby who had once showed a hysterical reaction against its rider. Everything looked perfectly normal for Ugley and his companions. They seemed to comprehend what they were doing only so well. Then, all I had to do was to wait and see. Sitting on the back of Ugley I once speculated if they ever encountered Ella and the monster before meeting me.

Chapter 16
ANOTHER SMART TEAMMATE

It was not so long before I knew that we were not going back to the castle. Certainly, the king had nothing to do with the runaway hemabies. My next guess was the hidden dome. But in reality, I had no idea how to get there because it was the swarm of little fish who had taken me there. Then again, there was nothing I could do except looking at the waggling tail of the weird hemaby who was leading us.

By the time I was able to grasp the destination, my heart was panicked with horror by their intention. It was the home of light-devils, the deadly field of the game number two. The bright light in the distance was already atrociously tempting me again. I tapped Ugley's neck anxiously while pressing my bemused mind. However, it occurred to me that Ugley was determined to ignore whatsoever I argued. Sure enough, they entered the field (rather cheerfully) and halted in mid height from the center of the ground. The light sources were down below in the distance, but I had a strong suspicion that those hungry monstrous devils would come up to get us any second.

Now I kicked Ugley irritatingly to draw his attention. But once again, he only ignored me. I remembered how he had tried to save my life last time when I was out of the air supply. He had almost killed himself just to save me, jumping into the devil home to get one of those air-pockets.

No. He won't do anything silly. He knows too well about it.

I tried hard to convince myself, suppressing down the fear that constantly forced my mind from inside. It was the behavior of Ugley that kept me troubled; he came all the way from the graveyard without a single objection to his companion, and now he was highly spirited in his body expression.

Maybe these smart hemabies have a remarkable plan, I tried again, *which is nothing to do with light-devils.*

Really, I had already experienced light-devils more than enough to last in my memory for the rest of my life.

It appeared to me that they were waiting for something. Ugley and his friends were staring at the light for what seemed like hours. I was not sure what they waited for and why they stared so closely at the light down below. My only concern was the way they looked at the devil home. I was quite sure that their remarkable plan was really something to do with the light-devils, but there was nothing I could do. My stomach began to irritate.

And there was nothing I could think of, either, because they just started to dive into whatever the target. I looked down the target with a tiny bit of hope for anything other than the devils, but, surely they were heading straight toward the home of devils. My hairs started to stand, my skin changing its form, and my stomach twisting. After one last look at the target, I curved down my neck, my body glued as close as it could onto Ugley's back. I did not want to count how long it would take before my body being chopped up by the hungry demons. I just wanted to die before even knowing it.

Was there a dark spot on the ground? I asked to myself. It was something that I saw through like my mind eyes. Yes, there was, I considered. It was a dark spot right in the center of the lighted ground. It was certainly discernible, I decided. A tiny seed of hope started to grow in my mind. I settled on checking…before dying. I lifted up my head again, my eyes spontaneously moved toward the dark spot when we were already nearing the ground.

Wait! That's not a spot! I saw it now. It was blurry due to the surrounding light, but undoubtedly, it was like a hole or maybe a well. Now, the two hemabies folded their wings into their body tightly. I pressed my head to Ugley's back firmly again. Then, it all happened intriguingly in seconds.

The leader hemaby and Kittous dashed into the hole, followed by Ugley along with me. They dived gently and quietly, still fast. I expected light-devils to wrap up my whole body any second, but nothing happened yet. Then, somehow, I began to feel the fear inside fading away. I unbolted my eyes. I saw the fellow hemaby and Kittous moving down smoothly, and we were following them.

What the heck is going on? I questioned.

It can't be!

I looked around in disbelief. Then, a sharp chill came upon my back and froze my senses. *No, it really cannot be possible!*

It was not a well or a hole we were diving into. Unbelievably, we were passing right through the center of the home of hundreds of light-devils. I saw those nasty silver-colored demons lazily playing around in several spacious open caves. I perceived now hundreds of small holes on the ceiling of the caves. Each hole was packed with a number of devils which looked molten silver under the light coming from air-pockets above of them. They were spread around every spot in every direction, only except where we were passing by. It seemed that they did not even notice us at all.

Meanwhile, I was conscious that we were on a certain current flow running toward another dark hole down below. Yet, the light-devils were never aware of their big and health preys trespassing right in the center of their invulnerable territory.

The dark hole ahead of us was like a giant mouth which pulled us straight down. I felt instant fear, but my major concern was to get away from the devils ever peacefully. It would rather be safer once I entered the dark mouth-like hole.

In a moment I understood that the dark hole was only an exit from the demon home. The instant we were thrown into the hole, the current flow died away, and we were on a broad open space. I looked back almost instinctively at the passageway because I felt that some of the hungry demons followed us.

The experience with the current flow drew my attention back to our track once more. It was not a new phenomenon. I recognized it now. It was this current flow that took Ugley and me out of the passageway from the hidden dome. And it was near the home of light-devils... I looked around for any hint of familiarity, but I saw a broad span of a sea floor under dime light from the distance. And when my eyes returned back to the exit again, strangely what I saw was only a flat blank surface of something like a great wall of a sea valley. The mouth-like exit was gone without a tiny trace. Have we been discharged again from the excretory passage of the giant anemone? I wondered.

Maybe we were lucky enough again to be there, right on time.

Our two companions already set off to their next destination. Now I had an invincible desire to know where they were now directing after taking such a brave step. And if that was the only way to get into this place, it would be another world of wonder I had never been before. Surely, it had to be a new world.

Up ahead on our way I began to see bright light on the sea floor. And soon the area was bathed with brilliant light from thousands of air-pockets swaying cheerfully along with invisible current. I could not resist the temptation to pick one. I stretched my arm toward the dancing air-pockets, but the instant I felt them touching my fingers, I jerked my hand as if I touched the tip of a giant sea serpent's tongue. I only remembered light-devils that might be waiting for me behind the light with a gross smile.

Kittous must have observed me who was frightened by nothing but air-pockets. While keeping the distance with her fellow hemabies, she consciously tried to get close enough to air-pockets so that her body could touch them. Following Kittous, Ugley showed an effort to duplicate exactly what Kittous did. That was a good demonstration for me. Ugley was enjoying it. I could tell it from the way he moved his body, his wings half spread out, moving gently up and down, and his tail swaying along with air-pockets. Some of air-pockets were merrily patting my feet like they were trying to persuade me to enjoy it all. I stretched my arm again and snatched an air-pocket. I inhaled the fresh air out of the air-pocket as much as my lung could accommodate while my arms opened out like wings to imitate Ugley as much as I could.

My eyes and my soul returned to our way ahead now. The beautiful ocean world yet continued beyond my eye sight. While my eyes were captivated by the scene of a remarkable ocean world, my mind began to reason, if it was really anything to do with the present assignment; if it was really something to do with, the power scales which we urgently had to obtain, the power scales which would stop the monsters who have been threatening and killing innocent people like those petrified men and Ella... And I hoped, otherwise, at least it was anything to do with Ella's whereabouts.

Obviously, the monster had threatened Ella to obtain any information. And by now maybe, he figured out everything, and somehow they were already in the hidden dome... On the other hand, if Ella had told everything to the monster, there would be no reason for the monster to hang around the hidden dome.

Ella, have you already taken them to the center of the galaxy?

For every reason, I only hoped that they have gone to the hidden dome. If we would ever be able to get there, at least I would know, first, her whereabouts, and second, she had bravely bamboozled the monster with false information.

I only hoped she was still alive. *Hey, Ella, where are you now?*

Chapter 17
BACK TO THE SILVER CASTLE

Ugley seemed to know the way well now. His friend was behind, quietly following us. I completely lost sense of direction until we arrived in the valley of the giant anemones. And the minute seeing the anemones, I knew where we were, and I understood what Ugley and his comrades had planned. One way or another, Ugley's friend must have found the hidden path to this mysterious place. I could hardly imagine how the swarm of little fish had taken us here before.

Here we go again. I faced the anemones which were alluring us all with hundreds of hands waving softly. It was not new anymore, and of course, there was no reason for Ugley to wait for my signal at all. He dived in courageously. Passing through the damp gorge of the giant anemone, we were soon out into the hidden world under the dome again.

"Here we are again, buddy." I said joyously, patting Ugley's neck gently as if to show off our wondrous discovery to Kittous and our genius new teammate.

With mild light from the top, everything was quite the same. The silver castle in the distance stood silently. Remembering the puzzle game I did, now I almost convinced myself that the castle, which stood before me in the distance, was really the one I had completed. Such a peaceful and magnificent castle. I could hardly believe that the intriguing mysteries and the unbearable dangers were in there.

"Guys, we need to check around, first." I said nervously, my eyes yet surveying the castle in the distance.

If Ella really managed to come in, I would need to find a way of snatching her, I assured myself.

"I doubt anyone ever came, but one way or another, if anyone did, that's a good sign." I said anxiously.

"Kittous!" I called my little teammate who was gently flapping her wings, seriously scrutinizing the castle in a new world.

Then, I just realized that the name 'Kittous' was totally new to everyone, including Kittous herself.

"Uh, Ugley, my bad…" I apologized, soothing his neck. "Forgot to tell you."

My eyes shifting to the little hemaby, I said, "My dear teammate, I didn't get a chance to tell you… Kittous, that's what I decided to call you, if you don't mind…"

With this, wiggling his tail gently like a happy dog, Ugley sang out something that sounded really like Kit-to-us. The little hemaby replied in a soft voice, pulling out her neck toward Ugley as if to show gratitude to Ugley for saying, 'Nice name, Kittous.'

"Kittous, please, stick to Ugley, and don't get lost here." I asked, smiling.

And I carried the smile over to our new teammate.

"I really appreciate your help, buddy…" I faltered to ask a favor because of the memory of its abnormality at the launching hall.

"Look, I know you don't want," I said cautiously, remembering Chrom, "but I'm just wondering if you could do me a favor for a ride only this time."

The eyes of the hemaby looked complex. Was that fear or anxiety? I was not sure.

"I mean, only if anything happens..." I said tentatively, but I was pretty sure it understood.

"OK, everyone, please hide yourself somewhere...up there, maybe." I suggested to them, pointing to the ceiling which was covered with bubble balls.

"I will be off down there, Ugley, please."

Ugley swiftly raced toward the castle. As we approached to the castle, my eyes were busy to locate any indication of Ella or the monstrous figure. It would be technically impossible for them to know the trail, I decided. Besides, there was a very little chance for them to have another key of silver scale. I climbed down smoothly in front of the gate and waited until all my teammates were out of sight. I refreshed the air in my lung and inserted the silver scale into the slit. The gate cracked open for me.

Here I come again.

The bright hall and the stairs came into view, but no sign of any moving figures. Upstairs were also clear without any trace of anyone. Even the small silver castle which I had built out of the puzzle pieces was not there. The whole castle was empty. I confirmed. Obviously, they could not make it. No, maybe they did not even consider coming here at all. That would make a huge difference. Now, the chances were, Ella had told them everything and they now figured out the location of the power scales... I began to feel bad.

"Ella, where are you now?" I cried worriedly.

I could not avoid a lump coming up to my throat by the thought of a looming threat. I swallowed. They must have found the power scales by now. I could already feel their contemptuous laughter.

I went downstairs quietly, my mind fighting back with growing anxiety. Just then, there was a sudden crack at the door, and accordingly, the door opened before me. And I immediately spotted a number of figures, standing right in front of me.

"Ryan!" Shouted Ella, her face reddened, bearing a thin smile, behind which I could feel full of horror.

I was so happy to see her, first, alive, and second, right here. However, I could not have a chance to ask her anything.

"Aha! Our hero is already here! Well, well, well, Ryan!"

To my surprise it was the king, his face full of glorious cheers, standing behind Ella. And beside him was a man who I have never met in person before, but I guessed who he was right away.

"Ella and our security guard informed me everything about your discovery," said the king thankfully, looking around the scenery of the inner dome, "including this amazingly magnificent new world."

"To be honest with you, Ryan, I doubted your story when I first heard. Existence of another world like this! Who would have ever guessed, otherwise?" He clapped his hands.

"May I?"

I stepped aside for him, still at a loss, trying to understand the situation.

"Well, I can't thank you enough for your discovery, Ryan. Of course, the same for Ella's brother. Without Laxan we could just linger away a thousand years around the home of light-devils. Certainly, we can have a good celebration for three of you. Yes, I will see to it." said the king contentedly, entering the castle.

The king's two eyes were yet taken, traveling around. Ella's eyes followed mostly on the face of the king. Her face was now so pale.

Has she been threatened by...the king? No way!

The king was little of my concern at the moment. Somehow, I had a bad feeling about the man introduced as a guard. How could he suddenly disappear? And here he came again. Was she lucky enough to escape from the shark monster with the help of the guard? I questioned. I stole a few glances at the man's face and then Ella's for any clue. There was only one thing I could tell from Ella. She looked extremely nervous with both the king and the man. And under the circumstance, I reckoned there was no way for her to tell me her story, not to mention her brother's. Then, another question arose. *Laxan... Has he been really working for the king to find the hidden passage?*

"So, Laxan helped you, sir, Your Highness..." I asked cautiously.

"The brilliant boy, yes, he did. I have been looking for our precious treasure, the atlas of the castle, ever since it was stolen by a little mouse many years ago. But, one day, this boy had found it for us splendidly, and the next day he discovered the hidden passage just like that," exclaimed the king cheerfully. "So, tell me your story, Ryan. I can't compare anything with yours now, can I?" added the king brightly.

"Actually, I was on my way to update my discovery with you." I began now. Of course, I could not tell the rest as it had happened. "Then I thought you would want something more confirmative rather than another mystery, sir."

Now I had to make up a reason why I had come back here without mentioning Ella.

"And you found something more confirmative?" demanded the king, rather softly, like talking to a close friend, his eyes still wandering around.

I was not sure he was enjoying the wall full of pure silver or looking for something more attractive or valuable.

"Not much, hitherto, sir…" I attempted, but it only sounded stupid. "But, since you are here, I can review everything with you now…including the thing that had almost killed me." I was thinking about the jigsaw puzzle.

"Ha!" exclaimed the king, his eyes were away, yet he was listening.

"Nonsense! I wouldn't believe anything can kill a smart boy like you, Ryan."

He grimaced in disbelief, his expression altering more or less sarcastic. My eyes glimpsed Ella's still nervous-looking face once more. Her constant abnormal behavior commenced to trouble me.

"If you remember, sir," I began calmly, ignoring his doubt, "I told you that I had happened to know the history of the castle, sir."

I looked at his eyes momentarily, expecting a positive response. His dark brown irises were shimmering with a hidden joy. I remembered when I had first faced him I had a good impression on him with his pitch black eyes, energetic, but soft enough to attract me like an old friend at once. Now suddenly, I was confused with his eyes. *Were they brown or black?*

"Yes, yes, of course, and the power silver scales, which, as I told you then, are the only reason why we are here," said the king cheerfully, "and they should be near, I definitely feel it now."

Evidently the king was only interested in the silver scales; maybe, only the power he was after.

"So, what is everything that you wanted to show me, Ryan? The final key or a power map or something like that you wanted to share?"

"Actually," I went on, pointing to the silver wall, "I will need to explain the wall, sir. I mean the silver metal bricks which shaped like jigsaw puzzle pieces, if you haven't noticed."

"Jigsaw puzzle? Ah, that's the game you played?" asked the king. Certainly he looked confused with the puzzle.

"Well, sort of, but I am not there yet, sir." I said.

"They are the silver metal bricks. I believe, there are a thousand pieces in total to make this castle wall and everything. Yes, the game, or the clue, if you like, is hidden right in one of these thousand pieces." I explained plainly now.

"Somehow, I was lucky enough to figure that out by counting, sir." Stepping toward the gate, I continued, "If you excuse me, sir." And pointing to the very first brick by the gate, I added, "I started from there…, sir."

I spotted the note on the very first brick at once. The engraved words were nearly unnoticed on the silver surface, but they stood up like a warning banner in red light for me. And the last sentence aggravated my throbbing heart again.

It is not intended, however, that any human possesses all the scales. Peace remains only when it is controlled or never.

It was thoughtful and rightful, but I doubted it was the same to the king at all. I could tell how badly he wanted the power scales now. And I could feel that he would crave the absolute power whatever the cost.

There is no difference between the bad guys up there and the good guy down in the castle. Ruth was right.

"Sir," I cautiously pulled out a question for him, "you have some of such power scales?" I began to feel nervous again.

"Yes, I do have some, but that's nothing or useless without the remainders." The king smirked awkwardly with his answer.

"So, that's three-hundred sixty-five…, and the remainders are somewhere up…" I said pensively, like I was there alone.

Yes, somewhere up there… I remembered the brightest bubble ball up on the ceiling of the dome, which was only visible when the puzzle was complete. My eyes met Ella's for the first time since she came in, and I sent a barely visible smile, hoping she could find any seconds to relax. She must have told nothing much useful to this half haunted man for sure.

"Somewhere up there, Ryan. That's what we already know," said the king on my behalf. "You are making me confused." His voice was softly, but I could feel irritation in his tone.

"Indeed, he is," said the guard who stood beside Ella, looking awfully annoyed rather than confused. He unlocked his big mouth as if to yelling at me, but closed without a single word as soon as his eyes met the king's.

"You are going to tell me about your new discovery, I believe," insisted the king, trying to be very calm and gentle.

His soft voice only made me confirm that he would do anything to get the power.

"Oh, I am terribly sorry, sir. I must be out of my mind. Yes, the clue –."

"What is it?" asked the king impatiently this time.

"I am sorry, sir, but I must finish this puzzle in order to show you that."

Stopping there briefly, I checked his expression. I could tell he was trying hard, yet barely visibly. I turned to the cold silver brick wall.

"I was, sort of, silly to have an idea of counting the whole bricks one by one, but after all, I was lucky enough to find the one that contained the puzzle game."

I looked at Ella this time to sand a quick thank-you smile, but unable to do so. I felt king's awfully cold stare from the corner of my eyes.

"635th brick!" I exclaimed, sounding highly self-esteemed.

"That puzzle thing is in there?" asked the king annoyingly now.

"Yes, right in the chest box, sir. And you wouldn't believe that this is a deadly game."

"You are saying, if you win the game, you will get the clue or something?"

"Yes, sort of. An awesome thing up on the ceiling of the dome outside, but I did not dare to go and find out, sir. I deemed that there must be something remarkable or so compelling, but I was very scared." I explained convincingly.

I saw now that the king's eyes were flickered in delight.

"But again, if you fail, you lose both, the game and your life, sir."

I said apprehensively. But, it was nothing to worry about for the king. Instead, his face was now filled with visible exhilaration.

"Well, what are we waiting for? It is a piece of cake for you, my dear."

"This way, please, sir." I directed them toward the stairs, and to the second level.

The brick containing the chest box came into view, but I turned my head around the wall, like I was there for the first time and amazed by the silver wall. I needed some time to think now.

If I ever find the power scales before the king... I chewed over once.

Can I use the power? I only doubted.

For a good or bad will, eventually the king might be the only one to deal with it. Now the king came too far, and there was no way of concealing the inklings. The minute I would complete the puzzle, the king would get the picture of the bright bubble ball in a spiral... My mind ached again.

Can he really comprehend everything just with that? A tiny bit of hope arose.

No, he will be still in the dark unless one of us telling him about the meaning.

I considered once, but it was only a strained assumption for a knowledgeable and intelligent king like him who has hungered for the silver scales so long.

I attempted to have an eye contact with Ella for any hint of her intention, but her eyes were elsewhere, unfocussed.

Ryan, go for it! The positive side of my mind yelled at me.

Trust Ella and dupe the king!

"Sir, I am pretty sure it is one of these bricks here." I said confidently, while indicating the bricks nearby.

"If you, please, sir, don't mind, I have to count the bricks from the first one. I just don't want to guess here. Maybe, some crucial tricks, you never know."

"Well, go ahead," replied the king rather pleasingly.

Of course, it would not bother him at all. Waiting for a few minutes or even hours would be nothing but a pleasure for him before the victory of a battle which he has suffered for countless years.

I counted from the first brick to the one containing the chest box. All along the time he was merely a good and quiet observant. And ultimately, when I brought out the chest box in front of him, he could not hide his expression, or maybe he did not need to.

"Indeed!" snorted the king only when he saw the warning.

"Do not dare to open it unless…. Be prepared before you do it…"

"Sir, the gate will be bolted when I open this box, and I only have –."

"Time to fix. I see that. We will wait outside then," said the king idly, giving an eye signal to the man who gently tapped Ella's shoulder.

"Excuse me, sir. If Ella stays here with me…?"

I knew he would not let her, but I just asked, anyway.

"I can't let you take a risk with that. No." His voice was confirmative and cold. "But, once you have that done, I may let her in," added the king, sounding very generous.

I was excited with his words, but the excitement lasted only for barely a second. I found no reason why he would let her in and see me unless he wanted me to be exactly like horrorstruck Ella. Now I instigated to see the dangerous game he was playing with me. And it occurred to me that he comprehended that the game was absolutely in his favor. Then it was not a game, anymore.

I heard him saying hurry-up before disappearing behind the gate, giving the sweltering pressure on me. I sat quite tranquil, fear surging through my body. My eyes fixed on the chest in front of me unopened, my mind listening the uptight thumping of my heart. I tried to revenge my frightened mind with the courage within.

Three times with this game already and why I have to feel so much pressure?

"Ryan, just do it!"

Yes, I will.

"And as soon as Ella comes in, run away!"

Yes, I will.

I could smile tentatively with that.

Ugley, what is up to you now?

If he could only be here when I would need…

Here I am again. I breathed deeply in and packed the given air into my lung as much as possible, and I opened the lid of the puzzle box...

Did I have enough air in me?

I did not feel too much strain in my chest until the last piece was placed onto the miniature castle. And the roof above was, at last, slid open, retrieving tons of delicious air and fresh light. The gate must have been opened by now because I heard Ella calling me out.

"Ryan!" Her voice sounded urgent and desperate.

I managed to stand on my feet, looking at the way up the stairs where the light coming from.

"Ryan!" She called me again, anxiously, her voice horrified.

I could see her coming up the stairs, but I did not answer. My mind was with only one thing.

Ugley, where are you?

I just hoped that, he could hear me, and he could come and bus us right away out of this place. Now Ella came beside me, trying to help me moving up the stairs.

"Are you all right, Ryan? Are you? I am so sorry, Ryan, terribly sorry. It all happened because of me."

I could see her eyes welled up with tears.

"My brother..."

Tears rolled out of the pinky corners of her marble eyes.

"We must hurry up, Ryan," said Ella restlessly, stealing the tears swiftly with her sleeve.

I knew what she was going to say. They would lock us here in a worse case, I thought. But her words were much worse than that. In fact, they were the worst ever since I came to this land.

"They will kill us all. They are these…these evil monsters, Ryan! The king and the guard, they are all fakes. They said they would save my brother if I helped them…, but now I don't believe a thing. .They must have killed him already and they will kill us all!"

Her voice trembled with unstoppable horror. She was at least able to say something, but I was not. If I ever had a word out of my mouth, it would have been the worst. I could hardly believe it all. He deceived me just like that. Not only me, but all the nation has been under the spell of the malicious monster. And now we were all in great danger. I pulled Ella's hand hurriedly to the porch where the sparkling bubble ball was visible in the center of the universe. And there, I spotted two monstrous creatures vivaciously flying up toward it. I dropped my jaws instantly by the sight.

"They really are…" I said, but I lost words to follow.

"Ryan, Ugley!"

I immediately turned to the other side of the bubble ball clusters where Ella was pointing. Yes, there were the boy and the girl! With our new teammate they were flying toward us lively now.

"Listen, Ella. We must hurry to get out of this place. They will come right after us in furious disappointment," I said nervously, my eyes still following the evil monsters.

"I will go straight to find the silver scales. You should go back to the castle right away and inform them. And you should find a safer place as soon as possible for now."

The monsters were now waned behind the light of the bubble balls. I turned my attention to the forever-life-saver who just came beside me along with Kittous.

"Ugley! What took you so long?" I complained delightedly. "And you, too." I added, casting a glance briefly at Kittous who looked rather nervous.

"Oh, Ella, this is my teammate, Kittous, and that's our new teammate who will take you home...safely." I said to the hemaby, beaming with the last word as if to make sure what I really meant. "I will save my sincere thanks for later, buddy." I added.

But Ella was not listening. Covering her mouth with her hands, she stood there petrified by the sight of Kittous. Her marble eyes were blank as though they were hypnotized by an invisible power from Kittous.

"For real..." Her voice was barely audible. "Never seen for real," mumbled Ella.

"Come on, Ella!" I yelled at her, hopping on Ugley's back.

Ella climbed on the back of the hemaby awkwardly, her eyes yet stealing the sight of Kittous. Now as her hemaby set off to follow us, Ella petted her hemaby's neck gently as a thank-you gesture. Then, we shot straight toward the exit.

In the meantime, I looked back at the ceiling to check the situation of the monsters. To my surprise, I saw a big fighting scene up there near the bubble ball clusters. There was a huge figure shaped like a giant troll, fighting furiously with two evil monsters. I gaped for a few seconds, wondering what the ally was. It was only like a dark cloud, but one thing for sure was that its body was glittered with the light from the bubble balls.

"Is that...the swarm of little flying fish?"

Chapter 18
SURVIVAL GAME

At last, bubble ball forest was in view again. They looked ever gloriously gleaming now.

"Ugley, we are almost there!" I cried out loud.

Now I could see layers and groups for sure. If I did not know that all, I had been only a lost child long ago and never able to find even the first clue.

Thanks to Ugley. You are such a dedicated teammate.

Still, I could not believe what had happened in the last hours back in the hidden dome. *Such a dangerous game...* It was almost over. For sure the king could have killed Ella and me without any merciful traces. Then, holding the remaining silver scales in his hands, he could have returned back to the castle with his symbolic friendly smile as if to show that it was nothing but a blissful excursion. Furthermore, his piteous torturing, peaceful threatening, and mysterious killing could continue inevitably as an extended part of his amusing game.

Maybe on any special occasion when he has visitors, he eagerly tells his creepy fairy tale to every one of them as a sarcastic part of his subtle joy.

I tapped Ugley's neck gently in appreciation.

Yes, Ugley, you deserve all the glorious power scales. You can mount them all on your skin to decorate yourself and protect your wonderful spirit from the evil will.

Now amongst bubble balls, I could almost see a beautiful hemaby with a thousand silver scales all around the body. No ugly Ugley anymore... I sighed. I wondered if it would ever be possible in reality.

Ugley raced straight up layers over layers without hesitation. When we were passing through around ten or more layers, unexpectedly, he reduced the speed dramatically. At first I thought we were already nearing the location without realizing it, but when I looked around, it was strangely eerie. Unambiguously the bubble balls in the surrounding looked all twisted. It was maybe because of the silence in the area, I deemed. But it did not seem right. Then, I considered that we were already thrown into a deep bubble ball forest. But then, I changed my mind. There was no reason why a sensible hemaby like Ugley would go that far in this urgent situation.

I could feel Ugley's back neck turned very stiff, his eyes very tense now, engaged in scrutinizing through the bubble balls ahead. My stomach started churning. Ugley now wagged his dorsal fins gently, which I took as a warning. Then, I heard a deafening sound from somewhere.

"THERE YOU ARE!"

The instant I heard the voice, I felt an electric shock through my artery. Ugley immediately turned around to face the man of the voice. There unmistakably stood two horrendous monsters. Obviously now, I could tell that one of them was the flying shark called Ripper. Then, I presumed right away that the other one was his lord called Harfhas, or Safrah, whichever correct now did not matter.

It was quite difficult to describe the precise figure of Safrah as he shifted from one form to another every now and then. With a mane, a tail and four legs, apparently he was a lion. But with a pair of wings of an eagle, a broad face of a human, and gills of a shark, he was a spine-chilling monster. In addition, his light brown tail was very thick and long, and his solid brown legs were like human legs and arms with thick and long webbed toes and fingers. His mane with extremely thick, and its pointy hairs ran down to his tail. His chest and abdomen were sparkly with silver scales mounted on a dark brown vest.

"Well, well, well, my little guest! You tricked me very nicely. NO ONE ever did that to me before, I should tell," said Safrah bitterly, but with a nasty sneer curving around his big mouth.

"Well, what is done is done. In appreciation of your hard work, and no difference for me to leave your breath a little longer, especially when I know where the power scales are after all your effort."

His big mouth turned into a mean smile.

"But I believe it was way long for you to enjoy your rides."

Then he turned his interest to Ugley.

"How clever!" exclaimed Safrah, chuckling, his eyes shifting to Ripper as if to say, 'He is clever than you, Ripper.'

"Well, who would have guessed he was this cute and smart, Ripper? See my dear hemaby here, isn't he fascinating with one scale from my generosity?" He sniggered momentarily.

"Hilarious! Like his father for sure," exclaimed Safrah.

"Fancy that! In spite of your elaborate work, Your Highness, he certainly outsmarted to find a rider, indeed," hissed Ripper, looking thoroughly at me.

Stupid! I should have known that he was the nasty monster when I first saw him at the dome. Then I could have found a way of locking him and his lord there for good.

"Well, of course, without him, you wouldn't be here happily, Ripper. Probably you would be killing your precious time with those dumb riders, forever," said Safrah sarcastically.

"And now, you certainly came help us out one last time, I am sure." Safrah, the monster was playing with me now just like Safrah, the king.

"Yes, my lord, they came up to steal our silver scales."

"Shut up! You fool. They are MINE!" snapped Safrah, failing to defeat his anger. Turning his head toward us, he shouted in an angry voice, whipping his long tail.

"HOW DARE!"

That was more likely as an atrocious monster. My heart seemed now balancing the courage over the fear well enough.

"Do you think you will be OK after fooling me?" cried Safrah, his voice playful again.

"Allow me, my lord, please!" interrupted Ripper with a big fake smile.

"Well, you have my permission," granted Safrah proudly, casting a quick slant.

"BUT, don't you ever damage the scale!"

"As you wish, my lord," cried Ripper, and turning toward us, he hissed, "and as you wish, you, little fox!"

Ripper breathed briefly once and yowled grossly. Ugley sensed an attack at once and gave a warning scream. Right then, Ripper spat out a large amount of viscous liquid like a glue fall, if there was. Ugley made a sharp turn and managed to escape from the sticky fall.

"YOU, MORON! Can't you even finish the meal on your plate?"

Annoyance came up nearly to the top of his head, Safrah yelled at Ripper. "GET OUT of my way at once!"

I noticed now that Safrah's hairs started to erect straight like a porcupine's. He grabbed some of his dark straight hairs with one of his enormous hands. The hairs in his hand stood up even straight like a bundle of spiky long nails. Then, he threw them toward us with a thundering roar. They were indeed a huge bundle of arrows, aimed at us with a sizzling blue flame out of his mouth. However, Ugley was faster. He made a quick move down and ran off from the attack.

"WHAT? I never miss my targets! After them!"

We were already out of the site when Ripper started to chase us. But then, before I breathed a sigh of relief, Safrah unpredictably showed up in front of us again. Ugley sensed the danger and changed the courses at once. By that moment, I felt his powerful tail wildly sweeping by, passing right beside us. In a flash Safrah spat a dry red flame over us with a rowdy sound. It missed us only by inches. The bubble balls around us erupted violently. Now, Ugley quickly changed the directions one more time. Then, he dived straight down through the layers of bubble balls.

Soon, we ran off from the boundary of bubble ball clouds, and in the distance the land and the ocean were visible. In a little while, the castle was nearing, but behind us was a big laughter of Safrah. He was yet chasing us fast.

Now Ugley was heading toward the water. I heard Safrah yelling from my back.

"Ha ha! Caring move, you little fox!" His voice was gross with sneering.

"Dive into the water and save the castle! You think I will appreciate it? You think your hide and seek will work? I will burn your ass before you hide!"

"Hey, what's going on, buddy? Hey, Ugley!" I shouted to Ugley in perplexity.

"To the galaxy! Ugley, I am not –." But it was already too late.

"Whoa!"

There was a big splash that smashed me on the face. I only managed to hold one of his dorsal fins. With difficulty I climbed up on his back again.

Ugley was yet fast in the water. I held the dorsal fins as hard as possible, hoping to turn into part of his body, my eyes constantly checking the chaser. There came Safrah again with another bundle of spiky arrows in his hand.

I quickly slapped Ugley's back as a warning. Then he quickly moved down and let the attack pass by. That was very close.

"NO! Not again!"

His silent scream transmitted from his furious face to my eardrums. His anger loaded up ever high. This time, Safrah smashed a mass of rocks on his way with his long compelling tail. In just a moment, hundreds of sundry rocks were scattered all over the area. A big turbulence of dusty water swiftly covered us and our way, even before I could give another alert to Ugley.

The rocks flew every direction in the dusty water. I held myself on the back of Ugley as close as possible. But, not so long did I feel something strike Ugley on the head, causing him to jerk stridently down to the floor. This eventually set me off out of control, slipping away from his back. Then, I could not find Ugley in such a surrounding with dusty particles and foams. I searched for an air-pocket ineffectively. I rushed up to the surface.

It was so quiet and peaceful to make me feel even worse on the surface. *Ugley must be dead by the attack. Poor thing.* A guilty feeling emerged in my mind morosely. Worries grew helplessly. *I have to go and check.* After a deep breath, I submerged my head to view underwater. But, as far as I could see, there was no sign of Ugley. Instead, I just noted that Safrah was fast approaching to me, waggling his long tail gently, his bulging eyes fixed on me. No time to think now. I strived to swim away as fast as possible from his reach. But, it was only a stupid attempt. Now, when I was nearly within his grip, I heard a voice of an angel from heaven.

"Ryan! Quick!"

It was Ella on her hemaby, trying to reach me with her hand. I managed to seize her hand while her hemaby pulling me out of the water. Now, Safrah just missed the target, but he did not hurry at all; he did not even yell at me this time. Apparently, there was nothing for him to be embarrassed about. He looked much relaxed, lazily gazing at the target who was frantically trying to run away from him. Maybe he already knew that I would not make it in the end. With loud flutters, the hemaby worked hard to fly up, dragging me above the surface, but soon, my hand slipped off Ella's grip, and I fell back into the water helplessly.

Meanwhile, up in the sky there was a rescue team arriving in the battle field. The riders must have come to know my own version of the fairy tale, entitled 'Silver Castle and the Two Nasty Monsters.' Knowing that these ogres were responsible for all the tricks and the missing friends, they had turned into the brave knights of Ella's rescue team. Instead of bubble balls in their hands, they all had various weapons of their own choices such as swords and spears. Now, they were swooping down toward us fearlessly, but they were almost like chasing Ripper who was ahead of them.

Seeing Ripper coming along with the rescue team, Safrah frowned at Ripper disapprovingly.

"RIPPER! Can't you see what you are bringing here, you stupid!" shouted Safrah crossly. "Clean it up at once!"

"Ooookey, right away, my lord!" replied the shark man, turning toward the rescue team behind.

Then, after a deep breath he blew out spiteful glue all the way toward the riders.

"Watch out!" I shouted in alarm as soon as I saw Ripper packing air in his lung.

"Attack!" Ruth shouted immediately after my warning.

They swiftly turned their ways all at once. No one was affected by the attack. Ripper yowled loudly in disappointment. They were too faster for Ripper; they were skillful riders in the sky whereas Ripper was not a bird, nor a hemaby.

As the group soared up, Ripper chased after them, howling hysterically. Then it was the knights' turn to attack the evil foe.

"NOW!" Ruth's voice rumbled the surrounding loudly.

By that, all the riders turned around like acrobats to the chaser, and all at once they threw darts to him. Ripper abruptly turned around, but it was a bit late to escape from more than twenty darts aimed at him. Some of the metal pieces unmistakably went through his skin. Ripper seethed with anger and anguish, moving sideway. I was quite impressed by the maneuver of my ally, forgetting my situation facing the cruelest monster in a few yards.

The riders celebrated themselves with yahoos for a moment until Ella and I shouted out a warning at the same time.

"LOOK OUT!"

Now it was Safrah who silently took off and soared up to the riders. He pulled out a huge bundle of arrows from his mane and threw them to the group. At the same time, he opened his mouth about half and blew out sizzling blue flames to cook them down. All the riders were confused for the moment, like they have forgotten their next plan.

"Left!" shouted Ruth, pointing to his left.

A few of them could not make it on time, falling down into the water, wailing horribly with pain. In a jiffy, there was another attack of burning flames right upon their way to the left.

"Flame!" someone shouted in panic.

"Everyone, back off!" It was Ruth again.

Many of them caught fire now, racing down to the water for an emergency landing. Only a few were able to manage to get away from the attack. They tried to soar up to the sky. But, Ripper was now above them, groaning heavily with steaming hot air as if to show that he waited so long for the moment to come. His whole body was shimmering with streaming blood and the darts mounted deeply into the skin. But it did not seem to bother him at all. After licking a mean smile for half a second, he poured a bucket of buttery mucus over the troop without much trouble or effort. It was only a few seconds before all those remaining riders were petrified and fell down into the water like dead leaves. In the end, they only ended up bestowing hilarious smiles on the two evil monsters.

"What the heck!" I shouted, gaping at the sight in horror.

"Ryan!" shouted Ella, coming within reach of me once more.

"Hurry!"

I grabbed her hand again and tried to climb on her hemaby. Now Ripper was already on the way to us, inhaling deeply, getting ready for another spiteful strike.

"Quick!" Ella shouted again.

I was not completely on its back, but the hemaby in horror flew up with an instant flapping on the water, causing a big splash. Consequently, my hands slipped off the hemaby's fins, and I fell back into the water again while Ella and her hemaby flew away before the attack of the vicious mucus.

It was only an amusing game for Safrah. Now he turned his full attention to me. His wide lips curved into a hideous smile by the sight of a horrified boy like a cornered mouse shaking in fear. No mercy and no hope. He drew near to me, but very slowly as if to try to enjoy the view of a little prey who was about to depart this life in any second.

"You still don't know where the silver scales are!" I shouted, hoping this could be any help.

In fact, I even wanted to take him to the location if I could only save my dear life at present. My heart thumping was even stronger than my voice now and faster than my senses. It sped up fast by every inch of the unavoidable approach of the monster. While looking around for any chance to escape, I shouted again frenetically.

"Yes. I know the exact location and, and I am not interested in such things!"

"Is that right?" Safrah chuckled, gently letting himself down on the water. As he relaxed without any possible danger, his wings folded in and disappeared into his body.

"Seriously, I can take you there and, and I will be gone right away. I will be out of Bubble Land. I mean, without a single piece of the silver scales, I mean, YOUR silver scales."

My voice was shaking. I understood that I only had a very little chance to make myself disappear into my own world for real.

"That sounds not a bad deal, don't you think so, Ripper?" said Safrah to Ripper who just landed on the water gently beside him.

"Yes, indeed, my lord," said Ripper calmly.

With the injuries around, Ripper's whole body was still bloody, but Safrah or even Riper himself did not care much about it. Maybe both are yet too excited to see the power with no limit, which was ever close to them now.

"Well, that is a good deal, but not enough for me," said Safrah.

"Besides, I already know where the scales are." He added proudly, his eyes turning to Ripper as if to expect words of admiration from Ripper.

"Isn't it strange if I don't know the location of my own scales, Ripper?"

"Indeed, my lord," said Ripper with a big smile, "and if you please allow me?"

Suddenly my blood vessel turned upside down, and my stomach churned vigorously.

"No, not this one, I can't let you do it," said Safrah resolutely.

"I want to let him see me with the world in my hand. And a small fish would do better than a fossilized boy for that. Yes, I will do that."

"Yes, indeed, my lord. You can make a perfect little hemaby this time, and forget about your mistake with that little mouse," said Ripper jubilantly.

"It was an ACCIDENT, not a mistake!" snapped Safrah at once. "I told you many times, you fool!" His voice sounded very angry, but his expression appeared opposite.

Now staring into my eyes, he curved his mouth into a mean vicious smile. And in few seconds, the smile turned into a horrible sneer as his mouth grew bigger. I felt myself already half dead when I saw his unbelievably big greasy mouth so close. I only had to look at his eyes, looking for a mercy by any chance. But they looked as cold as frozen air. There was no more hope left...

Ugley, are you still alive?

Chapter 19
SEARCHING FOR THE HOPE

However, my hope and I were not done yet. This time an angel came from down below the ocean depth, probably sent by the Goddess. While I was waiting for Safrah's final decision hopelessly, something abruptly came out of the water and took me up to the sky. It just happened in a flash right in front of Safrah. Until I was taken away from his jaws, I kept looking at his awful face, my heart still thumping in fears.

It was the most pleasant surprise ever happened to me in my entire life. It was an unexplainable feeling when fear out of the blue turned into thrill. I never thought fear was that close to thrill. It all happened so suddenly, and I did not have a moment yet to think about the surprise-maker. Then I immediately knew, who that was, who brought my hope back.

"HOLY! You survived, Ugley!"

A sudden explosion of the energy bomb out of my energized body must have blown off countless numbers of bubble balls up in the sky for sure. You would not believe how gorgeous Ugley had looked at the moment. The most glorious save!

Safrah, in displeasure, shouted loud to Ripper who seemed irresistibly amazed by the scene, his mouth yet remained open wide.

"AFTER HIM, you stupid!"

Ripper quickly turned to us and chased along with Safrah. Soon, they both were fast approaching us. For a moment I thought they were so fast to get closer and closer to us, but in fact, it was Ugley who slowed gradually. It immediately came to my attention without knowing the reason.

"Hey, Ugley, what's going on?" I urgently demanded, trying to read his thought.

Definitely, Ugley was slowing down on purpose. Now, pulling out his head toward the castle, Ugley shrieked sharply. I shot a glance at the direction carelessly, my mind still in annoyance. Then, I spied something flying toward us. There was no mistaking of what I saw. That was our little teammate, Kittous, racing fast to us.

"Kittous!" I yelled in excitement which then turned into fear promptly with the view of even closer chasers.

"To Kittous, Ugley!" I shouted, pointing to Kittous.

Ugley sped up to Kittous. Shortly, Kittous was nearing, and I stretched my arm as far as I could to catch her with my hand. There was something dangling in her mouth, I just noticed now. And I instinctively knew what they were. In the next seconds, before even I grasped her, Kittous quickly jumped over my hand, and perched on Ugley's back in front of me. Then, she was transformed into her usual peculiar little cat at once. Momentarily, I felt weird, but I had to cuddle her to secure as Ugley turned, resuming his direction up to bubble ball clouds.

At that moment Ugley screamed sharply as if to call us out for a warning. Kittous turned her head around and handed over a small jar with a letter S on it. It was one of the two jars connected each other with a short string; a jar containing black chunks with a letter S, and another jar, red chunks with a letter R. They were originally delivered to me by Kittous a while ago. But without knowing what to do I had just left them on the table in my room. And here came Kittous again for the delivery. Now, she was even taking a risk of her life, which was yet an enigma for me.

I quickly grabbed the jar with black chunks in it. My impulsive thought told me that if it meant to be used in this vital situation, it could be some kind of chunk bomb for the chasers. *But, what should I do with it? Maybe I just open it in front of them.* I considered. Apparently Safrah was faster and soon he might throw some arrow stuff or flame.

OK, this is for you, Safrah. I decided now.

"Ugley, slow down now!" I requested with an urgent hope to be helpful.

"Come on, you gross monster!" I hissed, my eyes constantly checking the fast approaching Safrah.

"There!" I called out, opening the black jar toward him at once, hoping it would clean the whole sky.

The black chunks instantly dispersed, scattering like an explosion right in front of Safrah.

"Down!" I yelled like a commander, yet holding Kittous tight.

Ugley shifted the courses quickly. An easy job for him. He was certainly capable of reading my thought now.

That was such a surprising and unexpected way of attack. Safrah almost went through this unknown dark cloud, yet he was quick enough to change his ways before getting into it. However, shortly after, he came upon viewing problems and losing the sense of direction, shaking his head frantically as if to remove the clouds of another swarm of maddening, this time, black flies. Then he turned around, up and down with a deafening roar in annoyance.

Ripper, however, with his injury, was not able to make a quick move. Instead, he tried to blow away with the wind out of his mouth at once. Meanwhile, Ugley quickly moved down below Ripper who had an instant vision problem with the particles, constantly blinking and occasionally closing his eyes. I looked at the eyes of Ugley and noticed his intension of approaching Ripper that way. Right then, Kittous forwarded the remaining jar containing red chunks with a letter S on it. Now, I had to be ready for Ripper with it. Then, there came a chance.

"Now!" I hissed, opening the red jar quickly toward Ripper.

"There!" I exclaimed. *R for Ripper!*

Ugley swiftly budged down to get away from him. Ripper, without knowing it, in order to make a big blow, inhaled the surrounding red air deeply. Until his lung was full of such air, he did not realize that something was totally wrong. Now, nothing could be under control from the very moment. Losing all senses, he began to sneeze out his precious mucus through his mouth and nose, chaotically. Then, his eyes bolted shut, he spat out a large amount of sticky glue over himself almost automatically, nonstop, covering up his whole body like laminating himself. In just a minute or so, he was wrapped up totally with his own glue, and now he was not even able to move freely with his wings frozen. Only his mouth stayed alive. Until then, he constantly generated sticky glue to cover up the rest of his body. Eventually, he was like a ball, a big ugly-looking ball which was decorated well with black and red glittering sprinkles. Then, the ball in a lifeless form, span around and fell down all the way into the ocean without much resistance.

In the mean time, his lord looked okay now with the situation under control, except for the vision which he was still struggling for recovery.

"Now, Hurry up, Ugley!" I requested quietly, looking up at the bubble ball layers in the distance.

Ugley flew as fast as his wings could carry us, and soon, we were back in layers of bubble balls again. He kept on moving up ahead without even a stop for a glance at anything. And after a while, he halted at the sight of a cluster of bubble balls. He studied a bit and slowly advanced to them with caution as if to avoid disturbing their peaceful sleep.

By then, I tried to identify the spiral geometry of the bubble balls in the layer, but it was too ambiguous. We were too close to see the whole picture of the geometry, I supposed. The only thing I could do was watching the way on which Ugley was determined to proceed, and occasionally looking back to check if the evil monster was after us again.

Ugley was so engrossed in observing the scene ahead. He stopped without even a small flipping sound. For a moment I wondered if he was lost, because I only saw plain bubble balls along the way. As he looked so serious for any reason, I reexamined the groups of bubble balls on our way with intent. Then, my eyes grew big and bright. My mind was awestruck in no time by the sight of the bubble balls that lined up to the center of a spiral. The geometry was vague in the distance, but as we were near to the center where the spiral was smaller, it was clear to read. Unquestionably I would have missed it, if Ugley did not stop for it.

"Ugley..." I muttered.

I looked at his eyes, but they were firm onto the center area, like they were attached to it. With gentle flapping Ugley pushed himself forward slowly, his eyes still straight on the destination. As we approached to the center, I virtually felt a magnetic field that pulled us toward the spiral center.

Finally, we are right in the heart of the galaxy!

In a tick, however, I realized that the bubble ball in the center was neither shiny nor beautiful

It can't be. I frowned in disenchantment at the sight. Under the dome we had seen the brightest ball in the galaxy. On the display of the gallery we had witnessed a distinctive bubble ball in the center of a spiral way. And that was what I expected to see at the end of the day.

"Ugley, but, that is not what we expected to see, right? Kittous?" I asked stupidly in sympathy.

My imagination with the power silver scales began to collapse. It was just a dirty bubble ball. I could not even see a thing inside. My eyes absentmindedly wandered around Kittous' and Ugley's.

I grabbed and carefully took out the bubble ball. Of course, nothing happened as an ordinary bubble ball. However, it was exceptionally light that it almost slipped off my hands. It was as light as a helium balloon, and as dirty as a mudfish skin.

I shook it once just to confirm the emptiness. And I corroborated with the final conclusion.

We failed to find it, or there is no such thing as power silver scale.

I did not even bother doing anything with it after that. It was such a regretful feeling after all the painful efforts. Instead, I looked at Ugley's eyes for what was left inside to yell and tease him in a way of resolving my despair.

"Well, this is it, buddy! This is all we get after all!"

If it is still hidden somewhere, yet to be found, that's good for now. But, how can we stand against Safrah? Obviously he has his own prevailing ability, let alone the power of the silver scales he possesses.

Whichever way we would find, fighting with Safrah sounded very stupid. I only shook my head.

Chapter 20
UGLEY THE GENIUS

Ugley shot out of the site without delay like there was no more business left with the bubble balls. He swooped down through layers of bubble balls while I was pondering the most urgent matter to deal with.

Now it is only a matter of time that the whole land will be moaning with fears. But we have no option at present. If we ever have one, that will be again the power of the silver scales. By all means we have to keep our hope alive.

"Power silver scales, Ugley! That's the only solution, Kittous!" I cried out to the blank sky like talking to the chilly wind against us.

Feeling anxiety and regret grow helplessly in my mind, I shot another glance at the ball in my arm. *What has been wrong?* Yet, every piece of the information was directional, and every clue was indicative of the location; right in the center of the spiral galaxy. And it was the brightest bubble ball.

Now, I recollected the story on my birthday card which had turned out to be very informative on Bubble Land. There was something about the brightest bubble ball in the story of the sand castle. Yes, I remembered now.

"…the silver castle became a sand castle…" I agreed with it. "…and the brightest bubble ball was gone nowhere to be seen…" I was not sure about this part.

I stared at the ball in my arm once more. Then I took a crack at smoothing the surface, but failed. There was heavily loaded opaque dirt on the surface like many layers of thin films.

"Is it normal to accumulate layers of dirt over years?" I mumbled, attempting to find the answer in Kittous' eyes.

Now using my finger nails I scratched out some of the dirt from the surface of the ball. As my finger tips went deeper, to my surprise, it was brighter on the spot. Curiosity arose. Now with a substantial effort I scratched out the layers of the dirt until my finger tips touched the main surface of the ball. And right that moment, bright white light came out from inside through the unveiled area. It was like the life of light escaping from the bubble ball cage. Sudden thrill came over me with the appearance of the light.

Now I did not care about the sharp pain in my fingers. I quickly cleaned wider area to see more. Then, out came a beam of bright light, directly pouring on my face. And behind were a vast number of shiny silver scales, provoking burning sensation in my mind. My eyes and mouth were frozen. Wailing sounds came hilariously out of both my and Kittous' mouths almost automatically at the same time.

"You, you, ugly genius! How, how could you do that to me!" I shout at Ugley breathlessly. "You fooled me, Ugley, you did!"

With wild thrill, Kittous, the weird cat kicked out of Ugley's back. For a moment, she must have forgotten that she was only a cat. She was transformed into a little hemaby a moment later and flew awkwardly along with Ugley.

I could not help screaming every second.

Yes, we won the game and we saved the world!

Now, I had to save my joyous screams for a bit later, because Ugley tried to say something to me with his vigilant eyes. His head directed forward repeatedly. Provisionally, I thought he was asking me to see ahead, but it was something rather urgent.

"What?" I questioned. "Throw something?"

By now, I was quite familiar with his body signals. His eyes and head all seemed indicative of an approval.

"You mean…this?" I frowned in disbelief, holding the dear ball even tighter.

He approved with a nod again.

Throwing the most precious treasure? No! My mind refused at once. Ugley the genius must have a remarkable plan. But, I couldn't convince my stubborn mind.

"OK, you are the captain, Ugley." I said, sounding a bit dejected.

Now, Kittous, who fast swooped down beside us, suddenly shrieked piercingly, her eyes looking ahead. That was a serious warning from our teammate. Safrah just appeared from nowhere and waited for us, his atrocious appearance as monstrous as it could be. With his hairs all erect, he was almost a crazy porcupine now. His face fumed with rage as if his brain had seethed so long by the internal flame before burning us down.

I could see the urgency now, but there was nothing else we could do at the moment. Again, I would have to trust Ugley who has been always right.

"OK, say, buddy, this is the best option!" I cried out optimistically.

Safrah did not wait long. He cast a bundle of his arrow-like hairs with a sizzling flame. Right then, Ugley screamed deafeningly, pulling out his neck as much as he could. By half surprise, I threw the ball forward. Then, I saw Safrah who, by the sight of the ball right before him, seemed so shocked that his eyes were like fire balls, and his mouth, a dark hallow hole. Ugley managed to escape barely an inch above the attack. But just before then, the ball burst sharply by some of the arrows from Safrah. And several astonishing things happened right in front of me.

Enormous numbers of silver scales scattered all in the air, forming a glittering piece of silver cloud right below us. The silver scales! Yes, I saw they were real. They were slim and shiny, flying vividly like new born butterflies out of a huge cocoon.

Without warning, Ugley flipped over his body so sharply, throwing me away, and dashed to the silver cloud. Then, I was like a piece of lifeless wood, falling all the way down until there came an angel to rescue me again.

"Ryan!" A voice on the alert boomed my eardrums.

In some distance I spotted Ella on a hemaby, and ahead there was another hemaby rushing toward me. It was uncoordinated, but fleetingly I felt that I was playing the game number one, and this hemaby was running to me to save my neck. They knew the game would be over if I touched the water.

I managed to grab the hemaby who came just in time. Gratifyingly, it was our new teammate hemaby who had bused Ella at the hidden dome. I climbed on it safely. I briefly thanked to Ella, my eyes moving on to the battle field of Ugley and the evil king.

Now I could hardly see Ugley who was inside of the scattering silver cloud. A moment later, a certain form of spinning force was generated from the surrounding. And it sped up dangerously fast, sweeping all the scales toward the center. Safrah seemed confused, wavering for a moment for any further attack. Evidently, he was not sure about the strength of his own power over the force now. For sure he realized what mattered was the number of the power scales which were now in the favor of Ugley. 365 versus 635. That was it. He looked different now; he looked weaker before the superior power which he could not reach anymore. He covered up his eyes with his huge hands to avoid the light.

Now the silver scales, which gathered in the center area, were coating Ugley entirely. And this time, stabbing winds were generated from the center, dispensing outward vigorously to the surrounding. Safrah may have shunned well from the touch of the light, but there was no way of getting away from the touch of the winds. His hairs and tail were merrily boogieing around regardless of the owner's will. In alert, aiming to escape from the site, he flew fast up to the bubble ball clouds. However, he was too slow before the final justice, if it was.

Feeling half pitiful for the miserable ending for such a frightening monster, my attention came back to the core of the storm. Just then, the winds, the light, and even the silver clouds were disappeared all at once. Following a millisecond of blackout, there in the center appeared a beautiful hemaby with glittering silver scales all around the body.

From tip to toe I was stunned by the new born hemaby.

That was MY wish!

It seemed that it was only the beginning of another surprise. While I was immersed by the magical performance with a hemaby on the stage, the surrounding befell so bright. The bubble balls in the surrounding gradually brightened up enchantingly and suddenly produced sparkling light. Then in the twinkling of an eye, the light shifted to the hemaby as if he absorbed all the light sources in the surrounding. As the light touched the silver scales on the hemaby, the light instantaneously bundled up and produced a single piece of light; it was like a prism that gave a beam of light with many beautiful refractive colors in it. And it was this beam of light that traveled directly to the evil monster.

The beam only touched the tip of the tail of the monster. However, as soon as it did, all the light transferred over to his entire body. And now, his whole body was so colorful and bright as if he stole all the energy from the hemaby for the moment. The bright light was so strong that the bubbles around him burst in no time. The brightness steadily diminished. Now, he seemed regaining power, turning back to the hemaby.

Seeing him returning furiously, I felt qualms inside, but the hemaby was fearlessly still, remaining in the same spot, watching Safrah approaching. Safrah twisted his face with his glaring eyes and sharp teeth, dashing to the hemaby every second.

"Oh, no, no!" I cried helplessly, but that was all I could say for the time being.

However, in seconds I witnessed something far beyond my imagination. Starting from the tail, the color of the whole body of Safrah changed to silver, leaving Safrah as a silvery monster. He was, then, transformed into a black monster, again gradually from the tail to the head. His whole body except the silver scales on his armor now completely changed. It was wholly black. Despite of this dramatic change, yet Safrah was the same monster, dashing to the hemaby ever fast with his dark mouth widely open. He was only about a few feet from the hemaby when a sudden white squall was created against him. Then, something really weird happened to the black monster. It was this squall that swallowed the monster in a jiffy. As if it was dissolved, his body disappeared into the thin air as soon as it touched the squall, progressively from the dancing tail to the furious mouth which nearly touched the hemaby. The monster was vanished with the squall just like that.

Now everything became so peaceful like nothing ever happened before. Only the silver scales from Safrah's armor fell down, presenting appealing reflective light in the evening sky. The silver scales, with which once Safrah enjoyed in playing repugnantly over innocent nature and humans on Bubble Land, tumbled down remorsefully into the water. And there, Ugley, the most charismatic hemaby followed, swooping down toward the water.

"Is that…?"

I spat out a thin wail by the view of something small, chasing after Ugley. And for sure it was no one, but my little teammate, another mysterious friend, Kittous.

By the time I watched all this, Ella and I were already around the roof of the castle. Our hemabies were taking us back to the castle. I hoped that I could see Ugley, the hero, jumping out of the water, but all I saw were riders popping out of the water on their hemabies, soaring up into the sky. Each one of them looked so happy with a handful of something very shiny in their hands.

Chapter 21
A CHEERFUL YOUNG FELLOW

"My wish?" I asked blankly.

It was the question that the king asked me for the job I had done. I have not thought about that much until now. *But, I have a wish. The best one.*

"I want to go home and…"

The king smiled at me, nodding gently, wanting to hear my next words.

"And get my homework done before my mom kills me."

It sounded silly, but I meant it. For the whole summer I had only planed, but never touched the homework yet. I could feel my mother making a face like Safrah's. Then, I suddenly realized that the school should have been resumed long ago, and I have been missing many classes. *Holy, the classes!* And my mother should have been looking for me everywhere. How long have I been missing? I tried to figure that out once, but I gave it up as I suddenly saw myself standing in a dark aquarium with a bunch of invisible light-devils. I screwed up everything now. I did not go to grandma's house. My homework left untouched. My project still undone. I have been a missing child for many days since I left my room with my school bag. *My bag!*

"Holy light-devils!" I cried, remembering that I had left the bag in the phone booth.

"What?"

The king saw my face turning pale for sure. He woke me up from the panicking daydream with a half anxious look. He probably heard me mumbling in shock.

"Sorry, sir. I mean I have school homework due by, uh…tomorrow." I declared tentatively, forcing my pale face into a smile.

"That is a very interesting wish!" exclaimed the king, laughing cheerfully.

"Well, Ryan, you saved the entire world, and we truly appreciate your job done," said the king, his laughter turning into a broad smile. "However, we can do anything except that." His lips curved again. "So, I guess, you have to do the homework for us before your mom kills you." He failed to smother a big laughter.

"And meanwhile, you will have to figure out how to bring your wish come true. Otherwise, you will stay here right beside us," said the king cheerfully now, "and that's exactly what I wish." he added brightly before marching away from the site.

I have known him only for a while, but I liked him already. He was certainly very nice and wise. W.E.L. would suit him very well. It would be wonderful now for everyone on Bubble Land, I thought. What a dramatic change. It seemed only seconds ago when I had said the same for the other king, Safrah.

Earlier, soon after I had come back to the castle, the king came to thank me. He had cheerfully mentioned that everyone in the end returned to the castle home in one piece. He already knew all about what had happened at the castle. I only guessed that it was Ella who had told everything to the king, because she came back to normal.

I had hoped to see Laxan and Ella when I visited the rehabilitation hall, but, I only met the king there, cheering all the riders who had escaped from the grip of the death. The king had spiritedly encouraged them with examples of young and brave people in the history and the legends of Bubble Land. I had noticed that Chrom and his cronies were good listeners, not to mention Ruth. His story was quite amusing to me, too, holding my steps until he had finished (the first part, he'd said). Then I had thought that his own story would be even more interesting (second part, maybe). However, until the end he had not said anything about his story or his past. Of course, I could guess, but I did not dare to ask why he had ended up being petrified underwater for so long.

That night when everyone fell asleep, I went to the aquarium, hoping to see Ugley, the ugly – now the most beautiful hemaby for real. But, there was no indication of such hemaby in the aquarium. Of course I expected, but I felt a bit disenchanted by the absence of Ugley. I appeased my empty mind with the thoughts that he had gone happily to his home somewhere in the ocean.

I began to miss Ugley by just thinking about the moments of every experience with him. Yes, there was a moment of disgust to begin with. But then, he was only handsome from the next moment; he was in the center of, the moment of the wonder, the moment of the thrill, the moment of the excitement, and in the end, the moment of the happiness. Ugley definitely had such a delicate heart to accommodate and share all the moments. And the eyes… Yes, they were the beginning of our tie. They were thoughtful and intelligent to feel grief and cheers. If he could only speak, he would tell an incredible story of his mysterious life, I thought.

Now, pressing down the growing pain of the blues, I walked to return to my room when someone drew my attention with a cheerful voice from behind.

"Well, well, well. That must be the rider."

There was a young man, looking at me with a happy smile. I was pretty sure that I have never seen him before.

"So, you could not sleep tight, ah?"

"Do you know me?" I asked, instead of answering.

"No, no. Well, yes, of course. How do I not know the one who saved the whole world?"

"Your face…, somehow, looks familiar. Haven't we met before?"

"Well, not precisely. I came to the castle just now to deliver a message," replied the man. "I hoped to join the races once, but, it seems that there will be no more amazing races anymore. What fun without thrills and challenges?" He complained cheerfully.

"So, you are ready to go home now?"

I simply nodded, feeling a sense of lose.

"And you wanted to see around before you leave, I presume." He said brightly like an old friend.

"Well, yes." I gazed at the aquarium vaguely. "Just wanted to see the aquarium once more… He's probably gone home happily." I said with a smile, looking pleased. "And I AM happy to go back home." I added.

"So…, you met the king, I suppose," said the man friendly.

"Of course. He is already popular." I said brightly, beaming. "Amazing. He told us a lot of stories. They were not just interesting, but very inspiring." I said frankly.

"But, one thing…" I added hesitantly, mulling over the stories. "I was told the king had a son, but he did not say a thing about the son..."

"Oh, his son. Yes, he now returned," said the man radiantly.

"Did he now? Where is he?" I asked excitedly as if being energized by the beam of the power scales.

"Well, he had been detained for so long by the evil power. But now, he returned to his own form of life. That's what I meant," said the man.

"Oh..." I said, nodding, but then, I realized that I did not see what he meant.

"His son returned to what?" I made a face in enigma.

"Yep," declared the man with a broad grin. "In fact, I happen to know about the story of the son, if you are interested."

Of course, I want to know about him. Snooping began to prickle my mind.

"Please." I begged, just like a little child full of expectation. "I want to hear everything about it." I insisted.

He looked at my eyes joyously for a moment. "Do you want to hear about Ugley? That maybe more interesting to you, I mean, since you wanted to see him, I guess."

"Well, definitely!" I exclaimed animatedly, feeling excited already.

He gazed at the empty aquarium for a long minute before he began. His two eyes were complex, yet mysteriously pleasing, which, somehow, were so familiar to me.

390

Chapter 22
IDENTITY OF THE UGLY HEMABY

Despite of his suggestion, he did say anything about Ugley. Instead, he said about Hasyn and his son, Leinad. He finished the story by emphasizing their miserable ending; Hasyn was petrified and Leinad was detained.

"That's the sad part of the story, I should point out."

His expression was rather happy, and I knew why now.

"You are told the story at present, but it all had happened before you came, and so it is only the first part of, Ryan, your story, if you are considering," said the man, his voice was spirited and persuasive.

"The next is the main part which is really breathtaking with a remarkable turning!" exclaimed the man exuberantly, his hands up in the air, his eyes vaguely on the ceiling for a while as if to count the bubble balls on the ceiling.

"See, Ryan, you have been just right there, making the happiest part!"

He cheered me up gracefully. But I was overcome with chagrin when he said that. *Whatever you say, but indubitably it was Ugley who did it all.* My longing to hear about Ugley grew even more now.

"I thought you were going to tell me about the story of Ugley, but you did not mention anything yet..." I questioned demandingly.

"Ah, you want to ensure that I will," said the man, gazing at me in the eyes wittily. "Well, I will say, I reserved it for the last or ending part of the story, Ryan."

I was going to insist, but he read my mind.

"Soon after the monster had vanished, Ugley carried the power scales with him all the way across the ocean. He traveled underwater until he let go the last piece of the scales back to the ocean. He meant to return all the power scales back to the sea world, and that was the best solution to him," explained the man proudly, nodding his head.

"And eventually after that, Ugley was able to walk out of the water again."

His words were plain, but the impact on me was tremendous.

"What?" I exclaimed loudly by surprise. "Ugley what?"

I could not close both my mouth and eyes for a long time.

"Holy cow! For real!"

Yes, that was the most enthralling final part of the story, to my great, great enjoyable surprise, of Ugley. And that cleared all the questioned I had.

When I after some time settled happily with Ugley's mystery, another question, which I had almost forgotten, just popped out of my mind.

"Do you know anything about the little hemaby? I asked anxiously.

"No, I have no idea about her," replied the man naturally, but his expression perturbed.

"It was Kittous following Ugley, I am pretty sure…" I muttered faintly, feeling a bit disappointed. For a second

I was excited by the consideration that Kittous was also able to walk out of the water just like Ugley.

"Kittous is smart… She must have gone somewhere happily." I said positively.

I tried, but I knew that I would never feel happy until I would know about what happened to her in the end.

Ugley must know… Yes, Ugley knows everything about Kittous…

Ugley told the man everything except Kittous? *It doesn't make sense.* Why nothing about her? I questioned. Now, while looking at the man doubtfully, out of the blue, I came up with a simple query for him.

"How do you know all that?" I asked interrogatively, my voice was dry.

"Well, we have been close friends so long. In fact, I just came here to deliver the news to the king. Nothing can fill his empty mind when he is craving for news of his missing son, I guess."

He stood up to his feet like all have been said and done.

"Oh, by the way, the son asked me to give this to you. You can keep it as a souvenir, or else if you ever need it," said the man, handing it over to me.

Walking toward the door, he added, "If you decide to stay here longer, you might be able to see him. Then, maybe you can ask him about Kittous, as well."

His voice echoed cheerfully in the hallway. Now I just noticed the souvenir in my hand.

"Excuse me, may I ask your name, please, as, uh, a souvenir, as well?" I shouted toward the man who was already out of sight. And my voice bounced back through the hallway with one word.

"NAD!"

The souvenir was a silver scale. And it was very identical to the one I attained from the bubble ball. So much to do with one small scale, I thought. The most remarkable fellow prince, Leinad has honorably given me one symbolic hemaby scale.

It must be the one and the only one he used to have while he was Ugley. I decided.

Chapter 23
MAKE IT FAST

I walked back to the aquarium again, my mind completely blank. I was almost like a sleepwalker until someone woke me up.

"Ry!" It was the usual voice of Ella, sounding in seventh heaven.

"Hi, Ella." I said cheerfully with a big smile.

I was also very pleased to see her now as I had hoped to see her before I would leave. She was not alone.

"And Laxan!" I added, sounding very surprised.

"Hey, you came back, Laxan! Man, you missed all the thrill and fun." I said playfully, my eyes moving to Ella's to share the amusement. I knew that he had gotten into a scrape while investigating the hidden passage around the home of light-devils. But now, he got out of it, and I was ready to pull his leg. "Where the heck have you been all this time?"

Ella and her brother both exchanged silly smiles and said almost at the same time, "Can't tell."

Laxan seemed to have decided to keep his story in closet.

"What? Come on, what's the secret between us?" I complained teasingly.

"Don't bother it, Ryan, you won't believe it, anyway," said Laxan serenely.

"Hey," began Ella brightly, her face with a glimpse of pink, "we thought you were gone until a man came told us you were here... You know, I talked to the king,

I mean our 'real' king, whose name is actually Hasyn if you did not know... Anyway, he said that you were more than just welcome to stay here in the castle," cried Ella wholeheartedly with a weight on 'more than welcome.'

"He said that there would be a superb position for you, Ryan." She added, grimacing. Her eyes set on mine, inciting me for a positive reply, but she did not wait. "Considering, yes?"

"I will think about it, Ella, but..." I said unsurely.

Feeling in a sticky situation, I only scratched my head, for I had no reasonable exit to run away from the dilemma.

Momentarily, I once contemplated any rationale to consider it. I looked back what I have gone through up until now; I had learned about the remarkable history of Bubble Land, and I had been involved in fighting like a patriot for the peace of the country. And, looking at my future in Bubble Land, I could tell that I would have a bright and pleasing prospect. Then, of course, I would be happily able to do my provoking homework for the king; divulging the unexplained legendary rudiments and mysteries yet remained.

Above all, there was the prince, who once was an ugly hemaby and my awesome friend, and whom I was eager to meet again. I would have tons of stories to talk about with him. And at last, there was a girl, who had been my favorite friend, sharing all the delightful and bitter moments until the last minutes. She was now here right before me, wanting to hear something sweet (or better than adieu).

Yes, it is my second home that I will enjoy to live with no doubts. I definitely will consider it...but, not today...

"Yes, Ella, I will consider. And…" I did not finish, but I had to stop there, because she was already excitedly holding my neck, hugging me tight. It was more embarrassing to me than exciting. I only smiled at her brother awkwardly.

"Listen, Ella." I began calmly, pulling out the very first silver scale from my pocket.

"Familiar with this?" I asked, smiling tentatively, waving the scale in my fingers gently. Then, I held her by the wrist and placed the scale on her hand cautiously like handling a very fragile glass piece.

She knew what it meant. Her eyes meandered around my eyes and the scale.

"Ry…" She sighed, her voice was down already. "Please…, you said you would consider."

"I did, but just in case, you keep this, OK?"

Her eyes went down to her hand as though she dropped the answer there.

"Oh, don't worry. I have one, too, you know. My thanks to Ugley."

I made an effort to cheer her up, but she was still not happy. I knew she wouldn't.

"OK, I want you to have that, just in case, you know, you can visit me with that… It's the key to my world, if you didn't know." I said encouragingly.

Now, brightening up my face with that idea, I added spiritedly, "Actually, you guys can visit me on your next birthday. Then, you both can help me find my grandpa…" Feeling satisfied, beaming, I exclaimed, "See, I already have a great plan!"

Still, there was no hint of elation developing on her face. I only felt daunted for not knowing what to do.

"And of course, I will come back shortly with this invitation key!" I attempted again, pulling out the other silver scale.

Ella smiled at me for barely half a second in appreciation of my effort. Laxan looked at his sister once and tried to help with his own way of cheering.

"Hey, sis, that's great. We can go there next time, and, and you know, it's our turn to pinpoint the evil men who kidnapped Ryan's grandpa. We will petrify them in one shot, or haul them to here as a present for our dear light-devils, whichever you prefer. And of course, I don't mind giving you another ride, if it is, well, investigator Ellaxan will find a way for sure."

That was helpful. At least Ella smiled and decided to talk. "For sure you are coming back?" she asked, her smile turning into an anxious grin.

I could only say yes, which was true. "Of course, Ella. You know this is my home, too, and I like you people... very much."

She looked satisfied with my words, her face turned brighter, but I could tell that her sadness would last for a long, long time until maybe I would really return. I wondered if I had the same feeling.

"And I really want to go back and see the hidden land again, Ella. This time we can really appreciate the silver castle and the dome. Of course, we can fool around with the teeny tiny flying fish until they go crazy."

Now, looking at Laxan I just realized that I was talking about something that Laxan would not know; the hidden land.

"I am sure your brother will be taken aback with the view and all in there, Ella." I said eagerly, giving Laxan a broad grin.

By that, they giggled at each other, but precisely, I wasn't sure why.

"It will be fantastic, if I can join you, Ryan. Yeah, the sooner the better."

Ella's mood was back to more or less normal now. I could feel that right away, because she jumped on my neck and kissed me on the cheek for a good bye.

"Dare forget us!"

She whispered in my ear in a warning tone, but I liked it.

Ella let go of me, and then she pushed her brother Laxan toward me. "OK, brother, your turn. Go warn him seriously," declared Ella gallantly.

Laxan approached me to shake hands with me. Holding my hand, he bent toward me, and whispered, "I don't think I can sleep well…probably until you coming back. Hope you help me sleep tight soon."

Then he parted. Looking at my gloomy expression, he added. "OK, sis, better let him go."

Laxan pulled his sister's arm toward the door. Ella hesitantly followed her brother. Her eyes sparkled with tears, her mouth still full of words to yell out.

But she said only a few. "Make it fast, Ry, very fast!"

"By the way, Ryan," said Laxan lively, and holding the door open, he added, "thanks for taking me to the secret dome." Then, he yelled at me cheerfully before the door closed. "That was splendid, and I was really taken aback!"

I was not sure what he meant by that. *Maybe he just wanted to make sure I would come back and take him there.* I decided. As far as I knew, the hidden dome was the secret of only Ella, me, and of course, Leinad. My three teammates (Ugley, Kittous, and the unknown hemaby), who had also shared the experience at the dome, were inexplicably disappeared after the battle with Safrah and Ripper.

I stared at the door absorbedly now, and attempted to mesmerize the imaginary Ella who just left regardless of her intention.

Open the door, Ella. And if you ask me one more time, I will change my mind...

The door simply ignored me as though it turned into a wall. Looking around the hall, I found myself in an empty hall all alone. I suddenly felt very lonely. *I am the only person left on Bubble Land for sure...*It was quiet. It was so quiet that I almost convinced myself to believe that everyone has gone with either Ugley or Safrah.

However, my eyes stopped at the aquarium with a surprise. There, I saw a hemaby far in the dark side of the aquarium. For a split second, I thought that was Ugley, but it was just one of those hemabies. It stayed in the dark spot without moving as if to imitate its old friend, Ugley, wanting to see him once more.

"You miss him, too?" I whispered softly.

"Don't worry, buddy. He will be back very, very soon with a big happy smile." I said persuasively.

"In the mean time," I continued in a sincere voice, "can you please give me a ride?"

It stayed there unmoved, only its fins wagging peacefully as if to say, 'I am considering.'

"Can you, please?" I begged again.

A moment later, the hemaby now started to move more actively and smoothly swam out of the shade. It then circled around for a minute and jumped out of the aquarium at my service. And as I sat on its back, without even any further request, it flew all the way to the open sky.

The sky was still bright, resembling a big dome under millions of dim light lamps on the ceiling. I was only in a dome world. When I looked at the scenery down below, I suddenly felt that I was the only person who owned the right to enjoy the beautiful world. The enchanting castle, the glorious land, and the peaceful ocean that bravely stretched toward the darkness... I shouted at once with one obvious reason for all.

"I am coming home!"

Coming back home... But, how can I go back home?

I have nearly forgotten about the key until now.

"The invitation key!" I cried.

I automatically threw my hand into the pocket. Naturally, I fished out the souvenir. A thin line of thrill developed inside.

"This is it!" I cried out.

All this time, what I learnt was the subtle power of a little silver scale. Perceptibly it has been a magic key that worked for every door and gate. It even unlocked and let me go beyond my own world. Maybe that was what the gatekeeper had meant when I first came. He'd certainly said that I needed another key to leave.

I looked down the castle and the main gate which quietly stood in front of the tower and the castle building. On the other side of the gate was paved passageway on levee which stretched all the way to a peaceful beach. It was wonderful refreshment in my memory. Then, I noticed something shiny at a corner of the beach. It almost looked like a chest box containing puzzle pieces from the distance.

Was there anything like that before?

"Wait! That's the phone booth!" I shouted in glee.

It should be. I was positive. I deposited the scale back into my pocket and asked the hemaby gently again.

"Can you please drop me on the beach?"

The hemaby considerately took me over to the beach, and I landed on the sand intact. The hemaby, with loud flapping, soared up to the sky ever energetically as if to show how happy it was to complete the last duty for its favorite guest from the outer world. I gaped at the hemaby who was shooting up in the dim light toward the castle which stood with charming light gleefully. I could almost hear it bid me cheerful farewell.

"Silver castle?" I questioned in surprise.

Yes, unquestionably, it was a silver castle that I was seeing now. It was like the silver castle out of the jigsaw puzzle. It was so magnificent that I was petrified like I caught a sudden attack from Ripper. It enticed me to come. I even had a strong feeling that Ella (with Kittous in her arm) was right behind the gate waiting for me. I fought hard, urging myself on persistently.

"You must go home, Ryan!"

I managed to turn myself to the other side of the beach. There, I saw now a big chest box, calling me joyfully. After stealing one last glance at the castle, I shouted at the imaginary friends of Bubble Land.

"Bye, all!"

I ran straight to the phone booth, and I opened the door, feeing half nervous. And the moment I entered, I heard a very familiar voice that shook the phone booth. It was my bag, being so irritated, yelling at me.

"What the light-devils took you so long?"

Its grumble was only cute, making me smile a shameful smile.

The scale perfectly substituted a coin, displaying an ever sweet message.

"Well, well done, Ryan. A brave, smart,
and COOL lad you are!
Can't wait your next visit.
Until then, so long!"

I could almost see another sentence right below that. "Make it fast, Ryan!"

I picked up the scale from the phone ever happily this time, and I threw it into my pocket. Now, tiny bubbles and foams started to escape from the sandy ground. They grew bigger rapidly and filled up the booth from the bottom. It began to veil the entire view viciously, but there was no fear in me this time. They were only beautiful bubbles. As the sight became vogue, I closed my eyes and got ready for the long journey.

Time passed by. But, was it a second or two? When the bubbles were cleared away from my sight, a motion picture of a late starry night has just filled up my eyes. A cool wind delivered a complex of various scents to my nose. I could immediately tell what they were. Familiar smell and familiar view. Yes, it was my usual beach with plenty of late summer sense.

"I must run home."

Suddenly, hundreds of people whom I have known in my own world popped out of my memory and stared at me in a peeve. They yelled at me in one voice.

"Where the holy light-devils have you been all this time?"

Chapter 24
SILVER CASTLE

To my great surprise, my mother did not nag at me for the absence of such a long period of time without any note. Precisely speaking, she only assumed that I went to grandma's house. For any reason I was fortunate to come home at late night.

I quietly unlocked the door with the key which I kept in my bag. She was already in bed, but heard me sneaking in the house.

"Ryan?"

Her voice was very soft, but it was like a thundering roar to me.

"Uh, yes, mom. It's me." I answered, trying to sound as warm as possible.

"What happened?" asked my mother, her voice yet placid.

I would rather feel comfortable, if she yelled at me. At least I was ready to hear 'What happened to you, young man? Have you been lost, for heaven's sake?'

"Sorry, mom. I just –."

"I thought you would come tomorrow… Has she been doing all right?"

Huh?! Is she talking to me in a dream? I was not sure. But one thing for sure was that she believed that I had been in grandma's house.

"Oh, yes, mom. She's fine, yes…" I replied clumsily, pretending to be true.

"OK, honey, I will talk to you later. Make sure you get ready for school by tomorrow. It's the last day, you know that… Sleep tight." Her voice was half way to a sweet dream now.

"Yeah, I know. Don't worry, mom. Good night."

Then, I did not have to tiptoe to my room anymore. In marched Ryan happily. I breathed a big sigh of relief, throwing my heavy body on the bed. *How long didn't I have sleep? Who said that there was nothing like home, no matter what?*

I knew I was in a little bit tricky situation with my mother. *But at least for now, I am OK. The school has not started yet, also for now, I am OK. The home work… That should be the first thing I will have to do tomorrow before mother yells at me. And finally, what is left will be the project…* I had no idea what to do for that, and I had no words that could make my mother smile… She would kill me really.

By then, my mind began to drift on an ocean of a sweet dream.

Nothing matters before a sweet dream.

The bright sun light came through the windows in my room and woke me up in the morning. Then, I smelled bacon and roasted tomato coming from the kitchen. Out came noises of a flock of sparrows lively feuding with magpies for something. It took me five seconds to realize that I was not in the castle. At last, I was home.

Still lying on my bed, I opened my eyes and looked around. I saw the pictures and the characters of the framed jigsaw puzzles hanging on the wall. All very familiar. Sure enough, it was my room. I spotted the shopping bags with some of the items that I had brought before I left for Bubble Land. Then, the castle... The sand castle out of a jigsaw puzzle game was there on the table. I smiled bitterly at the sight of the castle. *Was that all dream?*

I suddenly remembered the souvenir.

"My pants!" I raced down to the kitchen like a flash of lightning.

"Mom, where are my pants?" I asked my mother with a brief smile instead of saying good morning.

"In the laundry machine. Where did you get so much dirt like that? Did you have to go to any sandy mine in Blue Forest to dig out precious minerals or something? What are those black and red particles coated all over the pants?"

I was not listening to my mother's complaint. Worries swept away all my joys with the thought of the laundry machine.

"Oh, NO!"

I ran down to the laundry room, wailing outrageously, and stopped the machine at once. I picked out my pants which were dripping soapy water with huge bubbles in every wrinkled corner. My hand was faster than my mind, swimming in the slippery pockets. And there, I fished out a small piece of shiny metal. The scale was there unharmed, to my great relief. And it was gloriously sparkling with vivid lines of colors in various forms. I knew it was because of the residual soupy water, but I decided to believe it was only because of the mysterious nature of the scale. It could open the door to a wondrous world, of which otherwise you would never know the existence in your life. It was only a magic scale. It led me to the world of bubble balls; let me enter the castle kingdom; opened the miniature silver castle; and eventually fetched me back to my home land.

"Yes, the castle! The sand castle!"

I dashed back to my room, pressing down the sudden excitement that overcame my mind. I threw myself into the room, my eyes straight to the incomplete sand castle with one last piece. Now I remembered that it was the gate of the castle that had a missing piece. But then, I realized that the empty space was much smaller than the scale in my hand. Certainly, all the pieces of the castle were much smaller, and thus it would be silly to try with the scale. However, I must have been fantasized to believe it was really a magic scale. I brought the scale into the empty space vaguely. And I carefully placed the scale on the empty gap in the gate of the sand castle. Then, I screamed.

"Wow!"

Astonishingly, it perfectly matched somehow. It was the right piece, indeed.

The silver scale I brought from other world completed my own puzzle at last!

I lay down on my bed and closed my eyes, thinking about the enthralling moments at the castle of Bubble Land. All were still crystal-clear in my mind like a breathtaking fantasy movie that has been just watched.

Now, I heard my mother calling me, but I did not bother until she came up to my room yelling at me.

"You are not even sleeping, young man! Now, why didn't you answer me like that? Come on down for breakfast, right away!"

"OK, mom, right away." I replied, still my eyes closed, wanting to hold the memory of the incredible world.

"Well, nice work, Ryan, you did a good job on this puzzle, at least, I should say. Where did you get this puzzle, anyway? It is a magnificent silver castle!" exclaimed my mother before leaving the room.

Silver castle? No way! I hastily opened my eyes and looked at the work that I just completed with the last missing piece. There was no mistaking what she said about it. Unless my eyes were swindling me, there stood a beautiful silver castle on the table. And as far as I remembered, it was the same work of art that I had completed in the stifling silver castle.

It must have been charmed, I decided. It was not just a plain souvenir from Ugley or a simple key to fetch me back home. It was a power silver scale for which I risked my own life. On balance, the birthday present from the old man in the store was not just a sand castle out of puzzle pieces. It was even more worth than a real silver castle. It took me many days of challenges and fears before completion, but now, it came with glorious joys.

Nad… He seemed to know all about what had happened to Ugley and Leinad.

But somehow, he knew a lot; he knew a lot more than someone could explain in a day or two. He had said that he just came to the castle to deliver the news about Leinad to the king. Then, how Leinad knew about the return of his missing father? And how Nad knew so well about it? Weird, Leinad and Nad.

"Hang on! Isn't Leinad Nad? Isn't that the same name?"

Suddenly, another question shot across my mind for this hilarious young man.

"How did he know that I called the ugly hemaby Ugley?"

While I was being thrilled to discover that it was actually Leinad who had told me all the stories, I heard my mother calling me again. When I was about to run downstairs, I heard an irregular sound coming from under my bed. In fact, something was groaning faintly. For a moment, I thought that a homeless cat came into my room to rest while I was away. I looked down the bed frame immediately, and the moment I did, I was nearly shocked to death. It was not just a street cat. But it was someone I knew and I cared ever since she had shown up to my room. It was my little buddy and teammate.

"KITTOUS!"

LaVergne, TN USA
30 March 2011
222078LV00001B/1/P